John's gaze trav[...] parted and her body tingled under that frank, male assessment.

"I remember that kimono," he said in a low voice.

Now, when he looked at her, she saw it. Desire. She'd seen it before. Not when men glanced at her. Lord, no! But when they looked at Denise they sometimes wore that expression.

And it mirrored her own feelings too well because it was mixed with other emotions. Regret. Anger. Frustration. John Callahan didn't like being attracted to her any more than she liked being attracted to him.

Except he thought she was Denise. What if he found out she wasn't?

Dangerous thoughts swirled inside Dinah's mind. Thoughts she'd never allowed. It would be delicious. Forbidden. Utterly out of her experience and she suddenly wanted it so badly her whole being seemed concentrated on that one, searing thought.

Then his hand cupped her chin. Warm and dry and possessive. He tilted her face upwards until she was helpless but to meet his powerful gaze.

"What *is* it?" he asked, his voice husky and confused. "What's so different about you?"

Dinah was powerless to answer. From a long, long distance away, she watched his lips descend to meet her.

"Oh, my God," she whispered the moment before his mouth touched against hers, at first tentatively, then with more urgency . . .

Tangled

Nancy Kelly

ZEBRA BOOKS
KENSINGTON PUBLISHING CORP.

ZEBRA BOOKS are published by

Kensington Publishing Corp.
850 Third Avenue
New York, NY 10022

Zebra and the Z logo Reg. U.S. Pat. & TM Off.

First Printing: November, 1994

Printed in the United States of America

Prologue

A Long Time Ago . . .

The body lay still. Strangely, almost comically, still. Eyes open, staring into a cold, star-studded sky. Arms flung wide. Head lolling slightly to the right, as if one ear were cocked, listening to the sporadic screech of the night's wicked winter wind.

Shivering, the woman looked down upon the naked body. He'd deserved to die. She was glad he was dead. There was no remorse inside her for this monster.

Feeling something cold on her face, she was surprised to discover half-frozen tears.

An owl hooted, a lonely sound that shot an icicle of terror into her heart. Time ticked loudly inside her head.

She grabbed his legs and started to drag him across the ground. One of his arms caught on a skinny, bare branch and she jerked hard to free him. Slipping on a patch of ice, she twisted her ankle and bit back a cry of pain. But she didn't stop. She couldn't.

Perspiration broke out on her brow and ran beneath her arms as she relentlessly pulled him after her. Her breath plumed in a stream of white fog behind her. Jaw set, she dragged his body over field stubble and dirt clods frozen hard as iron, stumbling a little for he was twice her size.

There was no way to bury him. She hadn't the strength nor the inclination to even try. But there was a storm drain at the far end of this lonely field, and she knew she could roll him down the drainage ditch and stuff his body inside. It would be simple. No one would find him until spring thaw, and maybe not even then. The chances were he'd be entombed in the storm drain forever.

Then she would leave. All of them could leave.

The torment was over.

Chapter One

Yesterday . . .

Two boys on horseback swayed slowly through Forest Service land in Central Oregon. They trailed deer. It was hunting season. And while neither one had a permit or rifle, they planned on finding themselves a spike or a four-point and letting their friends know that *they*, little Mikey Watters and shit-for-brains Matt Logan, had seen the *biggest* buck around. Sure, they couldn't shoot it, but they would have seen it, and that counted. It counted for a lot.

Dust puffed from the horse's hooves in grainy clouds. Matt wiped his eyes, leaving streaks of grime across his round, freckled face.

"Damn dust," he complained. Then, liking the sound of that, said even more loudly, "Fucking damn dust."

Mikey whipped around to look at him, eyes wide. Both boys listened hard, hearts tripping with fear. The "F" word was really bad. Though they were far enough away from home to almost be on a distant planet, there was still a chance their fathers, or snitching older sisters, *might* hear. Then there'd be trouble. Yes, sirree.

Matt hunched his shoulders. "Nobody out there." His voice was scarcely more than a whisper.

Mikey nodded. He was impressed with Matt's daring. Wished he'd been the one to say it.

The ponderosa and jack pines surrounding them staggered into a small field at the northernmost end of the property. A broken down wire fence, rusted and useless now, defined the line of the Daniels place. Some new people lived there now, but Mikey and Matt's parents still referred to it as the Daniels place, mainly because Daniels had disappeared one day without a word to his family or any of the townspeople. Matt had once heard his dad describe old man Daniels as the ". . . worst bastard I ever met. Half full of liquor, half full of hate, and chock full of Satan's malice . . ."

'Course Daniels was long gone now. Probably dead. Nobody much cared. Once Matt had told his Uncle Jack about the Daniels story, but Uncle Jack hadn't seemed too interested. That was understandable. Uncle Jack worked for the L.A.P.D. and didn't have time to waste on stuff like that. He was catching *real* criminals. Guys who scared people and did drugs and stuff. You had to be more than just a bastard to get Uncle Jack's attention.

At least Uncle Jack *used* to be on the force, but Matt didn't want to think about that now. He'd rather concentrate on Daniels.

"Bastard," Matt said, growing bolder by the moment.

"Who you calling that?" Mikey demanded.

"Old man Daniels."

"Oh."

The horses pulled at the reins and ducked their heads to the field grass. Mikey and Matt slid to the ground by unspoken agreement. "Let's go up by the ridge," Mikey suggested. "Bound to find some real deer there."

" 'Kay." Matt pulled some jerky from his pocket and the two boys munched in silence, their gazes sweeping the upper ridges. One of the horses moved toward a dried up drainage ditch and culvert, the culvert so overgrown with weeds only the merest trickle of water could seep through. Not a big problem. Central Oregon was dry, tons drier than the valley. No flooding here.

"Are those tracks?" Mikey demanded excitedly.

Matt eagerly followed his friend's gaze toward the scooped out ditch. There were no tracks, but some of the field grass was broken off. "Our horses broke that off, stupid!"

"Well, sorreee." Mikey walked toward the ditch.

"Geez, you're dumb."

"No dumber than you, shit-for-brains," Mike threw out daringly, repeating the oft-used phrase coined by Matt's most hated enemies, the sixth-graders.

"Little, dopey bastard!"

That did it. Mikey launched himself at Matt and the two boys rolled into the shallow depression that had once been the ditch. But they pounded and pummelled at each other without much enthusiasm because, after all, they were best friends. Five minutes later, spent and gasping, they rolled apart.

And that's when they saw it.

A human skull.

Neither boy was overly impressed. You saw skulls all the time on T.V. But nevertheless, it was a find, and Matt screamed out his special Injun *whoop-whoop-whoop* to announce his discovery. Two hours later, when they showed the skull to Matt's mom, their estimation of its worth magnified a thousand times. She practically came unglued! Called Uncle Jack right away who told her to phone Sheriff Dempsey.

Wow.

No more little Mikey Watters and shit-for-brains Matt Logan. They were on the front page of *The Buckeroo Gazette* by week's end. The ditch was checked out by important policemen and more bones were found, a whole body full. Somebody was checking out whose bones they were. The town was abuzz, but everybody was pretty sure it was old man Daniels, the worst bastard Matt's dad ever met. Half full of liquor, half full of hate, and chock full of Satan's malice.

Chapter Two

Today . . .

"Come on, you worthless piece of junk," Dinah Scott muttered in frustration. The Fax machine's innards were grinding as if the damn thing were warming up for take-off. The whole room was practically humming, but nothing was happening. Two minutes earlier crumpled papers had spewed across the room like shrapnel—which was alarming in itself since Dinah was *sending*, not receiving.

She glanced at the clock. Four-thirty. Flick would be dragging steadily on his last cigar of the day, his chair creaking ominously under the bulk of his tremendous weight, a steady stream of abuse about *"Dinah Scott's irresponsible need to help any no-gooder who crosses her path"* and how he knew this would happen and she might as well start *"sending out resumes because she sure as hell wasn't employed by the* Santa Fe Review *no more!"*

"Damn, damn, damn!"

Snatching up her purse and sliding into a pair of ugly, but well-loved sandals, Dinah raced down the hall of her sister's Spanish-style home, skidding a little on the front tiles as she hauled open the front door and made a beeline for her car.

It was a 1974 white Fiat, aged, battered, and temperamental, but Dinah refused to even consider purchasing a new car. The very thought made her want to rip out her hair. She was too impatient to go through the trouble. She just wanted things to work. At least twice a day she screeched, "I just want things to work! Is that too much to ask?"

Apparently it was.

Muttering in frustration, she swung her bare legs into the driver's seat and twisted the ignition. The Fiat's engine sputtered madly before it finally caught. Breathing a silent prayer of thanks to the machinery gods who were apparently smiling down on her—at least at this particular moment—she downshifted, and with a jerk, the little car leapt along the brick drive. As far as she was concerned, until the Fiat's repair bills ate up every cent of her disposable income, she would hang onto the old rattletrap, even if this very afternoon the damn thing died on the Santa Monica freeway.

But it sure as hell better not.

She drove like a woman possessed. She wasn't a Los Angeles resident, but she knew where she was going. She'd been housesitting for her sister, Denise, since the latter part of July, and she'd made sure she'd learned how to negotiate the freeways with all of the proficiency of the other crazy drivers and commuters.

Denise. Her sister. Her twin. Denise had flitted off to parts unknown to put her torn-apart-self back together (something she did on a regular basis) and Dinah was making certain Denise's ex didn't try to assume ownership of the house while she was gone. It was just the kind of thing His Highness, John Callahan, would do, and

Denise didn't need any more aggravation in her life. Sure, she brought most of the trouble which surrounded her upon herself—in fact, attracted it like a magnet—but Denise wasn't all bad. She had problems. Hell, everyone had problems. Dinah just wanted to ease her sister's a little.

A red light wavered on the dashboard, echoing the Fax machine's warning.

"Don't do it," Dinah snapped fiercely. "You're on death row already. This is not a good time to gamble with fate."

The Fiat, ignoring her threat, backfired and died. Dinah heard its tires spinning on the pavement amidst the sound of thousands of surrounding automobiles. The Fiat's engine faintly ticked, its last death throes.

Dinah guided the car to the edge of the road and glanced at her watch. Four-fifty-seven. Flick wouldn't wait past five. Damn it. *Damn it!*

Grinding her back teeth together she stepped from the car, staring down at the automobile in hard fury as she considered her fate. If she didn't get Flick this column her career was over.

Flinging her arms wide she stared toward the heavens and silently demanded, "Why me?"

A car slid out of traffic and eased behind the Fiat. She glanced back with renewed hope. A blue BMW.

"Need help?" the driver asked, poking his head out the window. He was a handsome enough man, somewhere in his early thirties. Probably a killer or rapist if one could believe the statistics concerning Good Samaritans in Los Angeles.

"Looks like my engine conked out." Dinah didn't move. Her inner security system was on red alert. She didn't trust strangers. She didn't trust *men*. She would rather walk the breadth and width of the United States, go on a starvation diet, *and* take up bungee jumping as a profession than climb into a car with a man she'd just met. "Would you mind making a call to a towing company for me?"

"I can take you to the nearest service station."

"I don't want to leave my car."

The passenger window slid downward. What Dinah had assumed was another man was really a young woman with close-cropped hair gelled flat to her head. "You sure you don't want a ride?" he asked again.

The woman added, "You'd have to sit in the back next to Jimmy, but he's asleep and won't bother you." She twisted to glance in her back seat.

Dinah walked toward the passenger side and peered through the window. Jimmy looked to be about two years old, sound asleep in his car seat, achingly angelic.

"I think your car'll be safe for a little while," the man added, eyeing the passing traffic suspiciously, as if he doubted his own words.

"Maybe I *could* leave it," Dinah agreed with relief, unlatching the car door. Miracle of miracles, she'd actually been rescued by normal people.

Fifteen minutes later she was dropped off at a small convenience store with a sign in the window advertising: SUPER SODAS! MORE THAN EVEN *YOU* CAN DRINK! Flipping open the door to the phone book she called the towing company, then phoned Flick and explained her plight.

He was rude and to the point. "You're a lying bitch, Dinah. And you're late."

"It's not like I missed the deadline for the second coming," she responded evenly. It irritated the hell out of her whenever he swore at her.

"Your column's in syndication, babe, just in case you've forgotten. Don't mess with me, or you're out."

Dinah rolled her eyes and glanced through the dusty glass of the hot, sticky phone booth. Across the street was a Mailboxes, Inc., where for a seven dollar fee she would be allowed to use their Fax machine and send Flick her latest column. "I'll be sending to you in five minutes. Just hang in there."

"I haven't got all night."

"Five minutes." She hung up. "Bastard," she muttered, slamming back the door to the booth. Flick, so-named for his uncanny ability to flick a half-eaten cigar into an ashtray from nearly any distance, was about as understanding as her stepfather had been when she'd come home two hours late from her first date. For that infraction she'd endured a sound slap across the face, among other things. The fact that her beau of the moment's car had been sideswiped by a drunk driver and she'd been forced to wait while the accident report was filled out hadn't mattered in the least. Thomas Daniels had blamed her totally. So did Flick. The reasons clearly weren't important. She'd screwed up and had to pay the price.

She shivered a little despite the warm temperature, rubbing her arms. Luckily, Flick was at least a human being, an attribute she would never have ascribed to her stepfather, but when Flick was in the right he was so goddamned justified it made her want to scream.

Dinah dashed across the street, gave the attendent the Fax number and her typed column, paid the seven dollars, then waited impatiently while the machine sent Flick her latest discussion of how to deal with love and sex in the '90's.

Flick would probably hate it, she thought with a faint smile as she walked back across the street to the phone booth. He hated anything soupy and dopey, which was everything that didn't have something to do with crime or money.

Of course, Flick's negative attitude hadn't improved when she'd explained about her trip to Los Angeles. "Let your sister handle her own problems," he'd sniffed in disgust. "You've got a job to do."

"Six weeks," Dinah had answered. "Six weeks and I'll be back in Santa Fe. Los Angeles is crazy. I don't want to be there any longer than I have to. I'll get all my work in on time. Cross my heart and hope to die. Relax, Flick, nothing will go wrong . . ."

Now she grimaced as she punched out Flick's number and waited for him to pick up the line. Famous last words.

"It's on its way," she said without preamble as soon as she heard the connection go through.

Flick grunted. "Just get your pretty little ass back here and all will be forgiven."

Dinah clenched her hand around the receiver. She considered making a remark about his "fat ass" but decided prudence was called for. "As soon as I can, you macho pig," she responded mildly. "As soon as I can."

He snorted and hung up.

She caught a taxi back to her sister's house. Soul-weary, every bone aching, she slowly climbed the front tile steps. Instead of that good "closure" feeling she normally got after each hurried, sometimes brilliant/sometimes pathetically so-so assignment, her thoughts churned uncomfortably. A pit of feeling swallowed her and she realized it was those horrors from long ago, still dogging her. Best forgotten. Best never remembered. Drawing a deep, nurturing breath, she unlocked the front door.

Safely inside the cool white-walled interior of Denise's Spanish-style home, Dinah sank backward against the six-paneled door and closed her eyes. She couldn't shake the past. It was right there. Nearly tangible. *No, no, no!*

Her hands clenched, but it was no use. She was too uptight. Always had been. But her obsession with wanting the world to work right—to *be* right—was what had saved her sanity through those long, horrible days, nights, and weeks of misery when she and Denise and their younger sister, Hayley, had still lived at home with Thomas Daniels, the stepfather from hell. Two and a half years of torment. A sense of displacement when home wasn't a safe place. She understood teenagers running away and becoming street people. She'd considered it often enough herself. But that would have meant leaving Denise and Hayley and their emotionally frail mother to face the horrors alone. So she'd stayed.

Their mother's death had been a mixed blessing. The three sisters had mourned her passing, but had been inwardly jubilant that now, finally, they would be free of Thomas's iron-handed discipline and torture.

Only it hadn't worked out quite that way.

Dinah drew another long breath, holding it until her lungs were filled with fire, burning. She exhaled on a gasp, slowly opening her eyes, seeing the entryway's arty floor lamp with its smiling, wrought-iron snakes coiled around it and the clean, cool expanse of russet tiles that swept to the inner hallway. Thomas was dead now, she reminded herself, and his soul was in hell. He couldn't corrupt their lives anymore.

She just wished Denise understood that.

Heat shimmered above the pool, bright and dancing and blinding. Her arms were hot, tingling, broiling. She sank them into the water and languidly splashed water over the plastic raft, cooling off her baking limbs. The raft squeaked beneath her weight. Her mind was a blank.

A niggling thought intruded. *Don't think, don't think, don't think,* she warned herself furiously. *You're tranquil. Serene. Nothing matters outside this moment.*

Sun caressed her forehead, soaked inside her flesh. It bathed her like a seductive blanket. It seeped inside her bones. She was currently interested in self-hypnosis and was amazed to find it somewhat effective. It actually seemed to help keep a lid on those devils clamoring inside her head.

Don't think, don't think, don't think. Imagine all the poisons in your body reaching your center. Your being. Now fist your hand. Feel the poisons run down your arm to your fist. You are cleansed. The poisons are inside your fist. Feel them beat, hot and terrible. Now open your fist. Outward, outward, outward! Expelled into the universe. Shot into the black void of space. Away, away. Gone and forgotten.

Something splashed loudly at the other end of the pool. Denise's eyes flew open in alarm. Ripples cascaded outward and a dark form swam beneath the aqua surface. Denise paddled wildly for the side of the pool.

It was a man. Peter something-or-other. Heart beating heavily, she watched him swim the length of the pool underwater, surface, shake water from his black hair, then haul himself to the edge of the pool. Water ran down his hair and across his face and shoulders. Catching her eye, he stared at her across the rippled blue surface of the pool, absently running a hand over his bronzed, muscled chest, his gaze sliding thoughtfully over Denise's bikini-clad body.

He'd been eyeing her all week. He was Carolyn's "friend." Denise had had her own share of friends in her eventful life and knew how complicated and disastrous those kind of friends could be. Carolyn was married to Kevin, but then Denise had been married to John during the course of some of her own friendships. And Peter something-or-other had that predatory on-the-make look. His body was superbly muscled, his movements purposely sinuous, his attention focused so intently she felt as if she were under a microscope.

"You're that actress," he'd told her last week when he'd first appeared at Carolyn's swimming pool.

Denise had ignored him. She'd accepted Carolyn's invitation to come to Houston and get away from her miserably ruined life in California because she'd needed to forget who she was. This whole year had been another disaster. The fights with John had turned from hot and passionate to cold and distant. He didn't love her anymore and hell, she didn't love him. But she hadn't been ready to give him up. And then he'd gone ahead and hired that young bitch for the part in *Fortunata* after explaining without much interest that he wasn't even going to let Denise audition!

Bastard. Two-faced, smirking bastard. Let Dinah handle him. Dinah didn't give a damn about men and John was self-infatuated enough to be really annoyed by her.

Denise chuckled to herself. Dinah had unwillingly agreed to pretend she was Denise should anyone ask. It was the only way to maintain possession of the Malibu beach house, since John was bound and determined to divorce his has-been wife and claim ownership of everything they'd shared. Miserable, cheating, cold-hearted bastard!

"Want some suntan oil?" Peter called from across the pool.

"No, thanks." Her voice was barely above freezing.

What an unbelievable scuz, she thought, her lips curling in distaste. Suntan oil. Good God! Peter was low enough to remind her of his despicable actions three days earlier. He'd been lounging on a chaise across from her in a pair of electric blue bikini trunks, rubbing his limbs with Hawaiian Tropics oil. Catching her eye, he'd pulled out his penis, squirted enough oil over the damn thing to make even an Arab take notice, then slicked it from tip to shaft while she'd watched in fascinated revulsion.

Sicko. Goddamn revolting male.

"Carolyn says you're taking a much-needed vacation."

She considered refusing to answer but decided it wouldn't help. Anger boiled inside her, driving out her therapeutic thoughts. "That's right."

"Things pretty tough out west?"

"I needed a break."

"I always liked your pictures. Especially *Willful*."

"Good for you."

He laughed, and there was a nasty quality to it Denise recognized deep within her marrow. That "I know you" element that men used when they were sure they had you.

A sense of inevitability cloaked her, suffocating, hot, intense. The image of a glass cage enclosing her filled her mind. You couldn't scream. You couldn't struggle. It was your fault for being there, for enticing them. There was no escape.

Her raft had been drifting to the center of the pool. Gently she moved her hands through the water, pulling the raft to the opposite shore. Where was Carolyn?

SPLASH!

Denise shot to attention, nearly overbalancing herself. A silent scream froze in her throat. She struggled to reach the edge of the pool, but Peter's dark head surfaced beside her. He lunged for the raft, shaking water from his black hair, grinning like a beast.

"Get away from me!" Denise ordered.

"Come here."

"Get away!"

He hauled himself atop her on the raft in one fluid motion, pushing them both under, nearly drowning her. She screamed and her lungs filled with water. Coughing, she gasped for air.

"Don't move," he commanded.

"Get *off* me!"

He was moving. Circling her hips with his, driving himself against her. She could feel his erection. She could see it in her mind's eye, big and thick and covered with oil. Something hot beat inside her. She scratched his back, dragging skin beneath her nails. He laughed again. His hands slid between her legs. She squirmed and cried out, his thumb moving hard at her crotch, her legs opening of their own accord. His tongue filled her mouth. His hands ripped at the bottoms of her bikini, pulling it off her legs.

She thrashed, choked, and bit. He slapped her hard. She tasted blood. Then he shoved himself full-length inside her. She ceased to struggle, knowing what would happen if she did. Instead she endured his laughter, deep-throated and knowing. And then . . . and then . . . no, no, no! Her treacherous body began to respond!

"Carolyn told me," he gasped, pushing himself deeper and deeper inside her. "You want it this way. You always want it this way."

Denise didn't have the strength to argue.

She awoke suddenly, heart pounding, tears streaming down her cheeks. Above her was a faded gray Texas sky, beneath her a lounge chair, the plastic rungs soaked with her sweat. Her body was aflame.

"You okay?"

Denise started, realizing the man lounging on the chair beside her was someone she'd never seen before. Heat swarmed up her skin, staining her neck and cheeks. Had she been dreaming? Oh, no. No. Peter couldn't have been a figment of her imagination.

Could he?

It had been a dream, she realized vaguely, miserably. A dream mixed with reality. He hadn't raped her. But he had displayed his wares earlier.

She'd been the one who'd let the scenario unfold in her mind. And now her body was alive with shame and desire.

It was her fault. It was always her fault.

"You all right?" the man asked again.

"Um . . . yeah. I'm sorry . . ." What had he heard? What had he *seen?* Had she been squirming away on the lounge chair. God! He would think she was some kind of pervert!

"I've—I've lost track of time. Is it noon yet?" Denise asked, her voice shaking.

"Six o'clock," he answered, staring at her.

"Tuesday?"

"Friday the thirteenth."

"Oh, right," she choked out, grabbing her towel. "Wow, what a dream."

She scurried toward the poolside door, stepping through the marble bathroom and running down the hall to the back stairs of Carolyn's fabulous home. No one knew she was here, not even Dinah. Friday the thirteenth? She'd seen Peter at the pool—literally seen Peter, as a matter of fact—on Tuesday the third. What had happened to the ten days in between? And who was that man?

She ran up the back stairs to her private room, locking

the door behind her. Each bedroom had its own bath and in the privacy of hers she washed away the sweat and memory of her nightmare. God, her imagination was vivid! She could practically feel his hands still on her. Her skin crawled. Grabbing a washcloth, she twisted it into a rope and bit down on it as hard as she could to keep from screaming.

It was worse this time, much worse. Ten years of steady regression had taken its toll; her last therapist had told her that sterling bit of information. Denise gazed dully at her reflection. Reality. That was her problem. Difficulty distinguishing dreams from reality.

No kidding, Doc. Tell me something I don't know.

"You suffered great trauma as a child," one of The Therapists had intoned gravely.

Big fucking surprise.

"Your dreams are of a sexual nature because you're reacting to some base, primal inner torment."

No shit.

"You have yet to come to terms with the problem."

That's why I'm here, you ignorant ass.

"This may take some time."

Read that to mean, break out the checkbook and credit cards. This is going to be expensive.

Removing the washcloth, Denise dared to really look at herself in the bathroom mirror. She was still naked from the shower, sleek as satin, firm, youthful, and seductive. Her hair was blonde. Her eyes such an unusual shade of aquamarine she'd been accused of wearing tinted lenses. She was—in truth—staggeringly, remarkably, unforgettably, drop-dead gorgeous. Even more so than her twin because Dinah refused to wear the least bit of make-up, refused to do a damn thing with her hair other than twang it back in a rubber band, refused to wear anything but the most ill-fitting sweats in the hopes of hiding her to-die-for figure, refused to be anything like her hopeless, helpless, loony, ridiculous twin.

Denise had tried it Dinah's way, but she hated being overlooked. There was the problem. She *wanted* male attention in the worst way. Craved it. Lived for it. Especially the wrong kind of attention. She wanted it even if it meant sleeping with her best friend's husband. She wanted it even if it meant cuckolding her husband, whom she'd once loved with every ounce of her being.

But the bastard had slept around on her, too, hadn't he? She still wanted to rip out the throat of that whiny redhead who'd written him all those love notes. And what about that new starlet who was spending all that time with him on location for *Fortunata?*

Dinah. Dinah would take care of everything. Dinah was good and smart. Dinah would make John pay for all the pain he'd inflicted on her squirrel-crazy twin sister.

"Denise?" A knock sounded on her bedroom door.

It was Carolyn, her host. Wrapping a towel around her torso, Denise cracked open the door.

Carolyn Lenton was into helping others. At least into helping the privileged. The sick, twisted privileged who possessed oodles of money to spend on their recovery. Denise had originally wanted to consider her a friend, but had learned Carolyn was too whacked out to trust. Almost as whacked out as she herself was. Carolyn had invited Denise to recuperate at her Houston home, then had offered everything from cocaine to Dom Perignon to Peter's ever-ready wanger as a cure.

"Larry said you ran away from the pool as if you were spooked or something."

"Larry?"

"Larry Cummings. I introduced him to you yesterday."

"What happened to Peter?"

Carolyn's penciled brows lifted and a smile played at the corners of her mouth. "Shame on you," she said in a sing-song voice. "I knew you'd like him. He's still around. I could have him back here by eight o'clock, if you like. He's a real fan of yours, you know."

"He doesn't have a Texas accent."

"Well, of course not. He's from L.A. Of all the things you could say about him, that's it?" She grinned wickedly.

Denise felt herself tighten up inside. "Did Stone call?"

"Uh uh. Should he have?"

"I had an appointment I missed. Last Wednesday."

"You didn't miss it. You went." Carolyn looked puzzled.

A terrible sensation engulfed Denise. An anxiety attack. She couldn't breathe. Then memory returned in a wash of regret and annoyance as she realized the last ten days were there, a haze of sunshine, Perrier, and wasted hours, with maybe a few recreational drugs thrown in.

"Stone was preoccupied," she remembered.

"You said you asked him for a date," Carolyn laughed.

"I'm sicker than I thought."

Patting her shoulder, Carolyn started for the door, then stopped, examining Denise with eyes that saw far too much. "Maybe you should call him."

Dr. Hayden Stone. Her shrink of the hour. The man would listen for weeks on end as long as the meter was running.

But he was good looking.

"Maybe I will," Denise choked out.

"Baby, is there something wrong?"

"Nothing more than usual. Thanks."

Alone again, Denise listened as Carolyn's footsteps receded down the upstairs hall. Drawing a breath, she collapsed on the bed. Somewhere inside herself a thousand wings had begun to flutter. More anxiety. Deeper still, she sensed something dark and evil reach upward, its malignant fingers grabbing harder, closer. Someday they would grab her soul and squish it like a grape.

Self-hypnosis, she thought, panicked. Let the poisons collect in the center and then push them out. Push them out.

She closed her eyes and concentrated on John. Her powers of concentration sometimes astonished her because it felt so real. He was there. John Callahan. Her lover and husband. John whose maleness enveloped her, John who turned her to melting fluid.

"Make love to me, John." She reached for him beseechingly, but he stared down at her dispassionately. Unwrapping the towel, she placed his imaginary hand on her breast.

"I tried, Denise. I'm not going to try anymore."

"John, John, John." Her hands climbed up his torso and she rubbed against him like a kitten. Soft, smooth, tactile. The sweetness of love.

"What do you want this time, Denise?"

"Just the lead in *Lady Paradise*. That's all . . ."

He grabbed her hair in a tangle, pulling her head back, glaring at her. He stared at her so long and hard that her pulse rocketed. He was going to give in this time. He couldn't resist. His hand slid down her back, over her hips. She was wet and waiting for him. She guided him down to the bed, until he was sprawled atop her, his mouth like fire kissing her all over.

She squirmed deliciously.

The vision changed. It wasn't John. It was someone else. Someone who wanted to hurt and punish her. "Please," she moaned. A black, buried memory rose instead, smothering her. She cried out and sat bolt upright, fully awake, drenched anew in sweat.

Completely alone.

Crazy. Sick. Sexually deviant.

And why had she blown it by asking him for the part in his next film when she knew he would never consider her?

"Because everything you touch turns to shit," she muttered furiously. The Sadim Touch. Midas, spelled backwards. She had it in spades.

With shaking fingers, she reached for the telephone and dialed Stone's number.

Hayley narrowed her gaze on the brown-haired man standing behind the cameras in the dense California heat. The sleeves of his blue workshirt were rolled to his elbows. His gaze was directed at the lithesome actress draped across the table as if she were tonight's special entree. It wasn't a bad scene, really. The dialog made up for the cliche. But Hayley wasn't interested in Act II, Scene III of *Fortunata*. She was interested in the man in the workshirt and jeans. He was one of the top producers in Hollywood, a chauvinistic, arrogant, sexist, self-important boor.

He was her brother-in-law, John Callahan.

And he was her ticket to stardom.

"Unbutton the top couple of buttons of your jeans," Callahan said to the actress who instantly complied. The actor leaning against the table, glanced at him for direction.

Callahan might be only the producer at this party, but

his directing credits were pretty impressive, too, and since the actual director of the picture, Frank Carello, was standing to one side and schmoozing with some losers from the studio, Callahan was doing the work.

"Go," Callahan said.

The scene began again. A love scene. Hayley supposed it was passionate but there were so many people standing around, of which Callahan was her main focal point, that she had difficulty even paying attention. And the actor himself seemed so robotic. Good God, he couldn't fart without checking with Callahan first. Did he have no sense of timing, of creativity? About the kindest compliment she could give him was that he was dead-on Marlon Brando. The youthful Brando, that is. All smolder and growl and intensity. That cool fifties stuff that was so powerful in the nineties right now. God forbid the man might actually *smile* either on-camera, or off.

She moved slowly to the other side of the camera, checking another angle.

Didn't the guy get it? You had to go after something—really go after it—to achieve it. If he didn't improve, and soon, *Fortunata* would be his last stop on the track to stardom.

She, Hayley Scott, knew what to do. Whatever it took. Whatever price must be paid. She could do it. More importantly, she *would* do it. Without a whimper of protest.

Since the moment she could think, Hayley had yearned to be an actress, to be *the* actress. She play-acted everything. All the world was her stage . . .

But tricky, despicable fate had intervened and dropped opportunity at Denise's feet like an unwanted, unloved child whom Denise had then abused and abandoned. Hayley had followed her sister's short-lived, disastrous career, consumed with envy and horror. Furious with Denise, furious with fate. It should have been *her* chance, *her* opportunity. Her sister had squandered it, for God's sake. Tossed it away and stomped on it. Sucked all the life from it so now Hayley was starting below zero, having Denise's failure attached to her own name like a bad smell.

But Denise had married John Callahan. And Hayley's connection to her sister might serve her in good stead with him.

Or, it might boomerang.

"Move back," one of the lower-than-low assistants to an associate producer commanded her.

Hayley gave him a bright smile and stepped back. She was determined but she wasn't stupid. Today's nobody was tomorrow's most powerful producer in Hollywood. She wasn't beautiful like her older sisters, and, though she loathed admitting it, she wasn't as naturally talented as Denise. But she possessed something neither of her sisters did: a single-mindedness as hard and brilliant as a diamond. She cultivated friendships as if she were to be tested on her proficiency at it. She planned her life to the instant. She organized and worked and charged toward her goal with machine-like purpose.

She *wanted*.

Fortunata's director, Frank Carello, was a bear of a man with a nauseating manner of hugging people and acting as if they were part of his family. But John Callahan, the film's producer, had the slow walkin', slow-talkin' appeal of a cowboy. Had Hayley been interested in men as something more than a stepping stone to success, she might have fallen a little in love with him herself. As it was, she calculated just how she could use her connection to him to her advantage. He might be willing to cut her a break simply because she was his sister-in-law, but the irony of it was he didn't know they were related! Denise, bless her screwed-up soul, had long maintained the myth that she was the only child of a pair of luckless Indiana farmers who'd died in a fire when she was nineteen.

Neither Hayley nor Dinah had been invited to the wedding. She doubted Callahan even knew they existed.

"Mr. Callahan?"

The voice came from Tonja Terkell, the breathless first assistant who wore such tight shorts Hayley imagined she could read the brand of her underwear. Callahan favored Tonja with a distracted smile and shook his head to whatever gibberish she was going on about. The director looked pissed. Chastised, Tonja gingerly tiptoed out of the way.

Hayley inwardly groaned. She was here at Tonja's invitation and if Callahan or the director chose to rescind it because Tonja was too much of a pain in the ass, all her hard work would be for nought.

Grabbing Tonja's arm, Hayley wheeled her out of earshot. "What are you doing?" she hissed.

Tonja looked surprised and hurt. "My job, thank you very much. What's the matter? Nobody noticed you yet?"

"I can't get to Callahan."

"Why don't you work on Frankie? He loves everybody."

Hayley glanced at Frank Carello and felt weary. She didn't want someone who loved everybody. Besides, Carello's thick arms reminded her of her stepfather's muscular biceps, and that in turn reminded her of Thomas's beefy hands. Ugly hands. "I don't want to be part of the family."

"Well, okay," Tonja relented. "I got some good news for you."

"What?"

"Callahan's newest project."

Hayley zeroed in on Tonja. "You know what it is?"

"You bet. I heard him talking to Frankie about it yesterday afternoon. They don't pay much attention to me, but I listen."

"So, what is it?" Hayley demanded with increasing excitement.

"*Lady Paradise.*"

"*Lady Paradise?*"

"Uh huh. I think it's about a hooker." She shrugged. "Serious stuff?"

"No, more like *Pretty Woman*. You know, 'hooker with a heart of gold and a few bad breaks finds the man she loves and changes her spots.' The usual bullshit."

"*Pretty Woman* was a huge success and made a lot of money," Hayley said reflectively.

"Not to mention what it did for Julia Roberts."

Magic words. Magic, magic words. Tonja had no idea what her innocent comment did to Hayley's equilibrium.

"But I think there's a darker side in there somewhere," Tonja went on. "John said something about interviewing real hookers."

"Are you sure you didn't overhear them making plans for the evening?" Hayley demanded sarcastically.

"Frankie's wife's here and he would never screw up that relationship. And John Callahan has too much class." She eyed him longingly, with a bit of hero-worship thrown in.

"Can you get me a copy of the script?" Hayley asked.

"No way! I could lose my job!"

"Is it that much of a secret?"

"I don't know. But until Mr. Callahan starts sending out copies himself, I'm not messing with it. You want a flunky to take risks for you, find somebody else."

Empty words, since Tonja practically owed Hayley her job in the first place. It was Hayley who'd encouraged her to follow her dream, and it was Hayley who'd pushed her toward Callahan Productions.

So, she had her own best interests at heart. So, what? This was Hollywood.

"Calm down," Hayley soothed Tonja. "I don't want you to lose your job. I just want a chance, that's all, and I'd be perfect for this role."

"Yeah, well, half of Hollywood would be."

Hayley shook her head, her gaze pinned on John Callahan, whose father had run one of the most powerful movie studios in Hollywood before his death, and had made his son famous and successful in the process. John Callahan, whose reputed womanizing had led to two paternity suits, both unsubstantiated, and whom insiders claimed had married Denise Scott as a means to staunch his playboy image, was successful in his own right, but no one could forget his roots.

Was the man really as reformed as he would like people to believe? Hayley asked herself as she watched him squat down, lean his clipboard on one jean-clad knee and scribble madly. He radiated sexuality. She knew for a fact that he and Denise were over; the tabloids had trumpeted their break-up for weeks.

So what did he do for female company these days?

Hayley toyed with the idea of finding out personally, but she broke into a cold sweat at the mere possibility. Men were not her cup of tea. Neither were women for that matter. She'd come to the conclusion years earlier that she was asexual, and though it sometimes felt like she was missing out on some vital part of life, most of the time she was simply grateful. Too much anguish, too much worry, too much gnashing of teeth.

Love and sex got too tangled up with what was really important. Witness Denise, who gave the term promiscuous new meaning. Even Dinah had had her one, mortal heartbreak, although she'd turned misery to her advantage by writing about the foibles of romance.

For no particular reason Hayley thought about her mother. Had she really loved Thomas Daniels, a man to whom abuse came naturally?

For a moment something happened. Raw pain flooded through her, startling her. An ugly memory burned brightly: Daniels slapping Mama, laughing like a maniac as Mama cowered in humiliation; Daniels's cruel eyes sliding Hayley's way, her feet pounding across scarred linoleum; his laughter sweeping after her like a foul wind.

Hayley took a breath and followed John Callahan as he sauntered off the set to one of the studio offices.

If Thomas Daniels wasn't dead yet she hoped with every inch of her heart someone would kill him.

The Logan household had calmed down after the initial discovery, but Matt still felt like a pretty big wheel. He'd embellished the tale a bit now. He'd told that whiney Sherry Mesner that the skull had chattered at them. Just a little bit. Coulda been the wind, but more likely it was Daniels warning them away.

'Course Sherry had acted like she wasn't scared, then went and tattled to the teacher. Still, it had been worth seeing her eyes bug out while she'd screamed that he'd made the whole thing up.

But that was kid's stuff compared to this. Uncle Jack was here, standing in the kitchen. Flew in this morning and drove from Portland all the way to Wagon Wheel. Talked to Sheriff Dempsey—an old friend of his since high school, Mom said—about Daniels' skull. It wouldn't be long before there was bound to be another picture in the paper.

"So, how much are you really going to get involved?" Mom asked Uncle Jack. He was her younger brother and she always used that older sister tone on him. Were all older sisters the same?

"Depends."

Uncle Jack never said too much. Wore jeans and looked like a regular person, but you just *knew* he was thinking real hard about putting somebody away.

"Matt, go upstairs. I want to talk to Connor without an extra pair of ears."

"Ah, Mom!"

"Go."

Connor was Uncle Jack. Connor Jackley, but Matt thought Connor was a stupid name and had called him Uncle Jack from the moment he'd realized he had this special, beloved uncle who was a real police detective. Or at least he had been. For some reason he wasn't on the force anymore and there was fear in Matt's heart that Uncle Jack had quit for good. But it had to only be temporary. Matt simply couldn't bear to think of Uncle Jack as anything but an honest-to-God law enforcement officer.

"Do as your mama says," Dad spoke from the end of the table. He was leaning over a newspaper but that didn't mean nothing. He always knew what you were doing, and like Uncle Jack, he didn't say much but when he did, BLAM! You'd better run for cover 'cause it did mean something, yessirree.

Still . . .

"I'm the one who found the skull," Matt reminded them all.

Uncle Jack smiled in a way so that Matt knew he was on his side. But then he said, "I do have to talk to your mom and dad."

"Can't I—?"

"No," Mom cut him off.

Matt stomped away, then retraced his steps and hovered on the other side of the kitchen door, one eye peeled for Heather, his rotten, snitching older sister.

"Was it murder?" Mom asked softly.

"Yep," Uncle Jack said.

"And you know who did it?"

"Dempsey's got some ideas. One which leads right to Los Angeles."

Sheriff Gus Dempsey and Uncle Jack had gone to school together in Bend, or something. Matt was thrilled that they were both working on the case. His case. "The Case of the Rotten Skull."

"Well, it's bound to be someone from here," Dad put in. "Daniels pushed too many people, too hard."

Uncle Jack breathed in slow, like he was thinking real hard. "According to Gus, Daniels had three stepdaughters. One of em's Denise Scott, the actress."

Mom stared. "You're kidding."

"She's Denise Scott from *Wagon Wheel?*" Dad demanded.

"Yep. She married John Callahan, a producer of some fame, but I think they're divorced now."

"She's from *here?*" Mom just couldn't seem to get over it. "I thought that was all rumor."

Uncle Jack kinda snorted, like he was having trouble believing the whole thing, too. Matt wished he knew who this actress was. He didn't pay too much attention to girls.

"Dempsey says people in this town remember the Scott girls, but it's all kind of vague. He wants some help and since I'm from L.A. . . ." Uncle Jack left the thought unfinished.

"Gus Dempsey called you here specifically to help, huh?" Dad asked.

"He knew who to call," Mom added softly.

"It's not going to make me go back," Uncle Jack said suddenly, as if he thought Mom was pushing. She probably was, Matt thought darkly. She had that way of just going at something that could drive you crazy. But Matt desperately wanted Uncle Jack back on the force, too.

"I'm familiar with the case, so he wants me to check it out," Uncle Jack went on. "That's all."

There was a long silence where Matt could hear the tick-tock of the grandfather clock. He held his breath and wished himself invisible.

"How long do you think you'll be here?" Dad asked.

"Awhile."

"Matt, honey," his mother said with tight-lipped tolerance, "Go upstairs."

Shit. He skidded away to the worn back stairs.

"I said I'd help, so I guess I will," Uncle Jack's voice trailed after him. "I've got an address for Denise Scott in Malibu. I'll start with her. But while I'm here, I think I'll pick up the threads of their lives in Wagon Wheel. I mean, after all . . . if they know anything about Daniels' death, it all started here."

"Damn right!" Dad's harsh tone caught at Matt's heart. He stopped short, straining to hear. "And it ended here. And I don't think there's a person in this town who'd say they're sorry Thomas Daniels rotted to death in a culvert!"

Chapter Three

Dinah scanned her column, pleased that Flick had left it relatively intact. You never knew which way that man would jump. Sheer orneriness could keep him from printing it. If there were a person on earth guaranteed to shoot her frustration level to all new highs, it was Flick.

She folded the *Santa Fe Review* and left it on the table. Through windows paned with rust-colored metal inserts, she could see the beach and restless, gray ocean. Everything was gray today: the sky, the water, the sand, the chunks of ragged driftwood.

She absolutely *hated* Los Angeles.

Her article had scraped pretty close to the bone this week. She'd fashioned it along the lines of her experiences with her ex-love, Glen Bosworth. She'd lived with Glen, made love with Glen, kept house with Glen, and, after a spate of co-habitation, he'd kicked her out, claiming he had to find himself. What he found was another woman with a bigger bank account.

Her article had been titled: "Falling In Love With A Bank Balance."

Funny now, but achingly painful during the process. It had, in fact, nearly killed her emotionally, and now, four years later, she was still picking up the pieces of her self-respect. She would never, ever allow someone to use her in that way again.

Not liking her own thoughts, Dinah headed for the refrigerator, poured herself a glass of wine, then wandered aimlessly around Denise's sumptuous home. Decorated Santa Fe style, Denise's decorator had at least had the good sense to keep the aquamarine and pink to a discreet minimum, capitalizing on the colors of adobe, ivory, rust, and black. In the corner of a living room was an adobe fireplace with a garnet-colored tile seat. A butterfly chair with a black enameled steel frame and tapestry cushion sat by a mahogany side table. Atop the table was a photograph. Denise in a black and white picture. A curiously reflective pose for her wild twin.

Dinah mounted the stairs. Denise's bedroom was to the right of the north end stairway. Here the aqua and pink colors invaded every corner. Subtlety had never been Denise's strong point, Dinah reflected wryly. The place smelled faintly of Chanel #5 and the closet was full of expensive clothes. Denise had worn Chanel #5 since high school, and her lust for expensive gowns and jewels was nearly as great as her incredible naivete and charm.

Dinah had chosen to sleep in the innocuous bedroom sandwiched between the main bath and the master bedroom, but now she passed by that door and strode along the gallery to the room at the south end, the room that overlooked the ocean.

John Callahan's room was as masculine as Denise's was feminine. The king-sized bed was covered with a chocolate-colored comforter and mounted with creamy white pillows. The dresser and chest of drawers were dark Tuscany wood, and the closet was empty of clothes except for several suits packed in garment bags.

There was another photograph of Denise on the nightstand. Dinah had only glanced inside this room once since she moved in, but now, barefoot, she squinched her toes into the sinfully thick ivory carpet and stared down at Denise's photo. In this one Denise was more herself: one brow was arched, a red sweater fell seductively off one bared shoulder, one finger was crooked in a come-hither gesture to the photographer. John, no doubt.

Dinah glanced around. There were no pictures of John in the house. He was definitely a behind the scenes kind of guy. Either that, or Denise had tossed out all traces of him along with his memory.

Retracing her footsteps downstairs, Dinah headed for the library where the errant Fax machine and sophisticated computer equipment were arranged atop a black enamel worktable and bookshelf-cum-desk. John was a producer, directer, and sometimes writer. Dinah had used his equipment to write her articles these past few weeks. Apart from the temperamental Fax machine, everything was first-rate and ran smooth as glass.

And the Fiat was running again. Four hundred dollars it had cost, half of Dinah's life savings, but apart from an annoying little hiccup when it was idling, the car was holding off the Grim Reaper—at least until next time.

Dinah wrinkled her nose. The paperweight on the desk was a thunder egg. A pale gray chalcedony quartz with translucent crystal-like particles in its center which made it look like a petrified blue egg. Dinah picked it up, balancing its weight in her palm. John's? Probably. Might even be a gift from Denise.

Shivering slightly, she set the thunder egg on a short stack of John's forgotten notes. The egg slipped and the notes shifted. John Callahan's bold masculine signature was scrawled across a short page. The unexpected sight of it caused the hair to raise on Dinah's arms.

"You horrible bastard," she whispered softly.

Denise had once compared the man to Thomas Daniels. If John Callahan were even half as bad, Denise had lived in sheer hell.

It was next to impossible to get close to Callahan. She'd been at it for nearly two weeks and nothing. *Nada.* She'd phoned, and hung around, and tried in every way she knew to make contact. Callahan was just too immersed in *Fortunata.* She was going to have to wait until the damn thing wrapped, and she was terrible at waiting.

The bedside phone purred. Hayley snatched it up, grimacing as she glanced at the time. It had to be the deli. She was late for the third time this week. No doubt she was about to get her walking papers.

"Hey, girl. You a 'Miss Scott'?"

The tone was condescending and disinterested.

"Speaking," she answered crisply.

"You wanted ta see me, right?"

Hayley blinked. Her attention sharpened. "Is this Mrs. Carver?"

"Nobody else."

Her heart beat hard. "Could we get together? I've got something I'd like to propose to you."

"You're wastin' your time. I ain't no babysitter. And this ain't no method acting class."

"Tonja told you what I wanted?"

"Look, sweetcakes. Ya wanta get into the life, I still don't wan'cha. But I especially don't want no snot-nose actress who don't know shit."

"Five o'clock. Stanbury's Deli. I'll buy you dinner."

"What's that? Like corned beef on rye?" She snorted. "You gotta be kiddin'."

"I work there. You can have whatever's on the menu and fifty bucks besides." Hayley did a quick mental calculation. Jason was going to scream! And her job was on the line already, but hey. . . . This was her chance.

A pause. "I know I'm gonna regret this. Shit." She hung up.

Hayley carefully replaced the receiver. "Mrs. Carver" was a hooker from Hollywood Boulevard—Julia Roberts' *Pretty Woman* in living color. There would be no whitewashing the character; Mrs. Carver was the real down and dirty article. And she was going to show Hayley the ropes.

Hayley drew a deep, slow breath. Shelve your sensibilities at home and get ready for a wild ride. Next stop: a quick fuck with a nameless john.

"God," Hayley muttered, her hands like ice as she pressed her palms to her face.

The phone rang again. In a trance, Hayley lifted the receiver.

"You want a job, you get down here. Now!" Jason bellowed.

"Don't have a hemorrhage," she answered, pulling on her courage as if if were a coat. "I'll be right there, sugar . . ."

Dr. Stone's office resembled something scripted from a movie. It possessed the requisite desk, cushy chairs, and yes, unbelievably, a small couch, more like a loveseat, really, settled crosswise in one corner. The couch and chairs were white leather; the desk either pine or oak stained to a dark brown that was nearly black.

Feeling perverse, Denise slouched against the loveseat, her ankles crossed in front of her, her short, straight blue, minidress hiked up to reveal an ample expanse of tan thigh.

She had no intention of trying to seduce the doctor. Good Lord, no. But the man seemed so damned fixated on S-E-X that Denise was pretty fed up with his whole routine. He acted as if she were an uncontrollable nymphomaniac and seemed to believe that if they talked S-E-X nonstop—in serious, dulcet tones, of course—that she would learn some incredible truism of life and would CHANGE HER WAYS, HALLELUJAH, LORD!

She had problems, heaven knew, but even whacked-out, semi-sex-crazed loony that she was, Denise was completely aware that sex was not her only problem. Maybe it wasn't even the *real* problem. She suspected, though her mind shied away from any real attempt to delve into the issue, that her sex drive was just average and that she used sex as a shield for some deeper, murkier reason.

Well. She'd be damned if she'd reveal that little kernel of insight to Sigmund here. God knew what he'd come up with as a cure. She'd rather he thought she was trying to seduce him.

"You've had more delusions," Stone said, as if it were understood between them already. Maybe it was.

"That's right." Denise was torn between the desire to truly confide in someone or hang onto the last vestige of her self-respect.

"Want to talk about them?"

He looked so professional, even in the blue denim shirt and casual tan slacks. He listened with that learned casualness that Denise had come to distrust. She'd been through a slew of psychiatrists, psychologists, and various and sundry other mental health experts. Stone was better than most, but hey, nobody could have such black hair and not color it. *She* knew. And though his dark eyes simmered with compassion, Denise suspected it was all a sham; Stone's paternal persona, guaranteed to breach defensive walls, loosen tear ducts, help sinners howl out confessions, open pocketbooks . . .

"There's a man at Carolyn's. Let's call him Mr. Hawaiian Tropics. He's not exactly the modest type," she said dryly. "In fact, he's a downright exhibitionist."

"What's he done?"

"He's very proud of his genitalia. Likes to show it off at any available opportunity. I've gotten more than a few glimpses myself."

"And?"

"One day I was in the pool, on one of those blow-up rafts, and he dived into the water and jumped on me. He was naked and I told him to get off me, but he didn't. So then he—we—sort of fought, and then . . ."

Stone waited impassively.

What the hell was it about recounting sexual experiences that was so deadly embarrassing? She had this sense that the good doctor got off on these private testimonials; his own perverse way of vicariously getting his jollies. *And he thinks I'm the sicko.*

"Then he stuck it to me," Denise said matter-of-factly.

"Did you give your consent?"

"Sort of."

He waited. Clearly Dr. Stone believed that if he waited long enough she would crack wide open, throw herself on the floor and howl out a confession.

Well, maybe she would.

"In the dream, I didn't feel like it at first, okay? I don't think I did later, either, really. I slapped him and he hit me, but things kind of went on and I just gave up."

His gray eyes examined her clinically. "A lot of rape victims give up when there's no recourse."

"Yeah, well it wasn't like that." Denise looked around the room.

"What was it like?"

"I don't really know," she snapped back. "It wasn't horrible, okay? I didn't *hate* it. It freaked me out, but then I kind of accepted it."

"Sometimes guilt makes the victim feel like it was her fault, like she asked for it somehow."

"I know all this," Denise said with forced patience. "But it wasn't even real. It was a dream." She almost added "wet" dream but decided Stone wouldn't see the humor. God, these professionals were humorless!

"So, what do you think?"

"Maybe I want to be raped." Denise slid him a look from beneath her lashes, judging his reaction. Nothing. "I'd seen this guy showing off his equipment and I made up this whole scenario. It was great. I even got a thrill out of it. In fact I recommend it to anyone who's sexually frustrated. Works wonders."

"You think your dream suggests that you would welcome being taken forcefully?"

Jeeeezus, this guy was worse than her third grade math teacher. "That's what I just said, isn't it? I'm hardly going to endear myself to the women's libbers now, am I?" She sat up straighter, crossed her legs, and tugged ineffectively at her hemline.

"Have you had sexual relations with this man?"

"Not yet," she said pointedly. Yep, the guy was fixated on sex. Maybe all shrinks were.

But he was damned good-looking. When she asked him out she'd laughed airily, as if it were all a huge joke. The patient seducing the psychiatrist? Come on! It was such a cliche even she didn't believe it.

But a part of her had been serious.

And Dr. Hayden Stone knew it.

Now she examined the strong, masculine column of his neck. His skin was deeply tanned, as if he spent a lot of time in the sun. That, and combined with his body-type, prompted her to ask, "Do you golf? I bet you spend every Wednesday and Saturday afternoon on the links."

He smiled enigmatically. Another psychiatric trick. Oh, yes, she knew them all.

"What are your feelings for him?" he asked.

"For Mr. Hawaiian Tropics?" Denise laughed. "Well, I'd say he's loathsome, but interesting in a twisted sort of way, if you know what I mean. I don't think I could really call him my kind of guy, though."

"Denise, are you acting?"

"What?"

"Are you putting on an act for me?"

Her opinion of him took a sharp nosedive. The nerve of this guy! "I don't know what the hell you're talking about. You're the one who wanted to know what my feelings were."

"You sound angry."

"I'm goddamn furious. I don't know why I even come here. You can't help me. The only thing you think about is your dick and where you'll stick it next."

"Now I know you're acting," he said softly.

"I'm outta here." Snatching up her clutch bag, Denise headed for the door. Tension was a coiled spring inside her. Therapy. Bullshit. It was all a goddamn trap.

The walls of the corridor waved and swayed. Denise

hurried blindly for the door, gulping in hot, humid, sweaty Houston air as soon as she hit the street.

She found her car by rote. Carolyn's car. A shiny black Mercedes trimmed in gold. The damn thing could be trimmed in fur for all she cared. It was a worthless trinket paid for by sleazy perversions and false altruism.

Inside the leather seats were slick with heat. Denise's skin stuck like glue, squeaked when she moved. She had to get out of here and back to Los Angeles. Back to John. Back home.

"Shit," she muttered, slamming the Mercedes into gear. Maybe she should drive there. Would Carolyn put out an A.P.B. on her for grand theft auto? Hell, she probably wouldn't even notice the car was missing.

Stanbury's Deli could have been attractive and chic if the owner gave a rat's ass about its operation. But Jason, the manager, had full control, apparently, because Hayley had never seen the mysterious owner ever materialize. And Jason was both a bastard and a jailer, and when Hayley skidded across the semiclean black and white tile floor and behind the counter, Jason sent her his coldest, meanest glare.

"Oh, hurt me some more," Hayley muttered. "I had car trouble."

"You don't own a car. Why don't you just say you got run over by a truck?"

Hayley half-smiled. "Okay, I got run over by a truck."

"You really are a pain." He snapped a towel at her, stinging her hip. "And you're going to be out of a job soon, because I'm going to fire you."

"No, you're not."

"Yes, Hayley. I am."

She had to bite her tongue to keep from sending back a snarly retort. Jason thought he was teaching her a lesson. Well, okay, she could let him believe he was doing something good. Besides, pain that he was, he didn't hit on her or do anything else disgustingly male, so she was safe here. She didn't want to lose this job if she didn't have to.

"I'm sorry," she said, mustering up her best sincerity.

"Like hell." He laughed without humor. "Clean up this shit-dirty floor and I'll let you stay."

Hayley got out the mop and swabbed away dust, dirt, tossed cigarettes, and leftover food gunk stuck to the tiles. Thirty minutes later the place looked reasonably tidy and she was filling salt and pepper shakers when her "date" strutted in.

At least, she suspected it was Mrs. Carver. The woman wore a dark blue silk blouse and white leather skirt. The skirt was short enough, and Mrs. Carver was tall enough, so that it would meet some folks at eye level. Hooker shoes completed the outfit: white alligator with at least six inches of heel and covered with rhinestones. Her hair was her own, Hayley guessed, but it had been permed so badly it looked like carnival cotton candy dyed gold. The best thing about the woman was her skin. Lined a bit, yes, but satiny nevertheless. She had to be in her thirties but the skin might fool someone who didn't know.

Of course the whole effect was ruined by the inches of electric blue eyeshadow and black mascara and liner that emphasized a pair of slightly protruding, rather pretty, green eyes.

"Mrs. Carver?" Hayley asked.

"You got me." She sized Hayley up with practiced ease. "You sorta look like that actress."

"Denise Scott. I know."

"You tryin' to capitalize on that, honey? Let me tell ya. It don't never work. I should know. People tell me I look like Michelle Pfeiffer."

This was said straight, but for just a second Hayley almost laughed. Michelle Pfeiffer? Give me a break! Mrs. Carver bore a slight resemblance to Barbara Walters on a very, very bad day. Not that she couldn't be pretty; the raw material was there. But Hayley suspected there wasn't much of a chance for Mrs. Carver to be anything more than what she was today.

Which gave her a bad feeling. A premonition that made her feel slightly sick. Was this it for her, too? A downhill slide from Stanbury's Deli into the depths of prostitution, drugs, and God knew what else?

The past filtered in: a black shadow dogging her heels. Hayley couldn't prevent a sharp glance backwards before she pulled on her composure once more.

"What would you like?" She gestured to the menu as Mrs. Carver slipped herself into a narrow, blood red booth.

Shooting a sly glance Hayley's way, she asked, "What costs the most?"

Irritated, Hayley snapped, "Read the menu and see."

"Can I order two sandwiches?"

Leaning close to her, Hayley responded quietly, "I'm giving you a meal and fifty bucks. That's it. You wanna do business, or not?"

"I haven't decided. Where's the money, sweet-talker?"

With careful deliberation, Hayley pulled two twenties and a ten from the pocket of her black cords—Stanbury's uniform. Mrs. Carver stuffed the bills into her slim, black clutch purse.

"You wanna come out Saturday night?"

The question was offered so casually, Hayley almost

missed the implication. Her pulse rocketed, making her feel slightly weak. She was strong, invincible, except when it came to sex and men. She wanted to run from this situation she was setting up that would be nothing less than intolerable.

But then she saw herself receiving cheers, adulation, and awards. She pictured herself immersed in scripts and challenging scenes, working until she dropped, surrounded by people as driven and insatiably ambitious as herself. Everyone yearned to be Hayley Scott.

She could taste it, and it tasted sweet.

"Just tell me where, and I'll be there."

Rubbing her hands over her face Dinah pushed aside the hard copy of her latest article. It wasn't due until Thursday and she didn't feel like editing right now.

Alone again, she poured herself another glass of wine and sat out on the beachfront deck, circling the bottom of her wine goblet across the pebbled-glass table, spreading the condensation into little droplets. She drank slowly until she was a little drunk and a little sad. Her bones felt like water and she was half-convinced that if she sank down into the squeaky cushions of Denise's outdoor love-seat she would melt.

It was at times like these—those few moments when she stopped and reflected—that she thought about, wallowed in, the ruins of her youth. She was a fraud. A total flim-flam. What the hell did she know about love, anyway? Yet, she wrote about it every day. Every goddamn day as if it were her driving force.

Love makes the world go 'round. All it had done for the three Scott sisters was create pain and destruction.

But then, it wasn't really love that had motivated

Thomas Daniels, although that couldn't be said for Mama. Mama had fallen deeply, obsessively, in love, and when Thomas's conquests had become more common knowledge than Friday night's high school football score, Nina Scott Daniels had spent her days and nights lying on her lonely bed, lights out, claiming her despair and listlessness were all part and parcel of the trials of raising three headstrong young women.

Oh, Mama, we all knew better.

Denise had been a handful, that was true. And Hayley's stubborn determination could be unbearable. She, Dinah, had always harbored big dreams and planned to scale insurmountable walls. But, so what? They were all normal. Healthy. Possessed of women's own peculiar strengths and weaknesses.

Except . . .

Dinah gulped her wine too fast and tears came to her eyes. She coughed and coughed, then absurdly, lusted for a cigarette though she'd given up smoking five years earlier. Thomas Daniels. If she believed herself capable of true hate, he'd be the reason. She also suspected he was a closet pedophile, though he'd never laid a hand on her or her sisters. Anyway, he'd never touched *her,* and Denise and Hayley had both vehemently denied the charge that fateful night Dinah had been forced to bring it up.

But, oh God, those glittery, lustful stares! She'd been on the receiving end of those a time or two and it was enough to freeze your blood right in your veins. *That's* what Mama had seen and understood, and *that's* what had sent her to the dim sanctuary of her bedroom.

Thomas had worked as a carpenter and made more than a few conquests in the privacy of his victim's homes. He'd been a handsome man in a rough, base sort of way.

Dinah had found him particularly disgusting and whenever she met a man with that kind of burly build, with just the right color of near black hair, with that hint of a hidden smile, a judgement on women as a whole, she was repelled.

Glen Bosworth had been Thomas Daniels's exact opposite: aesthetically slim; sandy-haired with an appealing, studious look accentuated by a pair of wire-rimmed glasses; dry; clever; and sensitive.

And avaricious.

Dinah smiled wryly. The sun was setting, turning the water into a murky shade of iodine. It was glorious. Maybe there was more to Los Angeles than varying shades of gray, she could admit grudgingly to herself, but she still looked forward to the beauty and dry heat of Santa Fe.

She thought about her current article. Flick would like it. She was good at writing clever stories about relationships with the opposite sex, great at delivering anecdotes about failed love affairs, ones she'd sometimes experienced, but more often something imagined. Surfacy stories. Vignettes about why *she* was mad at *him*, or why *he* went crazy when *she* did this or that.

But she never scratched beneath the surface. She was too afraid.

Still, letters poured in. Lonely people wanting to know how she resolved her problems. She sometimes worked with a psychologist to make certain her answers were fair and helpful. Lord knew *she* was no expert. She hadn't the faintest idea how to make a real relationship last.

Anyway, maybe love was all an illusion. As insubstantial as dust motes. As deceptive as this silly charade she was playing for Denise's benefit.

She looked around herself. At Denise's house and beachfront property. If someone questioned who she was and what she was doing, would she tell them the truth?

Dinah considered. Hell, no. She could be Denise for a while. Why not? Maybe she'd incorporate in it one of her later stories: "Role Playing to Spice Up Your Sex Life."

Oh, yeah? She laughed aloud. Well, she could manufacture something up; she was an expert at manufacturing something up. Better than revealing the plain, boring truth.

Twenty minutes later she trundled up to the guest room. Slipping out of her clothes, she fell into bed, asleep inside of five minutes. She was so deep in slumber that later, when the tickle of air over her bare arms penetrated Dinah's sleep-fogged brain, she incorporated it into her dream. She was on a windy beach, immersed in sunshine and idle time. Snuggling deeper into the covers, she drew the slippery satin sheets of the guest room bed up to her chin, refusing to be pulled into reality just yet.

The breeze feathered the hair at her temples—a cool, chilly breath. She couldn't ignore it forever. Sighing, Dinah lifted one sleepy eyelid. Had she left a window open? Reluctantly raising her head, she saw the light was on in the hall.

Her heart jolted. She distinctly remembered turning it off.

Throwing back the covers, she fumbled for the switch to her bedside lamp, then bit back a scream when a huge hand clamped over her mouth.

"Don't scream," a very male, very low, nerve-tingling voice commanded.

She screamed anyway, a pathetic, pinched sound behind hard fingers. The smell of alcohol was heavy and rich. Oh, God. Her head swam with fear.

"I've tried to be fair, but you're a bigger bitch than even I thought. You're not going to ruin *Lady Paradise.* I won't let you. So forget about that audition or so help me God I'll throw you out on your cute little ass right now."

With his free hand, he switched on the lamp. Dinah gazed in wide-eyed silence at the lean, masculine face bending over her. Steely blue eyes regarded her without humor. Thin lips formed an uncompromising line. An incredibly perfect, aquiline nose looked out of place on that otherwise rugged countenance.

Realization dawned. John Callahan in the flesh.

He slowly lifted his hand from her mouth, but Dinah couldn't find the breath to speak.

"Don't look so petrified. The last thing on my mind right now is *you,*" he snarled in an ugly tone.

"What are you doing here?" she demanded, clearing her throat when she heard the shaky timbre of her voice.

"Your choice, Denise," he responded in a deep drawl. "Make it."

Dinah stared at him. "What?"

"The audition." His teeth were set. "That goddamn Sandberg called me today and I told him to shut up about you. You've really got your nerve. I wouldn't put you in the role of Toni if I was guaranteed an academy award!"

"I don't know what you're talking about."

"Bullshit."

That did it. Why was she arguing with him? She was supposed to be Denise, and since he didn't seem to realize she wasn't, well . . . "Get the hell out of my house!"

The look on his face changed suddenly from cool tolerance to hard-eyed fury. Dinah automatically shrank back, but he pinned her shoulders against the bed.

"Don't," she murmured, suddenly frightened.

He swore something unintelligible, then with a deft

muscular twist, tossed her over his shoulder. Her stomach slammed into hard bone and muscle, knocking the breath from her lungs. She shrieked in surprise, legs flailing. Rocklike arms clamped against her legs as he strode toward the door. Her nose bumped into a cotton, blue workshirt as she bounced against him.

It happened so fast they were in the hallway before she started to struggle in earnest. No use. His arms were too strong. His determination too deep.

"Goodbye, my love," he mocked.

"You can't throw me out!"

For an answer he strode along the gallery toward the stairs.

"Wait!" she cried. By God, he meant to actually do it! He was going to literally toss her out of the house!

"I'll ship your things later," he said with a first note of humor. "Leave an address."

In impotent fury she pummelled his muscled back with her fists. She kicked wildly and he tightened his grip around her legs and grabbed one wrist behind his back. "This is my house!" she yelled. "Put me down or you'll be the sorriest man that ever lived!"

"I already am. And for the record," he added through clenched teeth as Dinah attempted to bite his wrist. "This is my house. You're a guest."

Dinah struggled to knee him in the crotch. "You— god—damn—bastard!"

One knee connected square and his groan of pain intensified her struggle. But his strength was phenomenal. He squeezed her wrist and ankle so tightly she was certain she'd have bruises.

He carried her outside, to the deck where she'd been peaceably drinking her wine scant hours before. Waves crashed somewhere beyond. Dinah twisted violently.

White-ruffled breakers leaped against a deep, black sky. She kicked, but John Callahan's strong hands were iron manacles.

"Let go of me!" Dinah screamed in fury.

"You incredible bitch," he said in wonder. "You don't know when to give up." He swung her upward.

"Don't! Wait! My God!"

"Goodbye, my love," he said again, this time with a twinge of irony.

Then she was bodily thrown over the deck rail to the cold beach sand, three-feet below.

Chapter Four

She screamed with all her might!

A half-second later she hit the cold, dank beach. Sand went up her nose and grated against her teeth. She couldn't believe it. Could—not—believe it! He'd thrown her over the side of the deck as if she were so much garbage.

Clenching her hands, Dinah gathered up two fistfuls of the grainy, gray stuff, so infuriated she was almost afraid to move, certain she would combust into a pile of super-charged atoms if she so much as twitched.

How dare he! How *dare* he!

Sputtering, she leaped to her feet, ready to climb over the deck rail and hurl herself at him.

But he was gone. She heard the deck door slide closed and the lock click with cold finality behind him. He'd dumped her unceremoniously and turned on his heel.

Bastard!

Quick as a cat she dashed through past the birds of paradise and draping bougainvillea that lined the brick pathway to the front door. She knew where the spare key was; she'd hidden it herself. With a speed that defied belief, she snatched the key from a tiny hidden hook beneath the cantilevered siding, twisted it in the lock and half-stumbled, half-fell inside.

She was in the foyer before John Callahan's small brain and long legs had connected that she might be wily enough to find a way back inside. But he must have heard her because determined footsteps approached from the kitchen almost immediately. Frozen, Dinah hovered in the center of the tile foyer, undecided and alarmed but with her anger spiralling into the stratosphere.

Who the *hell* did he think he was? No wonder Denise had asked for her help! Dinah was tougher, generally cooler in the midst of a fight (though her limbs were shaking with such fury right now it was hard to tell) and incredibly sharp-tongued and incisive when she was certain she was in the right.

And she *was* in the right. No question about that. This was Denise's house and her *ex*-husband had bodily thrown her out, dumping her with such cool disdain onto the beach below that Dinah could scarcely believe it even now. She could have been hurt. Seriously hurt.

For the briefest of moments a glimmer of junior high revenge brightened her thoughts. She would feign injury. Cry crocodile tears. Or better yet, stoically fight back the pain that his thoughtlessly cruel actions had wrought, proving how brave she was and how sadistically wrong he was.

The footsteps grew louder, closer. Dinah held her breath, fighting an absurd impulse to run. Then Callahan appeared in the archway between the lower hall and the foyer.

But he didn't stop there. He strode purposely forward, his strides devouring the space between them in less than two seconds. It was a move meant to intimidate and Dinah, had she been any less strong, would have shrunk into herself as a means of protection. Perversely, her own hardships were what saved her now. Years of dealing with a sociopathic stepfather followed by Flick's acid-test in the business world had honed Dinah's strength to a pure, fine point. If he took one step nearer she'd gouge him with all her fiery willpower. Her eyes narrowed in anticipation.

Five feet away he stopped short to stare at her. It was then she realized she wasn't acting anything like her sister.

John Callahan was facing a woman he didn't know.

Dinah's throat closed in fear.

"Denise?" His voice was slightly rough, just short of gravelly. The hair on her arms stood on end.

"I could have you arrested," she accused, her tone so steely it brought his eyebrows crashing together.

Once more she smelled the subtle fragrance of hard alcohol, a musky, dangerous scent that nevertheless Dinah found perversely attractive. It had been nice when Thomas Daniels drank. He was less vicious, more inclined to fall into a dumb stupor than predatorily follow after her and her sisters with his mean little eyes. It was ass backwards, she knew; most people shuddered at the destruction that living with an alcoholic caused. But Thomas hadn't been an alcoholic. Alert and at the top of his senses was when he'd been the most unpredictable. Stone-cold sober he was a predator who made Dinah feel insecure and who sent Hayley and Denise scuttling to the corners of the house in order to escape his notice.

Dinah had forced herself to face off with him. Afraid, but unwilling to show it, she'd refused to back down when she'd sensed one of his "moods." It had served her, and her sisters, well. Thomas's cowardice had prevented him from doing all those things she read in his eyes that he wanted to do.

Now, she sized up Callahan. A bully. Like good old stepdaddy, Thomas Daniels.

Her eyes narrowed to aquamarine slits. Callahan's jaw locked, hard as stone and just as unyielding. Dinah's pulse fluttered but her expression remained challenging and full of icy indignation.

"How long have you been here?" he demanded into the dueling silence.

"Been here? This is my house. I've always been here."

Did he hear the faint, telltale shake in her voice? Lord, she hoped not. You couldn't give a man like Callahan the least little hint that your emotions weren't as secure as they looked.

"Really," he stated flatly.

"Yes, really."

She didn't like his tone. And the way he stared at her! Did he know? *Could* he know? She wasn't the actress Denise was, but by God, she was going to give an Oscar-winning performance now if it killed her. *What was he doing here?*

"So, my promiscuous wife has developed a backbone," he murmured. "Congratulations."

She didn't answer. She would have liked to defend Denise's honor, but it would have been wasted effort.

"That doesn't mean you own this house," he pointed out coldly.

"I *own* this house," she disagreed.

He raked a hand through his hair, a thought-gathering gesture which was curiously seductive. *Probably practices in front of a mirror,* she thought with an inward snort.

"That won't get you in *Lady Paradise.* I'll cut off my right arm before I ever put you in a film again."

He was obsessed with this film idea. "My claim is to this

house. That's all I want. Except that I want you out of it," she added as an afterthought.

His expression changed to weariness mixed with annoyance. Dinah had the feeling she'd stumbled onto worn ground. "You're so damn free with lies," he bit out. "It's nearly your least attractive trait." At her stony look of incomprehension, he added, "Ah, come on. We both know what the other one is."

"I think you'd better spell it out," she said stonily.

"Well, let's see. The last spelling I cared about was D-E-R-E-K. But then I'm sure to be behind the times."

The rumors surrounding Denise swirled inside Dinah's head. Callahan wanted her to believe them. He acted as if he believed them totally, but then, maybe that was merely a matter of blame shifting.

"Leo called me, y'know," Callahan said accusingly. "Begged me. Tried to threaten me. And you know what that did? Forced me into an untenable position."

Leo? Dinah thought, the precariousness of her masquerade sending thrills of anxiety through her veins. Who was Leo?

"I had to air a little dirty laundry to get him to back off."

"I don't know what you're talking about," Dinah declared truthfully.

"Yeah?" He wasn't buying it. "I told him about good ol' Derek." He drawled out 'Derek' in a way that left no question about his feelings for the man. "Told him what I found you two doing to each other on the last film set." At Dinah's stony look, he said, "Do I have to spell this, too?" Instead of words he gave a pretty accurate depiction with his index finger and loosely curled fingers of his other hand. "Leo got the picture a little quicker than you, but he didn't care." Callahan stopped, swayed on his feet. "Maybe I should have used gutter language. Maybe describing your little affair with Derek in filth would have been more suitable. But I think that would have lessened the impact somehow. I went clinical on him. You know it's funny when you use words like penis and vagina and tongue all in the same sentence, people get squirmy. Good old Sandberg's got the message, now. Hopefully, he'll be able to explain it to you."

Dinah was outraged. He really was scum. Suddenly her mind clicked. Leo Sandberg. Denise's agent.

"I don't want an audition," Dinah said. "Just the house." Her words rang with determination but inside, in her most protected self, a seed of doubt and suspicion had germinated. Denise hadn't played fair. There was a lot more at stake than possession of the Malibu home. A hell of a lot more.

His look was pitying. "You want an audition as much as you want to see me fail. But it's too late, Denise. Eons too late."

Callahan examined her through eyes that had seen it all, where his wife was concerned. She felt naked, somehow. As if Denise's transgressions had been visited on her. She felt soiled, too. And low. It was a distinctly unpleasant sensation and though his words had reduced her rage to a low simmer—there was no hope in knowing which perception was correct, his or Denise's—she disliked him on sight.

From pure, selfish desire, Dinah wanted to metaphorically kick him in the balls.

Metaphorically . . . and physically.

He read her mind and quickly stepped forward, clasped her by the shoulders, and gave her one hard shake that set her teeth rattling. Memories danced like fireflies behind her eyelids. Memories of another man shaking her, slapping her.

Dinah saw red. She swung with a closed fist, connected with a hard chest. Swearing, he pushed her up against the wall, holding her tautly, negating her violently struggling form by the sheer weight of his own.

"God . . . damn . . . it!" he spat through clenched teeth.

"You sick bastard," she panted. "Let me go! Let me GO!"

Crash! Beside them, the funky wrought-iron snake floor-lamp smashed onto the russet tiles.

She was drowning, going under into a black, familiar, clammy numbness which caught at her heart. The fear inside her was so intense she was a wild thing, inhuman, ready to inflict mortal damage.

John Callahan had never seen this side to his ex-wife and frankly, her wriggling and near spasmodic squirming shocked and frightened him a little. She must have finally gone over the edge. Headfirst. Right down into the black hole she'd been aiming for since they first met.

He let her go as suddenly as he'd grabbed her, his liquored senses clearing as if he'd taken an ammonia hit.

"Touch me again and I'll kill you," she choked past a heaving chest.

John stared in amazement. This certainly was a new tack.

Her eyes were wild with burning rage. Not acting, he realized with a faint jolt. This was real. His ex-wife meant to attack him.

He was literally saved by the bell.

Jarring chimes peeled loudly through the house, stilling both of them as if they'd been hit by a freeze ray. Denise pulled herself together with difficulty and John, eyeing her thoughtfully, yanked open the front doors to find a uniformed cop standing on the step.

"Good evening, sir," he said diffidently. "A neighbor reported screaming coming from these grounds and requested we check it out. Is everything all right?"

"Minor domestic dispute," John drawled, shooting a sideways glance at Denise. He expected her to toss out one of her dry, ironic zingers, those inappropriate and blackly humorous remarks that had made a fool of him on more than one occasion. But apparently she was in the throes of real emotion and for once in her life remained remarkably silent.

The cop turned to her. John steeled himself. In the face of the authorities, one of Denise's most sought after audiences, she tended to come alive. She could be teary-eyed and weak, or sweet and kittenish, or a blisteringly cold bitch. God, how she loved a stage of any kind!

The cop's eyes widened as he recognized her. Inwardly sighing, John waited for a spate of overdramatized histrionics. Denise was in her element.

But Denise didn't respond to the cue. Instead, she collected herself with an effort and asked, "Which neighbor complained?"

"Ma'am?"

"The people on the left or the people on the right? I want to know who's watching me."

John's head swiveled in surprise. What the hell was going on here?

The cop hesitated and Denise pressed, "Don't I have a right to know? Or, is that privileged information? Do *you* even know?" she finished, before she gave him a chance to answer, gazing at the cop with such microsopic intensity that the young man shifted uncomfortably, as if *he* were involved in some transgression, not Denise. Good God, the kid was green.

Either that or he'd succumbed to Denise's charms in less than five minutes. John inwardly snorted. It happened.

"Looks like everything's okay here," he mumbled, beating a hasty retreat.

"Nothing that can't be worked out," John agreed, closing the door behind him.

As soon as they were alone, he turned his attention back to Denise. Premonition crept over his skin. Something wasn't right. He'd seen a lot of sides to his ex-wife, but this was a new one. Her interests were always self-involved and generally self-destructive. Why did she give a damn about the neighbors? She adored a scene!

"Did I, or did I not, obtain this house in the divorce settlement?" she suddenly demanded, confounding him again because she sounded so serious.

"You did not," he stated.

She blinked. "The house was awarded to you?"

"What is this? Sudden amnesia? You know goddamn well what the settlement was."

She gazed off into space, totally perplexed. It was an incredible performance even for Denise.

"I had every right to throw you out," he added, "and you're lucky I didn't turn you in just now for trespassing. Our deal was you stay away from me, and I stay away from you. And *Lady Paradise* doesn't fit in there anywhere."

She didn't answer. She was absorbed in thought. John watched the play of emotions across her mobile face and thought with a jarring shock, *she's changed*. Her hair was different. Less blonde and a bit longer. Straighter than he'd ever seen it. And her face was rounder, fuller. And her skin was whiter—as if she didn't spend hours in tanning booths which he *knew* she did.

But the change was deeper than cosmetic. Something different. Something indefinable and curiously magnetic that reminded John what had attracted him to Denise in the first place.

Something he didn't want to be reminded of at any cost.

"And what's with the questions about the neighbors? You know how nosy they are," he accused.

"I just want to make sure I apologize for tonight's disturbance," she stated flatly.

"Since when?" He laughed. "You hate them all! Every one of 'em wants to write a book about your sordid sex life—and mine, too, as far as that goes."

"It goes pretty far," she reminded him.

"Paranoia on your part," he said with a disinterested shrug. This was clearly well-worn territory. "You're the one with the indiscriminate hormones."

Dinah bristled but bit back a hot retort. After all, it was nothing to her.

Callahan lifted a brow at her silence. "You're—different," he said, thoughtfully.

She visibly jerked, as if he'd touched some secret part of her not open to the public. And then, wonder of wonders, a scarlet tide of embarrassment swept up her neck and flooded her cheeks.

Denise Scott blushing like a schoolgirl?

John's bafflement turned to out and out amazement. He'd seen Denise cry, and act coy, and feign hurt, and feel true emotional pain. He'd seen her faint, and had been the recipient of her infantile fury more times than he'd like to remember. He'd tried to save her when she'd been going down for the third time in a mire of low self-esteem

and destructive behavior. He'd witnessed the brilliance of
her acting skills, been awed by the depth of her perception, been disgusted by her selfishness, humbled by her
unexpected tenderness.

But he had never, ever seen her blush. Not this guileless
kind of embarrassment over her actions. Not this awareness of her own humanity, her own simple mistakes.

"Do you honestly expect me to believe you forgot who
the neighbors are, and that I own this house?" he asked.

"No." Her voice was taut and faraway. "Maybe I just
. . . hoped and wanted . . . things to be different."

"They're exactly the same as they've always been."
This was the unpalatable truth.

Nodding, she inhaled through her teeth, shaking her
head. "Everything I own is here."

"Everything you own is packed up in storage or at
Derek's place or somewhere else. It's not here."

Her mouth twisted. "It is now."

He honestly didn't know what to say to her. He didn't
want her here. She'd caused too much destruction and
pain already, and his patience was all used up. But he had
crucified her during the divorce and some twisted, chivalrous part of himself still smarted with guilt at cutting her
down so thoroughly—a knife through butter.

"You can stay the night," he said brusquely, moving
away from her to right the lamp and put some distance
between them. His jaw was hard as he gazed down at the
bits of broken glass. "But you're out of here tomorrow."
Turning, he met her lovely wide, aquamarine eyes.
"That's the final word on it."

Oh, yeah? Dinah thought as His Highness bent down to
pick up the larger pieces of glass. His denim shirt strained

against his back and nearly separated from his low-riding, dusty blue jeans. Urban cowboy. Dirtbag. Slimy Hollywood ass-kisser. All producers were ass-kissers and John Callahan was no exception.

In measured silence, she waited until he'd twisted on one booted heel and disappeared in the direction of the kitchen. Then she exhaled a short, angry sigh. A detached part of her mind seemed fixated on those dangerously low blue jeans, the "cowboy" sway of his hips, his long legs. The man dressed as if he'd stepped out of a western film himself, a look he clearly cultivated.

He was so damnably *cool*, whereas, *she* was shaken to the core.

Could he be telling the truth? Did he own this house? His certainty had knocked her sideways, and she still felt unsteady.

Could it just be an elaborate lie on his part? Because he sensed how off-balance she was?

No. There was no point. What *was* the truth?

"Arrogant monster," she muttered under her breath, furious with herself for being such a coward. Where was her anger now? Where was that wave of indignation she'd been riding? How had he turned his own actions into a dissection of hers?

She heard him rummaging in a cupboard and then the clink of glassware. *That's right. Pour yourself another drink. Drink every last drop of liquor in the world and die of cirrhosis of the liver, you slimy, shit-kicking monster.*

Dinah drew a breath. She had to talk to Denise. Immediately. She needed answers. She needed help. She was running blind and it was a distinctly disadvantageous position to be in with the likes of John Callahan.

But she had a terrible feeling this was exactly the kind of pickle Denise had envisioned. That's why Denise had lied. To get her sister to commit to all this because there was no way Dinah would have allowed herself into this position if she'd dreamed for one second that John Callahan would show up and demand possession.

And Denise had wanted Dinah to fix everything for her. Again. Just like always.

With a supreme effort of will Dinah swallowed back her emotions, tiptoed around the remainder of the broken glass, and headed for the sanctity of her bedroom.

Scottsdale, Arizona. Hot, ugly—unless you were into saguaro cacti of which *she* definitely was not—and full of resorts and scattered housing developments. The landscape was so barren it could have been on the moon. Hell, even the saguaros looked otherworldly. It might be the chi-chi thing to buy a clay replica of one and top it with a little western hat and sling a scarf around its center finger, but Denise found them slightly obscene. If one were into phallic symbols, the way these guys thrust their stuff skyward, prickly with thorns or no, you couldn't hope to miss the open come-on.

The Mercedes slid to a halt in the circular brown-tile drive beneath the hotel entry awning. Two attendants rushed out to help her. Denise slid out, touched one attendant's waiting hand, and was jolted with enough static electricity to stand her hair on end.

"Electrifying," she muttered ironically as the attendant's eyes widened in recognition.

"Denise Scott!" he exclaimed.

His thrill at meeting her was just the medicine Denise needed right now. No tricks. No guile. Just an honest excitement at meeting a film star.

Yesterday's film star . . .

With an effort she ignored her own nasty conscience. Gesturing to the landscape, she asked, "Is this place really as ugly as it seems?"

"You don't like the desert?" He looked stricken.

"I don't like anything," she admitted, her lips twisting to take the sting out of it.

The other attendant was searching vainly in the backseat for some sign of luggage.

"I travel light," Denise added, handing over the keys. She was wrinkled and sore, and longed for a shower, or better yet a thick bubble bath surrounded by candles.

She strode inside the hotel, hit by air-conditioning so cold it felt like it would freeze her in mid-stride. She made a minor sensation at the check-in desk when spied by the obviously new girl on duty. The more seasoned employees were discreet to the point of absurdity, acting as if she were a longtime customer but trying their damnedest not to seem too interested in her.

Denise was used to it, but her internal radar for fakery, always on high alert, picked up every nuance, every sidelong look, and overly disinterested attitude. Only people who truly didn't recognize her acted normally. Perversely, upon encountering them, Denise wanted to shout: *Don't you know me? Don't you recognize me? I'm Denise Scott, you uninformed shit!*

"The California Suite is one of our nicest." The clerk smiled, handing her a key. She was young and possessed of curly, black hair and a practiced smile and even more practiced self-possession.

Denise sized her up. "But it's not *the* nicest."

"Pardon?" The girl blinked.

"What's the nicest suite? The best?"

"Our Presidential, ma'am. But it sleeps twelve. There's a center suite with four bedrooms, one on each—"

"I'll take it."

"I'm sorry?"

Feeling bitchy all over, Denise sighed and said, "You have nothing to be sorry about. Just put me in the Presidential suite and all will be well."

Now all the employees were listening. Hands stilled over keyboards. Conversation ended. Denise fantasized ears growing huger and huger as they all sought to eavesdrop. She made it easy for them. "Is there a problem with that?"

"I'm afraid it's been booked," the girl said in a chastised voice. "For over a month."

"Is it occupied at this moment?"

"The guests are arriving late this evening."

"Then they'll have to go someplace else."

Silence. Utter silence except for the soft gurgle of water from the circular fountain in the center of the foyer. *Why are you doing this?* she asked herself, panic starting to itch beneath her skin again. *Why?*

"Could I help you, Miss Scott?" a friendly male voice asked from behind her left shoulder.

Turning slowly, Denise encountered a serious-eyed man in a green golf shirt which sported the Desert Paradise Hotel logo: a saguaro blooming with tiny white flowers.

"I'm Brent McCaffey, general manager of Desert Paradise," he introduced himself, offering his hand which she accepted warily. "The party in the Presidential Suite paid in advance. It's a fiftieth wedding anniversary and they've also booked several other suites and a dozen or so hotel rooms. Actually, they also wanted the California Suite, but Maggie—" he pointed to the girl Denise had given the rough side of her tongue "—thought we should keep

at least one suite open, if possible, in case someone important stopped in at the last moment." He paused, letting his
words sink in. "Would you like the California Suite?"

Suddenly Denise was weary. Bone weary. Soul weary.
She'd driven straight from Houston without sleep. She
didn't even know what day it was. "Why is it called the
California Suite?" she asked.

"I don't know," he admitted, holding out a hand to
Maggie for the key as he sensed victory. "Let me show it
to you."

She had no extra clothes or shoes or toiletries. The
events of the past few days blurred into a dusty gray haze.
Brent McCaffey was speaking as he opened the door to
the suite but the words were indistinguishable to Denise.
She answered him but knew not what she said.

Fifteen minutes after leaving her alone, McCaffey
knocked on the door again. Denise could barely find the
energy to slide off the chain lock, then was pleased and
touched to realize he'd brought her several votive candles
from the gift shop. She'd made her wishes known, apparently, and McCaffey had appointed himself her personal
gopher.

The bath was glorious. Hot and seductive and surrounded by flickering light that danced shadows on her
sleek, wet skin. Denise's mind was numb. Too filled with
torment to be anything but a gauzy mist right now.

She'd been on her way home, she remembered with a
start, as if it were a long forgotten memory instead of a
recent plan. Home to John.

Only John wasn't there for her.

Pain seized her in a sharp, relentless grip. Turning her

face to her shoulder, she squeezed her eyes closed, fighting back tumultuous emotions that threatened to explode from within.

At length a long shudder swept her body and some of the pain eased. Reluctantly, she pulled herself from the bath water, towel-dried, and fell into bed, naked.

Much later she awoke, jerking bolt upright in bed to a room black as pitch, a scream issuing from her throat. Her heart thundered in her chest. Her skin was drenched in sweat. Her lungs felt tied down by steel bands.

Frozen with fear she counted the seconds, nerves jangling, senses searching through the blackness, seeking out danger. For the space of a full minute she was completely lost; she had no idea where she was or if, in fact, she was alone.

Gradually she realized the illumination at the end of the room was from a faint crack in the curtains that covered the full length of the wall. Climbing off the bed, she was somewhat disconcerted to realize she wore no pajamas. Cold by nature, she always wore *something* to bed. More than one lover had commented on her prudish behavior—after all, she, Denise Scott Callahan, was known for being a hot ride in the sack.

How little men know . . .

She padded across the carpet toward the sliver of light, her toes digging into its luxurious thickness. She was somewhere nice, at least. Better than some sleazy motel.

Banging her shin on a low table, Denise bit off a stream of vituperative fury before throwing back the curtains.

It was night. Deep night. The illumination came from floodlights trained on a fountain in the center of a hexagonal desert garden bounded on all six sides by separate buildings.

"Desert Paradise," she remembered with a rush of

relief, pulling the memory out with almost painful effort. She was at the Desert Paradise Hotel in Scottsdale.

Opening the glass door, she stepped onto the balcony, encountering a coolish night. The soft breeze felt good against her bare skin, and she closed her eyes and drank of the sweet, dry air, savoring a rare moment of perfect harmony and solitude.

It was at times like these that Denise felt like she'd been sleepwalking for eons. This then was reality, and it was such a welcome change! One moment she would be lost in a virtual haze, the next—wham!—something woke her up. The trigger could be anything. A certain smell. A snatch of music. A sudden inexplicable feeling of *déjà vu* that threw her into happier times.

But it didn't happen near enough. Less and less she opened her eyes to this incredible sensation of being truly alive and free. So, she stood on the balcony in utter nudity and didn't give a rat's ass if the whole compound woke up to see.

Carolyn's Mercedes.

Groaning, Denise realized she'd basically stolen the woman's car. She was lucky she wasn't being hauled in right now for Grand Theft Auto. Wouldn't that be a hoot! HOLLYWOOD ACTRESS STEALS GOLD-TRIMMED MERCEDES FROM FRIEND.

Yeah, a real yuk a minute.

She was going to have to call Carolyn and explain, though what explanation she could give was anybody's guess.

Second, she had to call Dinah.

Denise grimaced. Poor Dinah. She'd really done her dirty. She'd left her in John's house—although technically that house belonged to *her!*—without a word of warning. Not that John would bother her. The mysogynistic devil was deep into production of *Fortunata* according to Leo, and Denise knew it would take a tsunami large enough to drown the state of California to pry John away from his film now.

But she needed to come clean. Now, while she was in total control, without those increasingly frequent and terrifying delusions to screw up everything.

Your delusions are of your own making.

Hunching her shoulders, Denise slipped back inside the room, feeling her way to the edge of the bed. Well, maybe they were and maybe they weren't. At this point, she didn't really care. She just wanted them to stop.

Oh, Dinah, help me.

Denise had promised she would call. She'd sworn she would let Dinah know where she was staying. She'd vowed that her sister would only need to housesit for six weeks.

What did you hope to prove?

Glancing around, Denise read the digital clock on the opposite nightstand. 2:30 am. 1:30 in Los Angeles.

Her hand scrambled along the wall for a light switch. Encountering nothing, she fumbled for the bedside lamp, her fingers beginning to tremble. Why did she suddenly feel so panicky?

A snatch of the nightmare that had woken her came back. A hand clapped over her mouth. Foul breath on her face. A sense of drowning.

"God . . ." She shivered violently as her fingers encountered the twist-on switch at the base of the lamp.

The room charged into blinding light, made more so by the mirrored wall behind the bed. Biting off an aborted scream, Denise realized the reflection was hers—and the chilling sight of it sent thoughts of calling Dinah and Carolyn right out of her head.

She wasn't Denise. She was an older, tarnished woman with worn-out eyes and shaking limbs. A broken spirit. A bloodless ghost. Dead already. Beaten, spiritually and physically, by a monster.

She was her mother.

Stop lying there like a piece of meat. Get out of bed!

For a vivid instant she saw her stepfather standing over her resting mother, his shoulders tense and wide, his big hands itching to slap her around. Then he did hit her, she remembered, all the while belittling her. He'd done his damnedest to kill her. He'd finally succeeded, too. She'd slipped away to some other place one night and never came back.

Denise recalled her face. Unearthly still and pale as porcelain. Removed from life's painful blows. At peace, just like all the preachers and ministers and priests and rabbis predicted. Her mother finally found peace.

Shivering, Denise pulled herself back from that precipice. She couldn't think about Mama without falling. That's what it was. Falling into a pit, or hyperspace, or endless night. That's what it felt like, and Denise had learned she'd best avoid thinking about any part of the past if she wanted to hang onto the last shreds of her own sanity.

Dialing Carolyn's number from memory, Denise realized it was 3:30 a.m. in Houston. Bad idea to call this late. She almost hung up but decided that a hang-up in the dead of night would probably scare Carolyn worse. To her amusement, she got the answering machine.

"Carolyn, it's Denise. I borrowed your car. I'll be back in Houston tomorrow . . ." *Or the next day,* she thought, wincing. She wasn't sure how long it would take or when she'd actually find the energy to drive all the way back. What was wrong with her? How had she thought she could just drive home to L.A. and expect John to be waiting there with open arms? "Sorry," she added lamely. "See you soon."

She found herself dialing Dinah's Santa Fe number before she remembered Dinah was at the Malibu House. Shaking her head in frustration, Denise asked herself how she could be so sharp about some things—like remembering phone numbers she'd only dialed once or twice—and be so dull about other, much easier, things.

It was all part and parcel of her screwed up brain. She had a fabulous mind for trivia. An almost photographic memory. When it came to learning lines, no one was her equal. She had it down upon one read through. It was easy. Dead easy. And acting out those fantasies even easier.

She was made for Hollywood. A blonde beauty with oodles of talent and an unformed inner self which made it easy to slide down the chute to sex, drugs, and ultimate destruction. One of her shrinks had used that phrase, somewhere along the line.

But then, sleeping with the myriad of shits who ran the entertainment industry, from her first agent to her last director, hadn't been as easy. Contrary to popular belief, Denise was pretty sure she had a low sex drive.

Try that on for size, Dr. Stone. Your sexed-crazed patient is really bored of the whole damn thing! Hey, a good fantasy can take the place of all that silly panting and thrusting any day.

Derek Sather. The director of *Cosmos*. Her latest, and possibly last, picture. Lean and good-looking, and certain of his attractions, Derek had come on to Denise during contract negotiations, making it clear she owed him some favors of a very personal nature. He had a way of whispering guttural nonsequitur sex-talk in her ear when no one was around that Denise had found more amusing than tittillating.

"Big cock, sweetheart," he'd moaned against her earlobe. "Big, big cock."

You're an asshole.

"Creamin' yet, baby? Doin' it for me?"

You're a persistent asshole.

"Chewin' Juicy Fruit gum, baby. Got sweet juices to fill you up with."

You're an inventive, persistent asshole.

She was a big name. She could have said no. But then, he would have made her life hell during production in a thousand little ways. And by this time John had washed his hands of her. If they spoke at all it was to hammer out the details of their divorce, and even that was mostly done through their lawyers.

So . . .

So, she'd slept with Derek and learned that his sex-talk was the best part of the experience. With Derek it was more slam, bam, thank you ma'am. Not exactly the trip to Kinksville, he'd promised.

And she'd never seen him with a pack of Juicy Fruit gum.

Still, for that section of time while *Cosmos* was being filmed, she'd made herself believe it was Derek who could offer her the "Secret To Happiness"—that mythical state for which she was on a perpetual quest.

Abruptly Denise's mood darkened. She recognized it as the beginning of the end for this period of precious reality. The edges of her brain grew muzzy and unclear.

Hurrying to finish her tasks, she dialed the Malibu house and prayed Dinah was spending an evening in.

"Hello?" John answered, sounding wide awake and mean as a badger.

Denise bit back a cry. John? John at the house?

She slammed down the receiver and leaped to her feet. John was there? With Dinah?

Denise switched off the light and collapsed back down on the bed. She curled into a fetal position and dragged the bedspread over her cold limbs. Dinah and John. John and Dinah. What did it mean? What did it *mean?*

You are truly paranoid, she reminded herself. *Truly paranoid.* Biting down savagely into her lower lip, her stomach hot with fear, she slowly fell into uneasy slumber and thankful oblivion.

The club was dark and noisy and permeated with some scent Hayley couldn't identify and was pretty sure she didn't *want* to. Standing at the bar, she tried hard not to stare at the U-shaped runway in the center of the room which was flanked by tables teeming with men. Ugly men who made even uglier gestures. Ugly thoughts. Ugly needs.

But what could she expect in a place dominated by hookers, pimps, and the various low-level dregs of society?

The runway was studded with five translucent plastic poles filled with red fluid. The poles ran from floor to ceiling and within the fluid, silver glitter twisted, floated, and shimmered beneath the hot lights. Attached to each pole were some of the most well-built young women in history—thanks to good old plastic-surgery-miracle-grow —and they were gyrating and panting and sliding on the poles in a way that was euphemistically called "dancing" on the exterior marquee.

Occasionally one of the ugly men would grab at one of the women and he would be summarily yanked to his feet by a huge, totally bald, black man and tossed out the door. No wheedling or begging could get the bouncer to change his mind. Screw up once and you were out.

The bouncer was the only thing about the place that made Hayley feel safe.

"So, whad'ya think?" Mrs. Carver asked for the seventeenth time.

"I've seen worse." Hayley smiled ironically. "And I've seen better."

"Well, don't tell Danny. He might get his feelings hurt."

"God forbid. Who's Danny?"

Mrs. Carver, whose first name had turned out to be Gloria, pointed to the sharply-dressed, around thirty-year-old man behind the bar. Danny sported a small black mustache and a face that was carved in granite. He gave Hayley the creeps for reasons she couldn't quite explain and didn't want to analyze too closely.

"So, what's next?" she asked.

Gloria Carver sucked on her teeth, a gesture that meant she was giving the situation hard thought, or so Hayley had determined after several hours in the older woman's company.

They'd walked and strutted and stood around on Hollywood Boulevard, talking and flirting and generally trying to scare up business. It had nearly sent Hayley into an adrenalin overdose. Her emotions running rampant, a jetstream of hormones that made her limbs shake, her eyes tear, and her heart beat quadruple-time. It was a testament to her ability as an actress that she'd managed to hide the effects of her fear behind a stone facade, but she felt drained and exhausted from the effort. And the evening had only just begun.

"Come on," Gloria ordered, jerking her head toward the back of the club.

Hayley followed, her legs woolly and uncoordinated. She was in peril and she knew it.

But Tonja had gotten her a copy of *Lady Paradise*. Hayley had read it thirteen times; she already knew the part of Toni by heart. It was tailor-made for Hayley Scott. It was perfect. God, so perfect!

But it had "Big Star" written all over it. The role of a lifetime for whomever landed it, and no one as savvy as John Callahan would waste it on an unknown, even if that unknown had a famous sister who just happened to be his ex-wife. *Especially if that famous sister were his ex-wife.*

Still . . . not an actress in this town would be as qualified, rehearsed, and prepared with actual life experiences as Hayley would.

If she could just make it through this night . . .

She sashayed behind Gloria Carter, teetering only slightly on her black platforms. She'd actually picked up her red spandex skirt and stretchy black lace tanktop at a costume store—an inside joke only she could appreciate. She'd thought about a straight black wig but had changed her mind at the last minute. Instead she'd streaked her light brown hair with bleach and teased it mercilessly until she looked ready to walk onto the set of an MTV video.

And hey . . . she fit into her surroundings seamlessly. Another hooker on patrol. *Hey, baby, lookin' for something tasty?*

A line straight out of *Lady Paradise*. Did she dare use it?

The back hallway stank of cigarettes and the scent of burning grass. Hayley had taken one toke from a friend's joint during those misty high school years and had coughed herself into a vomiting fit. So much for drug abuse. She hadn't fared any better with alcohol; the sour smell of beer was revolting and wine left her with a three-day headache. Forget hard alcohol altogether. Apart from the sexy bottles, it all tasted the same: bad.

She was the virgin's virgin—and she was about to change all that in one fell swoop.

With a quivering heart, Hayley followed Gloria into a low-ceilinged room at the end of the hall. Three men waited inside. All standing, facing the door as they entered. Chairs and tables were scattered around. It looked more like a meeting room than the set of an assignation.

"What gives?" she murmured to Gloria.

"Shhhh."

Hayley subsided into silence at her sharp hiss, concentrating instead on her own galloping heart and quavering knees. Eye on the prize, she reminded herself harshly. Eye on the prize. No matter what the means, the end would be justified.

"Over at Keith's," one of the men told Gloria, not even glancing at Hayley.

"She okay?" another asked, ignoring Hayley even while he discussed her.

Gloria shrugged.

"Keith wants her," the third man put in.

Panic seized Hayley. This was it. This was really it!

"Okay," Gloria turned around and Hayley quickly followed after her.

"Who's Keith?" she demanded as they headed back to the club's main floor.

"The man of the hour, sugar. The man of the hour."

She followed after Gloria, past the women making love to the red poles, outside to the street and a black, late model sedan. Hayley slid into the backseat next to Gloria. The driver was a heavyset man who shifted the car into gear the instant the door closed behind them.

The air was suffocatingly close. Gloria's cheap perfume nauseated Hayley. She cracked open a window for air and turned her attention to the passing neon lights and traffic.

Eye on the prize.

"Keith's" was a nondescript apartment complex turned condominium. The driver pulled into an empty handicapped spot and put the car in park. Hayley looked at Gloria who signaled for her to get out of the car.

As soon as they were standing on the asphalt, the black sedan pulled away.

"You ready?" Gloria asked, her red lips glowing strangely blue in the cast from the nearby streetlight. She was smiling, completely aware of Hayley's doubts.

Eye on the prize.

"Lead the way."

They walked into a breezeway that smelled of mildew and grime. Gloria punched the button for the elevator. "Let me do the talking. One word outta your mouth, and they'll know you ain't real."

"I'll be quiet."

"They're gonna want you to perform, sweet-cakes. Don't think nothing else."

"I know."

"I don't think you've got the balls."

Hayley bit down on the inside of her cheek as they stepped into the empty elevator. The doors thunked shut and with a belated jerk, the car lurched upward.

They walked in tense silence down the fourth floor hallway and Gloria stopped in front of a forest green door. She knocked lightly, twice.

Almost instantly the door opened. Smoke billowed out like welcoming fog. Gloria stepped inside and Hayley followed, hovering close.

The place was furnished like a refuge for low-life

lounge lizards. A fake zebra-skin rug lay in front of a black naugahyde couch. Framed posters of cheap prints featuring women's lips and body parts adorned the walls. The paraphernalia on the coffee table, whose veneer was scorched from cigarettes and smattered with coffee rings, must have been purchased straight out of *Drug User's Weekly*.

Two men and a blonde woman who looked as if she might be stoned sat on the chairs and couch. The men eyed Hayley and Gloria.

"How do you want to do this?" Gloria asked them.

"Who's that?" the thinner, scrawnier man asked, pointing to Hayley.

"A friend. A friendly friend," she added.

"I'm a watcher," Hayley said.

Everyone turned to look at her. Gloria's mouth was a tight line of fury. The men just waited. Hayley, herself, was amazed to hear her own voice. It was as if the words came from someone else.

"Yeah?" the other man asked. A cigarette smoldered from his loose fingers and threatened to burn into the naugahyde.

"I don't participate. I watch."

"Sister, when you're here you *do*."

"Who the fuck is she?" Scrawny demanded without heat.

"I'm a watcher." Hayley sat down in the nearest chair, crossed her legs and prayed to a divine God she hadn't recognized in years.

Gloria Carver was in a rage. "And she don't get paid for it, either. I get her share and mine. She just enjoys the show."

"This sucks," the blonde chimed in without enthusiasm.

What a group of losers, Hayley thought, her fear changing to contempt. Drugs had burned out their minds and their energy. Movements in the room were so slow, she could have walked to the phone, dialed the police, and had the narcs at the door before anybody blinked.

"Okay, sugar. You first." Gloria pointed to Scrawny who thought for a minute—a whole damn minute—then obligingly undid his zipper.

Hayley focused on those two rows of zipper teeth, stalked by a bad memory she refused to address. Gloria leaned down to her.

"I told you, don't talk," she hissed in her ear.

The man with the cigarette passed it to the blonde and Hayley saw it was a joint. The blonde dragged on the skinny joint until it burned the opposite end in a rush of crinkly, red ember.

Gloria slid to her knees, stuck her hand inside Scrawny's fly, then moved inexhorably forward with those red, red lips.

And Hayley focused on an inner scene that sometimes came to her in times of desperately needed tranquility. A dry meadow surrounded by pines cut by a dusty trail. Huckleberry bushes. A lone eagle circling in a pale blue sky.

Somewhere from her past? Or maybe some future destiny.

Whatever it was, it kept her from bolting from the room, vomiting, and screaming.

Dragging herself up from the depths of sleep, Denise was vaguely aware of something wrong, but her mind shied away from learning what that something was. She was warm beneath a heavy bedspread. Trapped. Something dark and menacing swelled inside her head, swelled and receded, then swelled again. A man's voice. Like caramel. Soft and squishy and sweet. But evil.

She whimpered in her sleep, and then John's arms surrounded her. His breath fanned her neck. John, the good. John, the wonderful. She snuggled closer.

It can't be John. I'm at a resort in Scottsdale. It's a dream.

But what a delicious dream. No worries. Just safety.

Denise hovered on the brink of wakefulness but then John began kissing her nape, his fingers trailing strands of hair that fell along her shoulder.

"I hate being alone," she murmured, her breath choking.

"Denise . . ." he whispered softly, enthralled, his fingers growing bolder as they tiptoed down her arm to the curve of her waist.

She arched her back against him, suddenly so anxious for his lovemaking that she ached.

"Are you sure?" he mumbled, his mouth hot on her skin.

"Yes . . . yes . . ."

There was no more waiting. He turned her toward him, a bit rougher than usual. John was generally so sweet; it's what she loved about him most. His tender lovemaking. His slow "I'll make you want it so bad you'll die" method of stroking and teasing her.

But not this time. Now he was all muscle and strength and desire. A kernel of fear tightened inside her. This wasn't the way it was supposed to be.

"I was hard for you the moment you walked in," he said, his teeth gently biting her skin. Gently, but with repressed passion. "I've been thinking about you rubbing against me, riding me, grunting and moaning. Both of us screaming . . ."

"Stop," she whispered, alarm bells ringing.

"You like it rough. You said you like it rough . . ." She could barely make out his voice, it was so low and thick with sexual thrumming, base desire.

Blood thundered throughout her body. Denise felt as if she'd already run a marathon.

He took her fast, bucking and thrusting and fighting his way inside her as if he expected some resistance. Fear dissolved, changed to weary acceptance. This was the way it was for her. Always. Except with John.

Instead of fighting, she lay quietly, accepting his alien male form and the harsh, guttural words of degradation he slapped her with as if it were her due. She deserved it. She always deserved it. And her sick, netherworld self fed on it.

Later, much, much later, she opened her eyes to the dim gray shapes around her. It must be midday now; the slit of light coming through the drapes was a bright glare. He'd come to her in the early morning smelling like scotch, a new scent for him because John always came to bed tasting and smelling like peppermint mouthwash.

He was awake. She could sense that he was watching her even before she turned to look at him. Her lips curved into a secretive and knowing smile.

"I can't believe it," he said in a worshipful tone. "I just can't believe it . . ."

Then Brent McCaffey closed his eyes and leaned over to nuzzle Denise's bare breast.

Denise's mind went black. She was in Scottsdale and this wasn't a sick dream. This was happening! *Right now!*

Her whole body trembled. With a sudden thrust, she pushed Brent away. Breathing hard, she wrapped the blankets around her as she scrambled from the bed, dragging them with her.

"What?" he asked, dazed, his arms outstretched for her.

He was naked on the bed. Well, nearly naked. A green condom whose latex surface was dotted with round, funky-looking bumps adorned his rather stubby looking dick.

Denise's gaze was riveted to the condom. Then her eyes swept past Brent to the nightstand where a green box with a smiling saguaro cactus cheerfully extolled the virtues of:

"CACTUS CONDOMS. ALL YOU PROVIDE IS THE PRICK."

Truer words were never written.

She collapsed into hysterical laughter.

Chapter Five

Autumn had settled over central Oregon in a blanket of gold, sienna and orange. The colors were too intense to seem real, the air dusty and dry during the day, clear and crisp in the evening. The earth was red from the jack and sugar pines' bark; the whole area a high-mountain paradise, too arid for a stranger's idea of Oregon, too beautiful to be so sparsely populated.

Connor Jackley had grown up in Bend, the nearest city of any size to Wagon Wheel. He'd roped and ranched and done the high school football routine and gotten laid the first time in the back of his girlfriend's Ford wagon. He'd set fire to a clump of sagebrush and damn near started a forest fire for which his father had hit him hard, once, across the face and told him you had to earn respectability by responsibility.

Law enforcement had fascinated him from the moment he could recall his first thought. This was at the age of five, when he'd watched his mother smile and flirt her way out of a speeding ticket. The traffic cop had succumbed with a knowing smile of his own and a sidelong look at Connor's sister's curly blonde head.

That incident had staying power. While so many ultra-

violent or poignant or downright life-threatening scenes
in his life blurred together like a video run at fast-forward,
it still hung fresh and vivid in his memory. It was the
traffic cop's choice that had touched Connor's young
mind. Should he, or shouldn't he ticket the pretty woman
with her two pretty children? The answer, in that case,
had been no.

Years later Connor still pulled this page from the file
of his memory every so often. Should he arrest the
sniffly, cocaine-abusing prostitute so that her pimp
would have to pay to have her released on bail, or let
her go? Should he tolerate the cruddy, verbal filth spew-
ing from the mouth of the street kid, or haul his ass into
jail? Should he shoot to wound the vile pedophile who'd
infected one of his innocent victims with HIV, or kill
him on the spot?

It was that last incident that had lost him his job at the
force. He *had* shot the bastard even before the HIV results
were in. Shot him in the knee. Crippled him.

Oh, he hadn't gotten thrown off the force. The prick
had been running away, trying to shield himself with his
kidnap victim, a young girl of nine. As soon as he shoved
her away, Connor had aimed for his yellow back, his hand
dropping at the last instant, whether by design or chance
he still couldn't rightly say, but the bullet's trajectory hit
the guy in the back of the knee, ripping up the tendons
and ligaments and shattering the patella inside out.

It wasn't enough. It wasn't near enough. Especially
when the child's blood test bore out the cold, fatal truth.
Positive. A death certificate disguised as a medical report.

It wasn't enough even that fateful night. Connor had
walked to the screaming, yowling perp and aimed at the
wretch's face. Should he kill the souless insect? Should he
end his violent, unimportant life?

He'd wanted to. Itched to. Had held the barrel of the gun between the miserable bastard's fear-crazed eyes.

The memory brought a grimace to Connor's face. Fiddling with the radio of his rented Jeep Cherokee, he pondered the tricks of fate. He hadn't pulled the trigger. He'd just sighted his crying, fear-ridden victim and waited.

Cowards. They were cowards. Every last one of them. Some hid their cowardice behind stoic, dead expressions. Some cried and carried on and even pissed in their pants.

"Cowards," he said aloud, as the twangy, bittersweet sounds of a country-western ballad warmed the interior of the Jeep. His mouth twisted into a smile of remembrance. It was hard to escape a country-western existence in a city like Bend, Oregon where every signpost and banner seemed to allude to horses, rodeos, mountains, range, and livestock.

The encounter with the HIV rapist had been the last of Connor's fifteen years with the L.A.P.D. He'd walked away after that, amidst protests from his pals and co-workers. But Detective Jackley of homicide didn't listen. Now, here he was two years later, leading a part-time, quasi-legal life as a private investigator, the kicker of the story being that some of his buddies on the force still relied on his help to solve their cases.

And so . . .

He was headed to some dusty, sagebrush-landscaped trailer park to the address of one Candy Daniels Whorton, Thomas Daniels' daughter by his first wife, Jane. Jane herself had died this last spring from a massive heart attack brought on by a combination of heredity and a terrible fondness for food and drink. By all accounts, the luckless Candy was halfway to the Grim Reaper herself, having developed her mother's fondness, and outstripping her love of food based on her 300-pound-plus size.

He felt sorry for her already and he hadn't even met her.

His thoughts dark, Connor turned into the drive of the Valley High Trailer Park and bumped over the gravel-strewn ground to the dusty single-wide at the far end of the park. Sunlight burned on its weathered salmon and white exterior, showing off patches of rust that were creeping from beneath the rivets and around the screen door.

"Candy Dandy," Connor muttered, wincing at the thoughtless cruelty of the name that had fallen from Gus Dempsey's lips this morning. The sheriff sure wasn't sub-tle about his feelings for things. Connor had forgotten about Gus's baldly stated, politically incorrect opinions, but an hour with the man this morning had reminded him with technicolor brilliance.

"Candy's the one who told me about that actress, De-nise Scott. Said they were stepsisters. I thought she was lyin'." Dempsey had snorted, grinning hugely. "Wouldn't you? I mean, think about it! It's a *National Enquirer* story in the makin'!"

"The facts of Denise Scott's history have probably been written up hundreds of times," Connor disabused him.

"Uh-uh." Dempsey poured himself another cup of coffee, gestured to Connor who shook his head, then settled on the edge of his desk, as if he were getting reading to launch into a deep yarn. "Candy's got clippin's you wouldn't believe. Keeps track of those girls. She al-ways knew who they was when the rest of us was still scratchin' our heads and wonderin'."

"Girls?"

"Three sisters. Denise and Diane, I think. No, that's not right and the third one's Hildegarde, or somethin'. I don't give a good goddamn. It's the actress that killed him. Candy said so."

"If you were certain of that you would have brought Denise Scott in for questioning. You just don't want to make a mistake and have the whole world laughing at you for being such a backwoods fool." Connor's smile kept his old friend from taking offense.

"You're right as rain, as always. I don't want nothin' to do with this thing. I like what I've got here." He gestured to the less than opulent surroundings of the county offices. "You're here to make sure I keep it."

"Meaning?"

"Ah, now, don't be dense, Jackley. This thing could be a big mess if it isn't handled with extreme caution. I don't want to deal with it at all. I'd rather it just flew away home and never saw the light of investigation. That's what you're here for."

Connor half-smiled. "Are you telling me you're lazy and corrupt?"

"I ain't no Urganis," Gus snorted, referring to the previous sheriff who'd been caught with his pants down and a few other things as well. Sheriff Urganis had gotten booted out of his house, and out of office as well.

"I'm just lazy," Gus went on. "But you gotta understand how things are. Thomas Daniels . . ." Gus's happy, homely face fell into a grimace. "Well, people around here practically declared it a national holiday when he disappeared. I don't want to see anybody get hurt who doesn't have to."

"I hate to break it to you, Gus, but you just catch the baddies. Juries decide who gets punished."

"Don't I know it!" He snorted in pure disgust. "Damn screwed up system!"

"So, I'm here to learn a few facts, keep a low profile, then steal back to Los Angeles."

The intelligence he hid so well glimmered briefly in Gus's bright eyes. "I suppose we're going to have to keep after it, huh, Jackley? You go to L.A. and chase those girls down, but first . . ."

He'd handed Connor a piece of paper with Candy Daniels' address.

And so here he was.

Connor slid to a stop, his tires crunching gravel, the Cherokee humming at a high, anxious whine as if it wanted to get far away from here, to the action, to the future.

Outside the air was too cool for the hot, angry sun. Connor stretched his arms over his head, then strode to the half-rotten wooden porch that led to the door. Boards squeaked ominously beneath his booted feet. Lifting the unlocked screen, he rapped on the door.

A shuffle and a thump alerted him to someone's presence within. Slow footsteps moved deliberately to the door. A moment later the door cracked open and a suspicious female voice demanded, "Who is it?"

"Connor Jackley. Sheriff Dempsey asked me to talk to you about the Daniels murder."

"Yeah?"

"If you wouldn't mind," he added patiently.

The door widened a bit further and Connor's nerves went on red alert when his eyes met the dark, menacing nose of a .38 special. Lifting his gaze, he met a pair of black-lined blue eyes where suspicion, distrust, and hostility vied for supremacy. Candy Dandy had been kicked hard by life, and her tremendous bulk made her a stand-out whether she wanted to be or not.

Cruel, cruel fate.

"I wanted to talk to you about Denise Scott and her sisters. I understand they're your stepsisters."

"Like they'd admit it," Candy sneered.

"Could I . . . come in?"

Eyeing him carefully all the while, Candy pressed the door open a little wider with the barrel of the gun, then gestured him to enter.

He hoped to high heaven the damn thing wasn't loaded.

Dinah was up with the birds. Last night she hadn't slept the proverbial wink of sleep. Furious thoughts and worries circled her mind and she'd thrashed around the bed until she'd started worrying that John Callahan might come back to her bedroom to see what all the ruckus was about.

That quieted her down in a hurry, but then she lay wide awake and still, listening to her heartbeat, attuned to the littlest squeak and creak of the house. She'd heard the phone ring in the middle of the night but Callahan had answered it before she'd even lifted a hand. She'd half-expected him to throw open her door, level a finger at her, and holler, "Fraud!" but nothing had happened.

So far . . .

Now she tossed on jeans and a black T-shirt, snapped her hair into a ponytail, and was in the process of brushing her teeth when it occurred to her that she didn't look anything like Denise. Oh, sure, the raw material was the same, but Denise never looked anything less than glamorous, no matter what. Dinah, on the other hand, was plain as Brand X.

Grimacing at her reflection in the bathroom mirror, she thought about digging through Denise's clothes, then rejected the idea straight out. Okay, she could wear some make-up. But she worked in blue jeans and by God, she wasn't going to change her apparel even for the sake of keeping up this charade.

"You didn't ask for this," she whispered, pointing at her frowning image.

Part of her wanted to come clean and explain the circumstances, but she had a strong feeling that wouldn't cut much ice with His Highness. God knew what punishment he would inflict—more on Denise than herself, she was sure. So, maybe she could brazen it out. Callahan didn't know Denise had a twin unless Denise had told him, and Dinah had an equally strong feeling Denise kept that fact a secret. Denise was good at keeping secrets.

But if this were his house, she had to leave. She couldn't pretend to be Denise and hang around here all day when she didn't belong. What was the point? Plus, given enough time, John Callahan would undoubtedly start to grow suspicious.

And what was he doing here anyway? He should be on the set of that damn movie; Denise had been very clear about how obsessive the man was about his work.

Narrowing her eyes, Dinah sorted through various scenarios, rejecting them all. There was nothing to do but to keep up appearances—at least for now. And that meant appearing more like Denise.

Feeling like a sneak, Dinah gingerly pulled open several drawers until she found a stash of lipstick, blush, mascara, eyeliner, and several small instruments of torture for plucking brows and curling lashes. Most everything was still in its original package, purchased and forgotten.

Unwrapping the various and sundry pieces of make-up,

Dinah carefully applied a soft bronze eyeshadow, followed by medium brown eyeliner and mascara. A touch of blush and some lip-gloss with an aromatic peach scent finished the transformation.

Sliding a sideways glance at her reflection, a shiver rolled down her spine and Dinah unconsciously trembled. Apart from the hair, she did look like her twin. Too much so. Yet, it still might not enough to fool John Callahan.

The thought of curling her smooth blondish mane was more than she could stand, however, so she twanged it back once more and dug through Denise's drawers for some kind of scrunchy or decorative band.

No such luck. Would Denise just wear a rubber band in her hair?

Adjusting the three-way mirror and turning her chin, Dinah surveyed her profile. Inspiration struck. Quickly she wrapped her hair in a tight bun at the top of her head and dragged loose strands to frame her face. Sorta tacky, sorta trendy. It had been Denise's style in *Blindsided*.

Stepping back, Dinah's lips parted in awe at the transformation. It had been years since she'd dressed like Denise. Eons, if measured in experience and growth. She'd never wanted to be her twin. Had always shied away from emulating her in any way. Jealousy? Because Denise had been prettier, wilder, more daring? Probably. But also a desperate need to discover her own talents and needs. Her own self.

Stepping from her bedroom, she glanced both ways along the gallery. Not a sign of Callahan.

Quietly, ears sharpened for the slightest noise, she tiptoed barefoot past Denise's bedroom toward the back staircase that led to the kitchen. The house was silent and wrapped in the coldness of early morning.

At the bottom step, she hesitated, peeking around the

corner. The kitchen was empty and dark. The digital clock on the oven read 5:30.

Dinah heaved a sigh of relief, belatedly aware she'd been holding her breath. She headed straight for the coffee machine which was already perking, having been set the night before when she'd thought she was the one and only occupant of the place.

Now she had to be out of here by sunrise or face pistols at dawn.

Or something like that.

Suddenly she thought of all her work scattered around Callahan's library. How could she explain Denise's sudden interest in writing?

Heedless of noise, she ran through the shadows to the library. Heart pounding, she half-expected Callahan to be seated at the computer, poring over her latest article.

But the room was dark. Empty.

With shaking hands she pulled up all her files on the computer and purged them. Then she gathered the backup disks and grabbed up all the papers she'd tossed into the trash. She threw the paper in the fireplace and set fire to them.

Firelight danced in spooky orange flickers that touched on the corners of the room as the papers ignited and flamed out. Dinah's mind raced. Switching on the desk-lamp, she glanced around, searching for more signs of Dinah Scott's writing career. Apart from the disks, she was safe.

At the kitchen, she clutched the small pile of disks tightly, thinking hard. Childish fear made her slip them inside the cookie jar, just as a precaution in case His Highness should appear.

She suddenly realized that she would really have to leave today. Flick would be thrilled, but surprisingly, she

wasn't as anxious to shake the dust of L.A. off her boots
as she thought.

Watching the coffee drip into the pot, Dinah frowned,
considering her options. She *had* to talk to Denise, but she
didn't know where to look. Had she run off with this
Derek person? Callahan seemed to think so. But that was
during the divorce and a lot of water had run under the
bridge since then. Denise had insisted she was getting
psychological help and that was why Dinah had agreed to
this sham in the first place!

But where?

The coffee finished perking and Dinah poured herself
a cup, annoyed to see that her hands were shaking. She
was angry. Angry at herself for letting Denise dictate the
terms of this alliance. Denise knew where *she* was going,
but Dinah didn't have a clue where her flakey sister was.

And what kind of trouble she might be in.

And with whom . . .

"Damn, damn, damn," she muttered, balancing the
extra full cup as she turned toward the table. She needed
a shot of caffeine like another dose of bad news but hey,
she felt like it.

The sight of a belt over low slung jeans brought a
scream to her throat. Coffee sloshed. Burned her wrist.
"Shit," she bit out as Callahan jumped forward to save
her, the coffee, or maybe the tile floor should she drop the
cup. "What the hell do you think you're doing?" Dinah
demanded furiously. "Sneaking up on people!"

"I thought someone had broken in. I just wanted to
catch them."

"It never occurred to you it might be me?"

"No," he admitted honestly. "Since when do you get
up so early?"

"Since I . . . I got . . . since you said I couldn't stay here anymore!" Dinah sputtered.

He grinned, more a smirk of disbelief, actually, but it was inordinately charming and Dinah had to look away from its magnetic power. "Like you would listen to me," he said ironically. "For Christ sake, Denise, the last time you pulled this it took the National Guard to get you out."

"The last time?" Dinah queried, unable to stop herself.

He waved that away impatiently. "On the set. You know."

Dinah gave him a faint smile, at sea once again.

"Well, it wasn't exactly the National Guard," he admitted, watching her closely. Then, when she didn't respond, "So, this early morning coffee moment is because you're getting ready to go?"

"I didn't feel like being bounced out of here like last night. I make my own decisions."

"Yeah, right." This amused him and and his amusement irritated Dinah.

She didn't want to go. And she certainly didn't want him to have the last word. Pursing her lips, she realized the only answer was to stall. "If I asked you some questions . . . about the terms of our divorce, do you think you could give me some honest answers? Could you pretend that I really don't know, so I could hear it all again?"

Callahan slowly shook his head, his blue eyes searching hers for some kind of explanation. "Why?"

"Because . . . it's all kind of a fog to me," Dinah said, pleased by her ingenuity. "I'm in therapy, you know."

"You're always in therapy."

If it hadn't been so tragic, she might have laughed. How well they both knew Denise! "Humor me, all right? My therapist says it's good for me to hear the truth spoken again and again." She was out on a limb here, but it sure as hell sounded good. "It helps me keep on track."

"Who is this therapist?" John demanded.

"Dr. Runyan," Dinah pulled out. Runyan was the name of Flick's bloodhound.

Instead of answering, he poured himself a cup of coffee and took a tentative swallow. His face twisted into a comic mask of surprise. "Ouch! This is strong!"

She opened her mouth to say, "I like it that way," then opted for, "I needed a jolt."

"I guess!"

"Too strong for you?"

His eyes narrowed intently. "What's with you?" His gaze slid scathingly over her black shirt and jeans. "And what's with the clothes? Buy stock in The Gap?"

Dinah stared coldly. The best defense was a good offense. "So, are you going to help me, or what? It's up to you. Will you talk to me about the divorce?"

"You're the one who can't talk about the divorce. You always start screaming, name calling, and throwing blame."

"I won't do those things."

"Bullshit."

"I promise."

"Yeah, that and a quarter will buy me a local call. Give it up, Denise," he added wearily, as if he were tired of the game. "I don't have time. I'm in the middle of production."

"So, why are you here?"

"Just a bit of R & R."

"Yeah? I thought you lived and breathed the film during production. Something must have happened to bring you home."

"One night in Malibu isn't exactly a world tour vacation. I can still go to work." He stared at her over the rim of his coffee cup. "I don't get you at all."

His interest sharpened and she felt his assessing gaze as it scoured her face. Heat flooded her face. To this point, he'd treated her with contempt, annoyance, and a bit of amusement, as if she were a mere frivolity instead of a thinking, feeling human being. But she was starting to get to him. A bad sign. Time for retreat.

"I'll get my things together and leave."

She brushed past him but hard fingers suddenly circled her upper arm, turning her toward him. Her pulse fluttered nervously. This close, she could see the flecks of color in his eyes, gold and green against a deep, radiant blue.

And they say my eyes are beautiful, she thought inconsequentially, recalling all the press about Denise Scott's aquamarine orbs, identical to her own.

"No fight?" he asked softly, huskily.

"No fight." Her own voice was breathless, shaky.

She could feel every hard fingertip pressed into her skin. Glancing down, she looked at those long, tanned fingers wrapped around her black shirt.

"When I asked for a divorce, you swore you'd cut off my balls and serve them to Lauralee Gentry for an hors d'oeuvre." He paused, studying her closely.

Lauralee Gentry. Red-headed model with a little girl's voice. One of Callahan's conquests. A bad feeling stole over Dinah as she remembered there was some kind of scandal involving Denise.

Callahan enlightened her. "And then you called the press and told them Lauralee's implants were filled with champagne, not silicon or water."

For a wild moment, Dinah nearly burst out laughing. She remembered the incident clearly, though at the time

she'd thought the write-up was a misquote; even Denise
had her limits, after all. Now, she wondered.

Denise, you crazy nutcase!

Not that Lauralee was such an angel. She'd been
screwing Denise's husband behind her back and telling
the press that she and John Callahan were as good as
engaged—long before divorce proceedings began.

"Did you love her?" Dinah asked curiously.

John's brows lifted. *"Love* her?"

"Is that why you cheated?"

"I did not sleep with Lauralee Gentry," he stated flatly.

She heard the implication even though she was certain
he hadn't meant her to. "But there were others."

"There were others in your bed," he reminded her in
a cold voice that warned that if she wanted to play with
fire, she was bound to get burned.

Dinah subsided into the safety of silence. This apparently was a new tack for Denise, because John Callahan's
puzzled surveillance intensified even while he released her
arm. He sat down at the table, seemingly unaware that he
still held his coffee cup, his gaze fastened like iron on her
face—as if he'd never seen her before.

Which wasn't all that far from the truth.

She didn't know whether to leave or stay. She wanted
to leave. She *really* wanted to leave, but her feet couldn't
seem to get the message. They were planted firmly, and
a bit belligerently, on the terra-cotta tile floor.

"I got the house," he said. "And you got the money for
Cosmos even though you didn't earn a penny of it. I got my
freedom and you got Derek. Per the prenuptial, I kept
my possessions and earnings; you kept yours. Clear?"

"Clear."

"And you slandered me with accusations about Lauralee Gentry and Tia Martinez."

Tia Martinez. Starlet with a 19″ waist and 38 Double-D's which were purported to be real. Tia Maria, as she was known to the press, who loved to report on every detail of her life.

"Isn't she in your latest film?"

"She's a *Fortunata* costar."

Dinah snorted.

"You know damn well I don't get involved with anyone during film production."

"Any woman who's named after a drink is probably available after hours," Dinah stated loftily. "But I'm certain your scruples are so high that you stay away from her."

"Higher than yours."

"Okay, enough of this." Dinah didn't like to fight any battle she couldn't win, and this was one of them. "Let's face it. After the divorce, you kept a stellar career, but the name, Denise Scott, will be forever linked with scandal. It doesn't matter what you did, it's what the press thinks Denise Scott did. The double standard sucks."

This was where Denise had taken it in the shorts after her split from John. Not monetarily. Not immediately, at any rate. But her self-respect, never much to begin with, had been beaten to death. The press had pummelled her while John Callahan, the superior male being, had come out unscathed.

It really was a man's world.

"You deserve every negative comment ever printed about you," he answered remorselessly.

"Do I?"

"Yes."

"And did I deserve to lose my home?"

A flicker of emotion crossed his eyes. *Aha!* Dinah thought triumphantly. *A chink in the armor!* His Highness actually felt guilty about screwing over Denise. She was amazed he was capable of the emotion.

"What do you want? What do you really want?"

"I want to stay here," she heard herself say. "I want a part of this back."

His gaze darkened. Lines formed beside his mouth. In lieu of answering, he swept up yesterday's paper which was lying on the table where Dinah had left it. The *Santa Fe Review*. Folded open to Dinah Scott's column . . .

"Fine," he bit out. "I won't be here much and you can—"

Dinah snatched the paper from his hand. His jaw slackened in surprise as she tucked it under her arm. "I was reading that."

For half a beat he just stared, then he threw back his head and deep laughter rolled from his chest. Dinah's cheeks flamed. God! What he must think! But she hadn't had time for a more subtle plan. How would she have explained her name and the *Review?* He would have wondered and wondered and wondered until he finally decided to go after the truth. He was made that way.

"I don't know what's gotten into you, and I really don't care. But I'll say this, it's sure a helluva lot more entertaining than your usual tricks. Stay as long as you like." He stood and swept an arm in grandiose invitation.

With that he disappeared back upstairs, his chuckles drifting down the stairs after him, rich, husky, and irresistibly male.

Dinah snatched her disks from the cookie jar and ran to the safety of her own room, the echoes of his laughter hovering in her mind like a curse.

* * *

Six o'clock a.m. Too early for Connor to check with Dempsey and compare notes, but it had been near midnight when he'd finished with Candy and he hadn't felt like disturbing Dempsey's wife by phoning the sheriff in the middle of the night.

Now he sat over a cup of coffee at the counter of the early morning doughnut shop. Yep. Gus Dempsey was a regular here. Often times the stereotype fit the group; more times than was politically correct to admit, Connor had learned. And Gus sure liked to chew his way through doughnuts and coffee.

He watched the two aproned women yawn as they slogged from the coffee machine to the back room where they brought in trays of doughnuts. Connor, who'd sworn off deep-fat fried food long ago could feel his mouth water despite his good intentions. He was whip-lean and tough now, a product of a self-imposed regimen of exercise and healthy eating. He rarely drank and his vices were few. You couldn't be in L.A. Vice and then Homicide without a certain amount of self-control. Weaker men succumbed to the seductive dark side.

Besides, he'd gotten his daily shot of adrenalin-high with the sordid images and life and death decisions thrust upon him working for the L.A.P.D. Who needed more thrills than that?

"Can I freshen that?" the younger woman asked, holding a glass pot of coffee above his cup.

"Sure."

He hadn't sworn off caffeine yet. There was, after all, a limit.

Dempsey strolled in a half-hour later. His stomach slipped gently over his belt just enough to prove he was a man who liked life's little indulgences. "You didn't show up last night after seeing Candy Dandy."

"I couldn't get away."

Dempsey smiled faintly. "Be careful now. She's got a bit of a reputation around here."

They moved to a booth by silent agreement. The waitress brought Dempsey a cup of coffee and three chocolate-frosted doughnuts.

Gus bit into the first one, eating half in one bite. "She tell you she's a whore?" he mumbled, his mouth full.

Connor stirred his coffee. "She told me a lot of things."

He nodded. "She's a sad case in a lot of ways. What did she tell you about Daniels?"

"She had a lot of opinions—not as many facts. She's not the only link to the Scott girls, is she?"

"Nah. People remember Daniels even if they don't quite remember his wife. And the girls are memorable." Gus pulled a small notebook from his back pocket. "They kinda were in and outta school. Not a lot of supervision. But one of 'em got herself pregnant and tried to pin it on a local boy of good family."

"What happened?"

"Nothin'." He shrugged. "The boy's grown now and livin' in Seattle. I called him. He's proud of it—now that she's a star and all—but apart from us in Wagon Wheel, he can't convince anybody that he slept with Denise Scott, the film star. He's a braggart and she's got some funny history cooked up that doesn't say nothin' about Wagon Wheel, so it's all kind of a mess."

"I'm surprised he hasn't taken his story to the tabloids," Connor remarked ironically.

"Oh, he did. The story ran! But that lady's got so many stories about her now, nobody knows whether she's from New York City or Juneau, Alaska. And a little abortion in the past ain't no big deal."

"She aborted the child?"

"Well, some doctor said she'd had a miscarriage. Who knows? But I guess that's why nothin' came of the rumor. Miscarriages are kinda sad, and nobody wanted to feel sorry for someone as pretty and successful as Denise Scott. Her sleepin' around on that film king's son. That's what people want to know about." He eyed Connor thoughtfully. "Didn't Candy tell you none of this?"

"No, she didn't."

"Well, what'd she tell ya, then?"

Connor sighed. His interview with Candy Daniels Whorton had left him feeling unsettled and a little depressed. There were so many lost people in the world, the flotsam and jetsam of society whom the rest of the world treated with unconscious disdain and barely concealed sneers.

Candy's obesity was her least attractive feature and her most obvious one. She'd waddled away from the door, set the .38 on the cluttered counter, shoving dishes aside to make room for it, then sunk onto the couch, indicating a vinyl kitchen chair for Connor.

He could see some kind of dried red sauce stuck to the chair's back but he took a seat nevertheless.

She was eyeing him carefully. "Want a cigarette?"

"No, thanks."

"Sheriff said you'd want to talk to me. I've been kind of expecting you." She lit her own cigarette and filthy gray smoke added to the general air of debris and neglect.

"Thomas Daniels was your father?"

"Yep."

"He was a carpenter."

"He was good with his hands," she said with a smirk. "He'd go out on the job and spend more time with the wives than he needed to. Got hisself beat up a few times, too, but not enough to stop him. I was eleven when Mom kicked him out for good."

"And then he married Nina Scott?"

"Moved in before the papers was even filed." Candy shrugged. "I was glad. Good riddance."

Connor wondered if that were really true, but it was so long ago now it hardly seemed worth exploring. "Did you ever meet your stepsisters?"

"The three angels." She snorted. "I knew of 'em, but they came from somewhere else. Their mom divorced their dad and came to Wagon Wheel. I think they were from southern Oregon, somewhere like Medford or Roseburg. They was only here for about three years." Candy heaved a sigh and picked tobacco off her teeth from her unfiltered cigarette. "Nina was pretty. Dad went right for her and she was dumb enough to go for him." She laughed without humor.

"You told Sheriff Dempsey that you thought one of the sisters killed your father."

"Now, I didn't say it quite like that," she hurriedly corrected. "All I said was they had a lot of reason to hate him, that's all."

"Yeah?"

She sent him a look through the smoke, her eyes glimmering with hidden thoughts. "He was always putting his hands up their skirts." She shrugged. "It was all over town."

Connor wondered. Candy's reputation as a virtuous woman wasn't exactly stellar. Her mind seemed to run on one track, and he suspected he was hearing what she hoped was the truth more than what she actually knew.

"How old were these sisters when Thomas lived with them?"

"High school age. The twins had just graduated and the younger one, Hayley, was about a sophomore, I think. They all just disappeared at the same time."

"Where was the mother?"

"Oh, she died. She was kinda sorry-seemin'. Just kinda wasted away."

"You never went to school with the girls?"

"Uh, uh. I was younger. They were real pretty but kept to themselves, mostly. Who woulda thunk Denise would become a movie star!" A poignant bitterness touched her face. For a moment Connor could see her own extraordinary beauty, a beauty lost to fat and her own hardspent years.

"I've got pictures," she offered, a bit reluctantly, "if you'd like to see."

She waddled over to a scarred wooden end table and shook open a drawer. Inside was a cheap, but surprisingly clean, scrapbook. A bit shyly, she handed it to Connor and he opened it to find newspaper clippings yellowing with age. They were mostly of Denise, covering her film career, but Candy had pasted in all three girls' school pictures as well.

Blonde, blue-eyed, white teeth—the family resemblance was strong. But there was something remarkably joyless in the photos.

"They don't look happy," he remarked.

She made a noise of disgust. "They had my father living with 'em."

"You don't think your father's death was an accident?"

"Like he bashed in his head and stuffed himself in that culvert? Who're you kiddin', mister!"

"Maybe some jealous husband caught up with him."

"Maybe." She looked at him again and he sensed that same impression of secrets inside her.

Or maybe, since she was deemed to be something of the local town whore, it was her idea of a come-on.

"Why even bother lookin' for his killer?" Candy asked. "My dad was a piece of garbage. We're all better off without him, believe you me."

"A human life was ended," he said, trying it out on her.

"He was garbage," she repeated flatly. "And somebody finally dumped him."

Connor had traveled over the same ground about six different ways with her, but she didn't have much more to reveal. She knew nothing of Hayley and the other twin, whom Candy said was named Dinah.

In the end, his impression was that she just wanted to be deemed important, and that this was an elaborate way to see her name in the paper connected to the Scott sisters. She had no real interest in justice. Candy firmly believed Thomas Daniels deserved to die and he'd finally met up with destiny.

When he left her, she made a half-hearted attempt to get him to spend the night, then seemed almost relieved when he didn't. Her last words were, "It ain't loaded," as if he'd asked about the gun.

Candy Dandy was a miserable soul with a pathetic existence, and for no good reason he could name, he felt deeply sorry for her.

Now he looked at Dempsey who, despite his comment about her being a "sad case" clearly didn't feel anything for Candy but mild contempt.

"Is there anyone else around who could tell me more about the Scott sisters?"

Dempsey's sharp eyes glittered. "So, you do think one of 'em did it."

"I have no idea," Connor answered truthfully. "I don't even know why I'm continuing with this."

"I'll tell ya why." Gus had stuffed the other two dough-nuts in his mouth and eaten them as quickly as the first. Now he licked his thumb and set about picking up crumbs. "Because you don't know what on God's green earth you're gonna do with the rest of your life and this here puzzle is as good a pastime as any until you figure it out."

Connor didn't respond.

Dempsey slid the notebook across the table. "Every-body knows a little bit. You can practically go right down the telephone book and learn a little somethin' about each girl. But nobody knows much."

Connor accepted the notebook reluctantly, feeling he was on the threshold of something he really didn't want to discover. With a grimace, he muttered, "I've got time to kill. Might as well see what I can find out."

The taxi swept along the smog shrouded freeway, keep-ing up with the rest of the traffic as it ferried Denise from the airport to Carolyn's posh home. The Mercedes was in Brent McCaffey's capable hands; it would be shipped back tomorrow by truck.

Exhaustion weighed down her eyelids and made her shoulders ache. She was afraid to think too hard. She hadn't known what to do with McCaffey, though he'd been understanding enough to take his Cactus Condom and vamoose in good humor. She could just imagine the happy bastard telling all and sundry about his night with Denise Scott.

I went to bed with Denise Scott, the actress!

Yeah. Great. Another brilliant move.

Denise grimaced, glad the cabbie was sensitive enough to her mood to keep his mouth shut as they sped through the gray twilight.

She didn't want to go back to Carolyn's, but where else was she supposed to go? She had no home to speak of. She was a vagabond. A lost soul.

I am used up, she thought wearily. *Completely, utterly used up.*

Don't think, don't think, don't think. Fist your hand and push the poisons out. Outward, into the black space of nothingness.

"Goddammit, Denise," she bit out, tears forming in the corners of her eyes. It wasn't working. Nothing worked anymore.

The cabbie glanced into the rearview mirror. Made eye contact.

Denise tucked her arms close and huddled inside her sweater. She wasn't up to facing Carolyn, but she had no choice. Laying her head back against the seat cushion, she felt her body go limp. Her bones melted.

She let the tears flow.

Thirty minutes later she paid the fare and started up the long stone walkway to Carolyn's front door. The walk had never seemed this long but now it stretched into eternity, each footstep so heavy it took superhuman strength just to lift her ankles.

At the door Denise inhaled a deep, shaking breath. Her finger trembled as she pressed the bell. Chimes tolled inside like warning bells.

Exhaustion was closing her inside a cottony web. Swaying on her feet, Denise awaited her doom. Measured footsteps sounded, muffled against Carolyn's Aubusson carpet. A pause. Someone was peering through the peekhole at her.

The door suddenly opened. Denise swallowed. It was Peter. He of the oiled and lubed penis. Mr. Hawaiian

Tropics in the naked flesh. At least that was Denise's first impression, until she realized he wore a pair of black swim trunks.

"Well, hey!" he declared on a note of discovery. "Good to see you."

All of Denise's reserves failed her at that moment. She was crashing. As if she'd been on drugs. She stood silently, eyes huge, her vulnerability so raw that even she knew it must be visible on her face. Peter stepped forward and pulled her into his scuzzy arms, and she didn't have the will to resist.

"Where's Carolyn?" she choked out.

"She's here somewhere. Hey, you look bummed. Come on in and have a drink or something."

He walked her to the solarium and helped her onto a bright green lounge chair. Denise closed her eyes. Felt her mouth tremble uncontrollably.

"Could you call . . . Dr. Hayden Stone . . . ? Ask Carolyn to call him . . . please . . ."

"Hey, okay. You want a snort of coke first?"

With a long, desperate shudder, Denise lapsed into exhausted unconsciousness.

Chapter Six

Connor made short work of Gus's notebook. People were willing to talk but there was no new information, just more innuendo and the general consensus that the kid in Seattle had fathered a child which one of the sisters had aborted. The crowd favored Denise Scott; she was the most memorable. But amazingly enough, over half the people Connor questioned did not know she was the same Denise Scott as the movie star. The phrase he heard time and again was, "Well, that just can't be."

The good citizens of Wagon Wheel could not fit the two halves together. Denise Scott Callahan of the movies was too perfect to be the small town girl from the poor family with the revolting Thomas Daniels as a stepfather. Oh, yes, Connor heard a lot about Daniels. He was something of a celebrity in his own right. Fast with the women, mean as sin, and the man voted most likely to come to a "bad end."

"Bad blood," the elderly woman who'd lived closest to the Daniels place at the time the Scott girls were under Thomas Daniels' care told Connor. Her home was about a mile from Daniels'. "Born ugly and stayed that way all his life. Nearly beat his first wife to death, from all accounts, and took a swing or two at the second, I don't wonder. Those girls musta seen a lot. Felt it, too. He shoulda been done-in a long time before he finally got it."

The more Connor delved into Daniels' life, the more he felt he was sinking in quicksand. It was a no win case. Thomas Daniels was a thoroughly hated man, and he'd earned that reputation through all his violent forty years. Even the women he'd slept with—those who would admit to it, anyway—were heartily sorry they'd ever had anything to do with him.

No one admitted to killing him, but, to a person, they were glad he was dead.

And though they weren't as eager to express their opinions on who the killer might be, Connor learned that also, to a person, they believed one of the Scott girls had taken his life.

So, it was time to go back to L.A. to interview Denise Scott and see where that led him. And it was probably time to piece together a bit of his own life.

The road led to Hollywood.

He packed his few belongings into the bag he'd brought to his sister's house. She eyed him thoughtfully as he stood by the door, saying his goodbyes.

"You're going to put one of those girls in jail." She tried to hide her sadness but couldn't quite manage it.

"I hope to learn the truth."

"You're going to ruin her life for the sake of avenging Thomas Daniels'."

This was a side to his sister he'd never seen. It irked Connor, especially since she expressed feelings inside himself he was trying hard to ignore. "Murder is against the law. If I ever thought of going back, I'd have to believe I would uphold the law. That would be my job."

"So, this is some kind of test for you?"

Connor had about had it. Talk about your nagging conscience. Slinging his bag over his shoulder, he thrust open the screen door and walked onto the wooden porch, breathing in a hit of dust-choked late September air.

"Uncle Jack!"

His nephew, Matt, flagged him down. With him was his friend and perenniel sidekick, Mikey Watters. They pounced on Connor as if he were a special find of extraordinary significance.

"Where ya going?" Matt demanded, alarmed by his stuff red bag.

"I'm heading back to Los Angeles."

"What about old man Daniels? What about who killed him?"

Connor crossed to his rental car and tossed the bag in the back seat. Matt and Mikey trailed after him like lost puppies. "I'm still working on it."

"You gonna find that actress lady?" Matt's brow was furrowed.

"Certainly do my best."

"He got what was coming to him," Matt stated bluntly. "He was a . . . bastard."

Connor threw the boy a sidelong look, amused to see Matt's ears turn red with embarrassment. "He didn't win many popularity contests in Wagon Wheel, that's for sure."

"You think he deserved it?" Mikey piped in, his stubborn cowlick sticking straight off the back of his head.

Connor hesitated. Tricky stuff, dealing with such a malleable, young mind. "No one deserves to be murdered, no matter what his own crimes are. But certain people go through life aiming to make trouble and hurt others. Those people often die violently themselves."

Mikey nodded solemnly. "What goes around comes around."

The words took Connor by surprise, mostly because they came out of such a young mouth. "That's right."

Matt, intuiting that Mikey had somehow got a leg up on him, quickly jumped in, "His mom says that all the time! He's just a big dope."

"Shut up!"

"You shut up!" Matt glared at his friend. Four small hands balled into fists.

"I'm going to need you guys to help me," Connor broke in before this skirmish escalated into World War III. "Someone needs to report what's going on back here in Wagon Wheel to me. Think you could keep a notebook or something? Call me once in a while?"

The ruse worked so well Connor felt a tweak of conscience over tricking them. They both swore to keep excellent records and instantly started arguing about who would have control of the notes and who would get to talk first when they placed the call.

The squeak of the screen door announced Connor's sister, Mary. She stood on the porch, a slight frown marring her pretty face. He could read her like a book: she hoped he failed in his mission.

With a last wave he turned the car westward and began the two and a half hour drive to the Portland airport.

"Are you deaf, or just plain dumb?" Jason demanded, jerking Hayley back to the present. She was staring at the pile of menus in her hands but seeing a far different vision.

"You're so clever with words," she told him.

"Got a problem with work, Hayley? Those people over

there are going to walk out if you don't wait on them, and if they do, you're history."

"Management by tyranny," she muttered as she stuffed the menus under one arm, pasted on a bright smile and headed for the booth at the end.

The couple were in their late twenties. The woman didn't crack a smile as she watched Hayley approach. Her companion's gaze skimmed over her without interest and he said, "We've been waiting quite awhile."

"Really?" Hayley pretended not to have a brain in her head.

"How's the mushroom soup?" the woman asked, her voice so perfectly snooty that Hayley instantly memorized its intonation. It might work for her someday.

"The soup is superb," she answered in the same tone. "A delicate mushroom flavor with just the hint of sherry. Our chef adds bayleaf and, when the moon is right, a pinch of nutmeg. It's to die for."

The couple looked at her blankly, unsure whether she was putting them on or whether she was serious. Hayley kept right on smiling.

"I'll have the garden salad," the woman said frostily.

"Yes, make that two," her companion added, clearing his throat.

"Could I interest you in some wine or mineral water?"

They conferred and decided to both indulge in a domestic chardonnay.

"Excellent choice," Hayley observed, smile fixed in place. "Very plebian."

"What did she say?" the woman asked when she thought Hayley was out of earshot.

"She recommended the wine," he hissed back, leaving Hayley to fight a fit of laughter.

"So, they didn't leave," Jason greeted her as she wrote down their order.

"Yeah, and they think we've got a chef at this one star restaurant."

"Your attitude stinks."

Hayley slid him a sideways look. "Kinda goes with the smell around here, huh?"

Lines tightened around his mouth. He was the worst kind of manager: big on authority and criticism, small on help and praise. Since her night out with Gloria Carver, Hayley had learned a thing or two about lowlifes. Jason, though not as desperate and morally empty as the men she'd encountered, was still a lowlife. He was mean in a small-minded way that rubbed Hayley the wrong way. He enjoyed his petty insults and liked to see people squirm. It bugged him that Hayley was more impervious than most.

He reminded her of dear, sweet, old stepdaddy.

"You think you're so smart," he finally muttered, turning to bark at the newest waitress, a fumble-fingered eighteen-year-old who squeaked in fear everytime Jason growled at her. He slammed his way through the swinging cafe doors into the kitchen.

The eighteen-year-old raised tear-filled eyes to Hayley.

Yep. Jason had true class.

"Men," Hayley said by way of explanation. "Ever wonder why they populate the planet?"

She sniffed. "So we can have babies?"

The girl's innocence was almost unbearable. "They're here to make sure we never get away with anything. They've got to keep us in line. It's a male rule. And they like it best when they're hurting us."

Her eyes rounded. She stared at Hayley as if she'd said she was from Jupiter. "What?"

"Never mind." Hayley was brusque. She hated that kind of naivete. It was so easy to crush that type of soul.

At that moment the door opened and Gloria Carver herself sauntered to the nearest booth, licking her lips as she slid across the blood red cushion.

"I'll take this one," Hayley called over her shoulder, butterflies revving up for flight inside her stomach.

"So," Gloria said.

"So," Hayley answered.

After their evening at "Keith's," which actually turned out to be a roving address to keep the vice squad off Danny's—Danny of the the red pole club, that is—neck, Hayley and Gloria had been picked up by the same black sedan with the same stone-faced driver. They'd been dropped back at the club and Hayley had then hailed a cab to her apartment.

There'd been no other contact, so Hayley was curious and alarmed at her new "friend's" appearance.

"So, you're a watcher, huh? Dumbest thing I ever heard."

"Stick around here. It gets dumber."

"Kind of a smart mouth, aren't ya?"

"The manager seems to think so," Hayley admitted ironically.

"Wanna go out again?"

Hayley sized her up. For the life of her she couldn't see why Gloria Carver should care.

"They liked that," she enlightened Hayley. "Makes 'em feel like real studs to have a girl watch."

Hayley fought back visions she didn't want to remember. Gloria Carver was a professional and she gave good service for the right price, no matter who was watching.

"They already had female company," Hayley pointed out.

"Oh, her." Gloria dismissed the vapid blonde with a sound of disgust. "She just likes the drugstore. But you were stone-cold sober, weren't you? Sittin' there watching. Did you get what you wanted?"

"It was an education."

"Got off on it a little, too, didn't ya?"

Hayley regarded her coolly. Gloria Carver would probably hoot and holler if she knew how repulsed Hayley had been. Willing herself away from the scene had been the only way to get through the evening.

"Y'know, I got some other friends, too."

"What kind of friends?" Hayley asked cautiously.

"Expensive friends. Heidi Fleiss style, y'know what I mean? Money. Kinky. Really wild."

"Celebrities?" Hayley questioned, her pulse quickening.

"Oh, yeah. Hey, one of Danny's girls got a part by doing somethin' special with her little piggy toe."

"You're making this up." Hayley almost laughed.

"Uh uh. Come out with me again. I'll take you somewhere nice."

"Why? What's in it for you?"

"More money!" She was surprised Hayley was so dense. "I scored big the other night."

Hayley shook her head. "Next time, someone might want a different performance out of me. I don't need to risk it."

"How much do you want that part?"

Hayley met her knowing gaze. Gloria Carver was too smart and too insightful for a street hooker.

"We can go clubbin' at some hot spots."

Hayley eyed Gloria's street-walking duds but remained silent. Gloria read her mind.

"I got nicer stuff. You'd be surprised who I know."

John Callahan?

No, he wasn't into this scene at all. He might be a womanizer, but the only way he'd contact a hooker was for the same reasons Hayley was currently leading this double-life: a film project.

"All right," Hayley said tautly.

Eye on the prize.

Carolyn's party had hit that phase between fake smiles and kisses and down-and-dirty drinking, smoking, and turning on. It was the point when things could turn fantastic or ugly, depending on the makeup of the crowd.

It had been four days since Denise had collapsed on the sofa—and not a damn thing had changed. The initial excitement over her fainting spell had changed to boredom when the venerable Dr. Stone had made an uncharacteristic house call and ordered—as a prescription—a hearty bowl of soup. So, okay, she hadn't been eating regularly. Denise still didn't feel Stone had a right to be so irritatingly authoritative.

"You're going down," he said, another comment completely out of character. "You're not sinking. You're diving."

Denise had been lying on the chaise, a blanket tossed over her legs. Feeling vulnerable, she'd shrunk away from him. She'd never been so close to him before. No desk separated them. He was sitting in a chair right next to her, turned so that he could look square in her face.

And the light was so goddamn bright in the solarium. Jeeezus! You'd think Carolyn would have more forgiving illumination. Denise felt exposed and uncertain and afraid.

"How much is this house call costing me?" she demanded. "Double the rate?"

"I've listened to your flippancy for weeks. It tells its own story." When she didn't bite, he enlightened, "Your life is a cover-up."

Now, that was interesting. Stone, making a prediction? All she'd thought he could do was parrot other, better psychiatrists. "Okay, what do you want me to say? I'm sorry? From now on I'll remember to eat."

"Want to tell me what happened after our last visit?"

Denise considered. "I went on a little vacation," she said cautiously.

"What was it that set you off?"

"Set me off? Look, Doc, I think you've got me confused with someone else."

"You left my office and drove away in Carolyn's car. Were you aware of your actions?"

"Yes," she answered belligerently. Did he have to sound so arrogant and accusatory?

"You've been suffering from delusions. I just want to know if your decision to leave was made consciously."

"I was pissed after our last session, okay?"

"Because I accused you of acting?"

His gray eyes gave nothing away. No compassion there now. She had the sensation that he was angry with her. Maybe he actually got annoyed with his whackos once in a while.

"You really take your job seriously, don't you, Stoner?"

"Denise, do you remember what I told you at our first session?"

"Let me think. No, don't tell me. I bet I can come up with it."

"I said I was only in Houston temporarily."

"You didn't give me a chance to answer," she admonished. Damn the man. She hated it when he acted like he didn't hear her.

"My home's Los Angeles," Stone went on relentlessly. "I gave up my practice and moved for personal reasons, but I'm going back now."

Vaguely she recalled some part of this story. A wife. An ex-wife, maybe? And a life that seemed shallow and pointless. He'd left for Houston because . . . because . . .

Her mind shut down. Panic seized her. "You can't," she whispered, tortured.

He didn't answer, but his eyes saw everything. To her horror, Denise felt tears burn. She would not cry. Nothing could make her cry in front of someone except a director's cue. She damned well wouldn't let it!

"I'm sorry," he said.

Denise's throat closed in on itself. She stared mutely.

"But I didn't come here to talk about me," he added more gently. "We need to discuss you. Your therapy, and where we go from here."

"I'm not going anywhere."

"I haven't been your doctor long enough to make predictions on your illness."

"But I'm definitely ill, right? We've established that."

"You're symptomatic of a cyclothymic personality and—"

"Speak English, Doc."

"—I think you're heading toward a more severe bipolar mood disorder, such as manic-depression."

"Whoa . . ." Denise shaded her eyes against the glaring sunlight so she could see him more clearly. "Now there's a mouthful. Are you saying I'm a manic-depressive?"

"It's possible. It's also possible these delusionary spells and lapses are drug-induced."

She knew what he was asking. She didn't blame him. And she wasn't exactly drug-free. "Just say yes," she teased.

"Women are more prone to bipolar illnesses."

"Do say."

"Women have two X chromosomes, which is important in bipolar illness, if dominant X-linkage is involved."

The meaningless words were coming out of his mouth, but Denise was reading his eyes. He was saying, "Please, let me help you." She could almost believe his sincerity.

But that would be too risky. Too, too risky.

"You're going to miss talking about my sick, sex life," she murmured, her voice whispery and weak.

His brows pulled into a frown. For once in his life he seemed stumped for some professional platitude. Reaching into his breast pocket, he drew out a business card, holding it out to Denise. It took an immense amount of energy to accept the card.

"If you change your mind, this is my L.A. office number," he explained.

Hope surged inside her. She didn't live here, with Carolyn. Hell, no! She was a Los Angeles-ite herself.

But he was rejecting her. Call it what you will, he'd come here to personally drop her diagnosis on her, then to make sure she understood their relationship was over.

"You're also going to miss a big chunk of income."

He got the message. She saw him draw back and regard her thoughtfully, almost sadly. Well, why not? He was losing big bucks here. Did he really think she'd follow after him like a lovesick fool? Did he think she'd buy that mumbo-jumbo, psychiatric bullshit?

"Call me," he urged.

"You belong in L.A., Stoner. That dyed hair and that mock serious look. Now if you learn to curl your lip a bit,

you could do one of those '50's James Dean-Marlon
Brando jeans commercials."

To her intense surprise he reached for her hand. Denise's heart jolted at the contact, but he simply shook her
limp fingers in a gesture so poignantly symbolic of endings
that she nearly lost control of those bottled-up tears.

"Maybe when you learn to trust a bit more," he said,
bestowing one of his rare smiles on her before he left.

Well. That had certainly been a bad day. She'd spent
the rest of the afternoon sitting around with Carolyn and
dropping acid. She didn't normally do many drugs. But
she'd been so miserable since she'd run away from L.A.
and John, she'd simply fallen into whatever Carolyn was
doing. And Carolyn and her friends were doing acid.

She hadn't ever told Stone, of course, though now she
suspected he'd guessed as much. He would most likely
blame her delusions and time lapses on LSD, and there
was undoubtedly some truth to that. But he thought she
was a borderline manic-depressive. Now, that was fright-
ening. Because that was flat out crazy, no matter how you
sliced it.

Denise was viscerally afraid of being truly certifiable.

She'd surfaced sometime the following afternoon and
had been stone-cold sober ever since. No fun, but she'd
also experienced one of those short, clear periods where
life seemed to make some sort of sense and her destined
path didn't seem so bumpy.

She had to cut ties with Carolyn. It was time to move
onward and upward. She shied away from actually returning to Los Angeles and her career, but what else was
there?

She had to go back. And this decision had absolutely
nothing to do with Dr. Hayden Stone. Nothing.

Liar.

"Hey there . . ."

Denise surfaced from her reverie to find Peter smiling at her. He'd been fairly self-contained since he'd discovered her on the doorstep. At least she hadn't experienced any sexual delusions, nor had he displayed his endowments.

"Want something?" He gestured vaguely in the direction of the bar but Denise knew he was offering a veritable drugstore of delights as well. She'd already turned down cocaine, Ecstasy, and several others she hadn't bothered to learn the names of. Yes, Carolyn ran with the hot, young Hollywood crowd when she was in L.A. and some of them visited her in Houston when they were looking for a change of scene.

Manic-depressive. Shivers of fear slid beneath her skin. She'd read Patty Duke's accounts of suffering from it. She knew about Kristy McNichol. They came right out and admitted they were fighting the disease.

But I'm not like that. I'm not.

Peter was still waiting.

"I'd like some information on bipolar illnesses," she said. "Could you bring me a medical encyclopedia?"

"Is this a trick question?"

His gaze had slid from her face to her breasts. Her blouse was taupe silk and a line of black lace peeked out from the deepest point of the V. "Yes, it's a trick question. The trick is to see if you understand it."

"I understand."

Now his fingers were following the path of his eyes. Reaching forward, he drew a line from the hollow of her neck to the deepest point of the V, then back up over the mound of her left breast.

"I don't think you do," Denise replied, but a terrible churning developed inside her. Anger and sorrow and fear vied for dominance.

He moved closer. She could feel the heat of his breath against her ear. Then he moved around behind her. This was no dream. This was Peter The Proud, ready to entice her with drugs, alcohol, and oh, yes, let us not forget his favorite lure: Peter The Proud's Penis.

With a sense of inevitability Denise waited while his heat enveloped her. Her gaze lit on the luxurious appointments of Carolyn's home: the vivid tapestries; the pre-Columbian art; silk drapes; the mosaic tile inlaid with gold.

And the guests. Milling around, paying little attention as Peter's hands slid over her back and around the front to move up her ribcage and cup her breasts.

Like this, baby? You like this? Stop crying. I mean it, stop that blubbering!

Denise jerked as if from a sound sleep. Peter was silently thrusting against her, rhythmically bouncing against her buttocks, as if there weren't others in the room who were bound to notice any moment!

She didn't waste time on words. Just turned around and slapped him for all she was worth. The second afterwards she stared at her palm, shocked.

"Bitch!" Peter spat.

Denise trembled all over. She stalked from the room and ran upstairs, her whole body suffused with color. Shame. Shame that she'd let him touch her.

This was no delusion. None of it was a delusion.

Your life is a cover-up.

She pressed her knuckles to her flaming cheeks, biting her lower lip until blood flowed freely.

"Denise? You in there?" Carolyn's muffled voice

sounded through the bedroom door. "For Christ sake, you've got the whole party in an uproar. Peter smashed my favorite Waterford vase, the fucking bastard, and said it's your fault!" She rapped on the door. "Denise?"

Reluctantly, Denise opened the door. She looked at Carolyn. Really looked at her. Her red hair was artfully touched up but growing brittle, the telltale signs of too much tampering. Her face was unlined, to date, and she'd gone in for several sessions of permanent makeup so that now her eyes were always lined with a soft mink color of eyeliner and her lips were always pink rose. It was strangely attractive but Denise could never stop staring.

"The prick says you slapped him. You should have kicked him in the balls."

"I thought you liked him."

"He smashed that vase into my mosaic tile. A piece hit Ian Wallace on the chin. He's bleeding, goddammit!"

Underneath her fury at Peter was an accusation meant for Denise. Denise wasn't that nuts not to hear it.

And suddenly she was weary of this whole scene. Sick to the back teeth of Peter, Carolyn, and everyone else who'd cruised through the place these past weeks.

She could be gone and back in L.A. by morning.

As soon as Carolyn returned to the party, Denise packed up the clothes and personal items she'd bought since checking into Hotel Carolyn. An hour passed, an hour where the music downstairs swelled louder and louder along with the voices. Another night of revelry and self-indulgence and waste.

Leaving her bags at the top of the stairs, Denise tiptoed downstairs again, determined to avoid Peter at all costs.

No such luck. He was sprawled on the Aubusson carpet just inside the front door. Denise stepped gingerly over his legs, he was clearly stoned.

Carolyn stood beside a tall, slim man in a black T-shirt and gray sportscoat, her arm wrapped possessively through his. He was touching a handerchief to his chin. Ian Wallace, Denise remembered. He of the Waterford crystal debacle.

"Champagne?" Carolyn asked, her eyes too bright and wide.

"No, thanks. Carolyn, I've got to leave. Thanks for everything," Denise told her.

The thin man gazed at her intently. His hair was light brown and fashionably long, in that rock star kind of way. Denise pulled out a smile of acknowledgement though she'd never felt less like smiling.

"Denise Scott Callahan," he said. "I saw you slap our downed warrior over there."

"Prick," Carolyn muttered, staggering a bit as she glared at Peter's prone form.

"Sorry about the cut," Denise told Ian.

"Worth it."

"Whad'ya mean you've got to leave?" Carolyn asked, her sluggish brain finally interpreting the message.

"It's time to go back."

"To L.A.?" She tried to focus on Denise. "No, no, no, no, no . . ." Nuzzling against Ian, she asked, "Champagne? I'm dying of thirst."

"I'll get you a glass."

Ian disengaged himself from Carolyn, gently propping her against the back of the divan. He motioned Denise to follow him. Sensing trouble, Denise nevertheless complied. Ian was about the only person in the room who seemed in control of his faculties.

"Are you leaving tonight?" he asked as he uncorked another bottle of Dom Perignon. Half-empty bottles littered the bar.

"I hope to."

"I'm catching a midnight flight. Why don't you join me?"

"You're going to Los Angeles?"

"I live in Beverly Hills."

"Oh, well . . . I don't know."

"Don't say no. I might never get over the rejection." His smile was faintly mocking.

Denise considered. Why not? At least Ian was stable. Hell, he was a regular Rock of Gibraltar in this crowd.

"I hate being alone," she admitted.

He handed her a glass of champagne, Carolyn completely forgotten. "So do I," he told her, still smiling.

Touching the rim of his glass to hers, the deal was set.

Dinah squinted at the screen, wishing for her glasses. She'd left them in Santa Fe. She was always leaving them somewhere. But she hadn't planned to be separated from them so long.

If only Denise would call! She'd left message after message on Derek Sather's answering machine. Either Derek was simply ignoring her pleas for Denise to call, or he didn't give a damn that Denise was receiving urgent messages to call home, or . . . he didn't know or care where Denise was.

Maybe Callahan had been wrong in assuming Denise had run to Derek after the break-up. Maybe she'd left him and moved somewhere else. Somewhere better. Maybe she really was getting help this time, instead of bouncing into the arms of another man.

Fat chance, Dinah thought grimly, knowing her sister far too well.

But damn it all, Denise *had* to call. Dinah couldn't keep up this charade forever.

The low rumble of an arriving vehicle brought her up short. She was alone. John Callahan had swept in and swept out—his brief R&R less than twenty-four hours long. Curiously, she'd been strangely lonely since his departure; she hadn't realized how isolated she'd been until she'd had contact with another human being—no matter how loathsome that human being might be.

Maybe it was Federal Express or something, she decided, checking the clock. Noon. In the middle of the week. Not likely that His Highness would show up a second time unannounced, especially during the work week.

The phone purred on the desk. Dinah snatched up the receiver, distracted by the sound of the car's engine. "Yes?" she demanded. The only way this would be a call for her was if it were Flick, and she'd just spoken to him.

"Could I speak to Denise Scott Callahan?" a male voice asked.

Dinah hesitated. Sometimes she pretended she was Denise, other times she said she was housesitting. This time she didn't know which way to jump. "Who's calling, please?"

"Connor Jackley. I'm looking for Ms. Scott-Callahan because I have some information from Wagon Wheel, Oregon."

Dinah broke into a cold sweat so fast it was if someone had flicked a switch. "She's not here. She's away for awhile."

"Do you know if she's at the home of Carolyn Lenton in Houston, Texas?"

"Who?" Dinah asked.

"Do you work for Ms. Scott-Callahan?"

"I—yes. She's unavailable. Who are you?" she demanded, growing anxious. "What do you want? What kind of information?"

A cool breeze feathered against her arms. Dinah looked up to find John Callahan standing in the hallway, staring at her, taking in her jeans, her ponytail, her bare face, the fact that she was sitting at his computer . . .

The man at the end of the line was saying something else. Dinah dropped the receiver from nerveless fingers.

Callahan strode slowly toward her. Dinah clicked a finger on the computer mouse, closing her file, blanking the screen. Her heart revved into overdrive. The gig was up. Denise would never work on the computer. Never.

"What are you up to?" he asked in his slow-talking, sexy voice, his gaze flicking to the monitor. "Word processing?"

"It's none of your business."

"Yeah?"

"If I want to take up writing, it's my own affair."

He nodded. "Well, you're good at having affairs so go right ahead and have another."

A reprieve! Dinah's confidence began to return.

"Who was on the phone?"

"Nobody I wanted to talk to."

"Sounded a lot like a blackmailer to me. Have you got anything to be blackmailed about? Apart from the usual, that is?"

"Go to hell."

"You're not Denise, are you?" he said in a quiet voice.

Dinah nearly gasped, but she regarded him steadily, keeping her rollicking pulse to herself.

"You're playing a part, some strange new method acting that you bring right into your own life. What are you priming for? Nobody in this town'll hire you again. Nobody with any sense, anyway."

Dinah's gaze narrowed. Now that the disturbing phone call was over, and her deception intact, she felt curiously empowered. "Did you come back just to insult me? That's pretty weak, even for you."

"This little game is kind of interesting. I've got to hand it to you. I thought the thrill was gone, but, you've got my attention." His gaze hovered somewhere near her mouth.

"Why don't you just evaporate?"

"Sorry. I'm going to be here until Monday. I've got some things to do at home. Maybe I'll even get some time on my computer, if I set up an appointment."

His blue eyes simmered with humor. Humor at her expense, but it was still better than his steely eyed dissection of last week. "Don't bet on it," she muttered.

"And who's driving the Fiat in the garage?"

"I am," she stated flatly. "I'm changing my style."

"Uh huh."

Dinah stared at the dark screen, wishing he would go away so she could breathe easier. But his hip was propped against the computer table, his scent came to her in waves, and his tanned forearm was just inches from the keyboard.

"I'd bet a thousand dollars you would never even ride in a car like that. Whose is it? Don't lie, or I'll toss you out again and this time you'll stay out. I guarantee it."

"It's mine, you arrogant bastard. Now get the hell out of here and leave me alone. I'm busy."

Their gazes warred. Callahan looked ready to yank her out of the chair and do as he'd threatened. Dinah curled her fingers around the chair's cushion, childishly ready to hang on for dear life if he came one step closer.

"Why are you sleeping in the spare room?" he asked, throwing her for a loop.

"Because I like it better."

"Sick of the Santa Fe style?"

The mention of Santa Fe caused goosebumps to rise on her arms. *Who was that man on the phone? What information from Wagon Wheel?*

"Show me what you're writing," he demanded, leaning closer.

Dinah's pulse nearly shattered her eardrums. Then inspiration struck, "Will you set up an audition for me?"

He sucked air through his teeth. "I knew it!" he burst out savagely.

"No audition, no view of my writing!"

His eyes bore down on her, twin beams of bright blue fury. Dinah swallowed against a dry throat. She thought he might hit her. If he did, he'd live to regret it.

But instead he lifted one hand, slowly. She flinched as it came near her face but all he did was graze his knuckles down the curve of her cheekbone, his intense stare trapping her frightened one.

Then he turned on his heel and strode away, his footsteps echoing in the hallway.

And Dinah collapsed against the desk, completely spent.

I've got to get out of here, she warned herself desperately. *Before it's too late.*

Chapter Seven

The flight to Houston took three hours from Los Angeles. As Connor pulled his bag from the plane's overhead compartment, he reminded himself that he was wasting time. Carolyn Lenton's address was a longshot. One Derek Sather had dimly remembered only after Connor had used near bullying tactics.

Derek Sather was a stereotype. Quick track to stardom. Hot new actor-director. Quick fall into the fast life of drugs and sex.

His problems were the kind which ran rampant in Hollywood. Paranoid with low self-esteem. Concerned with appearances rather than substance. Never good enough to really make it. Hung up on all the trappings of stardom without being a real star. A regular walking time-bomb of anxieties and insecurities—and a horrible snob to boot.

While he was looking down his nose at Connor, he was also trying to impress him. It killed Connor how often this happened. Were they naturally this way, and somehow they came to Hollywood en masse, as if turning toward Mecca? Or did the Hollywood community subvert all other characteristics and leave only this jellied blob of neuroses, all packaged in the best possible wrapping, of course.

Because Derek Sather was a beautiful man. Even Connor, who'd seen a lot of beautiful people, recognized the man's attributes. Thick black hair, green eyes, a small compact body indicative of serious physical training, and an expressive mouth. He probably looked great on screen. But backbone? He had none.

"I'm not Denise Scott Callahan's keeper," he told Connor loftily. "And I'd appreciate your respect of my privacy in the future. I'm tired of the phone calls and the harassment."

Connor almost smiled. He'd considered calling John Callahan first, but in the end had decided to follow a more circuitous route to Denise. She was no longer living with her husband so his best bet was Derek Sather, whom *everyone* knew had been the reason Denise's marriage had broken up—as his buddies at the force had gleefully pointed out to Connor, apparently the last to know.

So Connor had left a few messages on Sather's answering machine, asking about Denise. Sather hadn't returned one call. Connor had toyed again with the idea of confronting John Callahan, but some sixth sense had warned him to wait. Start with Sather, Denise's last known ex, and work backwards. Except Sather had been worse than unresponsive, so Connor had decided to show up at the man's front door.

"If you'd called me back," Connor had pointed out to the scowling, young actor, "I wouldn't have made this trip. I have some information for Ms. Scott Callahan."

"Yeah, you and the rest of the world," he sneered.

"Do you know where she is?"

"Maybe. But you can go fuck yourself, man."

So, Connor had simply shouldered open the door and

pushed Derek Sather up against a wall. Hollywood's hot, young director had whined and flailed and threatened legal action like a true worm, but Connor had held fast and waited for him to crumple.

And crumple he did. Derek might be a total loser, but he wasn't completely stupid. Connor wasn't going to give up, no matter what he did. But Derek still gave one last stab of bravado.

"You're gonna be in jail, asshole! I'm gonna put you there!"

"You don't want to mess with me," Connor told him serenely. "You really don't."

"Fuck you!"

And it was then that Connor stole a look past his squirming, sputtering prisoner and glanced around the room. The living room's faux marble coffee table was littered with empty bottles of liquor and drug paraphernalia. A girl of not more than sixteen lay on the couch wearing only a pair of panties.

Connor turned his gaze to Derek who'd flushed red with indignation. But the gig was up and they both knew it.

"She's my daughter," he burst out. "It's the truth! I can prove it."

As if that made it all okay. "Give me Denise's address," Connor snarled in disgust, and so the information concerning Carolyn Lenton was imparted.

Further investigation revealed that Carolyn Lenton was nobody's friend. She had too much money and too little concern for anybody or anything other than her own unhealthy pursuits. She seemed to liken herself to some kind of psychological guru to the rich and famous. Her *modus operandi* was to seek out neurotic Hollywood types— of which there were an abundance in this land of sun and fun—and drag them off to Houston for God knew what kind of therapy.

Before proceeding to Houston, however, Connor had called John Callahan at work and at home. His attempts at reaching the man were unsuccessful, and the woman at the Callahan home had been paranoid and clearly lost when he'd mentioned Carolyn Lenton's name. The paranoia was probably the common Hollywood malady, but she hadn't recognized Carolyn's name.

So . . .

So, he'd decided to take the trip to Houston. His reasons were mixed. If word got out that he was seeking Denise Callahan over an unsolved murder, it was a media circus in the making. He wanted to avoid the press. The subtle, roundabout route was bound to be more effective.

And besides all that, he was certain he was on the right track, even though his rational mind told him he was on a wild goose chase. But his inner sense congratulated him and so he followed his instincts.

And once he connected with Denise—she would be the key to finding Dinah and Hayley.

From the airport he rented a car and drove without incident straight to Carolyn Lenton's home in River Oaks. He was surprised. This was a staid, well-established corner of the city. Old money. Conservative tastes. Not exactly a place you'd find the high-flying Hollywood types.

But Carolyn Lenton was from River Oaks, according to the information his buddies on the force had dug up for him. A throwback. A changeling. A pain in the goddamn neck for her hoity-toity parents who'd died of heart failure—both of them—within months of each other after Carolyn's first minor scandal with an older, local, long-married politician when she was barely out of her teens.

The result? A ton of money left in her greedy hands. A ton of free time to indulge whatever hedonistic pleasure appealed to her. And now, her own little bed and breakfast/drug haven for those so inclined.

At least that was the rumor.

Luckily for Carolyn, her guests were well-behaved. At least none of the neighbors had complained or even seemed aware that in the three-story home with its New Orleans style wrought-iron filigreed balconies and shuttered windows, a whole lotta shakin' was going on.

Connor pulled his rented compact to a slow stop across the street from Carolyn's home. The only evidence that the house was more than it seemed was the proliferation of automobiles parked along the drive which curved behind the house to a garage in the back.

It was four o'clock in the afternoon and beastly hot. Even with the air-conditioning, he could feel the dampness of his skin. Glancing in the mirror, he saw a taut line of disapproval already shaping his mouth. With an effort, he changed his expression. He'd seen a lot. Too much. Most often he could keep his face a careful mask, but the pure selfishness and waste of this situation annoyed him greatly. There were real problems in the world and the Carolyn Lentons didn't give a damn.

Striding up the mosaic-tiled walkway, Connor noticed how ultra-green the lawn was compared to the neighbors'. Carolyn Lenton clearly wasn't into water conservation. Hell, if she was anything like he suspected, the word to describe her was excess.

He chose the door knocker rather than the bell, slamming it hard several times.

Nothing.

Birds wheeled and danced overhead, chirping sharply. Once upon a time he would have stopped to watch.

Growing up in rural Oregon had made him appreciate simple pleasures. But years of police work had given him the sense that he couldn't enjoy nature. There just wasn't time.

It took three more bouts of incessant pounding before a voice came over the intercom.

"Who is it?" a male voice demanded with great irritation.

"Connor Jackley. Is Ms. Lenton in?"

"Who?"

"Connor Jackley," he repeated, unruffled.

"What do you want?"

"I would like to talk to the owner of this house."

A brief spurt of profanity followed. Minutes passed. Connor realized his missive had not been given to the lady of the house. Wondering if Carolyn would call the police on him, he pressed his finger to the bell and let the chimes ring over and over again until even Connor was nearly driven crazy with the noise.

The door suddenly flew open. A woman with red hair and an ugly, furious look on her face screamed, "Get off my property! I've called the police!"

"Are you Carolyn Lenton?"

Two men flanked her like bookends. Neither looked big enough to do damage. In fact, they were practically trembling at the knees. Clearly they hadn't expected to be called into service to protect their hostess.

Carolyn wore a silk wrap in peacock blue loosely tossed over a string bikini. "I'll set my pitbull on you if you don't leave right now!"

"Ms. Lenton, I'm trying to locate Denise Scott Callahan. I have some information from her hometown."

She was in the process of slamming the door, so immersed in her self-importance and fury it wouldn't have mattered if he'd told her he'd brought her a ten million dollar check from Publisher's Clearing House. But something stopped her. Whether his message finally sank in, or if it was something else, Connor wasn't quite certain. But instead of following through, she raked him with elevator eyes, giving him the once over from top to bottom and back again.

A change came over her expression. She waved the bookends away impatiently and pushed the door open with one finger, a sultry invitation Connor couldn't miss.

Inwardly, he sighed heavily. Now he knew what was going through her mind. He'd seen the signs too many times before. His own looks carried some kind of magnet for certain types of women. An ex-lover had once tried to explain, "It's that strong, silent thing you've got going. That minimalistic Bogart-speak. It drives us women wild, y'know. You look like you need someone to understand you. You're hard, but good, y'know what I mean? And you're sexy," she'd added with a sly smile. "Sooooo, sexy . . ."

It had been a good relationship. He'd enjoyed her humor, her way of teasing. But he couldn't commit in the way she'd wanted so the whole thing had fizzled out. He'd been totally involved in his work and she'd wanted the dream of a quiet, down-home lifestyle. Ironically, soon after they split he quit the force and became a private investigator.

Some things just weren't meant to be.

Carolyn steepled her fingers beneath her chin, assessing him as he walked inside. "So, what gives?" she asked. "Who are you really?"

"I'm a private investigator."

"Oh, my. What's Denise done?"

"Is she here?"

"Well, now, that's a good question, Mr . . . ?"

"Jackley."

"Do you have a first name?"

"Connor."

"Mmm . . ." Carolyn led the way through a solarium to the pool outside. Several people lay in lounge chairs, bronzed statues ignorant of anything but the heat of the sun on their skin.

Connor stayed beneath a slatted trellis where a scraggly vine sought to stay fresh beneath the beating rays. Carolyn sat in the sun on the opposite side of a glass-topped table and motioned him to sit down.

"How'd you know Denise was here?"

"It wasn't too hard to find out."

"You talk to her ex-husband?"

"No."

"Then that's who you should talk to. She still loves him."

Connor let that sink in. This was news to him. "Maybe I should talk to her."

"Well, that'd be great, but she left. Just a few nights ago, as a matter of fact. Back to Los Angeles." Carolyn twisted around and yelled to all and sundry, "Hey, get me a tonic, and bring something stronger for Mr. Jackley."

Nobody moved. The somnolent inactivity seemed almost surreal. Carolyn tried again then muttered an obscenity beneath her breath and went to get the drinks herself. Connor stared into the azure depths of the pool, watching the play of light on water.

She returned with a black enamel tray and two drinks, a tonic for her and a mug of ale for him, condensation dripping down the mug's frosted sides. She'd managed to lose the silk robe enroute and now settled herself on the lounge, one knee pulled up to show off her shapely thigh and calf.

"Would you rather have something else?" she asked, a hint of suggestion in her tone.

"No, thanks."

"All right, Connor. What can I tell you about Denise Scott?"

Connor lifted the mug. Its chill was heaven against the afternoon heat. He swallowed heartily and set the mug back down. Watching him, Carolyn Lenton pulled an ice cube from her glass, shook off the excess tonic water, then pressed it to her chest, smearing the small frozen block over her tanned flesh.

Plop! She dropped the cube into his mug of ale.

"What do you want to hear?" she asked in a husky purr.

"Everything."

"Every sordid detail? Every indiscretion and less than legal activity?" She leaned forward, her breasts straining against the triangular scraps of her bikini top.

Connor sized her up. He couldn't have stopped her now if he'd paid her. "Don't leave out a thing."

Three hours later he was on his way back to Houston International Airport without much more information. Denise was in L.A. Carolyn didn't know anything about any sisters.

"Sisters?" she'd repeated blankly. "You must be kidding. Denise has an ex-husband. A real prick, or so she says. But you never know. Denise is as screwed up as anybody. I should know."

Carolyn had gone on to tell him about Ian Wallace. She bristled at the name. It looked like Denise had scored him away from her hostess. Unforgivable, if Connor read the narrowed fury in Carolyn's permanently painted eyes.

To lesser extent, she'd also mentioned Dr. Hayden Stone. Denise's shrink, who, by coincidence had moved back to Los Angeles himself.

Glancing at the list of names and addresses on the notepad he'd tossed onto the passenger seat, Connor decided he'd better check with Dempsey. The sheriff was antsy. A part of him really wanted to brush the whole nasty story under the rug. But a part of him kept on plugging away. The last time Connor had talked to him, Dempsey had talked to Denise's ex-boyfriend again, one Jimmy Fargo, who lived in Seattle.

"He swears she had an abortion," Gus had informed him. "Seems obsessed with the idea."

"Did you ask him if he was sure he was the father?"

"Now, what are you thinkin', Jackley?"

"I don't know," Connor answered honestly. "I don't want to know."

"This thing's bound to blow up no matter what," Gus sighed with real regret. "Your sister sure doesn't like you pokin' around. Matt's been keepin' notes, y'know."

"She doesn't like him involved."

"Yeah, well, Matt feels kinda proprietary about the whole thing. Naturally so. But I got better things to do than worry about the eight-year-old murder of a lowlife mongrel like Daniels. Anytime you're sick of workin' on it, just let me know . . ."

Sick of working on it . . .

Now, Connor swept a hand around the back of his neck and rotated the kinks out of his spine. His mouth tasted sour after two glasses of ale. Carolyn had pressed more on him, but mostly Connor stayed away from booze of any kind. Once—only once—during his illustrious career with L.A.P.D., he'd let himself indulge in too much liquor. His partner had clapped him on the back and driven him home. No big deal. But later that night, that same partner had been first on the scene of a terrible automobile accident. Fog. Stupid drivers.

First on the scene. First to crash.

His death had nothing to do with Connor. But Connor's taste for alcohol of any kind had diminished.

Which was just as well since Carolyn had practically climbed atop him while her guests baked in the sun. Her hands had been strong, sleek and knowing and guiltily he recalled waiting just an instant too long before stopping her.

He needed a woman, but there wasn't one on the goddamned planet that held any appeal.

With an effort he pushed thoughts of Carolyn's nut-brown, oil-drenched body and exploring fingers from his mind and planned his next move: Ian Wallace of Beverly Hills.

Why did that name sound so familiar? And why did I have a hollow feeling in his gut?

This thing's bound to blow up, no matter what.

Grimacing, Connor wondered if Gus Dempsey and his sister might have the right idea after all. It was going to get messy and end badly.

They always did.

She'd gone straight home with him. It had seemed so right, after their long flight. And where else did she have to go anyway? Home? Where was that? Dinah was shacking up with John, and Derek, the putz, had only liked screwing the anal way. The man was a homosexual, if ever there was one, but try telling *him* that. Denise had jokingly said as much one day, and Derek had shrieked that he had a "teenaged daughter, in case you haven't noticed! I hate those sick, disgusting bastards!"

Denise had then pointed out that she had a lot of friends who were gay, and hey—you are what you are—but that hadn't cut any ice with Derek whose paranoia had reached critical mass.

Their relationship was dead anyway and so Denise, adrift and suffering from bipolar whatever-the-hell-it-was—Jeeezus, could you believe that?—had dialed Dinah and run off with Carolyn to the next bump on life's highway.

Walking into Ian's spacious home had been like coming home at the end of a long journey. She belonged here. She could tell. It was all beautiful. Sparkling windows. Antiques. Most culled from a house in Charlottesville that was now on the historic registry. Hardwood floors thick with area rugs. Rose blossoms floating in a pewter bowl on the hall sideboard.

Denise looked into Ian's face. He was smiling that inscrutable smile.

"You like it?"

"What do you think?"

"I think you like it." He clasped her hand and led her to the back of the house and the kitchen. Newspapers were neatly stacked on a chair.

"What the—Lina!" he screamed, his demeanor changing so swiftly it took Denise by surprise.

Footsteps scurried overhead. Moments later a tiny Mexican maid appeared, her eyes wide and frightened.

"Pick that up and get rid of it," Ian demanded coldly. He pointed to the newspapers.

"I take them with me," she said, nodding quickly over and over again.

She gave Ian a wide berth, going out of her way to avoid him as she lifted the huge stack in her arms.

Silence followed her exit. Then suddenly Ian pulled Denise into his arms, tightly. His heartbeat was strong and fast. Uncertain, Denise remained passive.

"Want to make love?" he murmured, his gaze intent.

She knew it would come to this. It always came to this. *Do I have to?* Denise thought wearily. "Do you have anything to drink?"

"Sure." Reluctantly he released her and walked to the refrigerator. A freshly made pitcher of martinis materialized in his hands. Lina might not know what to do with newspapers, but she seemed to understand her boss's other needs pretty well.

Producing two martini glasses and a stick of fat olives, he deftly poured them each a drink. There was something unnerving about the way he watched her as she lifted her glass, but Denise shook it off. So he got his jollies eyeing her. Half the nation's population had gotten off watching her in the midst of a fake orgasm in *Cosmos.* Jeeezus, what a sorry excuse for a film, even if it did make millions.

Denise had a nice buzz going when Ian reached out and tweaked her breast.

"I believe that's sexual harassment," she told him, trying to keep it light, feeling soul-weary with exhaustion.

He grinned and did it again.

Inevitability fell over her like a shroud. Same scene, different actor. Empty, empty life. But there was nothing else.

He slid a hand down the curve of her cheek. He bent down and kissed her ear. Hot breath. Urgent tongue.

You're gonna like this, baby. You're gonna like this.

Thomas Daniels' face swam into her vision, leering and cruel. Denise's whole body trembled. Misinterpreting, Ian wrapped his hands beneath her buttocks, picked her up, and set her on the counter, hiking up her skirt at the same time so her long bare legs dangled from skimpy, silk panties. He rhythmically ran his hands over her thighs, his thumbs brushing lightly against her panties, pulling away, brushing again. It was a move destined to generate heat and desire, but Denise couldn't respond.

Ian either didn't notice or didn't care. He simply jerked her hips to the edge of the counter, yanked off the panties, spread her legs, unzipped his pants, pulled out his erection, and went to work.

Denise braced herself on her hands and wondered desperately if Lina was about to reappear. But the maid stayed out of sight, and Ian was quick enough that before Denise had beaten herself up over making another bad choice, he'd zipped back up and even, gentlemanly, readjusted her skirt.

But the smile on his face worried her

Life could be far worse. Far, far worse.

"Been waiting to do that since Houston," he told her. "Thought about it on the plane the whole way back. Come on . . ." He took her hand and led her to his own magnificent pool and patio, where he settled her on a lounge chair.

Denise thrummed with tension. Haunting worries. Flitting ghosts. *Close your hand into a fist. Push out the poisons.*

Ian Wallace then stripped off his clothes, standing in front of her like a conquering warrior.

Swallowing, she wondered half-hysterically what he expected her to do now. She was *not* going to put anything in her mouth, if that's what he thought.

But he dove backwards into the pool and started doing laps. Denise watched him, almost mesmerized, and then she looked up and gazed at the mullioned French doors which led to the master bedroom. Lina stood framed in the glass, an unsmiling madonna with black hair scraped back.

And the look in her eyes was pure pity.

"He is the ugliest excuse for a human being I have ever seen."

"He's Emperor of the film industry."

"I can see sweat stains under his arms."

"So, he ain't Mr. Clean. Who cares? He's loaded."

"Which studio?"

"Titan Pictures."

"Damn . . ."

Hayley ground her teeth in frustration. The scene was the same as always: groups of people getting high, sprawled around in loose arms and legs, vacant stares, little interest. But this was at the home of Rodney Walburn III, a spread at the top of Mulholland Drive. Swank. Posh. Full of important players who were gorgeous, jaded, and pretty near lifeless human shells.

Rodney himself was a monster. Hollywood's "Be Thin or Be Nothing" attitude didn't seem to apply here. He rolled in fat, skin shiny with perspiration. His small eyes were nearly hidden behind flaps of fat. His pudgy hands looked small and his arms stood out from his torso, wedged like wings because they couldn't compete with his tremendous girth.

He was meticulous about his hair, however. He wore it greased down, not a single strand out of place. When he wanted something, he snapped his fingers and nubile Hollywood starlets ran to do his bidding.

Talk about Jabba the Hutt.

But he could make her career with one phone call. One phone call.

"What do I have to do?" Hayley asked Gloria.

"I thought you were a watcher. All you gotta do is watch."

Watch what? she thought a bit hysterically. If she had to see Jabba in action she was pretty sure she'd be sick. Mentally removing herself from a scene with him would be darn near impossible.

To make him even more repugnant, he used the F-word in every sentence. It was fuck this and fuck that, this fucking thing and that fucking thing, and you're a fucking idiot, you stupid cock-sucking fucker.

Yeah, he was a real piece of work.

As if reading her mind, Jabba suddenly snapped his fingers and pointed to Hayley and Gloria. Hayley swallowed her trepidation and followed after Gloria.

They approached Jabba together, Hayley slightly behind Gloria.

"Nice tits," he observed, staring at Gloria.

Well, she'd been wrong. He didn't say fuck that time. But the night was young.

"Yeah, they're honest-to-God silicon," Gloria smarted off.

Jabba snorted. His answer a chuckle. "You're a fucking ugly woman," he declared meanly.

This, from the Slime King?

"Who's the mouse?" he demanded, glancing at Hayley.

"New to the business," Gloria said. "She's a watcher."

"What the fuck's that?"

Gloria shrugged. "Ask her. She likes to watch."

This seemed to stump Jabba who was momentarily

silent. After all, you still had to formulate other words to make a sentence no matter whether fuck was a noun, adjective, or verb. This might be tough for someone so limited.

The head of Titan Pictures! How? *How?*

Licking his lips, he breathed heavily through his nose in an effort to move oxygen through those layers of fat to his overpowered lungs. Rodney Walburn—repulsive be thy name.

Hayley loathed him with a passion.

"Well, you're not watching me," he told her with thinly disguised Puritanism. "Go away."

Hayley's mouth nearly dropped open. So Jabba was a closet prude.

Gloria either didn't pick up on it or didn't care. She ran her hand over his head. Big mistake. Strands of oiled hair stuck straight up. Jabba's fat hand grabbed her wrist and he twisted viciously.

"Get the fuck out. Whores. You belong on the fucking street!"

Within seconds they were dumped on the doorstep like so much garbage. Gloria was infuriated. "I have friends!" she sputtered. "I know people. Fat bastard!" She shook her fist at the closed, locked door.

"Street walking never looked so good," Hayley muttered, more relieved than upset.

"He threw us out! Threw us out!" She was incensed. "Wait 'til I tell Danny!"

They both knew Danny had no power over Rodney Walburn. He was a small time pimp and Rodney was rumored to have earned his title through ties to organized crime. And Danny had considered it an honor that Rodney had been interested in his girls. He'd be more likely to blame Gloria for not delivering the goods than commiserate about what a pig the man was.

"Let's go," Hayley suggested, her mind already churning through possibilities. Okay, they'd bombed with this segment of the Hollywood crowd. Good. Hayley didn't really think anyone, no matter who they were, would cast an honest-to-goodness hooker in a part the calibre of Toni in *Lady Paradise*. Besides, Jabba didn't have creative control even if he was head of Titan Pictures. Hayley wasn't even certain Callahan's deal was with Titan. Wasn't there bad blood between him and the studio his father had practically owned?

Well, who cared anyway. Her best bet was John Callahan and her "Hooker for a Day" resume. This mixing with Hollywood royalty when she was disguised as a prostitute could only do more harm than good. Time to quit.

Time to make her move on Callahan himself.

Chapter Eight

The man's dark eyes held her in their grip. Emotion smoldered like black coals whose innards glowed red-hot. The room was barren. A cheap bed with squeaking mattress, a scarred bureau, a yellowed room notice attached to the back of the door.

"You're not gonna leave me," he sneered. "You're too fateful. You need a man like me."

Weary faced, she stood in the corner of the room, studying her lover. He was a real man. Top of the heap, all right. But as good as she was ever going to get.

When she pulled out a prop gun and shot him dead center in the chest it was a relief. The loud *blam* of the gun made the nearest production assistants jump in surprise.

The actress jumped too, but it worked in the context of the script.

Unfortunately, "fateful" for "faithful" didn't. The film's character was rough and low, but his mouth wasn't full of marbles.

John Callahan glanced at Frankie Carello, *Fortunata's* director. Frankie was nodding, signalling "go, go, go!" frantically with one arm. Apparently he liked what he saw.

John didn't. *Fortunata* had gotten away from him some-how and it wasn't even recognizable anymore. They should have never cast Justin Devers as Tom. The guy was a no talent. But he was Frankie's choice, some shirt-tail relative whose success on the television show, *Plenty of Trouble,* had somehow turned him from teen TV heart-throb to film leading man.

Not hardly.

But they were in too deep, he and Frankie. Way too deep. John's initial suggestions to recast had fallen on deaf ears. Frankie wanted Justin Devers and he was going to scream loudly and incessantly if he didn't get his way. Frankie could be as lovable as a teddy bear, and as fierce as a grizzly if his word were doubted. John would have fought harder, but at the time he'd been so mired in his own personal problems that he'd simply let Frankie have his own, bull-headed way.

Now it was too late. Too many scenes were shot to start over. They had to make this work and the sweat that stood out on Frankie's forehead and dampened the back of his white T-shirt was foreboding in itself.

The scene disintegrated. Justin kept blowing his lines.

And Frankie blew his top.

"You gotta have John direct you, is that it?" he screamed, waving his arms. "You only work for John? Who do you think the director is, huh? You think it's John Callahan? He's the producer, you dick-brain. *I'm* the di-rector." He jerked his thumb at his chest in rapid succes-sion, thunking his breast bone.

John inwardly sighed. He'd only directed a few scenes, more by accident than design since Frankie tended to stay up too late, drink too much wine, eat too much food, talk too much. Those early morning shots were killers for someone of Frankie's temperament and habits, and a few times John had taken over the afternoon shift as well.

Not that Justin Devers acted much better for him, no matter what Frankie thought. Nope, the guy was hopeless, and John would be lucky to get the scene down in five takes. Part of Frankie's problem was that he was a perfectionist (and a maniac) and though Justin was his choice, he'd made the poor kid's life a living hell.

Fortunata had been a debacle from the start—and now it was going down in flames.

"I know you're the director, Frank," Justin muttered, his face flushing angrily. "I'm not messing up on purpose."

"Really? You're doing a damn good imitation!"

"That's it." Justin stalked off the set, slamming out the nearest stage door.

"Little bastard," Frankie snorted. "Acts like he's a goddamn star."

"Do you want me to stay?" the brunette actress whined. When she wasn't acting, everything she said sounded like a whine.

"Go, go!" He waved her away.

"When are we going to get this?" one of the production assistants asked. "We're running out of time."

John sucked air between his teeth. Bad idea, telling Frankie what he already knew.

Frankie turned purple. He was in full grizzly bear mode today. "You're fired. Get outta my sight!" He swept past her, flailing his arms and muttering obscenities.

The production assistant, Tonja Terkell, blinked rapidly several times. John sighed, feeling sorry for her. He felt sorry for anyone who ran afoul of Frankie's unbearable temper.

"Not a good day," John commiserated, watching

Frankie slam from the set with even more affront than Justin Devers.

"Am I really fired?" she asked in a small voice.

"You work for me, not Carello, but Frankie's stubborn and unforgiving. This thing's about to wrap anyway. There's no need to come back."

Her eyes filled with tears. More kindly, John added, "Hey, I'll call you again when I need someone."

"Will you?"

He suspected she'd taken some scripts of *Lady Paradise* and either sold them or handed them to her friends. He was a stickler about keeping secrets, and he'd been tempted to fire her then. But she knew how to take orders and—generally—how to keep her mouth shut. Maybe she just needed a bit of polishing.

Or maybe he was a sucker for lost causes.

"Yes," he answered seriously. "I will."

He left before another production headache could surface, intending to go back to his nearby apartment, the one he kept near Titan Studios. But instead he headed north to Malibu, his thoughts, as they did more and more frequently these days, turning to his ex-wife.

Why? *Why?* What was it about her that got under his skin like an unbearable itch?

He'd first met Denise during production of *Willful,* Denise's first real hit, John's third. Denise was a costar but she stole the show. Sorta sweet, sorta sexy, and infinitely vulnerable, she possessed that mysterious essence known as star quality. It emanated from the screen and took over the film.

John had been involved with the leading lady, a screeching egomaniac whose unbearably diva personality disappeared when they were alone in bed. Undercover, she was funny and cuddly and almost shy. The startling contrast intrigued John for months until her temperamental fits slowed production so much that he grew embarrassed and angry. Her last day of filming was the last day of their relationship. She accused him of using her just for the role, forgetting entirely that he'd been against her for the lead and had only been reluctantly talked into it. She sued him for breach of contract. Breach of contract? She said they had a verbal understanding that she would be given a three-picture deal with Titan Pictures, his father's studio.

Titan Pictures . . . the bane of John's existence. He was intrinsically tied to the studio but loathed being any part of it. He hated the studio because he hated his father, and Sampson Callahan's death hadn't mellowed John in any way.

A dark cloud settled over him as soon as his memory touched on his self-centered, charismatic, overbearing father. Because John was the son of "Sampson Callahan, Head of Titan Studios," he'd twice been slapped with paternity suits. The claims were as ridiculous as his actress friend's breach of contract. He'd never slept with either woman.

But Sampson had. Along with a slew of others. Maybe he'd fathered their unborn children. Maybe they'd made it all up. All he knew was that he'd been chosen as the fall guy because Sampson Callahan was an uncaring, untouchable bastard.

And John was heir to everything.

The lawsuits came to nothing. John's turbulent relationship with his father continued. Sampson's womanizing increased.

Sampson Callahan had a history of sleeping with starlets, coercing some production company into giving them a bit part, then forgetting their existence. John's mother had stoically ignored the rumors even while she drank away her unhappiness. When John got old enough, those same rumors fell on *his* shoulders. He was accused of womanizing so often it was a miracle he had time to eat, sleep, and work.

At first he had vigorously denied the charges, but the press ate it up. Like father, like son, only the son screams about the injustice of it all! Big laughs and guffaws and sniggers all around.

John learned to keep his mouth shut.

Half of the rumors that surrounded him had something to do with Sampson, and John's reputation grew though he spent most nights alone.

His mother knew the truth. They never discussed it, but just before her death she pressed a palm to his cheek and said "Thank you," in a way that said everything.

The irony was, Sampson died not long afterwards. The robust studio head barked his last order—a firing of one of his most trusted yes-men—went home to dinner, complained of pain in his chest, and died of a massive coronary minutes later.

The funeral was attended by several thousand. John fortified himself with a shot of whiskey to make himself attend. His mother was on his mind. Her funeral had been small and intimate with only a few distant relatives from the east coast in attendance. This circus was all Sampson. Comparing it to his mother's simple ceremony made him sick. He couldn't stomach the hypocrisy.

And then John learned that a percentage of Titan Pictures was his, willed to him by his father.

That had *really* pissed him off.

He didn't want a nickel of Sampson's money. The old man had bullied him all his life, damn near cutting his only son out of his will when John refused to work at

Titan. In petty retaliation, Sampson refused to fund John's pictures. And when John received an Oscar nomination, his father publicly proclaimed how proud he was of his "gifted, talented son," and privately snarled rebukes whenever his and John's path managed to cross.

John had feared him when he was young. No kind words. No advice. Just belittling comments and criticism. But he'd grown tough. If that had been Sampson's plan, it had worked beautifully. But John believed—though it was impossible to guess how Sampson's mind really worked—that his father had really wanted to break him, ruin him, keep him under his thumb. It was fear that ruled Sampson Callahan. Fear that his upstart son would somehow surpass him. A fiercely, unnaturally keen competitive nature buried any and all fatherly feelings, thereby killing any love and respect John might have felt for the man who helped create him.

The irony was, if Sampson had been just a bit different, he could have experienced the joy of watching his son take to the business that he, too, enjoyed. How many men would give anything to have a son join them in their field? Maybe even work together to create a dynasty. To witness their own child realize incredible dreams and become wildly successful in the same field, different area of expertise?

So many children of successful Hollywood moguls lost their moorings along the way. Confused, aimless, they were cast adrift on a sea of their own self-doubt and fear, trying to live up to impossible standards. They died young or bobbed along a slow current leading nowhere.

John Callahan steered his own ship, but his father was an archetypal Captain Blye whose inflated self-importance left no room for other crew members. They waged a cold war of silent stares and locked jaws and neither budged a millimeter.

When Sampson Callahan had died, John had been surprised at his sense of loss. He'd lost his enemy. The reason he fought so hard and so long. He'd lost an important person in his life—the man responsible for killing his trust in others.

And then the studio named Rodney Walburn III as Sampson's replacement. Perversely, that appointment hurt. Though John wanted nothing to do with his father's empire, being summarily passed over by the board of directors even as a contender—and for someone as repugnant as Walburn—it had jarred way, way down deep.

Enter Denise Callahan: talented, irreverent, seemingly fragile, and full of love. The tabloids blared he'd married her to staunch his playboy image. The better papers declared the couple was deeply in love and dedicated to their craft and their new film endeavor: *Cosmos*.

John's belief in his love for Denise Scott lasted twenty-three days. Their marriage survived another ten months. On that twenty-third day, he walked into the deluxe trailer they shared at the New Mexico location and found Denise and a cameraman going at it as if sex were about to be outlawed forever.

To make matters worse, Denise didn't seem to even realize she'd done anything wrong. She accused *him* of cheating on her with Lauralee Gentry, and then listed every ex-girlfriend he'd ever had—real or imagined—and said it was time she got some of her own back.

He couldn't believe it. This was not the Denise Scott he'd married. But, oh, yes, it was. More affairs followed, some with disastrous results. An ugly, purple and black eye halted production for two weeks. John fired the lowlife grip responsible though the man, and Denise, swore "it wasn't like that."

Cosmos limped through its final stages with John scarcely conscious of anything but his amoral, alleycat wife and her string of lovers. Incredibly, she still looked great on screen, a surreal illusion that made the back of his throat hurt.

Messy divorce. Screaming headlines. A final push out of his life and out of their—*his*—home. He'd hurt and he wanted to hurt back. He wanted to destroy.

He took everything. She had no weapons to fight him, but it was a hollow victory, especially when he understood that she had real, deep psychological problems that were just beginning to manifest themselves. Guilt gnawed at his soul. He wanted to hate and hurt, but a self-destructive part of himself also wanted to forgive.

He'd thrown himself into *Fortunata* and laid the groundwork for *Lady Paradise*. No thoughts of Denise. No thoughts of anything but work. Work. His lifeblood.

But then she'd shown up at his house.

Their house.

Now, he parked in the drive of that house, cutting the engine and relaxing against the leather seat. He closed his eyes and inhaled air through his teeth.

He'd never thought he would be able to speak to Denise again without feeling deep, burning anger and a certain amount of humiliation at having the whole world know he was cuckolded. POW! A major wound to his masculinity.

Show me a man who says it doesn't hurt, I'll show you a filthy liar.

But over the past several weeks, and the few encounters he'd had with her, John had suffered a change of heart. He wasn't angry anymore. Not in the same way. And he didn't feel as personally injured. Was it time and distance that had soothed the pain? Or was it the realization that Denise's problems were so deeply rooted that she truly was incapable of distinguishing right from wrong.

Or maybe it was the change in her. A change so evident that John found himself staring fixedly at her, as if she were some strange, fascinating creature with which he'd never made contact before.

She looked different, she talked different, hell, she even *walked* different. She wouldn't sleep in her old bedroom. She wore a minimal amount of makeup. Her hair was dark blonde and thick with health. No bleach and touch ups.

It was as if she were consciously becoming a new person.

And he liked this person more than he should.

Stretching, he climbed out of the Jeep and strode slowly to the front door. Twisting the lock, he stepped inside, listening to the quiet. Vaguely, he heard a hollow tapping—the depressing of computer keys.

John shook his head. She was at his desk again. Anticipation mounting, he walked in the direction of the sound.

The tapping noises stopped. When John reached his office doorway, she was sitting poised at the keyboard, her head turned his way.

Suspicion swam in her aquamarine eyes. Her mouth tightened into a line. No lipstick. No visible makeup. The faintest dusting of freckles across the bridge of her nose. Pinkish glow to her skin, as if she'd gotten a bit too much sun. White tank top, frayed denim shorts, Birkenstocks.

Good God.

"Home again?" she asked, sounding irked.

John felt irked right back. "What's for dinner?"

The mouth grew tighter. "I bought some catfood."

"I don't have a cat."

"I do."

She pointed to a calico kitten sleeping in the den chair.

He stared. "You're allergic to cats."

"No, I'm not. I just never liked them much. I've changed my mind."

This last was mumbled into her hand as she began a fit of coughing John was sure was faked. "Maybe that cough's your allergies flaring up."

"I've got a cold," she said shortly. "I'm not allergic."

"Okay, okay." Who was he to argue? He believed she never meant half the things she'd told him in the past, why should she start now? Though she seemed to be making perfect sense.

"What's the cat's name?"

"Bobo."

"Bobo the cat?"

"Did you want something? Something specific, I mean?" she demanded. "I've got things to do."

He glanced at the screen, but his fishtank screensaver had taken over, and he couldn't see what she'd written. She lifted one fine, blonde brow, waiting.

Raising his hands in surrender, John backed away. Who was he to argue when she was in this kind of mood?

And when had Denise ever *had* this kind of mood before?

"By the way, this fax machine is a piece of shit," she called after him.

"Who are you faxing?" he threw over his shoulder as he strode up the stairs to the gallery.

"NONE OF YOUR GODDAMNED BUSINESS!" she hollered back.

In the sanctuary of his bedroom, John threw himself

down on the immaculate chocolate-colored comforter and stared up at the ceiling. Was she acting? Some kind of guru-induced method-acting disguised as psychotherapy?

"Screw it," he muttered, turning face down, infuriated that his senses were raw and even the slightest scrape of material against flesh developed a gnawing ache inside him.

Bad news. He was horny for his ex-wife.

Denise awoke with grit in her eyes, a sour taste in her mouth, and an overall numbness she usually associated with too much alcohol consumption.

"Oh, God, I feel like crap," she muttered.

The bed was huge. Acres of comforters and pillows and some kind of foam pad beneath the silk sheets guaranteed to give you a good night's sleep.

She buried her head beneath a pillow and sought refuge. It was too early. Her brain hurt. She wanted to whimper but was afraid to make a sound.

Consciousness slowly returned. What was she afraid of?

Cautiously she pulled her head from beneath the king-sized pillow and glanced around. An unfamiliar bedroom. Ian's bedroom, she remembered with a rush of panic. She'd slept in Ian's bed.

Now her aches and pains made a bit more sense. His lovemaking had been rough and demanding. She'd had terrible dreams. Evil spectres of leering faces and scraping claws. Talk about your *Rosemary's Baby*. Yuk. Just touching on the memory made her mind shy away even now, in the bright light of day.

Where was Ian?

Reaching out a tentative hand she examined the other side of the bed. No body and no warmth. Either he didn't sleep with her or he was an early riser.

She shivered. On shaking legs she headed for the master bath. Malachite green marble and gold fixtures. An actual bear rug as a bathmat.

Twisting on the shower, she turned the water as hot as she could stand, then stood beneath the burning, stinging spray and fought back sudden, hysterical sobbing.

An hour later she was more in control, her hand almost steady as she applied makeup. In the mirror something caught her eye. A soft discoloration near her collarbone.

She twisted to look at her skin but it was too close to her neck. Leaning forward, she examined the area in the mirror. A spreading bruise.

Memory slammed into her. Thomas Daniels' thick, red fist, smashing her cheekbone.

"No!"

That was a lie. Nothing had happened. It was her own fear. Fear, because he'd been such a sadistic bastard. He'd never touched her. Never.

Her hands spread protectively across her neck and collarbones. Not Ian, either. This was explainable. She'd had too much to drink. Tripped. No, stumbled into the wall. That was it! She could remember now. A drink. Something like gin . . . or something. And wasn't there an archway that was kind of narrow? Between the bar and hallway? She'd been clumsy. She'd always been kind of clumsy, and after a few drinks . . . well, it was bound to happen.

It made perfect sense.

Relief spread like liquid through her veins. Forcing a smile at her reflection, she applied hot pink lipstick. Her hand shook a little. Understandable. She was just going to have to tell Ian not to give her anything to drink. She couldn't hold her liquor. She was a terrible drunk.

Spying her suitcases and bags, she hesitated, unsure. Should she unpack? Was she moving in?

She should really call her agent.

"I'll have Leo get back to you," his snooty secretary told her.

"I'm not at home," Denise said, rattling off Ian's number.

"I'll give him the message."

For a moment Denise considered calling Dinah. She owed her sister a phone call.

The bitch. The man-stealing bitch.

Swallowing, Denise reached into her shirt pocket for the business card she knew was in there. Empty.

Panic struck her. *Where? Where?*

Frantically she threw open her cases, digging through her clothes, throwing them around the room, fighting a surging panic which threatened to engulf her.

She found Stone's L.A. number and address in the pocket of her kelly green shirt. Of course. She'd been here a few days already. She'd just kind of forgotten. Trembling, she placed the call, only to reach a receptionist.

"Please," Denise said, voice quivering. "I desperately need to talk to him."

"I'll tell him, Ms. Scott."

She hated begging. Hated it. Stumbling back to the bathroom she grabbed a washrag, twisted it into a rope and bit down on it. Shudders swept through her.

You are a total sick-o. You need help. Serious help.

A dull chime sounded through the quiet house. Dimly, she understood it was the front bell. She ignored it, but the smothered-sounding peals continued. With an effort she unclamped her jaw, removed the washrag, examined her pale face in the mirror, fluffed her hair, then headed downstairs on unsteady legs.

"Who is it?" she asked, peering through the peephole.

One helluva good-looking man stood on the stoop.

Without waiting for an answer she flung open the door.

He stared at her and she stared at him.

"Denise Scott?" he asked in a quiet voice.

When she nodded he offered her a warm, dry hand. Returning the handshake, she sensed the tremors that racked her and wondered if he could feel it, too.

"Connor Jackley," he said. "Private Investigator . . ."

He'd been to Wagon Wheel. He had a sister there. He'd grown up around Bend. He was an ex-cop. She sensed, though he didn't say it, that he was on some kind of furlough. The P.I. thing wasn't really him.

Lord, he possessed movie star looks. And that serious manner. Those soul-deep eyes. But he was no actor. This was his real self. A flesh and blood former L.A.P.D. cop with a mission.

What was he saying? Something about her family? *Her* family?

"I grew up on a farm in Indiana," she said rotely.

He was talking again but she couldn't make out the words. The buzz in her ears drowned out everything. Cold sweat broke out on her forehead.

"Ms. Scott . . . ?" His voice was wavery, dreamy, far, far away.

She awoke suddenly, flat on her back, staring up at the white molding surrounding the ceiling.

She was alone.

Oh, God!

"Ms. Scott?"

She gasped, shocked, then as she whipped around, disconcerted to see her visitor was seated on a nearby chair, watching her intently.

Her head throbbed. "What happened?"

"You passed out."

"What . . . what time is it?"

"Five o'clock."

Five o'clock. Denise collapsed back into the cushions and squeezed her eyes closed. She'd lost a whole day. Another whole day. And he'd been here the whole time.

"You didn't rape me or anything, did you?" she muttered breezily, but the effect was spoiled by her trembling lips.

There was a long hesitation. Denise peered at him through the corners of her eyes. Seeing him reminded her achingly of John for some reason, though they weren't anything alike in appearance.

She had to see John, she realized. Right away.

"Do you remember what I told you earlier?" Connor Jackley asked.

"Uh . . . no."

"I told you that the remains of your stepfather had been discovered."

Denise blinked. Her eyelids felt weighted down by the proverbial bricks. She blinked again. "What?"

"I'm investigating the murder of Thomas Daniels. I need your help."

Footsteps sounded, soft, pantherlike. Ian appeared in the doorway and gazed in a bored manner at the attractive Mr. Jackley.

"I didn't know you were here?" she asked, confused.

"Oh, yes. When I came home, your friend was here

and nothing I could say would get him to leave." Ian's lip curled. Denise realized she'd seen him look at her that same way.

"I called the police," Ian went on, "but it turns out, this man practically *is* the police." With that same predatory tread he came to sit on the edge of the couch. He handed her a glass of water and a pill. "Don't talk," he added, pressing a finger to her lips. "Just relax."

Denise couldn't help picking up the vibes of distrust and macho injury radiating from Ian. Connor Jackley had rubbed Ian Wallace the wrong way with a steel rake.

"What was it you wanted again?" she asked, ignoring the pill.

"Thomas Daniels," Connor reminded her with ultimate patience. "Your stepfather."

"I'm not from Indiana?" she asked, arching a brow.

She scared a smile out of him. "No."

"Okay, okay. You seem to have done your homework. Thomas Daniels was my stepfather," she admitted, the words so difficult they felt rusty inside her mouth.

"I need to know a little about him."

She shook her head. "Does the word 'vile' mean anything to you?"

"Vile in what way?"

"Am I under investigation?" she asked, fear shooting through her on the heels of sudden understanding.

"I'm not with the police any longer."

Ian snorted. Connor Jackley had LAW ENFORCEMENT stamped all over him—good looks, or no.

"You don't have to answer anything," Ian advised.

"No, no." Denise struggled to sit up. She was more than willing to set the record straight. "You said he was *murdered?* Are you sure?"

Jackley didn't spare her. "His skull was crushed."

The pain behind Denise's left eye was a needle, digging, digging, digging inside her brain. She covered the eye with one hand, willing the pain away. Unsuccessfully. "I don't know . . ."

"Your mother died when you and your twin were seniors in high school."

"My twin!" Denise gasped, appalled at his knowledge.

"Your younger sister, Hayley, was a sophomore? There was a few months when you all lived with Daniels before you moved away."

She narrowed her lashes. The pain was excruciating. The pain of memory. She couldn't find it. Couldn't find any of it, but in truth she didn't look very hard. It just hurt too goddamn much.

"I don't remember," she murmured truthfully.

"Do you remember your mother's death?" he asked gently.

Chrysanthemums. Gold and bloody orange and white. Smelling like weeds. The casket was open. Denise could see the top of her mother's head, the streaks of gray against the softer blonde-brown. "Yes."

"Do you remember anything after that?"

She'd left the funeral with her boyfriend, Jimmy Fargo, even though Dinah hadn't wanted her to. Jimmy had told her how sorry he was. He'd kissed her cheek and hugged her. It was fall. Hot and dry, and Jimmy had led her to their spot by the river where the Friday before they'd engaged in some serious making out. Denise turned her face into the side of his neck, her sorrow building into a terrible crescendo.

And Jimmy had felt her up.

"I don't remember much," Denise told Connor Jackley with a grimace.

"Tell me what you remember."

She looked at him. Should she tell him that Jimmy had then pressed her into the dry field grass, pulled at her dress with anxious, hurried fingers, then mounted her and shouted how much he loved her between grunts of pleasure?

Ah, yes. Sex. Her downfall. She'd let Jimmy Fargo take her without a peep of resistance. Even later, when she'd overheard him sniggering to a friend how he'd "fucked Denise Scott until she'd cried" she hadn't complained.

And still later, when she'd learned she was pregnant, and Jimmy Fargo, on the advice of his wealthy timber-baron father, had acted like he didn't know her, she still hadn't broken down.

Or, did you?

She couldn't remember much of anything after that until she was on a bus, months later, heading for the bright lights of Hollywood. Dinah'd been with her. And Hayley. And Dinah told her about the miscarriage, and only then did she recall she'd even been pregnant.

"I didn't know my stepfather was dead until you told me," Denise related carefully. "I guess I thought he was still in Wagon Wheel, but I really never think about him. At least I try not to. He was mean. Deep down mean. He used to scare me and my sisters."

"What did he do?"

"Oh, he'd threaten to beat us if we didn't mind him. That kind of thing. We tried to keep away from him. He hit Hayley once and Dinah nailed him with a bowling trophy he'd won when he was in high school."

"Was this after your mother died?"

"I . . . don't think so." Denise gazed directly into Connor's gray eyes. "No, wait, Dinah hit him on the shoulder, if that's what you're thinking! That didn't have anything to do with this."

"You're saying Thomas Daniels was alive and well when you and your sisters left Wagon Wheel."

"He was alive . . . I don't think he was ever well."

"Are you about finished?" Ian asked. His arm was looped familiarly over the back of the couch and he traced a finger along Denise's collarbone.

Shivering, she pulled in on herself. Connor's sharp eyes caught everything, but she couldn't tell what he was thinking.

"Do you have the addresses of your sisters?" he asked. "I'd like to talk to them."

"I don't even admit I have sisters, Mr. Jackley."

"It would help my investigation," he responded calmly.

He wasn't going to go away. Those gray eyes were going to wait and wait and wait. "I have an address for Hayley but I haven't talked to her in . . ." She shrugged.

"And Dinah?"

"I'll have to find her," she said quickly. "Really. She's hard to get hold of."

His expression said, "I know you're lying." She waited, heart beating hard, waiting for him to call her on it, but instead he gave her a number where she could reach him after she got hold of Dinah.

With difficulty she climbed off the couch and mounted the stairs to her scattered belongings and the tiny address book she kept tucked away. She was tired. So very, very tired.

Dictating Hayley's address and phone number to Connor, she watched as he rapidly printed the information in a notebook. Hayley would be able to handle Mr. Jackley. He wouldn't stop her from her goals. Nothing could.

"Whoever killed him did the world a favor," Denise heard herself say.

"It's still murder."

Ian showed him out and Denise listened to his receding footsteps.

"Take this," Ian ordered, when he returned, pushing the pill on her again.

"Why do I feel so hung over?"

"Take the pill and you'll stop feeling so awful."

"Did you put something in my drink last night, Ian?"

"Oh, for God's sake!" he exploded, his face bright red. "Take the damn pill and stop acting so neurotic!"

Denise sighed. She was sick of thinking so much anyway. Dutifully she swallowed the pill—a tranquilizer to calm her nerves—then just as her bones began to melt along with her troubles, he brought her a snifter of brandy.

And just as she lifted the snifter to her lips, she saw her stepfather as if he were in the room with her.

Like this? You like this? SLAP! You like this, you bitch? Say it! Say it now! Now, now!

"Ian . . . ?" Blindly she reached out a hand.

He wasn't there. She was alone. Alone with a monster.

She had a rock in her hand. Was it her hand? A rough chunk of gray and white granite. *Slam!* It broke against his skull. *Slam!* Blood poured, bright red and goddamn rivers of it! Over her hands and down his neck. Over his eye in scarlet rivulets. His eye rolled up. *Slam! Slam! Slam!*

And he staggered. Went down. And then the shovel. It took off half his face.

"Ian . . ." she whispered, sliding away.

"Right here, baby. Right here . . ."

"Okay, sugar, you want a thrill? You deserve a thrill. A thr-r-r-illlll." Her tongue suggestively circled a Pepto-Bismol pink painted mouth. She pursed her lips and kissed the air a couple of times for good measure. "Come on, come on. Whatcha waitin' for? An invitation? Baby, I just gave you one."

"How much?"

"What is this, a shakedown? Come on and show me some merchandise and I'll tell you how much it's worth," she teased.

"You gotta give me a price."

Was this guy green, or what? Hayley'd learned a few things from her nights of street walking and Rule #1 was never start spouting price until he was as committed as his intended hooker for a night. This young yahoo had to be a rookie cop.

It was a game. One she was damn good at, she'd learned. And strutting along Hollywood Boulevard was a helluva lot more entertaining than getting shacked up with some doped out loser with sick, albeit creative, fantasies.

The problem was, she was running out of time. Some of the prostitutes were onto her. They suspected she wasn't who she said she was because she didn't deliver. Right now, they were trying to figure her out. Pretty soon, they'd get rid of her. She made them nervous. Was she a cop, or what?

Gloria Carver had ceased to be her compatriot. She had business to take care of. Hayley's interests and goals didn't interest her.

So, now she was alone, but she'd watched the rest of the action long enough to get her patter down.

And it gave her a tremendous feeling of power.

"Come on . . ." Romeo touched her arm. "Tell me what you'll do for me. Whet my appetite."

"I'm gonna take you around the world."

"Yeah, how?"

"Use your imagination, baby. I'm your goddamned travel agent."

"I've only got fifty, sweetheart. Fifty do it for you?"

She clucked her tongue. "Oooh, boy. That would be one short trip."

"A hundred? What do I get for a hundred?"

He was standing too close. She could feel his breath on her neck. Unconsciously, she stepped away from him, needing space. Maybe he wasn't a cop. Maybe he was something else. Something worse.

A black car slid into the curb next to them. Hayley ran her hands down her hips. Her skirt was black vinyl as were her thigh-high boots. A tan suede vest, cinched up the front by leather thongs, was all that kept her breasts from spilling out. She'd ratted her blonde hair into a sexy, tossed tangle, caked on a ton of makeup, and completed the look with a pair of fake, black eyelashes.

"Let's go for a ride," Romeo said, jerking his head to the end of the block where a green sedan stood, its parking lights on.

"Nah . . ." She twisted away and pretended boredom. "I don't think I can agree to your terms."

"A hundred and fifty. Final offer."

"Bullshit. You'll keep going until you think I'll grab at the bait. But the department won't pay, will it? I don't think that's part of the budget."

"I don't know what you're talking about." He was angry.

Male pride, Hayley thought with an inward laugh. "Oh, yeah, you do."

Suddenly his fingers were hard on her upper arm.

"Hey!" she cried, surprised.

"Let the lady go," another voice snapped out, cold, hard, and masculine.

Hayley glanced around in surprise. A man had climbed from the car that had pulled into the curb and was staring daggers at her would-be john.

"Who the hell are you?" Romeo demanded, frustrated.

His answer was a strong hand wrapped around his thin neck. Romeo was jerked six inches off the ground then dropped back—all so quickly that if she'd blinked she would have missed it.

Instantly, Romeo began to whine. "Didn't know she was your lady, man. Maybe you oughtta talk to her about sending out signals, y'know. My throat hurts! I'm sorry, okay?"

Yeah, yeah, yeah, Hayley thought in annoyance. They were all the same. When the going got tough, the weak buckled under and whined.

"Thanks for the rescue, but I can handle my own problems," she told the newcomer as Romeo scurried to his flashing green sedan.

"You're soliciting?"

"What are you, a cop?" She raked him with cold eyes. "Oh, no, you are . . ." She should have seen it instantly. Something about the way they all acted. It was really true. You could tell one from miles away.

But he sure looked good. Hayley had always appreciated beauty in any form, and man, this guy had it in spades.

Except . . . that indefinable cop thing. A complete and total turn-off.

"What's your name, Mr. PO-liceman."

"That's Mr. Ex-policeman," he said, mouth twisting dryly.

"Oh, sure. And you're here for a date, right?"

"I'm looking for someone."

"Uh huh." Hayley studied her nails with exaggerated interest. "And who would that be?"

"You."

"The girl of your dreams, right?" She answered his smile with an ironic one of her own.

His eyes were gray. They had a way of looking right through you, but not that haughty "Do you have any Grey Poupon?" way. They were knowing, and, if she didn't know better, nonjudgmental.

"Are you Hayley Scott?"

She nearly swallowed her tongue. Hayley stared. "Who the hell are you?"

"Connor Jackley. *Ex*-cop," he stressed. "Private Investigator working with the Deschutes County Sheriff to find out more about the murder of your stepfather, Thomas Daniels."

Rapid-fire words. Bullets that zinged her brain. Hayley gaped, unable to take it all in. "He's . . . dead?" she asked blankly.

"Has been for a while."

She sensed him watching her closely. The street and noise and smells and filth receded. She was encased in fog. A thick soup of it. Somewhere somone was screaming. Crying.

"I hated him," she stated baldly. "He was such a bastard."

"Is there somewhere we could go and talk?"

"About Daniels? Forget it. I'm glad he's dead." A moment later it hit her. "He was murdered?"

"Someone crushed his skull."

The words jarred through her, painful and scary. Deep down scary. A door cracked open at the end of the long hallway of her memory and she slammed it shut so fast the whole thing was over before she realized what she'd done.

She wouldn't try to open it again.

"So long," she muttered, attempting to brush past him.

He grabbed her wrist, lightly, nothing serious. But something broke inside her. She snapped back and scratched him across the face, stunned to see welts on his cheek fill with blood, repulsed at the skin stuck beneath her fingertips.

He swore, soft and quick beneath his breath. Yanking her forward, he marched her to his car, dragging her to his side and shoving her inside, following quickly.

"Police brutality!" she screeched, scrabbling for the door handle.

Switching on the ignition, he tore into traffic just as she got the door partway open. For a millisecond she toyed with the idea of jumping out. The boulevard raced past in a neon blur.

Panic settled inside her. She glanced his way.

Rivulets of blood ran from the furrows she'd dug into his cheek.

Without looking at her, he said in a calm, disinterested voice, "If you're not going to jump out, close the door."

She did as she was told and they sped away into the darkness.

"Kidnapping," she accused, hands on her hips as they stood outside a four-plex unit in a fairly nice neighborhood. His place? "This sure as hell isn't headquarters. What *do* you have in mind?"

"Damned if I know," he admitted tersely. "I've got some questions that need to be answered. Your sister couldn't seem to put the pieces together for me."

"My sister?" Hayley asked cautiously.

"Denise Scott Callahan. She didn't know Thomas

Daniels was dead, either." His voice suggested he thought they were both telling a few fibs. "You're not going to try and tell me she's from Indiana and you're not sisters, are you?"

"I guess not." Okay, she *had* thought about it. "So, how'd you find me?"

"She gave me your address. I followed you. Stanbury's by day, Hollywood Boulevard by night." He shrugged.

"Oh, yeah, like you're shocked?" A small voice inside her head clamored to be heard. The voice of her innocence. A voice that wanted to scream, "I'm just acting! It's just an act!"

She staunched the voice. Hell if she was going to tell him anything!

"I think I have a good case against you," she pointed out, then said in a teary voice, "He forced me into his car against my will and brought me to a strange location . . ." She waited, gesturing to her surroundings.

"My apartment," he filled in.

She clucked her tongue. "His apartment. And there forced me to . . ." Again she waited for him to offer an answer.

"Talk about a man whom I believe beat and forced her and her sisters into sexual acts against their will," he said quietly.

That door at the end of her mind's hall creaked open. "No," she spat through her teeth. "No."

"A man whose actions may have directly led to one of his stepdaughters entering the world of prostitution."

"I'm no goddamned prostitute."

There. It was out. Better than talking about Daniels.

"You're a wannabe actress."

Hayley blinked. He knew. The bastard knew all along!

"The manager at Stanbury's has quite a lot to say about you."

"Jason!" She almost laughed with relief.

"What are you doing?" His gaze examined her outfit with puzzlement.

Hayley wasn't one to make friends or trust anyone, especially anyone male, but for some strange reason she felt a need for companionship. "Buy me a cup of coffee and I'll tell you."

He gestured toward the four-plex, brows raised in question.

"I need neutral territory," she said with a shake of her head.

"Some hooker," he muttered, but he held the passenger door for her and Hayley, wondering what demon possessed her, slid into the seat. "You'd better stop and buy some Kleenex," she said. "You're bleeding all over everything."

The place was loud, small, and densely packed with people and cigarette smoke. Hayley was grateful. No one paid a bit of interest in the way she was dressed. But it sure played havoc with their ability to hear each other, and as the evening wore on she learned she desperately wanted to hear what Mr. Connor Jackley had to say.

He *was* an ex-cop. She learned very quickly that the man didn't bother to lie. He was, what he was, what he was. She also learned he wanted Thomas Daniels' killer and nothing, and no one, would distract him.

By coincidence, it seemed, he'd been in Wagon Wheel shortly after Daniels' body was discovered. His *nephew* had found it, for God's sake, and Connor, at the urging of

Sheriff Gus Dempsey, a personal friend, was making inquiries in Los Angeles while the investigation proceeded—at a molasses slow rate, if Hayley read between the lines—back in Oregon.

Hayley learned more by what he didn't say, than what he did. Connor Jackley wanted Daniels' killer. He believed that Hayley, Denise, or Dinah (or all of them together) were either personally responsible, or, at the very least, involved. After Connor's inquiries, Greater Wagon Wheel apparently considered Denise, the most successful sister, and the one with the wildest reputation, the prime suspect.

Connor, for his part, cagily kept his feelings about Denise to himself. But his very caginess spoke volumes. Hayley knew what it meant. A conquest. A score. Another notch for her unfairly beautiful older sister.

Mr. Jackley had a *thing* for Denise.

"She wasn't all that informative," he told her, when she questioned him about his interview with Denise.

"Really?"

He nodded, his lashes narrowing thoughtfully. She knew he was remembering Denise. Her lushness. Her weakness. Her irresistibility.

"Did you sleep with her?" she asked, hoping to sound matter-of-fact.

He merely smiled, letting her know in his inimical way that he wasn't going to play that game. Hayley decided he hadn't slept with her. Not yet, anyway.

"Just bide your time," she counseled. "She's promiscuous as hell. Can't help herself, really."

"She didn't strike me that way at all."

He was baiting her. Putting her on. Expecting her to open up, bare her soul, and tell the tragic tale of the Scott sisters.

Wishing fervently that she hadn't marked him with her raking claws, she decided to give him a little something.

"Once upon a time there were three sisters who plotted to murder their stepfather. The oldest one—the smart one—didn't want to do it. Too dangerous. Sure, he deserved to die, but let it be someone else's problem.

"The second one was too screwed up to make a plan. She spent all her time digging herself out of her last mistake. Trouble followed her like a little black cloud, but she made it to the bigtime anyway."

"And the youngest sister?" he asked, when she hesitated.

The door swung wider, a black hole beyond. Dread ran through her like scalding liquid.

"The youngest sister is glad he's dead," she said slowly. "She hopes he really is dead, but it seems impossible."

"He really is dead." Jackley was quiet, sober, intense.

"Then let's leave him that way," she whispered, not caring whether he could hear or not.

They spent another hour at the coffee shop, neither bringing up again the reason they were together. For an investigator, Mr. Jackley was one patient, sensitive man.

Either that, or he was damn good at his job.

"Pay the bill, Jack, and take me home," Hayley muttered into the relative quiet of the now half-empty room. It was late and her throat ached from conversing at the top of her lungs.

He grinned.

"What's so funny?"

"My nephew calls me Jack."

"Uncle Jack?" she asked, grimacing, knowing it had to be true.

He lifted his palms in acknowledgement and Hayley groaned.

"Yeah. Well. Tell me all about your Brady Bunch extended family another time. I'm tired, and I've got to face Jason early tomorrow."

"All right. Let's go."

His hand lightly touched the small of her back as he held open the door and guided her from the late night coffee bar. Long after she was in bed, the lights out, the memory of that slight touch lingered like a sweet melody you couldn't forget, or the scent of perfume which conjured up images of a certain time or place.

Hayley wasn't much for self-diagnosis. She set goals and went for them. Period. Life was a challenge.

But tonight the memory of Connor Jackley's presence was a real, living thing that wouldn't let her rest. In a way she'd never understood before, she understood now. She was attracted to him. Truly, deeply attracted. The mystery of physical magnetism was now solved and it had a name: Connor Jackley, late of the L.A.P.D.

"An ex-cop," she muttered aloud in disgust. "Wouldn't you know."

And he had a thing for her ever-more-popular sister.

She'd taken the pill and slept away the early evening. Surfacing around nine p.m., Denise realized she was still lying on the couch. She staggered to her feet, resenting the fuzziness of her brain.

"Ian?" she called, but the house was empty. Barring Lina, that is, because she lived in the maid's rooms above the garage.

Wandering out to the garage, Denise checked out Ian's stable of cars. Three of them. A blood red Maserati. A Mercedes. And a late model blue Ford sedan—the kind used by surveillance operatives, cheating husbands, and people of all colors, creeds, and genders who want to blend into the woodwork.

And the keys were inside!

"You are under the influence," she told herself, but she slid into the driver's seat anyway. She had to see John and her cheating sister. Only Dinah wouldn't cheat on her. No way. Her twin was too careful. Too smart.

Denise eased into traffic aware that a) she had to drive slowly or risk an accident and b) she had to drive fast enough not to draw attention to herself. She was so immersed in her driving, in fact, that the miles cruised beneath her tires and before she could believe it was possible, she was on the last turns to the Malibu house.

Her head was clearer. Not *clear*, but clearer. She congratulated herself on her skill behind the wheel. No lousy traffic cops had pulled her over. She was here and she felt marvelous!

Except for that headache behind her eye. And a crummy all over feeling of anxiety that Connor Jackley had stirred up.

The gates loomed in front of her and she suffered a bad moment when she wondered whether John had changed the code. But punching out his birthday on the keypad sent the wrought-iron sentinels swinging backwards. Quickly, Denise jumped back in the car and drove inside.

The house was dark, not even a light left on to confuse prowlers. Dinah had to be out, Denise realized, because the only reason the house would be dark was if she were sleeping and she would never go to bed this early. Her sister, like herself, was a bit of a night owl.

Unless she and John are in bed together.

That sobered her up in a hurry.

Drawing several deep breaths, she tried to hang onto her self-control, then gave up in a rush of fury and betrayal. She ran for the front door and laid on the bell. The chimes rang maniacally, over and over, as her finger jammed the button incessantly.

Nothing.

Slowly, Denise realized the house was empty. No Dinah. No John. Maybe they were together somewhere. Maybe they weren't.

There was another keypad near the garage but when she pressed that code nothing happened. So, John cared a little bit about security after all.

"Damn." She'd given her only housekey to Dinah.

There was a window at the back of the house that never latched properly. And she knew the alarm system would be turned off; too many mistakes while she'd lived with John had prompted him to dismantle it.

"Let 'em rob us!" he'd hollered. "It's better than having the police driving over here every time you forget to disarm the damn thing!"

Yanking on the window, she felt the latch slip. Crawling inside, she was enveloped in smells and memories that reminded her of John and the few months of happiness they'd shared.

You ruined it. Remember Merle, the cameraman? Remember him?

But that was because John was doing that Gentry bitch.

Except he hadn't been.

She couldn't remember.

Yes, you can!

Covering her ears, Denise stumbled through the dark, banging her shin so hard on a table she howled with pain.

Swearing, she switched on the living room light, disdain-
ful of leaving traces of her break-in. Let 'em know she was
here. Too damn bad.

She wandered around the upstairs, flipping on lights,
examining rooms. To her surprise, Dinah was in the guest
room.

How did she explain that? Denise wondered vaguely.

John's room was unoccupied. It looked exactly as it had
when she'd left and possessed that same empty, unlived-in
sense.

He's not living here, she realized in surprise.

Back downstairs, she shook her head, waiting for the
cobwebs to clear, praying for a spell of lucidity. But depression dogged her like an univited guest and she found
herself standing in the office, staring at John's belongings
in the room he loved best.

The thunder egg paperweight caught the light, its inner
core of crystals glistening opulently, like some rich mine
where gems encrusted every inch of the walls.

Denise picked it up, judged its weight in her hands,
then suddenly panicked over what Ian might do to her if
he found out she'd stolen his car.

Driving like a madwoman, she made it back to Beverly
Hills in record time, screeching to a halt in the garage, her
heart thundering in her chest. Then she ran inside and
waited in the darkness.

A lamp was on down the hall. She walked slowly toward it, a prisoner approaching the firing squad. But
unlike Dinah, Ian had left a light on.

She was alone.

Breathing a sigh of relief, she glanced down at the
thunder egg, then she cradled it to her chest and closed
her eyes. She had a piece of John. Tomorrow, tomorrow

she would plan her next move to win him back, but for tonight she had a little piece of him.

Crawling into Ian's huge, fluffy bed, she cuddled the thunder egg as if it were a baby, and dreamed that everything was going to be all right now.

Chapter Nine

Dinner with His Highness. He'd extended the invitation and she'd turned him down, but then, while she'd been editing her latest column, she'd been so finely attuned to his presence in the house that she hadn't got a damn thing done anyway. He'd managed to invade every bit of breathing space even if he wasn't actually in the room with her. So, she'd buckled, and they'd spent a miserable two hours together.

She'd said next to nothing, picking at her food and worrying herself sick that he would realize the impossible: she was not his ex-wife. Not that he had much to say. She guessed he was as sorry as she was that they'd tried this exercise in futility.

Now they were driving back in his Jeep Cherokee. The situation was intolerable. She was near breaking point and far too aware of his masculinity. It seemed to seep into her pores. The seductive, musky way he smelled. The easy way he moved. The quirk of a smile. The storm of anger and puzzlement in his deadly blue eyes. The lean, good-looking overall maleness he exuded like a potent chemical meant to inflame her senses.

And inflame them he did.

Desire ate away at her like a cancer and Dinah could do nothing about it.

Unless I leave.

"The gate's open," John said in surprise as they turned off the main road.

"You left it open."

"Nope." He shook his head.

This was more conversation than either of them had made all evening. Dinah slid him a sideways look. She didn't believe all those things about him anymore. Things Denise had said. Lies meant to make her look better. Or maybe Denise believed them herself, but Dinah definitely did not.

Still, Callahan was dangerous. Dangerous to her. And there was no way to rectify the situation. None at all.

"My God!" he muttered, and Dinah snapped to attention. Lights blazed in every window. "Robbers?" he asked, baffled, sliding the Cherokee to a halt thirty-feet from the house.

"What kind of robbers leave on the lights?"

He shook his head, jumped from the Jeep and strode toward the house.

"Wait! Wait!" Dinah scrabbled for the door handle, scared. "What are you, crazy? They could have *guns!* Stop!"

He hesitated only briefly, then tried the front door. With an inscrutable look back at Dinah, he pulled out his key and gently pushed open the door. She held her breath. Her pulse pounded dully. He could be killed. Shot. Dead.

"Oh, God . . ."

Common sense won over masculine bravado. He jogged back to Dinah. "Get in the car," he ordered. She didn't have to be asked twice. The door wasn't even shut when he was backing down the drive, doing a 180 on the road and tearing back the way they'd come. Then he was on his cellular, tersely relating what had happened to 911. Police cars arrived in droves, sirens wailing.

They followed the blur of blue and red spinning lights, stopping the Jeep a few yards behind the front line of police cars. In the dark, he grinned at her, boyish white teeth flashing. Dinah grinned back. After a tense, taut evening where neither one of them could think of anything to say but the most meaningless small talk, it was a relief, a roar of adrenalin through the veins.

"Nobody here," the cop in charge related rather disappointingly. "Nothin' broken, maybe some things taken. Check it out. Might not realize what's missin' at first. Take your time." A pause. "No forced entry."

And then they were gone and John and Dinah were alone. They walked into the house together, cautiously. In silent agreement they stayed together as they checked every room. Discovering Bobo asleep under her bed, Dinah hugged the confused little kitten before laying him back on the bed.

Finally, in the kitchen, John and Dinah looked at each other in puzzlement.

"A prank?" John suggested.

Dinah lifted her palms.

"Want a brandy?"

"I don't drink brandy."

"Yes, you do," he said tiredly, as if he'd finally run out of patience with her, the robbery and everything else. He brought them each a snifter and gulped half his drink down, watching her closely. Dinah took a sip, held back a gasp as the stuff burned down her throat, then met his gaze defiantly.

Silence pooled between them. A living silence. Dinah

got a creepy feeling down the back of her neck. She was in trouble.

Callahan swirled his drink reflectively. "I'm done holding hands on *Fortunata*. It's Frankie's baby now and good riddance."

Frankie. The director. "What's wrong with it?"

"The cast. The screenplay." He regarded her moodily. "You should have been the lead."

"Really." In the midst of attempting another sip, Dinah choked on her brandy. She put the snifter down but her eyes teared and her lungs coughed and coughed.

"Not that I would have cast you, but hey, it would have been better than what I've got. I'm turning it over to Frankie and moving on to *Lady Paradise*."

"Is that why you've been coming here?" she managed between fits of coughing. "To escape."

"To gain a little perspective," he agreed with a nod. He'd produced the bottle of brandy from a kitchen cupboard and now he poured himself another healthy dose. Lifting an eyebrow, he silently asked if she wanted to join him.

"I don't drink brandy . . . very well," she amended.

"So, why aren't you pressuring me for a part?" he asked. "Thought you'd jump all over me. I just told you you'd have been better than what's-her-name."

"I don't want a part," Dinah replied flatly. "Besides, you wouldn't give me a chance anyway. I'm too big a risk."

"You're box office. Big box office. Probably bigger now, with all the scandal. I'm a producer. A deal-maker. I'd be crazy to turn you away."

Panic thrummed along her nerves. What was this? No way. No way could she test for Denise! "You're not serious. Not really."

Their gazes dueled and Dinah's panic escalated. But then Callahan shook his head, raked a hand through his hair and muttered, "God, no. I can't be that much of a masochist." His blue eyes searched hers a moment longer. She swallowed. With a muttered imprecation, he grabbed the neck of his beloved brandy bottle and headed upstairs. "Goodnight, my love," drifted down to her, and Dinah folded her arms around her chest and wished she hated him as much as she used to.

Life would certainly be easier.

Neosporin in the nailmarks Hayley had so generously given him. Connor examined the side of his face and grimaced. She'd really done it to him. He'd barely touched her and she'd come on like a wildcat.

Fear. He'd seen it in her eyes, and it was the fear of someone who expects to be abused. Someone used to it. A couple hours of her company had been long enough to convince him that she was deathly afraid of men in general. Thomas Daniels' legacy?

But she was also a go-getter. Almost obsessively so. She didn't want to talk about her sisters, her past, or anything to do with Wagon Wheel. Even when he'd mentioned that his hometown was very near hers, no response.

She wanted to talk about her career. Her goals. Her future.

He'd brought up Denise a dozen different ways but Hayley Scott didn't want to hear it. She was deaf, dumb, and blind when it came to any subject dealing with her childhood.

It didn't take a shrink to make this diagnosis: she was in complete, utter denial.

And Denise . . .

Connor's face darkened when he thought back to his encounter with her. Denise Scott Callahan's beauty was what had struck him first. Second, how pale and vulnerable she was. And Ian Wallace forcing pills on her . . . it had been all Connor could do to keep from strangling the man.

Ian Wallace. He'd asked his buddy, Bennie, in Vice why the name had rung a bell. Bennie was a veritable fountain of information.

"Ian *Wallace?* Man, you don't know shit, do ya?"

"The name sounded familiar," Connor defended himself.

"His old man left him a ton of money. Like oodles and oodles. But Ian was in trouble a lot as a kid. Sexual trouble. Fondling little girls, that sort of thing. Got himself sent to boarding school, pronto. Dad forked over a fortune to clear his son's name, and the victim's parents always dropped charges."

"Maybe he's changed," Connor said, playing devil's advocate.

"The only difference is, he controls the money, and his playmates are older." Bennie stroked his chin. "There was some other stuff, too. Want me to look it up?"

"Yeah. Let me know if something interesting crops up."

"You investigating the guy?"

"More like I tripped over him while checking into something else."

"Watch your step," Bennie said in all seriousness. "I mean it, man."

Connor was wired. All that coffee with Hayley. And thoughts circling his head. Not hungry, but bored, he hung on the refrigerator door, oblivious to half-empty mayonnaise and mustard jars and leftover pizza. In his mind's eye, he saw Ian Wallace and Denise Scott Callahan.

He was in a quandary. Gus Dempsey had lost interest in the Daniels case. He wasn't the kind of law enforcement agent who believed in championing an unpopular cause. Nobody liked Daniels. At best the man was a lowlife adulterer and sexual harasser, at worst a sexual abuser and rapist. His other charms included gluttony, loutishness, laziness, and general meanness. His death was a blessing to all.

Connor was certainly no idealist. He believed Daniels was as bad as painted. And, he, Connor, certainly had enough cases to fill his time while he decided whether he wanted back on the force or something else. Maybe something in Oregon.

But the meeting with Denise Scott had got to him. He'd never felt sorrier for another human being. Dependent personality. Too much too fast. Probable abuse at the hands of her stepfather and a sick relationship with Ian Wallace who possessed too much money and too little conscience.

Could he leave her like that? Just walk away? It was her choice, wasn't it? She was an adult. But Ian Wallace. . . . No morals. No respect. No ethics. Beverly Hills scum, but basically clean. Oh, yeah, money could buy anything.

Connor wanted to yank Denise away from him and clean her up. Denise Scott was under the influence of Wallace and a whole lot more. Drugs. Alcohol. God only knew.

Thomas Daniels' body wouldn't be the only corpse if Denise didn't clean up her act and soon.

Grabbing a piece of cold pizza, he stood over the sink and munched without tasting. His nephew had called this afternoon and left a long message, one that was continually interrupted by his friend, Mikey. The two boys wrangled on the phone until Mary shooed them off. Disapproval radiated over the line while she reported that the two boys, in their quest to provide him with "hot" tips, had followed Mr. Lancaster to his house and eavesdropped on the elderly man whose property abutted the Daniels' place. Mr. Lancaster, hearing noises, had grabbed his shotgun, stood on the porch flailing it around, and scared the living shit out of Mikey and Matt who'd dived into the underbrush as the old man fired his shotgun into the air.

Connor promptly got the boys back on the phone and ordered them to cease investigating. His sister's smug "I told you so" voice had irritated him, but the boys' actions were dangerous and had to be stopped. He'd then patiently explained to Matt and Mikey that he'd interviewed everyone connected with the case already and that he'd only asked them to keep a notebook to make them feel like they were helping.

Deflated, they'd mumbled they would be good and dropped the receiver. Connor was left with a major guilt trip and the realization that maybe he should drop the case entirely too.

Except now he'd met Denise and Hayley.

Hayley. . . . He hadn't known what to think about her. Fresh, bold, cheeky, and playing a dangerous game. She and Denise were both hiding information about Daniels, and why not? He'd tortured them. The hows and whys didn't matter; Connor knew he'd abused them.

They didn't want to talk. Hell, they didn't want to remember. Getting anything out of Denise would take a professional therapist; she needed serious help, that was for sure. But Hayley. . . . He couldn't put his finger on it, but he sensed, because she was a stronger personality, he might be able to break through her self-obsessed wall and get to the core of the problem.

But was it worth it? This was Dempsey's investigation and Connor was just helping out. With all the serious crime and bad news plaguing the country, should either of them worry unduly about what three tormented sisters did, or didn't do, to their abusive stepfather?

There was no good answer, but he aimed to keep on looking for one anyway. Maybe after the truth would come the healing.

Brrr-rr-ing! Brrr-rr-ing!

The funny little purr of the guest room phone intruded on Dinah's sleep. *Screw it,* she thought. The only person who ever called her was Flick and she damn well wasn't going to talk to him at—

She squeezed open one eyelid. 1:00 a.m.! Did the man have no respect at all?

Full wakefulness. A jerk of her heart. Not Flick. Not in the middle of the night.

Denise!

"Shit!"

Snatching up the receiver, Dinah answered urgently, "Hello?"

She heard someone pick up another receiver. "I've got it, John," she warned.

"Who is it?" he demanded.

Nothing. Dinah strained to hear, but only the *click* of a disconnection reached her ear. For a moment she stayed listening to Callahan's breathing. The miserable eavesdropper. Her own breath was fast and light. Dropping the receiver in the cradle, she huddled under her blankets, convinced, with that strange telepathy she and Denise occasionally shared, that her screwed-up twin was trying to reach her.

Well, it's about time.

She lay in bed, counting her heartbeats. A part of her half-expected him to materialize in her doorway. A part of her wanted him to!

Oh, good, Dinah. Good thinking. Get physically involved with John Callahan while he thinks you're Denise. Brilliant.

She couldn't keep up this charade much longer. He was wondering about a lot of other things. Her interest in the computer and writing baffled him. She didn't blame him. Denise wasn't exactly the esoteric, literary type, and she sure wasn't organized—at least not like Dinah. Callahan had to be thinking she'd metamorphosed into someone else.

Yeah, her sister!

Footsteps sounded on the gallery and stopped outside her room. Dinah sat bolt upright, clutching the sheets close to her throat.

The door opened and illumination from a lamp in the living room below the gallery silhouetted him in the doorway.

"You don't have to creep," she said carefully.

"Who did you warn away?"

Dinah fought a gasp. The man was nothing, if not direct. "I don't need you monitoring my phone calls."

"I'm going downstairs and getting something to eat."

He left on that, surprising Dinah because he'd sounded so . . . *mad*. Like it was her fault that he'd tried to eavesdrop? *Gimme a break.*

She lasted about five minutes, muttering in frustration until she leaped from bed, slid into Denise's pink mules and tossed on a silk, flowered kimono over her Coyote Cafe T-shirt and plaid boxers.

He was seated at the table, eating cookie dough ice cream out of the carton. He wore black sweatpants and a solid black warm-up zippered jacket. His chest was bare beneath the jacket; she could see a light dusting of dark brown curling chest hair. The hair on his head was uncombed and unruly and for some reason this sent a strange sensation into the pit of Dinah's stomach.

I don't like him, she reminded herself distinctly. *I don't!*

"I'm surprised you joined me."

He wasn't the only one. She must be out of her mind.

Annoyed with herself, Dinah poured the last of the orange juice into a glass, then leaned against the counter and examined him thoroughly, her brows drawn into a frown.

"I asked you to dinner so we could talk, but it didn't happen," he said.

"I guess there's nothing to say."

"Why did you really come back here?" he asked, ignoring her. "Did you think I'd just hand over the house if you started acting mysterious?"

"No." Dinah snorted.

"I looked up one of your files. 'Love Makes The World Go 'Round And That's Why We're All Motion Sick.' It reads like a newspaper column."

Dinah choked on the orange juice. Tears sprang to her eyes. She gasped and wheezed for breath. John calmly put down his carton of ice cream, walked over and slapped her on the back. Hard.

"You've got a habit of doing that."

She stumbled sideways, batted him away, and brushed tears from hot, blurred eyes. "Get . . . away! Get away!"

"You know, it wasn't half bad. I didn't know you were so Erma Bombeck about love and romance. That's if you really wrote it."

"What do you mean?" Dinah coughed hard once more and took another swallow from her orange juice. Her throat quivered. Slowly she drew a long breath.

"Come on." He went back to the ice cream, spooning it into his mouth and smirking. "That ain't you, babe. You can do a lot of things, but you can't write."

He was needling her. On purpose. To figure her out. To learn what game she was playing. She wouldn't fall for it. She wouldn't.

"I won a writing contest in high school."

"Uh huh. Before or after you dated the football team."

Dinah's eyes narrowed. "After."

He threw back his head and laughed. Dinah smiled, warily. Denise hadn't told him anything about her past. He was fishing.

"What was that guy's name?" he asked.

"What guy?"

"The guy you almost married."

Dinah held his gaze, calculating rapidly. She decided to err on the side of honesty. "Jimmy. And I did not 'almost' marry him."

John nodded. Did he really know anything about his ex-wife's past? Was this a test? For a moment Dinah almost panicked, but then her cool head came to her rescue. What could he know? Denise was a great story-teller—fiction, her specialty. So, she'd told him one thing and now Dinah's story didn't jibe. Big deal. Denise was so scatty about everything and Dinah was one hell of an accomplished liar when it suited her.

She could play this cat-and-mouse game as well as anyone, she concluded. She'd managed to so far while

Callahan popped in and out whenever he liked. And though it had played havoc with Dinah's writing, a couple of good glares at His Highness had kept him out of her office.

"His" office, he'd reminded her yesterday, but she could tell he'd been more amused than serious. Her most effective way of dealing with him, she'd learned, was simply to bully him.

"Stay outta my life," she'd told him a few days earlier when he'd asked too many questions.

"I'm not in your life. We're just talking here."

"Yeah, well, I don't have time. I'm working on a new career."

"Right."

"You were the one who told me I couldn't get an audition even if I slept with every male—would that be straight and gay alike?—in Hollywood."

That had made him smile. "Not exactly verbatim, but close enough."

"So, I've given up acting in favor of writing."

"Y'know, you're damn good. I never really appreciated how good, but this is really entertaining." He leaned his shoulder against the doorjamb, blue eyes lazily focusing somewhere near her mouth. "But it's not going to get you an audition."

Of course, that had all changed with tonight's revelation that he should have cast her in *Fortunata*. What a reversal!

What was happening?

She'd chosen to ignore him before. It had been easy. He could dangle the carrot of an audition in front of her nose until the second coming; it had no effect on her.

But she sure as hell wasn't going to actually *do* one!

Even when he wasn't provoking her, however, he'd

bugged her. He seemed so male and imposing. Just being around him made her itchy and uncomfortable and it wasn't just because he thought she was Denise—though that definitely had its place. It was something else, something she didn't want to identify.

Better to concentrate on her impersonation. He couldn't prove she wasn't Denise. Why should he? He didn't know she, Dinah, even existed, and let's face it, playing Denise was really pretty easy. Her twin was so mercurial, insecure, and needy that all Dinah had to do was pretend to call Leo, her agent, and whine, whine, whine.

Nothing convinced John Callahan faster, and was a quicker turn-off, than to believe she only wanted to be with him to score a part. And for John Callahan, producer and egomaniac, it was all too easy to believe.

So, she could be Dinah 99 percent of the time and still get away with it.

Except that he'd made noise this evening about offering her a part.

"Do you remember when we first met?" he said suddenly, grimacing a bit. Clearly this was not a fond memory.

"No."

"No?"

"No, I don't." This was *really* dangerous ground.

"What's with this obstinate thing you've got going? Just have a conversation with me, okay?"

"What do you want?" Dinah demanded. "I don't owe you anything."

"We're co-habitating. We've been cruel to each other. I'd like it to just . . . end."

He bit off the words with frustration. His blue eyes bored into hers. Dinah wanted to shrink beneath their power. Denise would, she was certain. But she couldn't. She just couldn't.

"We met on the set of *Willful*," Dinah said slowly. She'd read it in *People*.

"But do you remember it?"

"What are you getting at?"

His gaze traveled down her neckline to where her breasts jutted against the silk robe. Dinah's lips parted. Her body tingled under that frank, male assessment.

"I remember that kimono," he said in a low voice.

Now when he looked at her, she saw it. Desire. She'd seen it before. Not when men glanced at her. Lord, no! But when they looked at Denise they sometimes wore that expression.

And it mirrored her own feelings too well because it was mixed with other emotions. Regret. Anger. Frustration. John Callahan didn't like being attracted to her any more than she liked being attracted to him.

Except he thought she was Denise. What if he found out she wasn't?

Dangerous thoughts swirled inside Dinah's brain. Thoughts she'd never allowed. Her experiences with sex had been tepid at best. Good old Glen wasn't exactly the most accomplished or creative lover. A quick hump in the black of night. A slap on the rear when she was washing dishes. Oh, yes, he really knew how to woo a woman.

She'd known there was something missing but she hadn't really known what.

But the liquid, melting hot sensations sliding through her were warning signs. It would be delicious. Forbidden. Utterly out of her experience and she suddenly wanted it so badly her whole being seemed concentrated on that one, searing thought.

I want to make love to you, his flaming eyes and grim expression said.

God knew what her own face revealed.

She watched him rise from the table, his gaze locked to hers. It could be a script, she thought half-hysterically, the slow-motion movements choreographed so stereotypically as to cause a rewrite. Her own hypnotic hesitation too corny to be believed.

She shrank against the counter. His nearness overpowered her. Concentrating on those crisp chest hairs, she tried to block everything about him from her mind.

Then his hand cupped her chin. Warm and dry and possessive. He tilted her face upwards until she was helpless but to meet that powerful gaze.

"What *is* it?" he asked, his voice husky and confused.

Dinah was powerless to answer. From a long, long distance away she watched his lips descend to meet hers.

"Oh, my God," she whispered the moment before his mouth touched against hers, at first tentatively, then with more urgency.

And then his body followed, pressing her backward until every male contour and angle seemed seared to her flesh. Dinah felt faint. She couldn't take it in. Too many sensations. Too much.

And then she thought of Thomas Daniels. How he'd pushed her down on the bed. How his hot tongue had fought its way inside her mouth. How she'd flailed around for a weapon, connected with one of Denise's high heels and slammed him in the temple with the heel.

He'd never touched her again.

But this was different. Oh, so seductively different. His tongue was hot and slick and exciting and her mouth welcomed its invasion.

Was that her voice? Those frail, anxious gasps? She

could feel his hard male organ pressed urgently against her thigh. She wanted him to grind against her even while the thought scared her. Too primal. Too intense. This wasn't *her*. Not Dinah Scott. She was the smart one. The cool one. The one who cleaned up messes and took care of everything.

No, no, no!

His hand slipped down her back, circled to the front, squeezed her breast through the flowered silk kimono. She wanted to wrap her legs around him. She actually picked up one trembling limb and his fingers instantly came to help.

Then she was on the counter, lifted there by knowing, anxious hands. And the grinding she'd silently begged for started in small thrusts that rapidly slammed out of control and suddenly she was clawing at him, gasping for air, and he was ready, willing, and able.

Her robe fell open. Panties slipped off expertly. Thighs pressed together. His hardness sliding swiftly, effortlessly, deeply into her wet center.

The feeling was exquisite—and wrong. Totally wrong. Only how could something so wrong, feel so *goooood?* Didn't she write about the truth of romance? Didn't she believe that sex and love could be one and the same?

No. She didn't. Not really, but ohhhh God . . .

His hard, rapid breathing matched her own. Suddenly he lifted her again, still deep within her and then they were on the floor and the thrusting stopped.

"What?" she choked out.

He pressed his mouth to her neck, laughing slightly. "What're you doing to me? I gotta slow down or it's over."

"No, no, it's okay." Regret was coming in a big, sweeping wave. "Oh, my God!"

"Shhh," he murmured and then when he moved Dinah simply ceased to exist. Another person took over and this one strained and writhed and twisted to accommodate his male body until magic happened. An explosion of pure sensation that shot feelings through her she'd never believed in before.

And when it was over, he pushed back a strand of sweat-dampened hair from her forehead, mouth twisted into a smile of intense satisfaction, a symbol of pure, male pride and power.

"So, that's why they have fireworks in movies," Dinah said on a catch in her breathing.

For an answer he bent his mouth to one of her bare breasts and began a new kind of lovemaking which Dinah surrendered to completely.

She woke up with a start as dawn was creeping over the horizon. Shock ripped through her, zinging like electricity. She was in *his* room. In *his* bed. With *his* leg wrapped possessively around *her* naked body!

She'd slept with her sister's husband.

He's her ex, she reminded herself quickly, as if that somehow made it better. Good Lord, His Highness had simply looked at her in that sexy, penetrating way and she'd damn near laid down and spread her legs in invitation.

"Oh, no," she groaned in misery, squeezing her eyes closed at the horrifying image.

Her protest caused one of his arms to hug her waist. His lips moved against her hair, kissing, nuzzling. He was half-asleep but unwilling to let her go.

And she *liked* it.

Regrets and barely leashed desire.

So, this is a morning after.

And Denise had called last night. She was sure about that. Her sister had called and then she'd gone to bed with her husband.

Shit!

And it been so *perfect!*

She had to get out of here. Out of his room and out from under his spell. Glancing around, she caught sight of the picture of Denise and she groaned again.

His breath stirred her hair. She listened quietly. Her mind tiptoed through last night's recent memories: a reprisal of lovemaking in this bed with its chocolate-colored sheets and musky scent. He, giving her unspeakable pleasure in unspeakable areas. She, returning in kind without turning a hair, without hesitation, *with* enjoyment.

Once more she groaned helplessly, seduced by images, sick at herself and her carnal enjoyment. With someone else, okay. She'd jump up and down in ecstacy and take out a billboard: DINAH SCOTT HAD AN ORGASM AND IT WAS FABU-LICIOUS!

But not with John Callahan. Not with His Highness, the King of Conquest, Chauvinism, and Casual Sex.

More nuzzling. He'd found the back of her neck and his mouth tasted, his tongue discovered. Shivers slid down her spine. Gooseflesh rose on her arm. His fingers splayed across her abdomen, slipped lower, encountering the triangle of hair before touching into her feminine sex.

He was curved around her, his hardening penis pressed against her buttocks. It wouldn't be long before his lovemaking would turn urgent and demanding. She could already feel her wetness as her body readied itself.

Pregnancy! Oh, God. Or worse!

She hadn't used any protection.

She jerked bolt upright, shocked so deeply she could do nothing but whimper.

"What?" he asked, his voice husky with sleep. He lifted up on one elbow.

"Condoms," she whispered. "We didn't . . . we didn't . . ."

That stopped him. He blinked several times. Then, bitten off, "When were you last tested?"

"Me?" Her jaw dropped in indignation before she remembered who she was. "Like last week," she spat out in a lie because *she* wasn't the one who embarked in casual sex. "Negative."

"And when was the last time you took a lover?"

"Don't worry, it's not me with the problem," she snapped.

"I haven't slept with anyone in over a year," he snapped right back. "I was negative before that. And, as you well know, if I was stupid enough to have indiscriminate sex, it'd be with a condom."

"Not last night," she reminded him.

"You're the one with the string of lovers! Goddammit!" He leaped out of bed and his male beauty momentarily distracted her. "You're the one who always insisted *we* use a condom. What happened to that worry about having a baby? Change your mind?" A second later, he snarled, "Are you pregnant? Is that it? Some kind of trick to stick this on me, too?"

"Don't throw this on me!" Dinah leaped to her feet, remembered her nakedness and yanked one of those damned chocolate sheets off the bed, wrapping it around herself. *"You* made love to me. Not the other way around!" She was immensely relieved to learn he was sexually careful. If he was telling the truth.

"Oh, yeah?" He gazed at her in a way that made her blush. She wasn't going to get into that fight.

"I'm H.I.V. free," she said.

"Ditto."

"Excuse me if I'd like to have that confirmed."

"Fine." He lifted his palms in agreement. "We'll get tested together, just to be sure."

"Fine."

"Yeah, fine."

With that he slammed into the bathroom and turned on the shower. Dinah collapsed back onto the bed.

Welcome to sex in the nineties.

The sun beat down like a hammer. Unseasonably hot. The breeze was just more hot air. Everything steamed and seared and blistered.

Denise rocked back and forth in the sliding lounge chair, drifting, drifting, slowly drifting. Her big toe gripped onto the concrete surrounding Ian's azure pool and she rocked and rocked.

Leo, that overrated shit, had not returned her calls. Oh, sure, his brain-dead receptionist assured her that he was out of town but Denise knew better. Kissing someone else's ass. Denise Scott Callahan was old news. Washed up. OUT.

Hazy, hazy days. All running into each other. Languidly Denise reached for her iced grapefruit juice, her eyes encountering yesterday's *Variety*. Yeah, like she cared what was going on in that world. Without a doubt she would read about the ever-popular John Callahan, super stud.

Which reminded her of Dinah.

Dinah, won't you blow? Dinah, won't you blow?

She warbled softly, "Dinah won't you blow John's horn?"

Jealousy ran like green poison through her veins, followed by a backwash of pain so great she actually sobbed. She was glad she had the thunder egg. It was her little piece of John. The only one she might ever possess.

The grapefruit juice was in her hand. She gazed at it, slowly lifting it to her lips. Cold liquid ran down the front of her chest, pooling in her navel.

"Shit!" she shrieked, shocked that she'd missed her mouth. Setting the glass back down on the frosted glass table top she saw a series of white caplets lined up like little soldiers. Ian's gift. He was good at gifts.

Popping two in her mouth, she reminded herself that she didn't do drugs. Uh, uh. No way. They weren't for her. She was Denise Scott and she didn't do drugs.

Time floated. Powder blue sky. Cottony clouds. Blinding, starry brilliance bouncing off the pool and into her eyes.

She felt fabulous. No need to push the poisons out, so fuck you, Dr. Hayden Stone, and the horse you rode in on. And fuck you, John Callahan. And Dinah, too!

Hours later she realized she was holding a receiver in her hand, standing in the middle of Ian's bedroom. She wasn't alone. Lina was making the bed.

A voice on the phone. "Denise? Denise, is that you?"

Dinah! Sounding frantic. "Dinah?"

"Where *are* you? I've been going nuts worrying about you!" Dinah fairly shrieked.

"I'm fine." Her tongue was thick and woolly. Licking her lips, she said again, "I'm fine."

"Are you drunk? Are you listening to me? What's your phone number there? Are you at a hotel?"

Lina's dark eyes assessed coolly. Denise thought about flipping her off, except she remembered she liked Lina. "Do you know Ian Wallace?"

"Hell, no." Dinah sounded irritable.

"I'm at his place."

"In L.A.?"

"Yeah, well, Beverly Hills. You know us movie stars." She winked at Lina, lost her balance and fell to the floor. With an annoyed jingle the phone tumbled off the table and hit her leg leaving a nasty red gash. "Ooops . . ." Denise reached for the cut. Her fingers came away smeared with blood.

"Denise? Denise?"

Dinah's voice was tinny and small. Lina bent down and replaced the receiver, cutting Dinah off in mid-protest. "You're hurt, ma'am," she murmured.

"I need a band–aid," Denise told her.

She suddenly awakened, unaware she'd fallen asleep until she realized she was in Ian's bed, and she wasn't alone.

"Who are you?" she asked thickly. Her eyes widened. "My God!" It was Dr. Stoner. Her old shrink!

No. No, it wasn't. It was Ian and something about the look on his face made her shrink inside in terror. He was going to hurt her. She braced herself for the first hit.

Hours, maybe days later she awakened again. Senses still swathed in cotton refused to register her surroundings. Dully she listened to the labor of her own breathing.

Oh, Denise, Denise, Denise . . . what are you doing?

Dying. Killing yourself. Drowning.

With a whimper she fell back into fitful slumber.

Dinah sat on the deck and contemplated the rolling waves, dark and menacing in the midnight gloom. Bobo curled around her legs and purred, back and forth. She absentmindedly stroked the kitten's ears, her gaze on the exterior lights strung from the eaves which sent feeble fingers of illumination toward the ocean, adding to the sensation of darkness and mystery.

Her sister was in trouble. As bad as ever, if Dinah read the signals right and they were pretty hard to miss. Who was Ian Wallace of Beverly Hills? She didn't want to know. Yes, she did. She wanted to know so she could ring his doorbell, wait for the bastard to appear, then shoot a bullet right between his eyes.

God, how she hated men who treated women badly. She could sense it over the telephone wires, a telepathic message so intense she could taste its bitterness, smell its foul decay. The bastard was hurting her sister.

Not this time.

Conscience pricked up its ears. *You hurt her. You hurt her bigtime. You made love to her husband.*

Ex-husband, she reminded herself defensively.

No good. Doesn't count. You screwed him. You! You!

She sucked in air between her teeth. She'd made a mistake. A stupid, damn near unforgivable, and potentially fatal, mistake. She'd been tested. So had John. They were both negative which didn't meant anything until six months had passed because she didn't believe in his purported celibacy.

Yeah, right. Like His Highness hadn't sampled the side dishes around the set. What man wouldn't? And she knew from Denise that John Callahan was not above adultery—although, you had to consider the source, she reminded herself with a grimace. Oh, how she'd like to believe Denise was wrong! She wanted Callahan to be better than he was.

But maybe he's telling the truth, her naive, little-girl self suggested. *Maybe he's one of the good guys.*

"Fool," she muttered aloud, mad at herself.

Well, at least he was gone. Busy on post-production of

Fortunata (Yeah, like he was really handing the reins over to Frankie) and pre-production of that other one, *Lady Paradise*. Dinah didn't care much one way or another about the acting biz. She had to admit, she was pretty happy with her own career.

Longing filled her suddenly and unexpectedly. She had to go home to Santa Fe and Flick with his obdurate ways and crude manners. She was tired of L.A. and Hollywood.

Be honest. You're afraid you're falling for him!

"Yep," she muttered aloud, grabbing for her half-empty glass of white wine.

Hearing an engine, she sat straight up. John? Instantly she was mad at herself all over again. So, what if it was? So what? No more fooling around just because it felt good. She wasn't *that* stupid.

Coulda fooled me.

Footsteps. His footsteps. Entering the house. Then strong and purposeful and heading her way. Dinah sank back into the chair, heart pounding so hard it liked to deafen her. She started to sweat.

He stopped at the open French doors. The hairs on the back of her neck lifted. Every nerve tingled with anticipation.

"I've been thinking," he said, walking up behind her.

"Not a good idea, thinking. Too dangerous." She buried her nose in her wine glass, giddy as a schoolgirl.

His lips kissed her nape. A shudder swept through her, impossible to hide.

"I brought you a present," he murmured huskily.

"A present?"

He handed her a small box. Dinah glanced down at it. A box of condoms with stars and stripes in red, white, and blue technicolor.

"Couldn't resist," he added, turning her chair around, his mouth possessing hers. Dinah was torn between ecstasy and being greatly offended. "Seemed so patriotic."

"There are those who would disagree."

"The military should hand them out. Protect, serve, and all that."

"Who says we're going to need one?"

"We're going to need more than one," he countered. "No more Russian roulette."

"Just American apple pie?"

"Fast learner."

"I'm not going to go to bed with you," Dinah blurted out quickly. His lips, his hands, his body were making it hard to think!

His hand caressed her breast. He made a slight sound of pleasure in her ear. For the first time in her life she tried to conjure up images of Thomas Daniels—the coldest, harshest douse of ice water available to her—and for the first time in her life she couldn't. Her body responded as if primed, her hands reaching for him anxiously.

Bobo mewed out a sound of protest but neither John nor Dinah heard. Gathering her close, John carried her upstairs to the joys and intimacies of his bedroom, and Dinah lost the last vestiges of her will to resist as his body collapsed on hers and her body wrapped possessively around him.

Chapter Ten

It had cost a pretty penny but been worth it in the end.

Hayley sat on the edge of her twin bed, fingernails clamped between her teeth as she viewed her audition video. Okay, the guy with her—a friend from an acting class whose major talent was flipping a cigarette into his mouth from arm's length—was a waste, but who cared? He only made her look that much better!

Of course, the video was home-grown, courtesy of another acting class buddy, Ted Neusmith, who thought payment for services rendered ought to be negotiated while she was spread eagle on her back. Yeah, right.

Hayley had paid him fifty bucks plus the cost of the videotape. She'd given her costar another fifty.

But she, Hayley, came alive as Isabella, the down-on-her-luck prostitute whose lifestyle affects everyone close to her until she's alone with nothing but emptiness. Tonja Terkell had been wrong. A comedy, it wasn't. Oscar material. Damn straight!

Okay, she knew every actress in Hollywood would be after this role. It was too plum, too juicy, for anyone to leave alone. Hayley wasn't naive enough to believe she could be the star, but there were other, lesser roles tailor-made for someone with her ambition and talent.

Now, her primary concern was getting John Callahan to view the tape. She had no agent. More scuz. When she finally got a role, *then* she'd hire an agent. Oh, yeah, sure. She knew the drill. Nobody, but nobody, will touch you unless you're agented.

But not everyone's brother-in-law was John Callahan, Super Producer.

If only he knew it.

Sighing, she slipped the tape out of the recorder and stuffed it in her purse. Tonja was working for Callahan again. For inexplicable reasons, he'd taken an interest in her, hiring her as assistant, assistant, assistant producer for *Lady Paradise*.

Miracles can happen!

Hayley planned to push her videotape on Tonja this morning. It was early. Damn early. Five o'clock in the morning early. She could catch Tonja before she left for Callahan's building on the Strip and slip her the tape. Of course Tonja would protest. She viewed her job with Callahan as sacred, not to be defiled by clamoring friends.

This was new for Tonja—forgetting her friends—but Hayley wasn't going to let her get away with it. Tonja owed her and Hayley now intended to collect.

As a last resort Hayley planned on approaching Callahan himself, but it would be ever so nice if he'd at least viewed her acting skills first.

Buoyed by this small success, Hayley jumped in the rent-a-wreck she'd splurged for. She was nearly out of cash, but who cared? She felt energized and eager. And nothing, not Jason, the boss from hell, not Tonja and her insecurities, and not Connor Jackley, late of the L.A.P.D., was going to stop her from reaching her goal.

A tickle in her brain. Memories. Clamping her jaw, Hayley shoved the rental into gear, the tired vehicle grinding and chugging in protest, and flashed beneath the street lights in the early morning grimness of tawdry Hollywood, U.S.A.

Stardom, here I come!

He closed his eyes and counted to fifty, a practice he'd begun as a kid when his hormones were careening out of control and girls' tight skirts and lush, bouncing breasts occupied his entire mind. Now, it was merely a stress reducer. Other people might use cigarettes, alcohol, drugs, or exercise. Dr. Hayden Stone employed a common practice of elementary teachers: time out.

It had served him well. He'd passed through puberty and early adulthood with no serious mishaps, made his way through U.C.L.A. and medical school, internship, residency, and ten years of psychiatric practice before walking away from it all one bright, slightly smoggy Los Angeles morning.

Everyone thought he needed therapy. What? they cried. Give up his wife, Leesa, and a flourishing career making an indecent amount of money? Was he crazy? Certifiable? Too many years curing the nut cases. That's what it was. Take a vacation, they advised. It'll all be okay.

He possessed a license to practice in two states, California and Texas. When one of his patients made a half-hearted attempt to seduce him—a normal routine for Carolyn Lenton—he'd gently turned her down, but did not immediately brush aside her offer to move with her to Houston.

She had friends. A whole barrelful of crazies, to hear her talk, who needed professional help.

"Come on," she wheedled, crossing and uncrossing her legs, tugging ineffectively at her short red skirt. "I'm heading home for a visit and I think you oughtta come with me."

To her amazement, and a certain amount of surprise on his own part, he'd accepted. Not for a stay at her opulent home, however. He'd rented a one-room apartment, a complete change from his well-tended Bel-Air manor and the parade of housemaids and gardeners and workmen Leesa employed.

Leesa had filed for divorce. He'd read the terms—exorbitant—and complied. She immediately backed down, begging him to come home. Leesa was a wonderful woman, but there was something missing.

Wonderful woman. She's a wonderful woman.

How incredibly bland. Leesa deserved better than that from him.

Opening his eyes, Dr. Hayden Stone crossed to the window of his new offices. Ground level of an English cottage-style building not too many blocks off Sunset. Big come down. Very homey. Un-chic enough to cause embarrassment at parties.

Perfect.

He filed for divorce next. Generous terms, not exorbitant. Leesa signed, the document crumpled and bumpy from the tears she shed. Real tears that had ripped at his heart and he'd nearly reconsidered.

Except Leesa got married the Saturday after their divorce was final to a twenty-seven-year-old surfer. And she'd been two months pregnant.

Now *that* had hurt. He wanted children. Somehow he and Leesa had just never managed it.

Returning to L.A. had been a growth experience. Growth experience, he thought again, wincing a bit.

What did you expect? Some kind of epiphany? Get real!

His clients were waiting for him, anxious to fill him in on the last screwed-up year of their life, ready for new advice, new tricks, new something.

He settled in as if there'd been no break. So, here he was, unhappy, unfulfilled, and roaring down the lucrative road of success to some distant horizon he didn't care if he ever reached.

One regret. Denise. He shouldn't have left her. Huge blue eyes filled with hurt and fear and guilt. Pain so enormous it reached out and touched him. A crying, dying soul protected only by clever words and a sense of humor.

Why hadn't she called him?

Because you abandoned her.

Not true. He'd phoned Carolyn several times. His interest in Denise seemed to irritate her, however, because she refused to tell him anything but word games. All he knew was that Denise had left Houston with a man. If he wanted any further information he was going to have to confront Carolyn and find a way past her obstacle course of verbal weaponry to learn the plain truth.

Maybe he should fly to Houston.

His line beeped and the speaker phone came on. "Dr. Stone?" his receptionist's voice filled the room. "That woman's called again. She's on the line."

He frowned. "What woman?"

"The incoherent one. Since you weren't in conference I thought maybe you'd like to talk to her . . . ?"

Hayden suspected it was Angela Mercer. She habitually called whenever she was strung out, thinking he wouldn't charge her for his time if she phoned it in. And every month when he billed her for her two hour crying-jag calls, she refused to pay.

"Put her on," he said with a sigh.

"Dr. Stone's on the line now," he heard his receptionist tell the caller.

A weighty pause while Angela breathed noisily. Hayden waited, then encouraged, "Angela? Was there something you wanted to say?"

"Stoner?" Denise's voice wobbled.

He was at his desk in one jump, punching the button and snapping up the receiver. "Denise?"

"Where've you been? You son-of-a-bitch!"

The line went dead.

With more control than he felt, Hayden pressed the button for his receptionist. "When that woman calls again, interrupt me."

"Even if you're in conference with someone important?" This upset her business sensibilities.

"Even if you have to put the President of the United States on hold."

Disapproval.

Hayden reminded himself to fire the receptionist and hire someone with more heart than secretarial skills.

Slam! The receiver bounced out of its cradle, ricocheted off the edge of the table and knocked over an ivory figurine. Vaguely Denise realized she might have made a bit of a mistake there. Ian wouldn't like it.

Ian didn't like a lot of things, she'd learned. But Ian liked to hit. He hit Lina a lot. She made a lot of money off him because he assuaged his guilt with money and trinkets. Lina was saving up. And what he didn't pay her, she stole from his pockets. Lina had a lot of advice for Denise.

"Take the money and get out, madam," Lina whispered conspiratorially. "You don't have to stay. *I* do. For now. But I'm getting out, too. Very, very soon."

"Where will you go?" Denise asked.

"I have family. They don't know." She glanced over her shoulder, face full of fear, worried sick that Ian Wallace might magically appear.

"Why don't you leave now?"

"Need references. He won't give 'em. Gotta take what I can."

"I'll give you a reference," Denise offered magnanimously.

Lina gazed at her through dark, liquid, suspicious eyes. "You might be dead soon," was the disturbing answer.

Well. That had certainly sobered her up. What a thing to say! Ian might have his quirks, but Denise knew there were a lot of worse sickos in the world.

Wanna hear a story, Lina? A really good one? Let me tell you about dear old stepdaddy.

Her head ached. There was no story. What the hell was the matter with her?

"Bi-polar shit," she muttered, staggering around the bedroom. Catching sight of herself in the mirror, her hand flew to her mouth. She drew closer, awed and alarmed. That was her? That wild-haired, scatty, old woman. Jeeezus, she looked like poor white trash.

That's what he'd called her, she realized with stunning clarity. Along with bitch, slut, whore, and numerous other one word insults.

Thomas Daniels. He seemed to occupy her thoughts these days. Since Connor Jackley had appeared on Ian's doorstep and asked her all those questions, she'd thought about Daniels every waking moment. He was dead. Murdered. Denise shook her head, bemused. He couldn't be dead. He was too dirt ornery to be dead. He was too vile.

Weeds never die.

Homespun advice from her mother, but she believed in it. Thomas Daniels wasn't dead. He was out there, ready to jump her. When she thought she was alone and safe. When she was most vulnerable.

Denise gazed at her reflection unseeingly. She was lost in thought, swaying on her feet. When hands clamped on her shoulders she thought she was dreaming again, but then Ian spun her around so quickly she nearly lost her balance.

"You went out today," he accused, his voice sharp, staccato bursts of fury.

"I wanted to see someone." She cowered.

"Who?"

"A friend."

"Who?"

"My therapist," she admitted, drawing away. His fingers dug into her shoulders until she winced. "I didn't see him. I just drove by his offices."

"In *my* car."

"Well, Ian, you've got four. I just took the Ford."

"I didn't give you permission. You should have asked."

His anger was a living thing, well-hidden only when others were present. There was a big difference between the public Ian Wallace and the private one. But wasn't that always the way?

"Nothing happened," she murmured.

"Is that right?"

"Nothing happened."

"You'd better be telling me the truth."

"Ian, I've got to go back to work. I've called my agent and he's looking into something for me."

"You screwed up your career, Denise. It's over."

Pleasure in his voice. Sadistic enjoyment. Through the mirror she caught sight of his reflection. The self-satisfied smile as he gazed possessively down at her crown. How had she ever thought him attractive?

"I've got to call my sister. That detective . . ."

"A has-been." He sneered. "I've got friends in important places. That guy's career is dead."

"I can't stay here forever."

"C'mere . . ." He dragged her toward the bed. Denise reluctantly followed, mind numb, filled with sudden hate toward Dr. Hayden Stone and his bland disinterest.

Ian started removing her clothes. She stood silently, watching the pieces fall: her silk blouse, tan slacks, bikini underwear and black lace bra. She saw his long, strong fingers squeeze her breast, felt the sting of several sharp slaps against her nipples.

"You like that?" he asked.

She didn't respond. The next slap was across the face.

"Like that?" he demanded, his breath quickening.

"No."

"Yes, you do." His sharp, even teeth bit at her lip until she tasted her own blood.

Pushing her down he spread her legs, then those sharp teeth worked hard there, too. Denise jerked spasmodically until he mounted her, then she lay still, scarcely daring to breathe.

"C'mon, baby. C'mon." He pumped hard but true to form, his slack penis didn't respond. Denise stirred, aware that if she didn't help, she'd bear the brunt of his sexual frustration another way.

She reached a hand down to his flaccid member, gently

touching, trying to erase everything from her mind except for those wonderful times with John when he'd made love gently to her, breathing how much he loved her, how beautiful she was.

"Work harder, baby," Ian bristled. He pinched her neck, hard.

Denise clamped her jaw. Don't cry. Never cry.

His tongue nearly strangled her as he pushed it down her throat, one hand holding her hair so hard she couldn't fight the moan of pain. "C'mon, c'mon," he encouraged.

She knew what he wanted. It would be so easy to give in. Tears. Remorse. Fear. She felt them all but still she resisted.

"I'll hit you, bitch. It's what you want. What you want."

She rubbed him harder but it was no good.

Whack! The galaxy exploded inside her head.

Whack! Whack! Whack!

Now, he was pumping away, grunting like a pig, enjoying her choked breathing as she fought back emotion.

"Like that, don't ya?" he murmured. "Like that!" He climaxed with a howl of pleasure, flopping down on her, suffocating her.

Denise lay quiet beneath him. Moments later he stirred, climbed to his feet and went to the bathroom, bringing back a series of pills and a glass of water.

"Here," he said.

She took the pills, wincing at the pain against her mouth. Ian gently kissed her and brushed back her hair.

"I love you," he said, easing down beside her, stroking her hair.

Closing her eyes, Denise willed her tired body to relax. Inside her, changes were taking place. Blocks of her physical structure were breaking down and rearranging. With a clearer insight than she suspected herself capable of, she knew she was through with Ian Wallace and this course of self-destructiveness.

By hook or by crook, she was going to get back on track.

If she had to kill him to do it.

"You're fired," Flick growled into the phone.

"No, I'm not," Dinah argued, twisting in the narrow telephone booth and making a face at the impatient, heavyset man glaring at her from the outside. He could just wait. She had important business that needed taking care of. "I got you the piece right on time, and it was good, if I do say so myself."

"Nobody cares," Flick sniffed.

"I'm almost finished here," Dinah said wearily, grimacing at the almost lie. Was she almost finished? Who knew? But soon, very soon, she was going to have to leave L.A. for her real life in Santa Fe.

"Yeah, well, I'm hiring. Someone else's fanny'll be warming your chair by Thursday."

"I'm faxing as soon as I'm out of here," she muttered. "Hold on to your trousers."

The man outside the phone booth pointed to his watch. Dinah threw him a puzzled look, so he drummed his finger on the watch's face.

Yeah, right. Like she didn't know what he wanted. Shrugging, she pretended to be completely baffled. He swore a stream of pungent four letter words at her.

Was the whole world impatient?

"I'm serious, Scott," Flick added, his voice altering. "You said six weeks. It's been twelve."

"Ten," she corrected quickly. The guy outside rattled

the door. Dinah's glare could melt steel. He flipped the bird with both hands—a sign of true talent. She gave him another puzzled stare.

"Honey, you've used up my patience. Good luck in the job market."

He hung up before Dinah could protest. Feeling ornery, she dallied on the phone a few minutes longer, sending her buddy outside into a conniption fit. Slamming open the door, she met a stream of verbal abuse that ordinarily might have shocked her. Today, she was loaded for bear.

"Get a cellular, bozo," she told him, jumping into the Fiat and roaring away.

She sent the fax from her now favorite Mailboxes, Inc., annoyed all over again at the need for this subterfuge. If John Callahan would just LEAVE HER ALONE she could work in peace at the house and find out what the hell was wrong with his temperamental fax machine.

Outside again in air so smoggy you could taste it, Dinah turned to the convenience store and ordered a SUPER SODA!—MORE THAN EVEN *YOU* CAN DRINK! Then she settled into the Fiat, listened anxiously for the engine, popped the clutch and slid into traffic.

The super soda was more than even she could hold, the cup so wide it kept slipping through her hand. She balanced it on her thigh and drove one-handed, certain she was about to die on the maniac-congested freeways of L.A.

She couldn't bear to see John. One touch and she was a goner. She had to reach Denise. She had to get free!

For days now she'd toyed with the idea of telling him the truth. What would happen? Dinah shuddered. Even her fertile imagination had trouble envisioning that scenario. No matter what, she'd be the bad guy. Impersonating her sister. Taking over Denise's life. Sleeping with her husband.

Ex-husband. Dinah grimaced.

That excuse is wearing pretty thin, isn't it?

The answer to all her problems was Denise. Find her, straighten out this mess, leave town with her tail tucked firmly between her legs.

At the house she walked into her den. According to directory assistance, Ian Wallace possessed an unlisted number. Big deal. Everyone in L.A. did. Dinah had already ordered an incoming call scanner which listed the telephone number of each call that came into the house in case Denise phoned again. If and when that happened, she would be in possession of Ian Wallace's number, and she would know how to reach Denise.

And if Denise didn't call soon, Dinah would head straight to the police and tell them a tale they wouldn't soon forget. Because she knew her twin was in serious trouble. She sensed it.

Just like she was in serious trouble herself.

Chapter Eleven

Flick didn't publish her column. The *Santa Fe Review* introduced a new writer, Kate Patton, whose first endeavor concerned romance in the '90's entitled "What's Love Got To Do With It?"

Dinah scanned the article with hard fury, wadded up the paper, and flung it against the wall.

She had to go back. She had to leave this mess she'd made for herself in California and return to New Mexico.

She didn't want to go.

Muttering epithets directed solely at herself, she packed her suitcase, tossing in items unseeingly. She, Dinah, The Fixer, had created an ungodly mess and now she had to run out and leave everything!

"What is the matter with you?" she demanded.

Suitcase in hand, she stood in the gallery, listening to the sounds of the empty house. Callahan was at work, but he was coming back tonight. He'd been notably absent since their nights together, working like a fiend, or so he said in one of his numerous phone calls. At least once a day he checked in. He was concerned about her being alone. He worried about the break-in and considered reinstalling an alarm system.

Dinah assured him she was all right and then they sat on opposite ends of the phone with nothing—and everything—to say. Neither of them knew where to start. This cooling off period was good. Very good. Dinah felt like she was losing her mind.

He, like herself, had entered a phase of not knowing how to act. Protocol was lost. He believed he'd slept with his ex-wife, and he was mulling over that one. She knew he'd slept with his ex-sister-in-law.

Either way it was a disaster worthy of afternoon soap operas.

But he'd mentioned he was coming back tonight.

She was at the door when the phone rang. She hesitated. It could be Callahan, but it might be Denise.

Dropping her bags, she raced for the phone, waiting for the answering machine to pick up. The message sounded—Denise's voice merely repeating the number dialed. A beep.

"It's Carolyn. Are you there? Everyone here thought you left with Ian. Tell me it isn't true." The voice chuckled with feminine amusement. "Call me when you get a minute."

Dinah picked up. "Carolyn?" she asked warily.

"Well, my God! You *are* there. My sources told me your ex was living there. You're not co-habitating, are you?"

Without even trying, Dinah had convinced her she was Denise. "Your sources?"

"You don't sound like yourself," she said with sudden suspicion. "Who is this?"

Berating herself for being overly confident, she shot back, "It's me. Who else would it be?"

"Anybody, dearest, with *his* reputation." A beat, then, "Oh, my God! You got the part! That's why you're with John again!"

"No, no . . . I'm not with John. And there's no part. I'm just keeping an eye on the house."

"Oh." Disappointment bordering on boredom colored her voice. Slyly, she added, "Peter's been asking about you."

Peter? Treacherous waters, here. "Really?" she asked lightly.

"You still like him?"

"I . . . no . . . not that way."

"Well, I guess! Do you know his nose was broken? He whined about it for weeks!"

What was this all about? "Umm, how does he look?" Dinah asked curiously.

"Oh, you know. He's still parading the perfect cock. Thinks we're all standing in line." She sniffed, then subtly shifted gears. "Have you seen Ian? I need to get in touch with him, but I've misplaced his number."

"Ian . . . ?"

"Ian Wallace. Remember him?"

"Sorry." Dinah half-covered the receiver and coughed. "My ears are plugged with this cold." Here, finally, was a link to Denise's whereabouts. Treading cautiously, she heaved an exaggerated sigh. "I've lost the number, too. You don't have his address, do you? I could swing by and leave a message."

"Hey, all I know is Beverly Hills. I thought you two flew back together. Didn't you get those vital statistics?"

There was suspicion in her voice and more than a hint of jealousy. Not surprising, knowing Denise's penchant for attracting the male sex. "You know I'm not good at remembering the important things," Dinah said, guessing Carolyn was acquainted enough with Denise to know how unstable and volatile she was. The more you knew of Denise, the less you expected of her.

"Well, how are you doing?" Carolyn suddenly gushed with remembered solicitude.

"Coping."

"Stone helping you out there?"

"Not really," Dinah said, lost.

"Now, you didn't lose *his* number, too, did you? For God's sake, Denise, he *cared* about you."

"Do you have his number?" Dinah asked, wincing, afraid she was about to step over the line. She half-expected Carolyn to scream out, "Fraud! Liar! Imposter!," but all she said was, "The good doctor's probably listed in the phone book. Go see him, Denise. And get better."

The subtext was clear: *You total looney, you really need serious help.*

On that Dinah and Carolyn agreed.

A few more cryptic comments about Peter, and Carolyn hung up, frustrated in her search for Ian Wallace. But Dinah had learned something important.

Denise was seeing some doctor in town named Stone.

Hefting her bags over her shoulder, Dinah scratched out a note to John about feeding Bobo—he was sure to love that!—locked the front door behind her and headed for her beloved Fiat, aware she was running away from John Callahan and not certain whether she was sorry or relieved.

John Callahan was a happy man. Slogging through the last phases of *Fortunata* with Frankie bitching and screaming and the actors whining and sulking should have been pure hell. But John didn't really much care. Let 'em screw it up. He had other things to occupy his mind and keep him happy.

The script for *Lady Paradise* was on his desk. Smiling, he

thumbed through it, imagining Denise in the title role. She could do it. She could do it right—if she were so inclined—though dependability wasn't her strong suit.

His casting director, Susan Markson, had tested a dozen actresses, and she had several more interested who were "above" testing. If John brought up Denise's name, Susan would squint at him over the curl of her cigarette smoke, skewering him with cold eyes that had seen it all and then some. Susan was nothing if not opinionated. But John would win because it was his picture.

But did he really want Denise for Toni?

Yes!

A knock on the jamb of his open door and one of his assistants peeked in. For a moment he had trouble remembering her name. Tonja. Tonja Terkell.

She regarded him sheepishly, a videotape in her hand. "What's this?"

"An audition videotape," she admitted on a sigh.

"You want me to look at it?"

He'd offered her a job during production of *Fortunata* because he'd felt sorry for her. He felt sorry for a lot of them whose dreams of success in Hollywood turned them desperate and miserable.

"It's up to you," she said diffidently, afraid to commit. They were all afraid to commit. Too risky. The producer or director might disagree. Stick your neck out? Forget it. It'd only get chopped off.

"Leave it on the desk," John told her. Maybe he'd get around to watching it after the mountains of work he already had scheduled. Maybe he wouldn't.

He was at that phase of production where he spent 110 percent of his time on the phone. Shockingly, *Lady Paradise* had been purchased by Titan Studios. They'd come to *him,* if you could believe that. The only thing John could figure was, because he owned a percentage of the corporation, Rodney Walburn III felt compelled to acknowledge him.

Or at least that's what he'd originally thought. Because he despised Titan, John had blithely demanded total control and a budget one and a half times what he needed. He'd expected to be turned down—and how. But surprise! Good old Rod had agreed to all conditions, demanding only a Christmas release.

John's conclusion: Rod was sweating under those layers of fat. He became head of Titan Pictures by default and the board was sorry they'd appointed such a slug. A smart slug. A far-sighted slug. But a slug nonetheless.

But that was Rod's problem. John had signed the papers and the deal was set. He was driven now by two needs: to bring the picture in under Titan's generous budget, a mission he could easily fulfill, and two, to cast this picture brilliantly in as quick a manner as possible and get production rolling.

And there was Denise. Though he'd sworn long and loud that she would never get a part in *Lady Paradise*, there was no denying the main role fit her to a T. And why not? He'd purchased the struggling writer's fresh, fast-paced screenplay years earlier with Denise in mind. He'd reworked the main character himself thinking of her. He'd seen her so clearly. A more devious Denise, but possessing that strange inner vulnerability his ex could never quite destroy.

Maybe that was his fascination with her.

Nervously twiddling a pen fast and furiously between his thumb and forefinger, he barrelled through the first of his phone calls, then paced around like a restless tiger, anxious and tense. He'd told her he'd be home tonight. He needed her. God, he felt like an idiot!

The phone rang, and he ignored it, like he always did.

Four hours later, tired and irritable, he strode away from his production offices and unlocked his Jeep by remote. He should forget Malibu and work at his apartment tonight.

It was wasted thought. He turned the nose of the Jeep toward Malibu and Denise.

Through the windshield of her Rent-A-Wreck, Hayley watched John Callahan stride toward his black Jeep. Her window rolled down, she heard the soft *beep-beep* of his remote as he pointed it toward his car. Seconds later the man was inside and pulling into traffic. Hayley eased out behind him.

Okay, following the producer was pretty low. When had it ever worked for anyone? But he was her ex-brother-in-law and that, if nothing else, was at least an interesting point of conversation.

She could see it now. "Hey, Mr. Callahan! I'm Hayley Scott, Denise's sister. I know you didn't know about me, but it's all true. Could you look at my audition tape? I'd really like to be your next big star!"

Oh, sure.

But . . . nothing ventured, nothing gained.

He was heading to his Malibu home, Hayley realized. Tonja said he rented an apartment nearby, but no such luck today.

She almost changed her mind. She would rather catch him closer to her own home. After all, she was already running late for work and Jason would have a hemorrhage if she showed up late again. A trip to Malibu would definitely put her in the tardy category.

But such was the price of stardom.

Callahan drove at breakneck speed. A conservative, he wasn't. Hayley maneuvered as best she could but was in a thorough sweat as they wound the last few miles to his home.

The houses were set back from the road by wrought-iron gates. Whether this was Callahan's jealous way of guarding his privacy, or a testament to Denise's paranoia, Hayley couldn't say. What it did mean was that she was out of luck until she figured some way to get past the gates because they'd already shut soundly behind her quarry.

Honesty was the best policy. She didn't necessarily believe it, but it was worth a shot.

She was about to call on the intercom attached to a post when the wrought iron gates mysteriously opened again. Not bothering to learn why, Hayley gunned her Rent-A-Wreck inside the sanctum and cruised to a stop in the driveway of the unprepossessing home.

She'd expected a mansion, something more than this anyway. Not that it wasn't nice. By normal standards, it was an immaculate, beautiful home. But this was Hollywood and between them Denise and John Callahan were loaded. They'd bought this place at the height of their love affair, so Hayley had expected no expenses spared.

On the other hand, she'd give a lot to live in such quiet splendor. She'd just thought Denise would be more, well, *tacky!*

Swallowing the butterflies in her throat and stomach, she grabbed her audition tape and marched to the front door. She'd asked for Tonja's help and it hadn't worked. Now she had to rely on her own fortitude, intelligence and general *chutzpah.*

Chimes rang through the house, jangling her nerves with every reverberation. She trembled with fear and memory suddenly threw her back to her youth. With tooth-grinding effort, she squeezed the horrid thoughts back, refusing to acknowledge them. Instead, she used her favorite trick of denial: she filled her mind with the sight of a mountain stream, concentrating on the peacefulness, the total quietude and sense of sweet displacement.

The door flew open and John Callahan, his shirt off, stood in the aperture, glaring down at her.

The sight of his smoothly muscled body threw Hayley out of sync. She grinned stupidly.

"Yeah?" he asked, clearly annoyed. "How'd you get in? Oh, *shit!* I opened the gates."

"I'm . . . Hayley Scott," she said distantly, her ears crashing with thunder from the frightened beat of her heart and the screaming of her nerves.

"I was expecting someone else. What do you want?"

"I'm . . . I'm . . ."

"What?" he demanded impatiently, clearly distracted.

"I'm Denise's sister."

That caught him up. He stared, his gaze raking her from head-to-toe. The crashing in her head changed to a loud hum. She couldn't think. Struggling, she tried to keep the hum in her head from overtaking her. *My God,* she thought in amazement. *I'm going to faint.*

And promptly she did.

She awoke almost instantly, aware that she was in Callahan's arms and he was carrying her inside the house. Walls and furnishings flashed by and she was laid on a couch in a living room which was surrounded by an upstairs gallery. Above her head, paddle fans floated lazily.

John Callahan glared down at her, his slate blue eyes full of harsh questions. "Are you sick?" he demanded.

"No." It was a pathetic squeak. Clearing her throat, she said again, louder, "No."

"Let me get you something. Don't move."

She didn't. She *couldn't!* She thought she might freeze from embarrassment and be in a permanent cryogenic state. This was *not* how she'd envisioned her first meeting with the famed John Callahan.

He returned with a glass of water and a snifter of brandy, cocking an eyebrow and lifting each drink in turn.

"The brandy," Hayley decided with a faint smile.

"Smart choice."

Struggling upward she sipped the fiery liquid, choking a bit. Almost instantly she felt her color return and along with it, a suffocating sense of dismal humiliation.

"Okay, who are you?" Callahan asked with more patience than she would have credited him.

"Hayley Scott, Denise's sister."

"My ex-wife is an only child," he clipped out. "No siblings."

"A lie. You must know how Denise lies. She can't help herself. Maybe she doesn't even know what the truth is any more," Hayley added magnanimously.

His lashes narrowed. "She's not here right now. I don't know where she is."

She heard the worry in his tone but was too distracted by her own amazement. Denise *lived* here with *him?*

"So, you want to catch up on old times?" He was ironic.

The opportunity was here. All she had to do was pull a copy of her audition tape out of her handbag—which was somewhere near the front door, she realized in dismay—and wow him with her talent. But Callahan was in no mood to be sold on her acting skills. His concentration was all on Denise.

"Something like that," she murmured.

"She should be back." He consulted his watch, frowning.

Hayley realized that if she stuck around, she would meet her sister face-to-face. This was a wrinkle she hadn't considered. See Denise in person?

Emotions charged through her in shockwaves. They hadn't been together since their flight from Wagon Wheel. Denise had been crying and Dinah had shaken and shaken her, forcing her to get a grip.

Hayley shut down, heart pounding so hard she closed her eyes, woozy.

"Are you sure you're not sick?" His voice was the crack of a whip.

"I'm just tired. I haven't eaten today and it caught me. When . . . when will Denise be back?"

He shook his head.

In truth John wasn't sure. Telltale signs of flight abounded. Clothes were strewn around Denise's room and the beaten Fiat wasn't in the garage. A scratched out note on the kitchen table asked him to feed Bobo. No word on where she'd gone or when she'd return. It could be that she'd just gone out for a few hours; anything was possible with Denise. But the house felt abandoned and empty, bereft almost. John sensed it keenly, in a way that gets beneath the skin.

And so he was in no mood to deal with this Denise lookalike and her pack of lies, no matter how entertaining.

She seemed to have a lot she wanted to say, but there was a lock on her mouth. Another day, John might have been interested enough to solve the mystery.

But not today.

The color had come back to her cheeks. Her eyes

sparkled, a darker blue than Denise's but the same shape and size. Her hair wasn't as blonde. Maybe she kept it natural, although Denise seemed to have lost her bottle of bleach these days as well. If he didn't know better he would believe they *were* related; they certainly possessed the same look.

"Give me your name and phone number, and I'll have Denise call you," he said tersely.

"Can't I stay awhile?"

"I'll give her the information," was his answer.

She chewed on her bottom lip, a gesture that added to her resemblance to Denise even though his ex was too careful about her physical appearance to indulge in nervous habits. Still, there was something that reached him. What did she really want?

Even as the thought crossed his mind, she told him. "I'm a struggling actress myself."

"Oh, God."

That stopped her. She wasn't stupid, at least. "But I guess you don't want to hear that right now. Got a pen?"

He grabbed one from the office and when he returned she was holding a copy of *Entertainment*. She scratched down her information on the backside of the magazine and handed it to him.

"Have Denise call me," she said.

He glanced at the name. Hayley Scott.

"Tell her I've been in town awhile."

"You haven't tried to contact her before?"

"We kind of lost touch, Mr. Callahan."

He gazed at her expectantly. She wrinkled her nose. Now that definitely was Denise. This Hayley person had copied her movements so well it was uncanny.

"So, you still believe she's an only child?" she asked,

climbing to her feet where she stood unsteadily a moment or two. John automatically reached out to help her, but she jerked away.

"I don't really know," he admitted honestly.

"Make her tell you the truth."

With that advice, she headed for the door. He followed behind her and watched as she climbed into a car a decade older than Denise's Fiat.

"Where are you?" John whispered as soon as her taillights vanished around the corner of the drive. He'd left the gate open as soon as he'd realized Denise wasn't home. Now, with dusk approaching, he pushed the button to close the wrought-iron fence.

Two hours later, as he sat in his office, doodling pensively, the telephone suddenly buzzed.

"Callahan," he answered.

"John? Tha'choo?"

The hairs on the back of his neck stood on end. Denise. The slur in her voice was unmistakable. Memories tumbled over each other. Ugly memories of the times she'd been stoned and drunk and generally out of her head. His fury knew no bounds. She'd fooled him! He'd believed in her and she'd played him for a sucker again!

"Where are you?" he snapped.

"Don't be mad . . ."

"For God's sake, Denise, you just don't know how to stay clean."

"I'm sorry, I'm sorry." She started to cry. Or at least it sounded like it. Denise never gave in to true emotion, but she sure as hell played the part. "Don't be mad. I love you, and I want to come home."

"You should have thought of that before you left."

"No, John. Don't . . ."

A skirmish on the other end of the line. Swearing. Then a male voice demanded, "Who the fuck is this?"

He wanted to slam down the receiver. He was in the process of doing so, but he couldn't quite let go. His feelings were too tangled and raw. "Who are you?" he demanded right back.

Slam! The man on the other end smashed the receiver down so hard it hurt John's ear. In a cool rage John's fingers gripped the phone so hard his hand throbbed.

Slowly, he set the receiver back in its cradle. The bitch had done it again. Stolen his heart then left. Made passionate love to him, then jumped in the sack with the nearest, most repulsive loser she could find. A punishment to her or to him. He didn't know which.

But it was the last time it would ever happen. The very last time.

She wouldn't be allowed into his house—into his goddamned life!—again.

Through a drug-hazed vision Denise watched Ian slam the phone down. A second later he picked up the receiver again. *Thwack, thwack.* Pain exploded inside her head. Her vision grayed. Something warm and thick stuck to her eyelashes. Rivulets of her own blood. Swiping them away, she glanced down at scarlet-stained hands. Shocked, she turned her hands palm up, smelling the slightly sweet odor of blood, remembering the hot sticky feel.

Déjà vu . . .

"Call him again and you're dead," Ian hissed in her ear, shaking her.

Denise didn't respond. She waited until Ian's ragged breathing came under control. Seconds felt like hours as she stayed perfectly still. Rigid. Firm in the belief that if she didn't move, maybe he would leave her alone. Finally he left the room, locking it from the outside.

How had it happened? One moment she'd been at Carolyn Lenton's, the next in this nightmare. Ian had seemed like the ticket out of trouble, in fact she'd sailed into a whirlpool straight to hell.

With an effort she hauled herself to the bathroom to clean up. At the sight of herself, she didn't know whether to laugh or cry. The bastard had whacked the receiver on her head so hard he'd broken the skin. Lots of blood. Lots and lots of blood, but upon closer examination, not much of a serious cut at all.

"I am going to kill him," she said softly to the pathetic image staring back at her. The thought was calming. Just like before, when she'd decided to kill her stepfather.

Frowning, Denise scrubbed at the blood. Thomas Daniels was dead. He'd died and stayed dead. But she hadn't killed him. She'd planned to. God knew she'd wanted to! But then something happened and she didn't have to.

If only she knew what that something was. Delving into her subconscious, she carefully picked through pieces of memory better left untouched. A bad feeling invaded her every pore.

"Maybe I did kill him," she said aloud.

Maybe that's why it sounded so right to kill Ian.

The man in question sat at the bar downstairs, smoking a cigarette and watching Lina, his maid, move lethargically around the living room, ostensibly dusting and cleaning. He owned her ever since she'd been caught stealing from an uppity friend of his and had been *persona non grata* at the best homes in Beverly Hills.

She'd protested her innocence, of course. The pool boy, Juan Miguel, was responsible. Ian had assured her he believed her, hired her himself, and proceeded to be her best friend and patron. But he knew she stole from him.

She had a young son, Paolo, who lived with his grandparents in Colombia. Lina wanted to save enough money to bring Paolo to Los Angeles. Her husband, a bum who drank all her earnings, wasn't even part of the picture. Lina escaped him by heading to the land of opportunity and living with friends who had an eye on a sizable chunk of her wages as well.

Then the report of her thieving. Enter Ian Wallace, with offers of money and protection.

Yes. He owned her now.

The very first night of her employ, she had worked late. He'd offered her a drink and asked questions about her life in Colombia. She refused the drink, but slowly warmed up. Very slowly. It had taken several months to break down her defenses, but by the time he ran his hands over her sturdy buttocks, she didn't refuse him. She accepted him with quiet stoicism, her black eyes flashing with repressed emotion that both amused and inflamed him.

She didn't protest when his fingers crept up her leg. The first time he mounted her she was bent over, cleaning the marble entryway. The sight of her swaying hips and subservient position did him in. Yanking up her skirt, he pulled down her undergarments with shaking fingers, climaxing so quickly he could hardly get inside her before the deed was done!

A first gasp and she'd said nothing. Ian was in heaven. He liked sex, especially sex where he dominated. When he was eleven years old, a mistress of his wealthy father had turned him on to marijuana and mutual masturbation. He'd wanted sex with her but she'd tormented and teased, refusing him the ultimate act. Was it his fault he'd turned to Heather Newberger?

What a circus. Ian smiled faintly, sipping Courvoisier and reliving those early years. Of course his wealthy, puritanical father had hushed it up. And the Newbergers had made out, make no mistake about that. The cost of Heather Newberger's virginity? Well, it was a helluva lot more than it was worth, by God. She'd screamed and cried and made a real nuisance of herself.

The recriminations! You'd have thought he'd raped Mother Theresa. He'd told them she'd wanted it. He'd been pretty clear on the whole thing, but they didn't hear him. Sent to an all-boys school. Time passed. Boredom. Ian decided women were only on this earth for the pleasure and domination of men. He'd found a friend who believed the same, and the two of them had snuck out of school and met some girls as eager as they were. Then one of them claimed she was pregnant. More hush money.

And so it went until dear old dad flamed out with lung cancer. Mom held the purse strings for a while, but Ian made sure she knew he was the entitled one. He intimidated and threatened and made her life hell until she just gave up one day, signing over everything and melting into the woodwork like the pathetic little worm she was.

Adulthood was less interesting. Too many women who were too willing. No challenge there. Nothing shocking. Nothing to get the old blood pumping, the penis hard and throbbing.

That was the real problem, Ian reflected sourly. His sorry cock just didn't like those eager females with one hand down the front of his pants and another stealing his wallet. He'd had to go in search of tougher fare, and unfortunately, was still paying off that blue-collar jackass who'd caused such a stink in San Diego.

Sweet little Jenny with the red, red lips had been asking for it. Licking that ice cream cone in her polka dot dress, her skinny legs sticking out. Little white socks and shoes. Okay, maybe she was a little young, but she'd been more than willing to take off her clothes for a fiver. Jenny wasn't complaining, nosirree, it was her dad, breathing fire and saying nasty things about calling the police. It had taken more than Jenny's fiver to set matters straight, but in the end it had all worked out.

He'd been damn near bored stiff when he'd happened upon Lina. The last few years had been bliss. No problems at all. Until he looked at Lina one day and didn't like the way her teeth crossed. And her fingers were so stubby.

So, he'd gone in search of more stylish fare. He absolutely detested Carolyn Lenton. Avaricious, unprincipled, and loud, he'd first refused her invitation to decadence in Houston. He wanted something closer to home. But then Carolyn let it slip that Denise Scott Callahan was one of her guests, and Ian had always had a hard-on over her.

Ian had been on the first flight out. More sweet incentive. Denise belonged to John Callahan and Ian knew enough about that bastard to want to give his ex-wife a ride. Callahan was one of those holier-than-thou assholes who looked down on the rest of the world, especially if those others might have some extra money. Not that Callahan hadn't been born with a silver spoon wedged firmly down his throat. Oh, no! Sampson Callahan had provided plenty for his cool, independent son.

So, who was he to act as if he were better? It infuriated Ian the way women reacted to the man, too. Callahan's reputation as a womanizer should have turned them off—

women loved to play those kind of "you can't catch me" games—but instead it attracted them like free money.

But Denise Scott had slipped the leash. She was no longer John Callahan's private pet. And Ian Wallace couldn't wait to give her what she had coming.

It had been so easy. All it took was one moronic jerk-off named Peter, and Denise was putty in Ian's hands. She wanted out. He was her ticket. They left together and the rest was history.

Unlike Lina, however, Denise had some kick to her. He didn't trust her. She was too unstable and remarkably sharp of tongue when she wasn't high. Resorting to drugs annoyed Ian; he'd rather have her clear headed. But she was too unpredictable and this annoying habit of picking up the telephone had to stop.

God, but it was rich! She'd actually called Callahan today!

A shiver of excitement ran through him, remembering the sound of Callahan's furious voice. Maybe he should videotape him and Denise screwing away and send Callahan a copy.

The idea had merit, except Ian knew better than to involve himself. A pity. He would love to cripple John Shithead Callahan.

Maybe he'd go give Denise another taste of the old Wallace charm. He'd kinda lost interest lately, but if he imagined Callahan watching . . .

He heard Lina's heavy footsteps around the corner. Swirling his brandy, Ian listened to her movements. She was going into the dining room.

He was glad he'd thumped Denise with the phone. But that hazy look in her eyes, that disinterest—*that* really pissed him off. He wanted to see some fear, some real emotion. Maybe he'd take her off the drugs and get into a real, rambunctious winner-take-all-fight! She was strong though; he wouldn't get away unblemished.

Was it worth it?

Ian smelled the lemony scent of the oil Lina rubbed into the table. Sliding off the stool, he went to stand in the doorway, watching her as she methodically rubbed and rubbed until the patina was sleek and glossy.

She was aware he was there; he caught the slight, telltale tightening of her body though she tried to hide it. He'd left her alone since Denise's arrival, but right now, his eyes following her every move, he was pleasantly horny.

He'd go after Denise in a minute, but for now, well . . .

Lina wore black slacks and a black blouse. Her breasts were nice and big without being that terrible cowlike shape some men went nuts over. Ian was a connoisseur. He liked them big, but not monstrous sacks. Her hips were a bit too wide but that made them nice and squishy when he grabbed.

He moved in closer. She stopped rubbing. He could hear her breath catch.

"Keep going," he urged.

After a moment's hesitation, she returned to her work. Leaning over her, he grabbed one of those big tits and squeezed. She kept right on rubbing and rubbing.

Moving behind her, he started doing a little rubbing of his own. Closing his eyes, he smiled as he reached around for the zipper of her pants. Good old Lina.

"You like that?" he whispered in her ear, fumbling for his own pants.

She didn't answer. Quiet. Obedient. Lina, the good. Priming him for Denise.

Perfect.

Chapter Twelve

Parked outside Hayley's apartment, Connor dug inside his pocket for the cellophane-wrapped mint he'd received with his fortune cookie at Wu's, the Chinese restaurant where he'd eaten lunch. Munching on the mint, he considered his options. He could contact Denise again. He *should* contact her, if for no other reason than to assure himself that she was still hanging on. He would love to counsel her into leaving Wallace—and maybe he would—even though it was certain to be a waste of energy.

There was also another avenue: Dr. Hayden Stone. Though Carolyn Lenton had explained Dr. Stone was no longer Denise's shrink, it wasn't impossible that Denise had followed after him. Even if she hadn't, Dr. Stone probably knew more about her inner workings than anyone else, and though Connor was perfectly cognizant of the "confidentiality" code between patient and doctor, there were ways to learn things without forcing an actual confession. Some doctors, in fact, could scarcely contain themselves. In Connor's biased opinion, shrinks were a bunch of old gossips who just loved to hear the dirt first.

So, that was next on his list. For now, he wanted to

connect with Hayley again. She was so focused, so cold and driven in her wants. But she wasn't armored with a guard like Ian Wallace, and since Denise hadn't followed through with Dinah's address, Hayley was his best bet.

Swallowing the last bit of the mint, Connor settled back in the seat. Evening shadows cast by the ragged looking palm tree outside Hayley's apartment complex striped the hood of his car. Momentarily he thought about chucking the whole thing and moving to Wagon Wheel. Like his sister, he recognized this search for truth was going to hurt more than help. But damn it, he wanted to *know!*

A dilapidated vintage Chevrolet backfired into the parking lot and Hayley Scott climbed out, not bothering to lock up. Connor watched her slim legs climb the exterior stairs to her apartment. There was something "lost little girl" about her that struck him. Denise was openly wild, mired in emotional turbulence, but Hayley possessed a more sedate, though similar, quality.

He wondered what Dinah would be like.

Climbing from his car, he followed her at a more leisurely pace, losing sight of her before he reached the bottom step. Hayley Scott moved at double-speed, fueled by determination.

At her door, he rapped loudly, faintly amused at the sound of her bird-quick steps. She opened the door to the length of the chain and peered out.

"Well, hello," she said, frowning. "Just in the neighborhood, or are you planning to grill me some more?"

"Maybe a little of both."

"Your honesty's your worst quality," she told him, unlatching the chain.

"No more streetwalking?"

"No." Pure finality. Discussion closed. "I'm just waiting for the bossman to watch my tape," she revealed, unlocking the chain. As Connor entered the apartment, she glanced in disgust at the black VCR tape dumped unceremoniously on the couch. "I took it to him today but things didn't turn out the way I expected."

"He didn't like it?"

"He never saw it." She glanced his way. "It's complicated."

"I've got time."

Hayley shrugged. "So do I. I was late for work, and my old buddy, Jason, fired me."

For some reason that struck Connor as funny. He grinned, surprised at how long it had been since he remembered smiling.

"What's with you?" Hayley asked suspiciously.

"Come on, I'll take you to dinner."

"Who's buying?"

"I am."

"Will you save the psychoanalysis of me and my family until after I eat?"

He lifted three fingers in the traditional Boy Scout's honor.

Heaving a sigh, she capitulated, "All right. But only 'cause I'm broke and starving."

"I won't let it go to my head."

"I mean it. There's nothing else," she said fiercely.

"Your opinion of the male sex is duly noted."

For that he earned a hard glare that oddly made him feel like grinning again.

Scraping up the last forkful of chocolate-almond mousse, Hayley leaned back in the seat with a sigh of contentment. Connor fiddled with his water glass, smearing rings of condensation across the glossy black tabletop of the Immediate Gratification Cafe.

"Maybe I'll get a job here," Hayley said, stretching her arms above her head. "This would be a good place to be fired from."

"What happens if your acting dream doesn't material-ize?"

"Oh, it will. I'll make it happen."

He didn't know whether to be impressed or alarmed at her single-sightedness. "You ready to talk?"

"I don't have anything else I can tell you, but fire away."

"Let's go for a walk."

They headed outside into crowded streets. The cafe was located across from a trendy strip mall and Hayley, though she'd struck out with Callahan and lost her job at Stanbury's, felt positively light-hearted.

She knew what it was—stupid though it might be. Connor Jackley. Being in the company of a man whom she could trust was a totally new experience for Hayley. All he wanted was information. And though it was infor-mation she wasn't prepared to give, it was nice to know where she stood. No grabbing hands, dirty thoughts, wicked suggestions. The man was Mr. Clean with dark hair and good looks—a potent combination if you were the kind of woman who cared—which she, of course, wasn't.

"So, when are you going to start with the third degree again, Jack?"

He shrugged. "I'd like to talk to your sister when she's not under Ian Wallace's influence."

"Oh, Denise split with him already."

"She did?" Connor was surprised.

"Yup. Her ex was waiting for her at their house in Malibu. He told me he'd have her call me."

He looked unconvinced.

"Well, I suppose she could be leading some kind of double life, which, knowing Denise, is a distinct possibility. But Mr. Callahan acted like she'd been there awhile."

"What about your other sister?"

"Dinah?" Hayley shrugged. "Dinah takes care of things. You don't have to worry about her."

"Where is she?"

"I don't have a clue."

"Denise promised to get me in touch with her, but *nada* so far. I thought you could help."

"Sorry."

He shrugged, as if he didn't quite believe her. Oh, sure, she could tell him Dinah was somewhere in New Mexico, writing for some paper, but then he'd just contact her and stir up this hornet's nest even worse.

Better to leave Dinah out of it.

"Tell me about her," he said.

"Dinah?"

They stopped by his car. Connor opened the door, offering her a hand of assistance. Hayley stared at it a moment, shivered slightly, then got in her seat unaided. While he climbed in the other side, she stared out the window.

"I hate thinking back," she admitted cautiously.

"Because of Daniels?"

"Oh . . . yeah." She grimaced. "He made us all so uncomfortable. Particularly Denise. She had this boyfriend and I think the old man was jealous. He yelled at her a lot. She would run off to be with Jimmy and when she'd come back he'd yell and yell and yell!" She shuddered, managing a faint smile. "You get the picture."

"What about Dinah?"

"Dinah was cool." Hayley forced herself to talk. It would be safer if she gave him the history. Much safer coming from her than Dinah or Denise. "Dinah's the smart one. Just a few well placed words and he'd get furious! I used to envy her so much. He hated her."

"Your stepfather," he clarified.

Hayley nodded. "And then that would get Denise going. She'd start in with the sarcasm and he'd bellow and rant and rave. It was kind of funny really." Digging through her purse, she searched furiously for a mint. Where were the damn things anyway? "Damn it!" she muttered, slamming the purse on the floor.

"What about you?"

"What about me, Dr. Freud?" she demanded. "I just wanted it all to stop, okay? And eventually it did."

"What stopped it?"

"We left. We just packed up and got the hell outta Dodge. Dinah insisted I take my high school equivalency and that's the end of that story."

"You all left together."

"Yep, but we split up pretty fast. Dinah had places to go and she connected with Glen Bosworth." She made a face of disgust. "And Denise met a guy who was an actor and then she got a part and things happened for her."

Connor's gray eyes held hers. She didn't like what she read in them. It made her feel funny inside. Scared. "What about you?" he asked softly.

"I've bummed around taking acting classes and waiting for lightning to strike twice. It struck my sister, I figured it could strike me, too."

He didn't respond immediately and Hayley began to feel defensive. "Look, I didn't know he was dead, okay, but believe me, it's no big loss to the world. He was scum."

"Someone murdered him. The investigation isn't going to go away."

"Well, why the hell not?" Hayley demanded. "Can't *somebody* find something more constructive to do than churn up all this crap!" She exhaled in frustration, raking back her hair. She felt itchy and anxious inside, ready to push away from a subject too hot to handle and get back on track with the things that mattered in her life. But Connor Jackley clearly wasn't interested in the Hayley Scott of today. She could prattle on for hours about her hopes and dreams, if he cared to listen, but no, no. All he cared about was the past. Her past. And part of her detested him for it.

"Whoever killed my stepfather probably just couldn't take it anymore. He had a way of turning everything to shit. Denise called it 'The Sadim Touch'—backwards for Midas. I just steered clear of him."

"Did he abuse you?"

"No." The answer came swiftly. "But not for lack of trying," she admitted after a moment.

"What about your sisters?"

"Denise hung out with her boyfriend. Dinah stayed at school. I just stayed away."

Connor pulled the car up to her apartment complex and killed the ignition. Twisting so he could get a better look at her, he placed one arm along the back of the seat. Inside, Hayley shrank away, though she didn't physically move.

"There's been talk that Denise was pregnant when she left Wagon Wheel. Jimmy Fargo, currently of Seattle, said she had an abortion."

Hayley ground her teeth together. Reluctantly, she pushed out the truth. "She lost the baby."

"Miscarriage?" he asked.

"What does it matter?" she demanded, truly pissed. This was too much!

"I think Daniels abused her. I don't know about you and Dinah, but I believe Denise was physically, possibly sexually, abused. If he found out she was pregnant, what would he do? Beat her? Slap her around?"

Hayley flinched at every word. Connor watched, his expression stone, but inside his heart ached for her. Emotions flitted across her face. Emotions she denied, but they were there. Deep under the surface. Only available when he mined them with the picks of shovels of brutal truth.

"I hate this," she said. "I want you to go away and never come back."

"Will you give me Dinah's address?"

"No."

"I can get it from Denise. It'll just take a little more time."

"I don't care what you do."

"Are you protecting her?"

"I thought I liked you," Hayley said icily. "I was wrong." A moment passed. "You're not going to go away, are you?"

"No." After a pause, he added more kindly, "I can't."

Connor's appetite for answers was whetted. He was determined to get to the bottom of this mystery, at any price, though he knew that price would be heavy.

Glancing over at Hayley, he felt a moment of deep regret. In profile, her resemblance to Denise was uncanny. What would Dinah be like? The sister he still hadn't met.

"Goodnight, Jack," Hayley said on a sigh as she climbed from the car. "It's been real, but our association is at an end."

She walked away, less determined than before, less

quick and sure. A different Hayley was emerging. Courtesy of his constant badgering?

He wished he knew if he were helping or hindering, but it really wouldn't matter anyway. He wanted the truth, and in his pursuit, he was willing to pay the highest price.

The newsroom hadn't changed one iota since she'd left. The same zigzag of partitions, the same clutter, the same noise. Dinah stood in the doorway, oddly removed, and wondered if Kate Patton had taken over her desk as well as her column.

She strode to Flick's office, a glass-enclosed adjunct stuck in the corner. But Flick wasn't there, though the half-eaten cigar still smoldering in the trashcan was evidence he wasn't far away.

She let herself inside and settled into one of the uncomfortable chairs near the odiferous, smoking trash can. She felt tired all over, her thoughts so uncomfortable they physically hurt. Her own stupidity had landed her in this predicament and Dinah Scott was not stupid.

At least not normally.

Groaning, she rubbed her face and tried to forget images of John Callahan. Yet every breath she took reminded her of his scent. It seemed to have permeated her own flesh, and though she loathed to admit it, she was well on the way to falling in love with the bastard.

Only he wasn't a bastard. She, Dinah Scott, would not fall in love with someone as self-centered, despicable, and cold as John Callahan had been purported to be. She should have known better than to listen to Denise. When had her sister ever been right about anything?

"Oh, hell," she murmured, as the door flew open and Flick herded his considerable bulk inside.

He didn't so much as bat an eyelash at the sight of his errant reporter. "What do you want?" he growled around his inevitable, smelly cigar as he squeezed behind the desk and plopped into the chair. A shriek rose from the cushions—a last death throe? Apparently not because the chair held, at least for the moment.

"I want my job, a raise, and an extension on my long-distance job situation."

He harrumphed loudly.

"It doesn't hurt you that I'm in California. It just bugs you that you can't look over my shoulder."

"Nice attitude."

"I learned from the master," Dinah responded sweetly.

"You get nothing. You bailed out, and I don't need the grief."

Dinah knew he was bluffing. She was secure about her work, and she was syndicated by enough papers to have a career with or without the *Santa Fe Review*. "Are you making me move to Los Angeles permanently?"

That earned her an eyebrow twitch. "What the hell's that supposed to mean?"

"I'm getting acclimated. A little more smog. A little more traffic." She shrugged her acceptance. "A few more natural disasters, but it's a huge area. I've talked to several local papers and even the *Times*. I'm not an unknown, Flick."

This was a bold lie. Okay, she was syndicated, sort of. But the papers that picked her up weren't exactly the most well known.

Flick stared at her, scrunched up his face, then slid his cigar thoughtfully from one side of his mouth to the other. He puffed, filling the room with blue smoke and foul odor. "Nobody knows you."

"We could argue all week. Do I or don't I have a job?"

"You have a job if you stick around. No raise."

"I've got unfinished business in L.A."

"Shit." He scowled.

"I should be back for good in a couple of weeks."

They stared at each other for long moments. Flick finally broke the silence. "What's the matter with you?"

Dinah reacted. "What do you mean?"

"You're different. Less bitchy. Kind of distracted."

"Thank you so much."

The faintest smile glimmered in his eyes. Pulling the wet cigar from his mouth, he smashed the end in the nearest ashtray, then flicked the ugly remainder at the trashcan. It hit the rim and flopped onto the floor.

It was the first time Dinah had ever seen him miss.

Scowling, he muttered, "Two weeks! After that, forget showing your face around here ever again."

"You're a peach." Dinah grinned, then beat a hasty retreat before he could change his mind.

She was halfway out the door when she remembered her glasses. Hurrying to her desk, she encountered a young—very young—woman with a pinched mouth and a surly stare.

"Kate Patton?" Dinah asked.

"Who're you?"

"You're at my desk," Dinah told her, proprietarily yanking open the drawer and rummaging around until she found her glasses. "It's a temporary assignment, so don't screw anything up."

"Yeah, yeah, yeah." She yawned and walked toward the coffee machine. "Like anybody cares about this shitty newspaper."

Infuriated, Dinah bit back a sharp retort. *She* cared. This job meant a lot to her, and it really ticked her off that someone as young and inexperienced as Kate could get away with that kind of attitude. Flick would have a fit!

Instantly Dinah's mood improved. Another couple weeks, maybe a month, Kate would be history anyway. Hah! Two weeks, Flick had allowed her? Screw that. Dinah was safe until spring.

Well, at least her job was safe. Her heart—that was another matter.

The Fiat sat waiting patiently at LAX. Dinah paid the parking fee, offered up a prayer that the new clanging beneath the hood was something minor, then eased into traffic.

Driving was a disaster. A huge pile-up with blaring horns and a carnival of flashing red and blue lights added an hour to her trip home. Nevertheless, her heart was light.

Fool, she warned herself. But her careless heart refused to listen. She didn't know whether John would be home or not, but the anticipation was a powerful elixir.

Her breath caught when she saw the gates were open. He was there. Waiting. Unless of course the house had been burglarized again.

But no. The Jeep was parked in the driveway.

Be casual. No big deal. Act naturally.

As if gasping out its last breath, the Fiat died in the drive. Dinah coasted to a stop, yanked on the brake, then sat for a few moments inside the car, her fingers wrapped around the steering wheel, her pulse in overdrive.

She was an idiot, a helpless teenager, a reckless lovesick patsy. But she couldn't help it! Her whole being had been taken over by emotion, and her normally cool head, her most constant ally, had gone on vacation.

Yep. She was in serious trouble.

She walked quickly up the brick path to the doorway, her fingers clasping the door handle, her heart feeling like it would jump out of her chest. She had to press a hand to her breasts, then laughed shakily at the notion. God! She was nuts!

Inside, the house was quiet. She stood in the entryway, breathing shallowly. "John?" she called tentatively, hating the uncertain quality of her voice.

Her actions were so well scripted she could have been the star of a Denise Scott film. Life imitating art.

But he wasn't anywhere around. At least he didn't answer when she called. The Jeep was a mystery, but it wasn't impossible that he'd left with someone else.

Another woman?

Her heart leaped. She was instantly furious with herself. God! What a mind! Of all the things to think of.

"Don't be such an insecure idiot," she berated herself. He was probably with someone from his production company, or the studio, or *anybody!* The man had a job. A demanding career, as a matter of fact. And pre-production of *Lady Paradise* was behind schedule, shifting the whole thing forward and costing oodles of money. She knew that much.

Her pulse slowly recovering, she tossed her bag on the tile floor and walked toward John's office, determined to think positively and not be such a dope. Weariness invaded every pore. This double life was killing her. Something had to give and soon.

Lifting her arms, she closed her eyes and stretched, willing herself to relax. Time to forget everything. Time to unwind. Time for a hot shower and bed.

And maybe John?

Embarrassed, she muttered obscenities directed solely

at herself, opened her eyes and gasped. John Callahan himself stood in the doorway of the office, holding Bobo in his arms.

"Hi!" Dinah gulped on a squeak. "I—I didn't know you were here. Didn't you hear me call? God, you scared me . . ." Her voice trailed into oblivion at the look on his face. Iron fury locked his jaw and turned his blue eyes to narrow angry beams. Bobo squirmed, squeaked, and wriggled from his arms.

Dinah watched the kitten scurry away, then glanced back fearfully at John. "What? What is it?"

"Get out of my house."

The words were quiet, but each syllable was a hammer. Dinah flinched, her eyes round with confusion. "What?" she asked dazedly.

"You don't remember the telephone call?"

She slowly shook her head, a bad feeling stealing over her.

"Well, I'm not surprised. I'm not even going to ask how, why, or who. Just get the hell out of my life. I'm not your enabler anymore."

She could only stand there, shaking her head. Everything seemed to stop.

Denise had called, she realized.

No, no, no!

"I don't want to see you anymore," he uttered, slowly, as if she might have trouble hearing. And she *was* having trouble. Lights danced inside her head. So many things could have been said to him. So many terrible things.

It's not your problem. It's not you!

But I love him!

Guilt gnawed at her stomach, burned her cheeks. She glanced away, mortified. *You have to tell him the truth.*

"You are the weakest, most sorry excuse for a human

being I've ever met." Anger burned in his voice, but there was something else, too. Regret. Maybe hurt. Dinah's head throbbed. She ached—ached with a pain so huge she wanted to die.

"Get your adulterous ass off my property and out of my life."

She caught the faint smell of scotch. He'd been drinking. Dinah knew there was no way to talk to him. What in God's name would she say anyway? But she couldn't stop herself from trying. "It's not what you think."

How pathetic.

He actually laughed, the painful sound reverberating throughout the room.

"I need to talk to you . . . when you're sober."

"I will never be sober for you again," he said, shaking his head.

"John, listen, I've been trying to keep my life together even though it's out of control. You don't understand. You can't understand." The words sprang out, faster and faster. "I was working. I wasn't with anyone. I—"

Another burst of explosive laughter. He began pushing her toward the front door. There wasn't a lot she could do to stop him, but she tried every trick. At the hall aperture she dug her fingers into the molding and hung on for dear life.

John pushed inexorably forward. Dinah's temper rose in response. "Don't try to throw me out!"

"Watch me."

"I let you toss me onto the beach. I'm not letting you now!"

"Let me?" His hand came over hers, clawing at her fingers. Dinah struggled in earnest. John yanked one arm free and pinned it behind her back. She wrapped a leg around his knee and jerked hard. He swayed but didn't fall, then pulled on her arm again, wrenching it. Dinah gasped in pain.

"You son of a bitch!" she bit out.

"Now there's the Denise we all know and love."

She wanted to hit and kick and gouge. Surprised by her own passion, Dinah settled for an icy glare that didn't do jack shit where His Highness, John Callahan stood. "You're just like all the rest!" she accused acidly.

Blue eyes raked her with disgust. *Disgust.* That was it. That was the emotion. Angry words started to fill her head.

You silly, high-falutin' bitch. Think your shit doesn't smell? C'mere. C'mere . . .

She'd stayed where she was, balanced on the balls of her feet like a fighter. If Thomas Daniels so much as feinted in her direction, she'd go straight for his balls. One swift kick.

He'd sneered: superior, cruel, his lip curling with disgust. Disgust that she was a woman and therefore weak. Weak in strength, weak in spirit. Like he was such an icon of respectability and moral fiber.

He'd never touched her. Never hurt her. But it wasn't for lack of trying. Oh, no. It wasn't for lack of trying.

"You can't make me do something I don't want to do," she warned John Callahan.

For an answer he grabbed her arms and swung her over his shoulders in a fireman's carry, his favorite mode of transportation. This time she didn't kick and pound. She waited, counting the footsteps, eyes bouncing with each step until she heard him open the front door. With one easy move, he dropped her on her feet.

And she hauled back and slapped his arrogant, smug, too handsome face.

"Come back and I'll call the police," he snarled, the mark on his face changing from white to a livid red.

"I'm going to make your life a living hell!"

"You already have. I hope the bastard was worth it."

"You don't know anything about me!"

"You're a lying, conniving, sick piece of meat."

Dinah's breath caught. She was so enraged she was shaking. Her lips quivered and tears flashed in the corners of her eyes.

He lifted his hands. "Oh, no. I've played that game before. You want to get laid, go find somebody else. I know how you like it. Hard, fast, mean. Total domination. Well, here's a newsflash. It turns my stomach."

Words failed her. He was a thousand times worse than Denise had said. A million!

"I don't know how this ever happened," he added flatly. "I'm sick of you and your problems."

"Yeah?" Dinah finally discovered her voice. "You're not exactly the model of morality and restraint!"

"I've been too damn good. A fact I'm going to rectify right now."

He disappeared back in the house. Dinah marched after him, spoiling for a fight. He grabbed a lightweight jacket from the back of a kitchen chair and headed for the garage. "Where are you going?" she demanded.

"*I'm* going to get laid," he announced grandly as he pushed the button for the garage door and staggered through the empty room and outdoors to the Jeep.

"You'll get pulled over for drunk driving," she yelled, following after him.

"Too damn bad!"

"I'm calling the police. I'll give them your license number. I'll make sure they pick you up!"

"What the hell do you want?" he roared, dropping the keys in his fury. They fell to the cement drive and bounced into the surrounding lawn.

She glared at him, fists clenched. He glared right back, so undeniably handsome that something uncoiled inside Dinah. Something rich and dangerous and totally wanton. It must have shown on her face because he sensed it. His eyes narrowed, but he shook his head. Muttering obscenities beneath his breath, he bent down for the keys.

Then he was upright again, his gaze hot and electric. "Go away, Denise. Just . . . go away."

He swayed. She moved forward instinctively. His gaze dropped to the swing of her hips and he groaned like a condemned man.

"I think I hate you," she told him through her teeth.

His answer was to drag her close, smash his lips on hers, mold her body to his own hard contours, his own inflamed senses pushing hers sky high, until she clutched at him like a love slave.

Then his lips were all over her neck. His hands swarming her body; her own traveling over him just as eagerly. They fell to the grass as one, writhing and touching and gasping for air.

Dinah had no control over the person he brought out in her, but common sense wasn't completely lost. They were outside, and anyone who chose to drive through the open gates would find them in a tangle of arms and legs, as horny and oblivious as mongrel dogs!

"Oh, God, John! This is crazy!" Dinah shivered, half-ecstacy, half-humiliation.

His fingers dug at the band of her denim skirt, pulling it over slim hips, revealing french cut white panties and long, shapely tanned thighs. He groaned, burying his face low against her in a move that shocked Dinah to her ultimate core.

"Stop!" she cried, genuinely scared. With more strength than she would have credited herself, she suddenly flung John away from her, jumped to her feet and ran for the house.

Inside, she glanced this way and that, feral and panicked. A bell chimed and she shrieked aloud until she slowly realized it was the grandfather clock in the living room.

What's the matter with me?

She heard John behind her. He staggered into the entryway, leaned against the wall, and stared at her, raking a hand through his hair.

"You're so screwed-up, there's no hope," he told her, adding, "And so am I.

"Now get out," he ordered as he continued on his journey to the kitchen where she heard him pouring himself another drink.

"John . . ."

"GET OUT!"

She ran for the door, remembered her dead Fiat, and veered off for the kitchen telephone to call a cab.

Bastard. Asshole. Damn male.

She wished she could really hate him.

Chapter Thirteen

Callahan's production offices were bare-bones in the opulence department. Industrial grade carpet, scrupulously clean, fake leather chairs with chrome arms, a smattering of desks and lamps in the reception area. If Hayley didn't know Hollywood, she might have been concerned, but one of the few items she'd learned over her years here was that pricey exteriors didn't necessarily mean a damn thing.

The receptionist lifted one haughty brow. "Yes?"

"I'm a friend of Tonja Terkell's," Hayley alerted her, her tone matching that discriminating eyebrow.

Without another word, the receptionist turned to the blinking lights on the telephone, pressed a button, and called Tonja over an intercom. She received no response and therefore simply pretended Hayley wasn't standing in front of her.

Hayley remained on her feet. Backbone. She had plenty of it. More than most people possessed. She wanted this part and she was determined to get it—or damn near die trying.

What had come over her at Callahan's house? Thinking back, she shook her head in wonderment. It was as if she'd fallen under some secret spell which John Callahan had spun. A few words about Denise, a step inside her own past, and Hayley had been out of there. Zippo.

Now, she couldn't believe it. For years she'd been traveling with the speed and determination of a freight train toward her destination: stardom. And then she'd been derailed so easily—and the station had been within view! She didn't understand how it could happen. It was like stepping into a nightmare and finding you couldn't move your feet because they were planted in some thick, gooey substance that held you down.

She'd let Jason fire her, gone home in a daze, and run smack into Connor Jackley who was waiting with relentless questions she couldn't answer.

And later, after he'd left, she'd been restless and disturbed, her sleep fitful and haunted by images she faintly recognized from her own past. Some real, some imagined, she felt burned by the heat of some evil core within her, a place Connor kept urging her to visit.

Well, she simply wasn't going to. After waking from a miserable night, head aching and soul anxious, she determined she was not going to think about Connor Jackley or her sisters or her past in Wagon Wheel. She was going to focus on her ambition.

So, here she was, raring to go. Except this damn blockade of disinterest had been thrown up in front of her.

"Is Tonja in?" she demanded of the receptionist.

"She's not answering."

"Would you mind trying again?"

This time both brows lifted and the woman went mum. Ice cold. The big freeze.

"She left this at my place," Hayley explained, pulling out her audition tape. "I called her and told her I'd bring it to her."

"Leave it on the desk, I'll make sure—"

"Sorry. I deliver this one myself."

A poison look. Hayley glanced toward the hall and debated making a run for it. Sure, the woman would call security, but at least she'd have some time before she was booted out. She knew Callahan was here; she'd seen his Jeep. If she could just get to him, she'd be home free.

And then opportunity knocked: Mr. Producer himself strode from the inner offices on his way out and brushed within inches of Hayley. The receptionist straightened as if someone had shoved a rod up her back and Hayley threw on her best smile and said, "Hello, again."

The look he gave her nearly singed off her skin. Phew! The man was furious. At her? No way. But a niggling memory invaded her mind, and remembering a similar look on her stepfather's face, Hayley shrank back.

For a moment she thought Callahan would shoot right past without a word, but he stopped short and turned her way. She had the impression he was holding in some very nasty emotions with a very manly effort.

"You want to see me?" he clipped out.

"Well . . . um . . . yeah."

"Then, come on. I've got half an hour before my next meeting."

Hayley didn't need to be asked twice. She jumped forward as the receptionist gasped in annoyance and frustration. Hah! Score one for the good guys! She had her chance now and she wasn't going to blow it again.

At his Jeep Callahan ordered, "Climb in, talk fast, and don't lie. I'm not in the best of moods, so you've got twenty minutes to convince me you're not some conniving lookalike." He swiveled her way, pinning her with steely blue eyes. "And for the record, I detest my ex-wife, so don't count on any favors."

As a test, it was one of the most grueling of her life. Hayley was many things, but a revealer of truths wasn't one of them. But that, it turned out, was all Callahan wanted. Truths. Hurtful, soul-delving truths.

"Did you ask Denise about me?" she questioned once they were underway.

"Nope."

"Why not?"

"Didn't get a chance." His words were bitten off, as if they tasted bad. Whatever had happened between him and Denise was something she probably didn't want to know. "So, go on," he commanded. "Tell me all about yourself and your sister."

The worst possible subject, but the only one anyone cared to listen to. Why couldn't *someone* talk about *something* else? "I'd rather hear about *Lady Paradise,*" she said as the freeway zipped past.

The sideways slant of his eyes in her direction eloquently spoke his feelings on that matter. He believed she was lying. Lying in order to weasel her way into his film.

Well, hell. She *did* want a part. But she could see the only way to get one was to tell the unvarnished truth.

Swallowing her misgivings, she launched into her tale. "Denise is older than I am, by two years. We kind of moved all over as kids. I never knew my father and when I was about eleven, my mother remarried."

He didn't respond, didn't take his eyes off the road.

Hesitantly, Hayley continued, "We moved to a little town in central Oregon called Wagon Wheel."

"This doesn't match any of the fables Denise told me."

"Well, it's the truth."

"Go on."

It was time to bring up Dinah. Hayley had purposely left out mention of Denise's twin because hey, the guy didn't believe her already. This latest soap opera device would only gum up the works. And besides, it wasn't pertinent.

She decided to save that information for the moment.

"We lived together until my mother died and then we tried to stay with my stepfather but it didn't work, so Denise left and I followed her. We bummed around L.A. awhile and kind of split up."

Hayley swallowed, remembering. It had been too difficult staying together. Denise had split with her boyfriend and was going through some really weird stuff. Crying all night. Nightmares that scared the liver out of Hayley. Dinah had been there too, and she would shake Denise awake and demand that she "get a grip!" They all relied on Dinah—until Denise found another guy, a good-looking Hollywood hustler, who introduced her to a life that looked beautiful and good and like everything she'd ever wanted.

Dinah wouldn't let Hayley follow, but after Denise flitted off, Dinah had found Glen Bosworth. When she moved in with Glen, Hayley left. More bad choices. Now, years later, Hayley had taken acting classes until she knew more than the combined knowledge of all her instructors, Denise was—well—unstable as ever, and Dinah had run off to "Somewhere in the Great Southwest" after leaving Glen.

Hayley gave Callahan an abbreviated account—sans Dinah—and then wondered if the time was right to get back to *Lady Paradise*.

"Denise never even intimated she had a sister," Callahan said coolly.

Apparently, the time wasn't right yet. With a sigh, Hayley asked, "What did she tell you?"

"Lots of things. The Indiana story was first. Then there was talk of a love gone wrong and a baby."

Hayley stared. "She said she'd had a baby?"

"No . . . a pregnancy," he corrected himself. "The tabloids were on some hot story about her and some guy she went to school with. The guy said they'd had a relationship and she was pregnant. I questioned Denise. First she said it was a pack of lies, then she kind of waffled and finally admitted she'd had a pregnancy scare. Then she said she'd miscarried." He snorted. "I stopped caring what the truth was after awhile." Inhaling through his teeth, he added dryly, "And now you want me to believe you're her sister."

"If you'd just ask her, she'd tell you."

"Would she?" Irony deepened the lines beside his mouth.

Hayley managed a faint smile, realizing she honestly didn't know.

She found herself comparing him to Connor. As handsome as he was, Callahan couldn't quite match that smoldering something that Connor Jackley possessed. At least not for her. Callahan was direct and tough and moved with that slow-walkin', slow-talkin' way that drove women crazy. But Hayley was more seduced by Connor Jackley's laconic comments and quiet intensity.

She shivered involuntarily. But you couldn't trust men. Not any of them. "You might have to apply some pressure, but she'd tell you the truth eventually."

"Denise isn't good with the truth." His hands tightened on the wheel, and his jaw muscles tautened reflexively. Hayley realized he was under some severe emotion where Denise was concerned. So, what else was new?

"She's so screwed up, she'll never be right," he went on, as if she'd asked. "I don't give a damn about her childhood. It's too popular these days to blame everything on events from your past. Lots of people have been abused."

His callousness scraped her nerves like fingernails on a blackboard. "I hate thinking about Thomas Daniels," she admitted tautly.

That got a look from him. His brows drew together and she thought he was going to ask her something else, but he changed his mind.

And then they were at their destination. Titan Studios.

"What are we doing here?" she demanded, nearly jumping from her skin.

"I've got a meeting with the head of the studio, Rodney Walburn."

Jabba? The color emptied from Hayley's cheeks. *Oh, God, no!*

"I can call you a cab. This might take awhile." He smiled as the guard waved him through the gates. "Sorry I didn't tell you. I wasn't really in the mood."

Hayley's pulse jumped erratically. She was inside the studio lot! "No, I'll wait." She was safe unless Jabba decided to leave his air-conditioned environs to walk John to his car. No chance of that . . . was there?

Thirty minutes later she got her answer. Jabba himself waddled John back to the Jeep. Alarmed, Hayley glanced around frantically wondering where to hide. If he recognized her from his private party . . .

Oh, shit!

John introduced them. "Hayley Scott, Rodney Walburn."

Jabba managed to pull his lips into a smile. His hair was as neatly gelled as before. Hayley inwardly shuddered as she shook his hand. Her own was ice cold.

His mean, little eyes swept over her. "You remind me of someone."

Hayley gazed at him with wide-eyed innocence. Time to act, and give an award-winning performance. Her heart hammered. "Oh?"

John snorted. "She looks like Denise," he clipped out.

"Oh, yes." He glanced past her, back to John. Hayley's slamming heart slowed down. "Good to be working together, John," he said. "I like the deal. Fuck, it's the best in town! You know it, I know it. You're such a son-of-a-bitch you don't deserve it!" he laughed with forced heartiness. "Any other problems you've got, bring 'em to me. I'll take care of them for you, you know that. Who've you got for the lead? You know who comes to mind, don't you?"

"Denise," John offered flatly.

"Yeah, she's a fuckin' bitch, but you know she's big box office. I don't have to tell you."

His language hadn't improved much, Hayley silently observed. She hated offensive men. Positively hated them.

Callahan responded with a terse goodbye as he climbed in the driver's seat of the Jeep. If she'd thought he looked severe before, she hadn't known what the word meant. He didn't bother to wave as he tore out of the lot.

"Nice guy," she observed.

"I got what I wanted."

"Really? How do you look when you lose?"

"I don't lose," he told her flatly. "Not to Titan."

With that they wheeled out of the lot and headed back to his production offices. "What is it exactly that you want?" he asked her.

Time for the big plunge. "A part in *Lady Paradise*."

"Uh huh." He was surprised only by her candor, not her request. "And if I don't give you one?"

"What do you mean?"

"You tell me a tale about being Denise's sister, then you ask for a part. Which tabloid will you call first and what wild story can I expect to see if I don't take you seriously?"

"You think I'd blackmail you for a part?"

"Yep."

"All I want you to do is look at this tape." Feeling deflated, she pulled the audition video from her purse.

"I have a casting director," he replied.

"Then, give it to them," Hayley said with a return of spunk. "I'm good at what I do. Damn good. All I want is a chance, whether you believe I'm Denise's sister or not."

They pulled to a screeching halt in front of his production offices. John sighed and shot a glance at the determined young beauty in the seat opposite him. She could be Denise's sister; they certainly looked enough alike, but hell, with enough plastic surgery, everyone in Hollywood was a clone.

He accepted the tape from her outstretched hand with a certain weariness. The lengths people went to never ceased to amaze him. One guy had parachuted into a special preproduction party for *Cosmo* wearing a pair of suspenders, green Speedo trunks, and army boots, and singing *WHAT THE WORLD NEEDS NOW IS LOVE*. He'd tossed an audition tape John's way as he was led out by security.

He had balls, but no talent. John expected more of the same here.

"This might have worked better for you if I were fonder of my ex-wife."

"Don't judge me before you've looked," she replied. Sketching a wave, she departed to a dilapidated Chevy which wheezed and backfired its way out of the lot.

John watched her moodily, his mind already twisting to more painful thoughts. Denise. He'd pushed her out of the house and she'd left in a fine rage that had pinkened her skin and turned her aquamarine eyes to glittering gems of repressed fury. He'd then drunk himself into a stupor, paid the price by suffering mightily the next day with a queasy stomach and trembling hands, growled at the sympathetic gofers at his office, then done his damnedest to forget.

One look at this Hayley person, however, and he was done for. Snap decision. Invite her along. Pump her for information.

What information? *What?* He knew too damn much about Denise already and he didn't believe for a minute that this lookalike was really related to her. No. It had been grasping at straws. The wispiest, most fluttery, unattainable straws. This is what he'd been reduced to, just because she'd gotten under his skin, made him believe she'd changed, then sunk right back to her old habits so quickly and thoroughly that he'd felt like she'd ripped out his insides and left a hollow shell.

Well, the hell with her. And the hell with this Hayley, too.

Striding down the hall to his office, he tossed the videotape in the direction of one of his assistants.

"What's this?" she asked.

"An audition tape."

"What do you want me to do with it?"

"Send it to casting."

"Is it someone you recommend?" she yelled after him as he crossed the threshold to his office.

John didn't bother answering. Slamming the door, he slumped down in his chair, mentally swore at himself for being such a fool for love, then picked up the phone and called Frank Carello, *Lady Paradise's* director.

"Dr. Stone's unavailable at the moment. If you leave your name and number he'll call you back."

The receptionist's voice was bored and disinterested. Dinah considered, then decided against leaving any information. It would be simpler just to see the good doctor, maybe catch him off-guard. He could lead her to Denise faster than anyone, were he so inclined. Failing that, she'd have to hire a private investigator because Ian Wallace of Beverly Hills was a well-kept secret which Dinah Scott couldn't solve unless she gave away her identity—and that she wasn't willing to do.

She exhaled wearily. If only Denise had called again while she was still at the Malibu house. She could have caught the phone number on her scanner. But no, she—Dinah—had been summarily tossed out and now she was staying at this modest-rate hotel, about the only thing she could afford, and wondering what the hell to do first.

Bobo mewed and jumped from the edge of the bed, trotting her way and rubbing his head against her leg. Absently, Dinah bent over to pet him. Her one reminder of life with His Highness.

So, what next?

Doodling on the hotel notepad, Dinah circled and recircled Dr. Hayden Stone's name and office address. There were several doctors named Stone, three of them psychiatrists. Dinah wasn't really sure which one was the doctor Carolyn Lenton had referred to, but she had no intention of calling back and asking her. Carolyn would know she wasn't Denise, and Dinah was unwilling to subject Denise to the public scrutiny that would follow the revelation that she had a secret twin sister. Too many questions would follow. Too many threads to the past.

That could all come later. Or better yet, not at all.

From the notepad, Dinah's gaze switched to the rented portable computer where the text from her latest column, "The Myth of Sexual Freedom," glimmered in silvery waves at her. Its message: beware of letting emotion rule common sense and risking pregnancy or infection from a serious sexually transmitted disease. Its subtext: it can happen to anyone, even the most highly educated and motivated, if you let yourself believe the fantasy, even for a second.

Her own mistake lay heavy on her heart. Yet, foolishly, but with painful reality, another part of herself didn't care. *Didn't care!* Because it was John Callahan and she loved him. The stupidest reason of all. Truly high school. Truly fatalistic. A modern day *Romeo and Juliet* mentality which was the scourge of truth.

What we do for love, she berated herself, angry and shocked. She was smart. She was cool. *She* was in control!

"Oh, God . . ."

She knew, with dreadful certainty, that she would sleep with him again. That even though she'd be more cautious, if given the choice of risking her health or giving him up, she would choose risking her health. If she knew for certain he were HIV infected, she would still *want* to sleep with him, but she hoped she possessed the intelligence not to.

But she didn't know!

The recognition of her own lovesick craziness robbed her of strength. If this was how *she* felt, what hope was there for those millions of starry-eyed romantics who turned themselves over to their lovers, body and soul?

So, what answer was there?

No answer. Not when an individual was in the throes of love and lust. Protection. Cautionary advice. Counsel. And the hope that those at risk would listen.

This week's column was less frivolous. It held a real message. *Know thyself. Know thy own weaknesses.*

Well, she was getting a damn good look at herself and she didn't like what she saw.

But for her, Dinah Scott, it was a moot point. John had thrown her out. Correction: *Denise* out. And that was the end of that. Now, she had to pick up the pieces and sort out what she wanted. No easy task.

So, on to Dr. Hayden Stone and the rest of the shrinks and finding Denise. In fact, the need to see her sister was an itch inside her, an irritating need that she'd never felt before. When they'd fled Wagon Wheel, it was tacitly understood they would all split up and forge separate lives. Dinah had reinforced the notion, though pushing Hayley out of the nest so early hadn't set well. But then Hayley hadn't handled Dinah's relationship with Glen well (her younger sister was smarter than she'd ever credited), and she'd left when Dinah moved in with him.

Now it was time to get together again. At least it was for Dinah.

Damage control. If they didn't get their stories straight, who knew what could happen?

So thinking, she grabbed the list of addresses for the erstwhile shrinks named Stone of greater Los Angeles. She would start with the closest and work her way out.

Maybe her next column would be: "How to Introduce Yourself to a Man with Credentials."

Or, better yet, "Stalking the Big Bucks via a Man with a Medical Degree."

It was sad how many women readers lived for that advice.

But maybe it was safer than chasing after love.

"Take that doughnut out of your mouth and pay attention, Gus," Connor drawled, listening to the sheriff munch away on the other end of the line.

"It's carrots. The wife's got me on a diet."

"Yeah, right. More like carrot cake."

"No, seriously. She's worried I'm working too hard. We're on this friggin' campaign to lose weight and she means it. The woman's downright nasty when she wants to be."

Gus? Working too hard? Connor pictured his cozy little, slightly rundown environs and decided right then and there that he was quitting L.A. and the whole stinking ratrace and moving back to Oregon. With his L.A.P.D. credentials, he ought to be able to find something in a snap. And if not, who cared? He'd grown up ranching; he'd go back to it if law enforcement fell through.

"So, how's the Daniels' investigation going up there?" Connor asked dutifully.

Gus chewed noisily. "Truth?"

Connor grunted his assent.

"Let me tell you what's been happenin' since you left. I got some boys here who played tag with a .22. One blew his friend dead away by mistake. Families devastated all around. And then we caught ourselves a little drug lab workin' overtime last week with some kids from good families. And there's the usual Saturday night brawls from weekend cowboys. And I got me a principal accused of gay relations."

"So, nobody gives a rat's ass about Thomas Daniels," Connor concluded.

"Not much, they don't," Gus admitted. "But the investigation's still open, and I'd kinda like to know, wouldn't you?"

Connor thought about Hayley Scott's blue eyes, the determined thrust of her chin, and the overall sense of needing and wanting she emoted without being aware of it.

"I'll keep checking."

"No hurry," said Gus.

Connor grimaced as he hung up. *No hurry?* Then why did he feel like he was sitting on a time bomb?

"You sure as hell've got balls," Jason snarled, looking superior behind Stanbury's counter, as if he were King of the New World.

"I need a job. I'll be better. I promise I'll be to work on time," Hayley told him.

"Bullshit."

"God's honest truth."

She pleaded silently. Why she'd stooped to coming back to Jason was a bit of a mystery, but after interviewing at several other places, and having one man, if you could believe it, ask her if she'd ever considered another profession, his hand drifting down her arm as he leered, Hayley wondered if her street time might not be catching up with her. The guy sure as hell didn't mean an acting job. And he *did* look a little familiar.

So, back to Jason. Better the devil you know than the devil you don't.

"Make yourself useful," he muttered harshly, showing

a rare side of compassion. He'd been mad enough to commit murder when he'd fired her.

She hid a smile as she accepted a Stanbury's black apron. Jason, the bastard, was one of the few men she actually trusted! A sad, sad state of affairs.

At break, she wandered to the phone on Jason's desk and placed a call without asking. He caught her, snatched the receiver from her hand, and proceeded to tongue-lash her so thoroughly she almost quit on the spot.

"Excuse me for having another life," she told him tartly.

"Who're you calling?"

"None of your business!"

"Still gonna be a famous actress?" he taunted.

Hayley narrowed her eyes and glared furiously. No one messed with her dream. No one.

The truth was she'd called Callahan Productions and was lucky enough to get Tonja on the line. Her old buddy was starting to irritate her, however, because Tonja, now that she sensed her job was secure, had pretty much decided to dump Hayley.

But Hayley needed her. "I'll buy you lunch," she'd promised Tonja who'd tried a dozen ways to say no before finally caving in.

Of course, now Hayley had to leave Stanbury's in the middle of her shift.

Pressing fingers to a spot above her left eye, she moaned, "I'm going to have to get this sinus infection taken care of before it puts me in a coffin."

Jason snorted. "You've worked exactly four hours. A record for you, I believe."

"Don't exaggerate, Jason."

"Leave now, and leave for good."

"I'm taking a lunch break," Hayley told him. "I'll be back even if I feel near collapse, because that's the kind of employee I am."

Expelling a sound of pure disgust, he stomped off.

"I'll be back even if I get run over by a truck!" she added for good measure.

It wasn't any fun unless you pushed the bastard to the limit.

Tonja was waiting outside the building, looking pissed. She swung into Hayley's Rent-A-Wreck, the corners of her mouth bending down further, a nearly impossible task given how high her nose was pointed skyward.

"I really hate being pressured," she whined as they drove to a tiny restaurant that was big into chicken avocado burgers and sprouts. True Californian fare, though Hayley, raised in central Oregon, still believed in beef.

It was time for some home truths. "Tonja, who gave you the courage to get a job with Callahan Productions?"

"What do you mean?" She squirmed.

"I told you about Callahan, about my plans, about everything. Now you want to shut me out."

"You think I owe you something?" she screeched, overly incensed. Bad acting, Hayley thought. No wonder Tonja had chosen the production side.

"You didn't give him the audition tape. I had to do it myself."

"*You* gave him the tape?" Her eyes were huge circles.

"Mmmhmmm. Now, all you gotta do is make sure he views it. Do you think you can do that?"

Hayley chased lettuce around on her plate with a fork, eyeing Tonja. She didn't expect to have friends. Friends cost too much thought and energy, and then they stabbed you in the back anyway. You could only rely on yourself. Period.

But she did expect payback. And Hayley had felt sorry for Tonja when she'd met the down-on-her-luck screen-writer-cum-waitress who'd been turned down by Jason when she'd applied for a job at Stanbury's. So Hayley had wheedled and cajoled until Tonja was finally hired, then Hayley had pointed her in the direction of Callahan Productions and Tonja had been overjoyed when she'd gotten her first lowlier-than-low position.

All she had to do now was help Hayley a bit. Give a little push. But wouldn't you know that now, Tonja wasn't willing to stick her neck out.

But Tonja didn't know Hayley's connection to John Callahan.

"Okay, okay," Tonja muttered, uncomfortable under Hayley's hard stare. "I got you the script, didn't I? I can ask him if he's watched the video, but that's it. I can't force him!"

"I just want to know where I stand, that's all. If he doesn't like what he sees, he won't test me."

"I'll see what I can do," Tonja promised, succumbing to Hayley's will. Sometimes Hayley Scott made her really nervous.

Hayley dropped her off, feeling better than she had in weeks. Finally, everything was going according to plan. She knew that if Callahan would just take a look, he'd see she was the right person for the role of Toni, girl-next-door turned willing prostitute.

Back at Stanbury's, she worked like a dog for Jason who pretended he didn't notice. By the time she headed back to her apartment, secure in the knowledge that she would be able to at least pay her rent, she was so tired all she could think about was her leaky shower and collapsing on the living room couch.

Unlocking the stubborn front door, she suddenly felt eyes following her. Fighting a gasp she whipped around and there, in the shadows at the far end of the balcony, a man's shadow and steady footsteps.

Hayley pressed back in the doorway, heart slamming. The sound echoed, pounding at her skull. Fear shot through her, needle-sharp.

He came straight toward her like she knew he would. "Hayley?" Connor Jackley asked, stopping short.

Her legs turned to water. She crumpled in an ignominous heap.

He was there. Hand on her shoulder. Heat radiating from his nearness. "What happened?" he demanded, all cop.

She wanted to laugh. It was ridiculous! "You scared the liver out of me, you sneaky louse!" she accused sharply, finding her voice.

"Did someone hurt you?"

Memories tugged and her breath caught. Another man, Thomas, chasing after her, laughing at her fears. "Give it a rest," she muttered, refusing his hand as she staggered to her feet.

He stared at her in the gathering gloom, the shadows of his face entrancingly attractive. Her gaze flitted to his mouth and she had to turn away.

"I am not talking to you anymore," she warned as she finished unlocking her door.

"I've been to see Dr. Hayden Stone," he answered. "Denise's last psychiatrist. He thinks it's lucky Denise left Ian Wallace because he's a miserable excuse for a human being."

"Trust Denise to choose well," Hayley muttered.

"Dr. Stone didn't know about either you or Dinah."

He followed her inside, seeming to fill the space inside her tiny living room. It made her nervous, having him so close.

Hayley wrapped her arms around herself, hating herself for feeling so vulnerable. "So, she's not confiding in her shrink. Big deal. Did you enlighten him?"

"You're sure she's back with her ex-husband?" he asked, ignoring her question.

"You've really got it bad," she accused angrily. "You want to talk to Denise? Then go do it. I don't need to hear this."

"I'd like to talk about it with you," he said softly.

"I'm not interested. Go chase after Denise. Maybe you'll get lucky. I hear she's an easy screw," Hayley tossed out bitterly. "Just—go away!"

With annoyance and fear, she watched as Connor Jackley completely ignored her demands and stood, waiting expectantly, in the center of the living room.

"Don't mind me, I need an aspirin," she sputtered sarcastically as she left him alone.

It was going to be a long night, but she was secretly glad he hadn't left.

Lights twinkled on the inky surface of the pool like diamonds. Denise watched them idly as she sipped a diet cola. No pills, thank you very much. She was having one of her clear times and it felt great to feel everything, see everything, understand everything.

She was packed and ready to go; she didn't know where. But this cycle of self-destruction had to end.

You'd be proud of me, Stone! Star pupil. I learned good, didn't I?

Of course it had taken hitting the ultimate bottom first.

Lina had left. Denise vaguely remembered Lina begging her to leave, too. A thin stream of blood had been running from her left nostril and her lips were quivering with anguish. Half of Lina's words had been in Spanish, but Denise, even in her drug-altered state, had caught the gist of it: "Get out before he kills us both!"

Sooooo . . . she was taking Lina's advice. Especially because since the maid's departure, Ian had been in a bad, bad mood. Denise had the bruises to prove it.

For the life of her she couldn't understand what had taken her so long to come to this conclusion. Why had she put up with this abuse and degradation?

Because you deserve it, sick-o.

"No, I don't."

She'd called Leo this afternoon and the schmuck had finally taken her call. Said he'd just returned from Rome. So sorry it took so long to get back to her.

"They're casting for *Lady Paradise,*" he told her. "I've talked to Susan Markson. You've got a lock on it, Denise. For God's sakes, where have you *been* all these weeks?"

"Does John know that I'm being considered?"

"Hell, yes, sweetheart! He talked to Susan about you himself! Whatever you've been doing, keep doing it. He loves you!"

His words filled her with green poison. This was Dinah's doing. John loved Dinah, not Denise. John and Dinah. John and Dinah.

Her jealousy lifted the fog that had enveloped her for so long. Action. That's what she needed.

Lights! Camera! Action!

Screw Ian Wallace and his cruelty. It was past time to leave.

She *wanted* that part.

With that thought firmly in mind, she shook off her current lethargy and got to her feet. She should see Stoner. Now, in her current state of mind. No need to tell him about the last few weeks. It was all a blur anyway. She would check into the Beverly Hills Hotel and then she would call him again. Everything copacetic.

With new resolve, Denise climbed, light-footed, up the stairs. Gathering her suitcases, she glanced around, shuddering at the dark, sticky memories this place had given her. Hurriedly she returned to the foyer. She'd loved this house at first, but now she hated every board, nail, and slap of stucco.

Time to call a cab. She would have the driver drop her off at a different hotel, then switch several times before she landed at the Beverly Hills. She was taking no chances. Always before, she'd run from one man to another, but this time she was just running. Ian Wallace was something she'd never encountered before.

Except for dear, old stepdaddy.

Denise shuddered again. Not the time to think about *that!*

She was at the phone when she felt the familiar vibration of a car's engine in the adjacent garage. She froze, receiver in mid-air.

He was back.

Slamming down the receiver, she glanced around frantically, searching for a place to hide her suitcases. Nowhere! *Nowhere!* With a squeak of pure fear, she ran to the hallway closet and jammed the first bag inside. It tangled with long coats and she fought back hysterical screaming while she struggled to smash the second one inside and close the door.

Footsteps. Unhurried. Coming her way.

Gritting her teeth to control their chattering, she gently closed the door, grimacing against the soft click of the latch, then she tiptoed through the dining room and into the kitchen, away from Ian's approaching steps.

She was seated at the bar, flipping through a magazine, willing her fingers to stop shaking, when he appeared in the doorway between the dining room and kitchen. He'd followed her all the way around.

Denise drew on immense acting skills and merely gave him a cursory, "Hello." After all, what else was there to say? Through the corners of her eyes, she glanced his way.

He held one of her suitcases.

The shaking in her hands intensified. He deliberately set the suitcase on the floor, unlatched it and dumped the contents into a heap. "You want to go? Go!" he said in that deadly voice she'd come to fear. "Nobody's keeping you here. You don't have to sneak."

Denise kept flipping through the magazine, thinking hard. Panic whipped through her veins.

"Did you hear me?" He moved closer, directly behind her. One hand brushed her hair away from her ear, exposing it. Her whole body trembled. "What are you afraid of?"

"You," she admitted. Her ear felt cold, vulnerable.

He leaned over and stuck his tongue inside, wiggling it around. Grimacing, Denise tried not to move. "Just like Lina," he whispered, the sound reverberating inside her head. "Leaving, just like Lina."

In a swift movement he grabbed her by the hair. Denise cried out, flailing to free herself. He slapped her and dragged her outside to the pool, throwing her onto the surrounding tiles, dunking her head underwater and holding it.

Three times and she gave up. Unconsciousness, freedom, beckoned with open arms. She reached for it gladly and slipped in limp heap into the waiting pool.

Hours later. Maybe minutes. Maybe eons. She awoke to the familiar feel of rough sex. Good old Ian. Probably thought she was dead and was in for a little necrophilia.

Hazily she realized they were in his bedroom. Eyes closed, she tried to will herself away but for once she couldn't. She hated him and his grunting and sweat. She was far too lucid to put up with this. And too angry. It felt good to be angry. Rage ran through her like a life-giving balm, liquid fire awakening from the soles of her feet, spreading upward, revitalizing long submissive flesh, tingling furiously.

Like Rip Van Winkle, she'd been asleep for years and she was just now coming to.

And she hated. Hated like she'd never felt it possible to hate.

But she lay there, quiet and empty, while this animal rutted above her.

One of her arms was flung off the bed, an expression of total abandon. With each of his thrusts, her fingertips brushed the side of the nightstand. Slowly, slowly, she lifted her hand up the side of the polished wood, her palm drawing into a fist. How hard could she hit him? Where? How? To make him stop forever.

Her hand reached the top of the nightstand and encountered something rocklike and rough and familiar. John's thunder egg. Her palm closed around it, the pad of her thumb digging into one of its center crystals.

With a power born of pure fury, she raised it up, arm

shaking wildly, then smashed it as hard as she could against Ian Wallace's temple.

He collapsed in mid-stroke and Denise hit him again. And again. And again. And again . . .

She didn't quit until they were both drenched in his blood. The thunder egg rolled from her now lax fingers and she lay back, gasping and quaking.

It's over, she thought, just before she fainted beneath his weight.

Chapter Fourteen

It was dark as pitch when Dinah had the cabbie drop her off in front of Dr. Hayden Stone's offices. The Fiat was lost to her, courtesy of its advancing years and John Callahan's disinterest in it. The poor thing was probably still cold as a cod in His Highness's driveway. But she couldn't think about that now.

Luckily, the good doctor seemed to keep odd hours because a receptionist was still on duty as Dinah made her way inside. The offices were understated, understaffed, and underwhelming in a way Dinah found disarming. She smiled at the pretty (but not drop-dead gorgeous like they usually were) receptionist and opened her mouth to inquire about Dr. Stone when something on the woman's face stopped her short.

Excitement. Disbelief. Adulation.

"Hello!" the girl greeted her. "I'm so glad you finally connected! He's been anxious to talk to you for weeks."

Dinah smiled faintly. She'd seen two other doctors and no one had yet made made the connection between her and Denise. Not so here. This receptionist thought she was her famous sister. Ergo, he must be the Dr. Stone she was searching for.

"Is he in?" Dinah asked diffidently.

"He's just finishing up. Would you mind waiting?" She seemed embarrassed to even ask.

"Not at all. Is there a restroom where I could . . . ?"

"Oh, right down the hall. Second door on the left." She indicated a closed door. "Go right on through."

Dinah headed for the bathroom. Looking in the mirror above the sink, she examined her reflection. Yes, she was a dead-ringer for her sister, but only if you were looking for it. Denise never wore her hair in a ponytail—unless it was artfully coiffed by some hairdresser who was a celebrity in his own right—and she never, but never, wore grungy jeans.

Nope. She was plain Dinah Scott. Except to Denise's doctor, who was expecting to see his famous client.

And to John Callahan, who'd made love to her.

"Damn." Vigorously, she scrubbed her hands. *Lady Macbeth?* "Oh, screw it!"

Back in the reception room she thumbed through a copy of *People* and tried to ignore the sideways stares from the starstruck receptionist. Either the girl was new, or Denise was Dr. Stone's only famous face.

Five minutes later an extremely thin, opulently dressed woman whose fingers were weighted down with rings and upon whose neck a thick pearl choker looked like a dog collar, marched toward the reception desk.

The receptionist looked up, gave the woman a big smile, then turned to Dinah. "He'll see you now."

The woman turned to give Dinah a furious glare.

Dinah ignored her. "His office is . . . ?"

"Straight down the hall."

"Thanks."

"I have an appointment," the woman said icily. Her glare at Dinah changed to annoyed confusion. Clearly she thought she recognized her but wasn't certain, and in Hollywood it was always best to play it cool. Dinah had learned that much and more since becoming a part-time resident.

"He won't be long," the receptionist assured the woman as Dinah headed for the inner sanctum.

Dr. Stone's office was at the end of the hall, remarkably unadorned except for a small brass nameplate attached to the door. The man was definitely not into making a statement which surprised Dinah a little since Denise was so high-profile. What kind of a relationship did the two of them have?

Peeking inside the office, she was surprised by her first glimpse of Dr. Stone. He wore a blue denim shirt, sleeves were rolled up the forearms, and a pair of tan chinos. His hair was light brown; his eyes dark, either brown or hazel. He had the lean build of a golfer and an air of quietude that Dinah was certain shrinks practiced in medical school.

But he wasn't anything like the slick, eye-on-the-meter professional she'd expected. He was . . . well, *appealing*.

The look on his face was expectant, almost eager, but as soon as he saw her it changed to surprise. "Dinah?" he asked.

She was poleaxed! So, Denise had come clean with the doc! Thank God she didn't have to keep up pretenses for him. "Denise's twin," she agreed, reaching a hand across the desk.

He couldn't seem to connect. He stood like the proverbial statue. Dr. Stone turned to stone. Dinah felt a perverse stab of amusement. She bet it wasn't every day Dr. Stone got thrown for a loop, and he was definitely thrown now.

"She never mentioned you," he said.

"Then how did you know?"

"Someone else told me."

"Who?"

His eyes searched her face with an intensity that made her feel slightly uncomfortable. Dinah shifted her weight.

"Have a seat," he invited.

"Thanks." She sat on the edge of the cushion. "Who?" she asked again.

"Connor Jackley."

Dinah stared at him blankly. *"Who?"* she repeated.

"Connor Jackley. He's a private investigator."

A private investigator. . . . Dinah suddenly felt ice cold inside. She had trouble collecting her thoughts.

"He wanted to talk to me about Denise," Dr. Stone went on, "but I didn't have a lot to say. He told me about you and your other sister, Hayley. Apparently he's been in contact with her."

"What?" Dinah asked weakly.

"Would you like something to drink?" he suddenly asked. "You look like you're about to faint."

"Hayley told him about us?" she repeated.

"He was just here, as a matter of fact. I've been trying to reach Denise for a while. I thought you were her, of course, so I didn't call the house."

"The house?" Dinah felt like a parrot.

"The Malibu house. Denise and John Callahan's residence. Mr. Jackley said she's staying there."

"What? Oh, no, no. That was me. Until recently." At his blank look, she said, "I had to leave."

"Denise isn't with Mr. Callahan?" He looked disturbed.

"No. At least I don't think so." *Lord, I hope not!* But no, John was too enraged and disgusted to allow Denise—any Denise—back into his life. "I can see why this private investigator might have got the idea she was," she said. "But I was the one living there."

He frowned. "She was never there?"

"No." Dinah's thoughts whirled. *Private investigator! Good God, what was that all about?* "She left me there, stranded, playing a part which got too tricky to keep up with. So, I left, but Denise has been missing awhile." After a beat, she asked, worried, "You're her doctor, don't you know where she is?"

"I was her doctor."

"Was?"

"In Houston. But I haven't seen her since I moved back. She hasn't contacted me." Now, he looked as worried as Dinah felt, though for different reasons. "I wish she hadn't lied about her past."

"Well, Denise has her reasons," Dinah murmured evasively.

Dr. Stone was a true doctor. "Which are?"

"I didn't come here to rat out my sister. I'm looking for her, and I thought you could help. The last I heard, she was staying with a friend in Beverly Hills, but I can't get a lead on him."

"Who?"

"Ian Wallace of Bever—"

"Ian Wallace?"

"You know him?" Now that was truly redundant. Not only did the good doctor know him, he appeared to be shocked and concerned to the tips of his toes.

"I know of him," he admitted grimly.

"You're scaring me. What's the deal with Wallace?"

"Where did she meet him? In *Houston?*" He paced the room, one hand fervently rubbing his jaw.

Dinah waited quietly, sensing danger. Dr. Hayden

Stone struck her as a careful concealer of emotion, and he was doing a piss-poor job of it right now.

"Could you leave me your number and address?" he said abruptly, reaching for his jacket.

"Where are you going? For God's sake, you're making me crazy! If you're going to find Denise, I'm going with you!" She jumped to her feet.

"Mr. Jackley seemed to think she was in Malibu. Maybe she wasn't with Wallace. He said he'd interviewed her."

"Interviewed *who?*"

"Denise," he said patiently. "For his investigation, Mr. Jackley interviewed Denise."

"*Where?*"

"I didn't ask."

"What investigation?" Dinah demanded, feeling like her world was reeling out of control.

"The murder of your stepfather, Thomas Daniels."

Her legs collapsed. She sank back into the chair as if pulled down by ropes. "Back up, Doc," she said unevenly. "I need a little more information and time."

Half an hour later Dinah had been brought up to speed and though Dr. Stone's worry for Denise hadn't lessened, he wasn't as obsessed with the idea of chasing after her as he had been. Dinah was deeply concerned about the investigation into her stepfather's death, and she told Dr. Stone as much.

"It won't help. Thomas Daniels was a son-of-a-bitch who hurt us all in different ways. I am not sorry he's dead. I'm sure Denise and Hayley feel the same way, but raking it all up isn't going to solve Denise's problems."

"How do you know?" he asked curiously.

"I know that Denise's problems started with him." At his surprised look, she said dryly, "Let's not kid ourselves. I'm sure my stepfather abused her. But I took care of things," she added quickly. "Denise is still suffering, but mostly she's just unstable."

"Meaning?"

"She feeds on male attention. It's her nature." Dinah shrugged. "So, how do I find this Jackley guy?"

Dr. Stone fished into his pocket and produced a piece of paper with a phone number scratched on it. Meticulously copying the number, he handed the paper to Dinah.

"I'd like to believe Denise isn't with Ian Wallace," he said.

"Is he that bad?"

Dr. Hayden Stone's mouth tightened. Dinah wondered, somewhat fatalistically, if he'd fallen for her sister, too. "Everything I've heard is a lot of rumor and innuendo and it wouldn't be fair to repeat it."

"Come on. We're talking about my twin. Give me this guy's address."

He shook his head. "I'll try to reach her. If you talk to her first, tell her I want to reach to her."

"And you promise you'll call me?" she demanded, watching him closely.

Her suspiciousness brought a smile to his lips. Dinah realized Dr. Hayden Stone was a very attractive man. She suddenly wanted to warn him to be careful. She liked him and, knowing Denise, he was bound to get hurt.

"It would be better for me to be with you when you talk to her," Dinah said desperately. "Really."

"I've seen all her sides," he assured her. "Nothing she

does surprises me, or will make me think less of her. She's a patient."

She's a helluva lot more than that, Doc. I know it, even if you don't yet.

"Call me the minute you find her," Dinah demanded. "I'll be camped on your doorstep tomorrow morning if you don't."

Smiling enigmatically, he preceded her down the hall, informed the receptionist he was leaving, much to the squawking of the pearl-collared woman, then headed out without so much as a goodbye. Dinah flirted with the idea of following him, then decided she'd let him play it his way. She'd found her link to Denise, and she wasn't going to break it.

Patience was a virtue. She would wait.

You think you're sooo noble, her conscience smote her. *But you don't want to face her, do you? She's not going to understand about John. You'd like to keep that little secret, wouldn't you?*

"Bastard," she muttered.

"Pardon?" The receptionist looked alarmed.

"I was thinking of someone else," Dinah explained.

"Will Dr. Stone be returning?" the woman demanded imperiously. "I'm pressed for time as it is!"

"I think we'll have to reschedule," the flustered receptionist answered. "He had an emergency appointment."

"And I'm stuffed with green cheese!" she declared angrily. Turning on Dinah, she half-screamed, "I'm supposed to not care that you squeezed in ahead of me?"

Showing more restraint than normal, Dinah kept her tongue stilled. Life was too full of problems to stoop to the level of one self-centered woman.

"What about me?" the woman shrieked, working herself up to a full-fledged fit. "That's what I'd like to know.

What am I supposed to do now?" Turning on Dinah, she stepped in front of her, blocking her path. "You took my turn, so what am I supposed to do now?"

"Go suck an egg."

So much for restraint.

Connor Jackley's presence in her apartment made Hayley feel claustrophobic. The air was thick and still. She knew what he wanted to hear. She could go on all day about Thomas Daniels if she felt like it, but she never felt like it. Never ever.

His patience wore her down. He wasn't much of a talker himself, which made each syllable appear packed with extra meaning. How she'd managed to handle him the last times they'd been together was a mystery because she sure as hell couldn't handle him now.

"Dr. Stone wasn't a whole lot of help," Connor concluded, after explaining the rather unrewarding conversation he'd had with the close-mouthed doctor. "But he was glad to hear Denise was no longer with Ian Wallace."

"Wallace sounds like a great guy," she said wryly.

"I'm no fan." Connor was terse. "And neither's Dr. Stone." He shifted gears. "Apparently, Denise was pretty tight-lipped about you and Dinah."

"Denise didn't tell him?" Hayley was surprised. "He's her shrink, and she didn't tell *him?*"

"Guess not."

Hayley was heartily glad that she didn't suffer from Denise's problems. Her sister was one screwed-up kook.

But Hayley had had all she could take of another delve into the past. "Maybe you ought to leave," she suggested to Connor. "I can't talk anymore."

"You've hardly said ten words."

"I'm not feeling all that chatty, okay? If you're so interested in Denise, why don't you go bother her?"

He stared at her, as if he wished there were some other avenue of interrogation. But she was stonewalling him, and unless he just enjoyed her less-than-scintillating company, there was no reason for him to hang around.

Apparently he came to this same conclusion because rather reluctantly he got to his feet and said, "You think Denise will finally give me Dinah's address?"

"One can only hope."

Her sarcasm brought a fleeting smile to his lips. The guy was just not going to give up, and it both scared and irritated Hayley. She had better things to think about—like an audition tape that may have already been viewed by People Who Matter.

The phone rang, and Hayley jumped as if she'd been stabbed. *Tonja!* Snatching up the receiver, she said, "Hello?"

"Hayley?" a voice whimpered. A feminine voice. Denise's voice.

Instinctively she knew this was a call meant for her ears alone. No Connor Jackley, no matter how badly he wanted to talk to her sister. "Yeah, this is Hayley," she said off-handedly. She waved a silent goodbye to Connor who let himself out, moving so slowly that Hayley gnashed her back teeth together to fight back a scream of impatience.

"Hayley?" Denise's voice had climbed an octave.

"I'm here. Shhhh. Calm down. What is it?"

"I think I've killed him."

Surreal calm. "Who?" she asked, the hair lifting on her arms in a strange kind of *déjà vu*.

"Ian. Ian Wallace. Can you—can you help?"

"Is anybody there with you?"

"No . . . I'm alone at Ian's," she gulped.

"Give me the address," she stated flatly, committing it to memory as Denise haltingly dragged it past her lips.

It took over an hour to find the place and when she did Hayley inhaled a deep breath, expelling it slowly. A mansion, that's what it was. A goddamn palace.

Lights blazed as she drove through the open gates to the quadruple-car garage. Her Rent-A-Wreck was like a neon sign, inviting gawkers to look and remember.

She could hear it now. Some little bratty kid with an over-active imagination. "I saw it! I saw it! I know exactly what it looks like. And it was there the night he was killed. I even memorized the license plate number! And I saw the killer! It was a woman and she drove up, went in the house, and pumped him with lead!"

Or whatever. Denise hadn't exactly been specific.

She rang the front bell, fingers of apprehension dancing along the back of her neck.

Expecting nothing, she checked the door—and it opened beneath her touch. Quickly she stepped inside, locking it behind her. Her heart beat so loudly she could hear it in her ears.

With the presence of mind of a seasoned criminal, she walked straight to the garage, found the button for the garage door, opened it, then calmly and efficiently drove her car into the only empty slot.

Then she was in the house again, listening for sounds of life. The place was quiet as a tomb. Literally. Shivering, she crept upstairs, searching the rooms until she stepped into the master suite at the end of the hall.

Denise sat on the floor, catatonic, wrapped in a blanket, smeared with blood. On the bed, a man lay face down. So much blood! Pools of it.

Hayley's senses swam. *Oh, Dinah, help!*

"Denise," she whispered, but there was no immediate response from her sister.

Steeling her resolve, Hayley used her favorite trick of conscience, concentrating on a sweetly pastoral scene, somewhere in the mountains of Oregon. Then she strode to the body and lay her fingers against Ian's neck.

Faintly, a pulse beat.

"He's alive," she said in relief. "Barely. But he's not dead yet." She saw the thunder egg and debated on whether to pick it up or not.

"This is just like before," Denise said, her voice startlingly clear in the quiet room. "I killed him."

"You did *not* kill him."

"I wish Dinah were here. I don't know where Dinah is." A gasp, almost a cry. "Oh, yes, I do. She's with John!"

"C'mon, let's get you out of here," Hayley said, getting the heebie-jeebies. She gathered Denise in her arms, helping her to her feet. Briefly, she considered dialing 911. Ian Wallace needed help.

Then she saw the bruises on her sister's face and arms, and she remembered Connor Jackley's reaction to Ian Wallace's name.

"I hope he's dead," Denise stated chillingly.

"I'll take you back to my place." With that Hayley scuttled her out of the room and into the safety of her Rent-A-Wreck.

He felt irritated all over in a way he couldn't analyze. Hayley had done that to him and after examining the bareness of his refrigerator—furious with himself that there wasn't one goddamned beer!—Connor slammed out of his apartment and decided to take Hayley up on her advice.

He would go see Denise.

He made the trip to Malibu in record time, swearing at traffic all the way. Hayley Scott bugged him. He sympathized with her desperate need to keep her past a secret; if half the things he suspected were true, those three girls had led a miserable existence. But couldn't she let down a little? He *knew* that whole obsessive, goal-driven career stuff was her escape. One did not have to be a shrink of Dr. Stone's caliber to figure that much out. But was he, Connor Jackley, ex-policeman, so all-mighty threatening that she couldn't *give* just a little?

"Hell with it," he muttered, pressing the button at the gates of the Callahan beachfront home. She wasn't his problem anymore than Denise or the missing Dinah were.

No answer. Impatiently, Connor stabbed the button again, aware that he was acting out of character. What had she done to him, to make him feel this way?

You're attracted to her, Iron-man.

"Goddammit!"

A man's voice crackled over the intercom. "Yeah?"

"Connor Jackley," he answered tersely, assuming it was Callahan. "I'd like to speak to Denise Callahan. I'm a private investigator."

"Wrong place. She's not here." He was just as terse.

"Is she living here?"

"Not anymore."

Confused, Connor hesitated. "I've got information about her family," he went on cautiously.

"Is this the Indiana story, or have you talked to Hayley Scott?"

Connor's brows lifted. "I've talked to Sheriff Gus Dempsey of Wagon Wheel, Oregon, where Denise spent most of her high school years."

A pause. Then the voice asked cautiously, "What's this about?"

"Maybe it would be better if we talked face-to-face."

Another pause, then Callahan seemed to hear the enormity of the situation in Connor's tone. "Shit," was his muttered reply, but the gates began to swing inward.

Writing, usually a welcome escape, was suddenly a huge pain in the derriere, and furious, Dinah scribbled madly over a page of notes then tore and tore at the whole paper until it was pieces of confetti.

"Damn! Shit! Crap!"

Literary words. Necessary in times of great stress.

She needed John.

Frustrated, she prowled the hotel room until she couldn't stand it any longer. Waiting for Denise's psychiatrist to call was Chinese water torture, and she wasn't going to get any work done until she connected with Denise no matter what she'd promised Flick.

So . . .

So, she was going to the Malibu house on the off-chance that John might be there. Sure, he'd been living there—sort of—with her, but since he'd tossed her out, she somehow couldn't picture him rattling around there alone.

But she didn't know what else to do.

Forty minutes later she had the cabdriver stop at the

gates to the house which stood wide open. Clutching her purse, she debated on asking the driver to wait, but the open gates sure made it look like someone was home.

"Drive forward," she ordered, and as the cab slid to a halt beside a car she didn't recognize, Dinah's pulse began to pound with dread. Whose car? *Another woman's?*

"Wait," she said, then forced her legs to carry her to the front door. Ringing the bell, she called herself every kind of fool, then nearly bolted at the sound of John's approaching footsteps on the tile foyer floor.

He threw open the door and for a moment Dinah blinked in the light spilling from inside.

It was John. She could tell by the way he held himself, the turn of his head, his lean, cowboy ways.

I love you, she thought a bit desperately.

"Well, if it isn't *Dinah,*" he drawled in a way that sent gooseflesh rising on her skin. "Dinah Scott. My wife's secret twin. Come on in and let's get to know each other . . ."

Chapter Fifteen

It's been a hell of an evening. Come to that, it's been a hell of a week. Well, why stop there? Face it, Callahan. It's been a hell of a life.

He faced Dinah Scott in blessed numbness, inured to one more shock. His first thought was: *she's so beautiful.* His second: *her eyes hold more secrets than Denise's.*

What an evening!

He'd been pouring himself his second scotch, wondering idly if he were following in his mother's alcoholic footsteps, had decided he just didn't give a damn, and downed the drink, when the gate intercom buzzed and he unwittingly invited Connor Jackley, private investigator, into his home to talk about his ex-wife's past.

He should have sent the guy on his way. Who the hell cared anyway? But he'd been seduced by those comments about Wagon Wheel, Oregon—Bohunk, U.S.A., if he'd ever heard it—and let's face it, just the mention of Denise's name was enough to tickle his interest—and libido—though it hurt to admit.

But he hadn't expected the tale. Oh, no. He hadn't expected *that!*

A murder? With Denise at the center of the controversy? Shit! He should write the damn thing and sell it for mucho buckos.

He didn't believe it for an instant. Still, Connor Jackley, ex-L.A.P.D., didn't strike him as the kind of man who made colossal mistakes. And this would be a real biggee, were it not true. So, he had to credit the man's story as the truth. The murder part, that is. Denise's involvement? That was another story.

"You think Denise killed her stepfather, Thomas Daniels," John had clarified, rolling the empty old-fashioned glass between his palms.

"I'd like to talk to her again."

"You've already spoken to her, then?"

"Once."

"About this." John hated being redundant, but he was having a little trouble believing all this. Not once, in all her elaborate tales, had Denise mentioned Oregon as a place of past residence. Sure, there was that idiot who claimed to have fathered a child with her, but Denise's lack of reaction to that story had made John discount it as just another nut searching for his fifteen minutes of fame.

Jackley nodded.

"You talked to her about living in Wagon Wheel and murdering her stepfather."

"I told her Thomas Daniels was dead and that I was investigating," Jackley agreed.

"And what did she say about that?"

"Is she living here, or not?" Jackley countered.

"I'd say that falls in the 'or not' category. She's moved to a hotel."

"Recently?"

"Yep."

That seemed to get him thinking. Questions were racing through John's mind, too. Like, did this have anything to do with Hayley Scott's claims, or were the two stories coincidental?

"So, you *don't* think Denise did the dirty deed?" John asked.

"How long was she here before she left?"

"Well, I don't know. A month or two or three. You'd have to ask her."

"She's been *living* here for over a month?"

"That's what I said. What does it matter? You said the guy's been dead for years."

Did he really think Denise was capable of murder? No. No way. She was self-destructive, but she wasn't a killer.

John poured himself another scotch, bothered. The problem was, the idea had merit. Denise, damn her lovely eyes, was capable of anything.

"I had a different address for her," Jackley muttered, frowning.

"Yeah? Where?"

"You wouldn't happen to know how to get hold of her sister."

John lifted a brow. "So, you buy the Hayley Scott story?"

"If the story is that they went to school in Wagon Wheel until their mother died, then lived with their step-father, I know it's the truth. But there are a lot of gaps."

"You *know* it's the truth." John digested that, then stated baldly, "Denise would never murder anyone." Sure, he was pissed at her, but no, he wouldn't—couldn't —believe that.

"She and her sisters lived with Daniels until he disappeared. I think they know why he disappeared, and maybe who murdered him."

"Did you say *sisters?*"

"Hayley and Dinah."

John started laughing. He couldn't help himself. "Hayley and Dinah. Okay, I've met Hayley. Did she give you this cockamamie story, too?"

"The Deschutes County Sheriff, Gus Dempsey—"

"Yeah, yeah, yeah." John cut him off. "You told me about the sheriff. He filled you in?"

"He asked me to investigate Daniels' death, and we both decided the best place to start was with his three stepdaughters. His wife, Nina, the girls' mother, died earlier that year, and they were stuck together for a number of months before they left."

"What the hell is this?" John demanded. "You know how many histories Denise has? I don't believe any of this! You'll have to ask her what the truth is, and good luck. I don't even know if she knows anymore."

"How can I reach her?"

"She checked into some hotel." John shrugged, remembering with a stab of regret their last acrimonious words. "At least that's what she said she was doing."

"She didn't mention Ian Wallace?"

John did a slow double-take. "Ian Wallace," he repeated in a deadly voice. "What's that bastard got to do with her?"

"You know him?" Jackley looked interested.

"We crossed paths. There was a brief period when Wallace connected with my father."

There was a hell of a lot more to the story than that, but John didn't wish to elaborate. Ian Wallace, craftier than a mongrel dog, had pushed all the right buttons with Sampson, setting himself up as the son Sampson deserved to have. Money and power were the lure, and Wallace nearly had Sampson eating out of his hand. Oh, they were going to make so many films together! With Ian's

enormous personal funds and Titan's powerful distribu-
tion and promotion—they couldn't lose.

Sampson had nagged John about it. Thrown their relationship in his face. John would have liked to believe his
own disinterest had finally made Sampson realize he was
grooming Ian Wallace for a position John neither wanted
nor would ever take. But the truth was, the cracks in Ian's
personality began to show and Sampson's own shrewd-
ness rescued him from dire consequences. For dire they
would have been, if Ian had gained the upper hand. The
man was made of money but rumors abounded. He was
morally bereft and corrupt. No amount of good looks and
surface charm could make up for his basic emptiness.

Sampson had been lucky.

"Denise is involved with him?" John demanded, his
words a staccato rap.

"When I interviewed her, I got the impression she was
living with him."

"When did you interview her?"

"A couple weeks ago."

John stared. A couple weeks ago he and Denise were
sharing a bed together. His skin crawled.

Something was sliding around inside his head. Some
piece of information that made no sense. Something he'd
meant to ask about earlier. He tried to draw it to the
surface, but before he could, Jackley reminded him of
what it was.

"Do you have Dinah's address? I haven't got hold of
her yet."

The words formed though he knew he was going to
sound stupid. "Who's Dinah?"

Jackley's look was sharp. John watched him, could
practically see the calculations taking place inside his

head, knew he wasn't going to like what he was about to hear.

"Dinah is Denise's identical twin sister."

And for the second time John threw back his head and laughed, half sheer amusement, half hysterical reaction, and then the doorbell pealed through the house.

He had exactly thirty seconds to digest Connor Jackley's bombshell. Thirty seconds to put together information so sharp it cut. Thirty seconds to understand that Denise, his lovely, lying ex-wife possessed a twin whom she'd neither spoken of, nor alluded to in any manner. Thirty seconds before he threw open the door and came face-to-face with her. For he knew it was Dinah, as he'd known in some deep awareness of his soul, since he'd first encountered her sleeping in the guestroom.

Now, her lips parted in shock at his mocking, faux-friendly tone. And suddenly he truly believed and understood. This wasn't Denise! He'd been sleeping with a stranger, and she'd never once uttered one word of truth.

The writing. The Fiat. The lack of make-up. The quirks of her humor.

It felt like a blow to his solar plexus. He could scarcely breathe.

"John . . ." she murmured achingly.

Abruptly he turned back to Connor Jackley who now stood in the archway, his expression grim as he gazed at the blonde woman slumped in the doorway.

"Dinah?" he questioned and she gazed at him blankly.

John couldn't look. Couldn't speak. He strode straight to the bottle of scotch, poured himself a more than healthy shot, then sank down at the kitchen table. He was worse than numb. He didn't exist. It was unreality—and he welcomed it.

Jackley returned, and behind him, Dinah.

After a moment of intense silence, Jackley said, "I'm afraid Denise must still be with Ian Wallace. I'm going over there now."

"I'm going with you." Dinah erupted into action.

The phone rang and all three of them jerked, as if caught in some nefarious act. John reached for it. "Hello?"

"Hey, you're impossible to catch at work," Susan Markson's voice said easily. "I half-expected the answering machine. Guess what? I checked out that audition tape you sent. Looks a lot like Denise, doesn't she? She's dynamite, John. I say go for it. You've found your Toni."

"Is it Denise?" Dinah whispered anxiously.

He glanced at her. Even in her current disarray—hairs falling loose from her ponytail, eyes dilated with fear, mouth quivering—she was an aphrodisiac too powerful to ignore. He hated himself. He hated her.

"John?" Susan queried into the silence. "Is this a bad time?"

"Send the tape back to my office," John managed to answer.

"Sure."

"We'll talk tomorrow."

He wanted to laugh. Tomorrow. Work. The process of filmmaking. Hayley Scott as Toni, John Callahan's latest discovery.

Connor Jackley and Dinah—beautiful, lying bitch that she was—waited.

"We'll all go," John said, sliding the glass away. He would deal with all of this later. That decent, chivalrous part of himself which was only slightly tarnished still recognized priorities. Ian Wallace was scum and Denise was in his clutches—maybe where she wanted to be, but if there was a rescue squad, he was going to be a part of it.

* * *

Ian Wallace's house was brightly lit, squares of light illuminating the grounds from nearly every window. John and the private investigator, Connor Jackley, strode up to the front door but Dinah lagged behind.

She was in a cold trance. Everything felt sharp and dangerous. Memories danced of another time when she'd saved her sister. Only then no one knew. Then she could hide.

"Door's open," Jackley said in surprise. He'd rung the bell and pounded madly to no avail. Now, after the briefest of hesitations, he let himself in, John at his heels. Dinah followed at a discreet distance, every hair on her body standing on end.

The place was hollow, empty. She had no feeling of life. The men made a cursory examination of the main floor then headed upstairs. John never once looked at her. She couldn't blame him.

Eight years ago she'd felt this same robotic oddness. Eight years ago she'd done what she had to do. She never dwelled on it. It was the past. She was the caretaker, and she'd done what she had to do.

Now, she heard the muffled imprecation. John's, she reckoned, for she was certain Connor Jackley rarely reacted to anything less than world annihilation. *Denise,* she thought fearfully, her steps quickening.

At the threshold to the master bedroom she stopped short, a gasp caught in her throat, choking her. Blood everywhere. Smears of it across the bed and carpet. Covering the head of the man who lay face down atop the rumpled, brownish-red stained covers.

"He's alive," Jackley muttered tersely, his fingers at the

man's neck. Reaching for the phone, he called 911. Quietly relating the address, he shot a look Dinah's way. She stared back silently. Where was Denise?

John was grim, surveying the scene as if he were too horrified to speak. Maybe he was.

On the floor, nestled in the folds of the sliding comforter, a familiar blood-encrusted object caught Dinah's eye. The thunder egg, she realized with a jolt of her heart. The crystals were dulled brick-red and brown with sticky blood and hair.

A shudder ran through her from the soles of her feet to the crown of her head. John gazed at her, his eyes dark pits of emotional hell.

Maybe if he didn't see it. Maybe if she took the thunder egg and kept it safe. Maybe she could still save Denise.

Denise was the thief.

The thought gave her cold comfort. Denise had sneaked into the house. Denise had felt compelled to spy and steal rather than talk to her sister. Denise had to know about her and John.

"Where is she?" John rasped out.

Connor gazed at him, then at Dinah whose white face and bloodless lips revealed her agony.

He thought of Hayley's mysterious phone call. He knew.

The thin, distant wail of the ambulance was the only sound in the cloaking silence while each of them concentrated on their own private thoughts.

The showerhead sputtered and spit, soaking the back of Hayley's blouse as she leaned over her sister. She scrubbed furiously, so hard and fast it was almost spasmodic. Blood ran in pink rivulets off Denise's hands and body. She sat under the spray, teeth chattering, body twitching, silent and staring. Nearly catatonic.

"Stop it," Hayley whispered in her ear. "Damn it, Denise. Get a hold of yourself!"

She shook violently.

Hayley stood up, watching the water run. Denise was still in her clothes. No time to strip her. No time.

"I killed him," Denise said tremulously. "I killed him."

Hayley ran to her bedroom and yanked out a smokey blue jogging suit and some underclothes. No time. No time at all before they came looking for her.

"Wash up," Hayley ordered. "Do it now! I've got some clothes for you."

Thirty minutes later Denise leaned weakly against the cushions of Hayley's couch. She was propped up, but sliding down, as if her insides had turned to liquid. "I need Stoner," she whimpered.

"Who?" Hayley paced in front of her.

"Stoner . . . Dr. Stone."

"For God's sake, Denise!"

"He'll help me, since Dinah won't." Her voice was little-girl naive.

"Give me the number," she demanded, reaching for the phone. Her own fingers shook so hard she thought she heard them rattle.

A recorded message. An emergency number. Hayley called the emergency number and was told Dr. Stone would call her back. Expecting nothing, she jumped in fright when the phone rang back almost instantly.

"I'll be right there," he stated firmly and when he disconnected, the receiver drifted from Hayley's hand.

Dinah, she begged silently. *Help us.*

* * *

The police were thorough and inordinately tactful. They thought she was Denise, were confused when Connor Jackley informed them she was Denise's twin. John stood by, staring out the window, an integral part of the proceedings, yet as removed as the planets.

There'd been no hiding the thunder egg. It had been scooped up, bagged, and tagged. She could hear it now. Exhibit A. Denise Scott Callahan's fate was sealed.

Connor Jackley drifted to her side. "We don't know what happened," he reminded her quietly.

Dinah's smile lacked humor. "Yes, we do."

Connor conferred with the detectives. Dinah and John were released, though they were reminded that they would be questioned again. Big surprise.

Connor dropped them off at the Malibu house. "I need to call a cab," Dinah told John tonelessly.

He nodded. She followed him inside where he sat heavily at the kitchen table. His scotch was where he'd left it, ice cubes melted, but he didn't reach for it.

"Why didn't you tell me?" he asked.

Dinah scarcely had the strength to answer. "She wanted this house. She wanted you. And she wanted me to keep things in place for her while she got help."

His glance was swift and cut like a knife. He was thinking of their lovemaking. Dinah blushed painfully and looked away. "I only made things worse," she murmured.

There was a weighty pause, then he asked, "Where do you think she is?"

Dinah shook her head.

Another deadly silence, then he reached for the phone and said, "I'll get you that cab."

Wrapped in misery, Dinah could only stand by. When he was finished, John didn't look at her. Almost as an afterthought he retrieved his drink. In uneasy silence they waited for Dinah's cab.

She was floating . . . floating on a sea of memory. Bad memories, all bleeding together. She'd killed before. She'd killed again. Whoever said things got easier was right. This time she was anesthethized, numb, her limbs asleep in that familiar, slightly uncomfortable sensation, a billion tiny little needle pricks underneath her skin.

She wasn't alone. Hayley was here, she realized dimly. And someone else. A warm, male body, holding her.

"Stoner," she mumbled, her tongue thick.

"You're in shock," his voice sounded as if it were under water. Again that sensation of floating. "Can you tell me what happened?"

"Not now." She snuggled into his arms, breathing deeply. He smelled gooooooood. None of that clinical stuff, she half-expected of him. His scent was clean and crisp and tangy. A man's aftershave she was unfamiliar with.

Blurred voices all around her. Snatches of conversation. ". . . call the police . . . Wallace dead . . . turn herself in . . ."

"No!" Denise shouted, surfacing. "I don't want anybody to know."

"You've got to tell me what happened," Stone said gently. She could hear the reverberations in her chest, a rumbling she found comforting.

"I killed him."

"She keeps saying that." Hayley's voice, annoyed and scared.

"But he was still alive."

"Yes."

"And you dialed 911?"

A hesitation. "No," Hayley answered grimly. "I hope he dies."

"For God's sake!"

A scramble for the telephone and then Stone's terse voice, giving directions. Moments later, "Someone called for an ambulance already."

"Who?" Hayley, really frightened now.

"Whoever discovered his body . . ."

Drifting . . . swaying . . . rocking. Denise lifted an eyelid and realized Stone was across the room, eyeing Hayley in that stern, almost angry way he sometimes employed. Jealousy stabbed her. Stoner was hers and hers alone.

"Look at her," Hayley stated flatly. "You think I'd lift a finger to help him?"

They both turned her way. Vaguely Denise realized how fat and cumbersome her face felt. Ian had hit her. Hit her hard. Groaning, she buried her face in the pillows, realizing how awful she must look. The rub of the velveteen against her flesh burned. Tears of pain filled her eyes.

Stone was back, his hand on her arm. "Denise?"

"Go 'way."

"You can't hide-out here. Hayley says you've been living with Ian Wallace. Your fingerprints have got to be all over the place. It's only a matter of time."

"No time," Hayley muttered, sucking air through her teeth.

"He beat you. That's self-evident," Stone went on quietly. "You need to tell the police."

Awkwardly Denise reached for his hand, unable to lift her face from the sanctuary of the pillow. His firm palm clasped hers warmly. "Hold me," she whispered.

His arms surrounded her. For once his professionalism

wasn't warring with his need to comfort. Denise whimpered.

A loud, furious knock.

"Oh, shit," Hayley gasped.

Stoner relaxed his embrace. "Answer it."

A cool breeze against her cold flesh. Denise shivered uncontrollably.

"Dr. Stone," Connor Jackley's voice greeted grimly. "Ah, yes. I was hoping to find Denise here. The police want to question her regarding the death of Ian Wallace . . ."

Hayley drank the coffee black though she was a stickler for cream in any form, real cream, milk, Coffeemate, whatever. But cops were everywhere, swarming, hanging around, full of questions.

And the press! Word had leaked. They were outside in droves. Her apartment complex had suddenly become the hottest spot in L.A. Tomorrow's papers would scream!

Denise Scott Arrested for Attempted Murder.

Actress Bashes Former Lover's Skull

Superstar Chooses Real-life Role of Murderess.

Dr. Stone was running interference. He feared for Denise's mental health—with good reason. And Connor, well, he was in the thick of it as usual.

His gaze had touched hers all evening, but Hayley's eyes slid away. She couldn't handle the scrutiny. Not now.

As if hearing her thoughts, he came to her side. She stopped him before he could start. "This kind of shoves my stepfather's murder to the background, doesn't it?"

"I hate this kind of scene. This tragedy," he said bitterly.

"The bastard deserved it."

Connor nodded.

Denise's bruises had worsened. Her face was a caricature of itself. Luckily, a buddy of Connor's named Bennie, who normally worked Vice, had responded to a personal call, and he was shutting down the paparazzi single-handedly.

"Daniels deserved it," Hayley observed.

"Someday maybe you'll tell me the truth about that."

"I'd have to remember it first."

He half-smiled, his gray eyes tired but full of something Hayley couldn't name, something she was afraid to trust. "You already do," he said.

He walked back to Denise who was clinging to Dr. Hayden Stone as if he were a lifeline. Hayley's gaze followed the lines of his back, his familiar form.

I already do, she thought. *I already do.*

Chapter Sixteen

Dinah pounded on the keyboard of her portable computer until the monitor blinked alarmingly. She waited, breath held, expecting the worst. The Fiat—rest its soul—had been a nuisance. Losing the only word processor she owned would be devastation.

The screen cleared and her words jumped out at her. *". . . and what constitutes the right of privacy? Does the press have a right—or, as some claim, an obligation—to delve into the lives of celebrities? If a story's deemed newsworthy, does that mean no one's safe? How do we draw the line? Should it be drawn? And if it's not, what of the people who are dissected, tried, convicted, and discarded like so much carrion? What happens to the Tonya Hardings and Michael Jacksons and Denise Scott Callahans after we, the press and the public, are through with them? . . ."*

An editorial. Her new job. On the air no less, with KBLA, a local television station.

Nine months after the fiasco with Denise and Ian Wallace.

And John Callahan.

Nine months since Flick refused to print her impassioned, angry column about men who control women's lives. Nine months since she quit the *Santa Fe Review* and accepted a position at a Los Angeles paper for exorbitant wages. Nine months since *that* paper's editor rewrote her story on Denise's side of the Ian Wallace tale, embellishing it tabloid style and printing Dinah's name in the byline—all without telling her. Nine months since she told that sleazoid slob where to get off and took the position with the TV station.

God, she *hated* L.A!

But it was her home now. A one-bedroom apartment in Westwood, trendy enough to please her, small enough to remind her that she wasn't the sudden celebrity everyone else wanted to make her.

Oh, yes. It had happened: COME ONE, COME ALL! SEE THE TWIN SISTER OF THE CRAZED KILLER!

"Shit," she muttered, viciously hitting the print button. Paper began to chunk out from the tiny printer hooked up like an umbilical cord to the portable PC.

Walking toward the sliding glass door, she gazed across her balcony to the smog-shrouded surrounding buildings. All of a sudden she was big news with a capital BIG. Without meaning to be, without wanting to be, she'd become as sought after and famous as Denise. *A Current Affair* and *Inside Edition* had promised megabucks for a few minutes of her time. "Talk about whatever you want," a producer had assured her.

Oh, yeah. Right. That's how it worked. The topic would be the "D" word. Denise, Denise, Denise. And, oh, yeah, Dinah. Denise's twin. But who really cared about what *she* thought, unless it was what *she* thought about Denise!

Denise . . .

Abruptly Dinah's selfish thoughts tumbled to the truth of her real emotions. Denise was in trouble and, thank

God, in therapy. Dr. Hayden Stone had changed from footloose shrink to concerned and doting doctor. The cataclysmic volcano that followed Ian Wallace's hospitalization might have buried Denise once and for all if it weren't for Doc Stone.

And Ian had lived. Lived long enough to call Denise a scheming cunt whom he planned to put in jail for the rest of her life. Dinah's thought at the time was that Denise should have made sure he was dead before phoning Hayley. He was pounding the last nails in her coffin, pond scum that he was, and the tide inevitably had turned his—the victim's—way.

But then a raft of suits had suddenly landed at Ian's door. Old girlfriends who'd been beaten, raped, and humiliated, then paid off. Casual acquaintances who'd been unlucky enough to find themselves alone with a man who hid his monstrosity by average good looks, glasses, and a polished banter. Losers who'd once clung to someone as low as Ian only for the money, then had suffered miserably at his cruel hands. Everyone who'd been afraid to cross the powerful, wealthy, loner Ian Wallace. Now, they came in wave after wave, an unrelenting army of abused females who took up the battlecry in the name of Denise Scott Callahan.

Overnight Ian Wallace changed from famous to infamous, and Denise changed from screwed-up murderess to tabloid heroine. Delicious irony, except Denise was too unraveled to appreciate any of it.

Dinah had charged after Ian with words. The pen was truly mightier than the sword. She'd written editorial after editorial about the nature of sub-humans such as Ian Wallace. The man himself, recovering in a hospital, was bombarded with press and paparazzi. Those who knew him, like Rodney Walburn III, head of Titan Pictures, quickly washed their hands of any association with such a monster.

And then Ian was released and plagued by the press camped outside his home. No rest for the wicked.

Dinah, for one, felt no regret when the man's body turned up floating in his pool. Too many drinks—drowning his sorrows, perhaps? His final swansong was unlamented. But it had put Dinah in a reflective mood and hence the harsh words about her brethren, those perennial vultures, the press.

Ian was dead, but Denise was alive and well and acquitted of attempted murder by reason of self-defense.

Hollow, hollow victory. Apart from the excitement and frenzy of the whole Ian business, everything was remarkably the same.

Except Hayley was fast riding the vehicle of success.

Dinah made a noise of disgust through her nose. Hayley was John's latest find. The publicity surrounding Denise hadn't hurt the youngest Scott sister, and though Dinah wished the best for Hayley, her feelings were much more ambivalent about John.

And this latest twist! Two months into filming, *Lady Paradise*'s supporting role was suddenly up for grabs. The actress contracted to play Katie, the title character's close friend and the film's most tragic role, had been summarily fired by John. The film's director, Frank Carello, had gone apeshit, walking out because the fired actress was some shirttail relative whom he'd personally recommended, supposedly against John's better judgement. Apparently this was Frankie's *modus operandi* and John, not known for compromise, had just plain had it. So, now John was producing *and* directing, stepping into Carello's shoes without so much as a hiccup. More rumors. Everyone was relieved. Everyone happier. Until the costar's role was offered to—DA-DA!—you, got it—Denise Scott Callahan, the flavor of the month no matter how nuts she was!

Two days ago Dinah had made the mistake of phoning John and telling him exactly what she thought of his decision.

"You're doing it for the publicity!" she'd raged. "You're a sell-out."

"I'm doing it for Denise," he shot back coldly.

"Bullshit!"

"The goddamn truth!"

They'd both slammed down the receiver at the same moment. Dinah was beside herself, especially since Denise was recovering at the Malibu house and she could just imagine the cozy scenes being played out between *ex*-husband and *ex*-wife!

With a sick moan, she covered her face with her hands. Jealousy. A truly hateful emotion. She knew she was wrong. John didn't love Denise. Too much water under the bridge. Too much angst and misery and just plain everything. The blissful moments she—Dinah—had spent with him had been because they were two different people. If she'd truly been Denise, the situation would have grown too complicated and out-of-hand, but because she was a replica, a totally different human being inside, the brew that bubbled between them had boiled over into something delicious, dangerous, and unexpectedly tantalizing and sweet.

The stuff dreams were made of.

But it was over. Over, over, over. And all that was left for her now was newfound—albeit unwanted—stardom and a news career as hot as a comet. Hardly the dregs, but it sure as hell felt like it.

Weary all over, Dinah ripped off the final pages from

her printer and read over her latest editorial, angry and disturbed that her success had been kissed by the whim of fate rather than earned by her own sweat and talent.

"Have you ever made love to a patient?" Denise asked, her feet curled beneath her on the living room sofa.

Stoner barely reacted. He was distracted today, his brows drawn in concentration as he studied the inside of his coffee cup. He'd finished the coffee an hour ago, so she had no clue what he found so fascinating inside. She suspected he was avoiding her for some reason.

Well, hell, that was sure an exercise in futility. He came here to cure her, didn't he? Wasn't that why she was paying him?

"Do I get the pleasure of your company, or are you going to stay in your distant land?" she demanded sarcastically.

"What made you decide to take the part?"

"Ahhh . . . I should have guessed. You think I'm too sick to do it, don't you? Hey, that's what the lithium's for, remember?"

"Lithium helps, that's all."

"Yeah, yeah, yeah." Denise waved him away, bored. She knew all about her manic-depression. She didn't even believe it anymore. Lithium shmithium. She had a job now. A job with John, and she wanted to wallow in it. Savor it. And she didn't need some damn nay-sayer like Sigmund here screwing it up. "You know, you really piss me off."

He regarded her seriously, and Denise itched to touch him. These months of quietude, where she'd huddled in the eye of the storm and let Stone and Connor Jackley and her sisters battle the biggest winds, had made her aware of Dr. Hayden Stone in an entirely unacceptable way. She wanted him. Not sexually. Not really . . . though it was nice to feel strong vibes humming along those lines, too. (She couldn't remember the last time she'd really *wanted* a man like that!) But she wanted something *more*, too. Something tangible that didn't make any sense at all.

What if he wants you, too?

She couldn't bear it. She didn't want him to want her sexually.

Oh, sure! Like you aren't thinking about it right now?

God, it could drive a person crazy.

That struck her as funny and she broke into a huge grin. Stone didn't react and Denise jumped to her feet, padding barefoot across the rug to where he sat on the edge of the black leather armchair.

"I'm not suffering from delusions. I haven't had one romantic liaison in any way, shape, or form in nine months. I've been so good I hate myself. And I'm just lucky that John's giving me this chance. Damn lucky."

Stoner studied her, gauging how honest he could be with such a messed-up looney. Denise knew the look. "He told me your agent badgered him. Called every hour on the hour from the moment that other girl was fired."

"Do you think John would have buckled if he didn't think I was right for the part?"

"I think he feels responsible for you."

"He doesn't give a shit about me."

"He gave you this house. He wants you well. He just doesn't know how to go about it."

Denise couldn't handle this unflattering account of her effect on John. Especially not from Stone. She clenched her fists and had to fight an overpowering urge to run her fingers through his thick hair and drag his mouth to hers.

Schoolgirl stuff! Sick? You bet! And stupid, and romantic, and so juvenile she could hardly stand herself.

"Is my hour up?" she asked, placing a hand on her thrust-out hip. "I wouldn't want to keep you."

"When are you going to talk to me about Thomas Daniels?"

Denise stared, genuinely shocked. All these months and not one word. And now here it was again. The sticky, unrelenting past. How she hated it!

"Why?"

"Because if you don't come to grips with it, touch it, look at it, and understand it, you'll fall back into your old patterns. I can already see it," he added softly. "You're turning it on again."

"Turning what on, Doc?" Denise's jaw was taut. She wanted to clamp her hands over her ears! *No, no, no!*

"The sexuality. You know. Your way of putting up walls, but all it does is victimize you."

"Fuck you."

"You'll either find another Mr. Hawaiian Tropics, or, worse, an Ian Wallace. It'll start again. Maybe it'll be someone working on this picture."

"You don't get it! This picture's practically wrapped. I'm just working myself in around the edges because that talentless bitch made John fire her, and I fell into an enormous opportunity! Like Leo says, this is a perfect way for me to get back into it. I don't have to carry the picture. That's Hayley's problem." A brief flare of envy.

"Denise, you've got to be careful!"

"Why, Doc?"

"You've made progress, but it's nothing. It's waiting to be swept away by an uncaring, ruthless world. I want you to succeed."

Was that pent-up passion she heard? He definitely sounded more ruffled than she would have credited him for. Was she getting to him?

"Don't worry, I will," she assured him. She knew how to act. The one thing she really knew was how to be someone else. "You worry too much. It's kind of sweet. But that whole thing about my stepfather is over. I haven't seen Connor in weeks."

"That's because he's in Wagon Wheel."

A breath across her shoulders. Cold worry. She shook it off. "Nothing can hurt me now," she declared. "I've walked through the fire, okay? Besides, that's all old news. Nobody cares!"

"Denise," he murmured softly, shaking his head.

"What? What do you want me to do?" she demanded.

"Try."

"No." Her answer came swiftly, surprising her with its vehemence.

"It won't go away. It will never go away." He spoke slowly, meaningfully.

"I can cope without it."

The doctor climbed to his feet. He looked down at her from his superior height, and Denise responded to the defeat in his face. She touched the sleeve of his blue oxford shirt. He glanced down at her fingers. Acting on instinct alone, her other hand cupped his jaw, thrilling to the feel of bone and tissue and the beginnings of afternoon shadow.

"It's time to leave," he told her, moving from her tentative embrace.

"You haven't ever made it with a patient," she answered her own question. "Too many scruples."

He almost smiled. She could feel the warmth beneath

his ever-proper exterior. She had great radar for such things.

"Next time, we'll meet at my office," he told her, a warning.

"Maybe there won't be a next time," Denise challenged him. *How do you like that, Sigmund?*

For an answer he gave her his patented professional stare. Rage shivered beneath her skin. Giving into impulse she grabbed up one of John's vases and threw it after him as he walked into the foyer.

Crash! It shattered against the wall, shards of cerulean glass flying everywhere. Shocked, Denise cried out and ran after him, filled with remorse at the sight of him nursing a cut that was bleeding through the arm of his shirt—almost the exact place she'd first touched him.

"I'm sorry! I'm so sorry!" she stammered.

"At my office we're going to talk about Thomas Daniels, Hayley, Dinah, and high school." His voice was ice. "That's all I want to talk about."

She nodded, knowing this was not the time to argue. Then his gaze slipped to her mouth. *Aha!* she thought. *He does notice!* Her lips parted expectantly, hopefully, but he left without another word.

Denise sank against the wall and clutched her chest, fighting down her hammering heart. She closed her eyes. What could she do to make him realize she really cared? *What?*

Dr. Stone was not made of stone. Maybe, if she were really, really lucky, she could get him to care. Care in a way she needed and craved. Care for her and her alone.

Her senses swam, the thought so heady she felt scared. *Clench your fist. Push the poisons out . . .*

Except she wanted to feel this. She wanted to feel this burgeoning sensation. *Love?* No! She loved John.

"The hell you do," she said, her mouth twisting in irony. "You love Dr. Stoner."

A hiatus. Two days of down time while the location crew returned and his production team filmed the final scenes in the studio. A good thing, too, because his new star looked wrung out, as if she were shriveling in on herself a bit more each day.

Twisting the Jeep's steering wheel as he negotiated a traffic light, John viciously punched the stop button on his CD player, thoroughly annoyed with Kenny G, though normally he was one of his favorite artists.

He felt as if he'd walked through hell without being cleansed.

It was incredible how quickly one's life changed. In the space of an hour, a second, the blink of an eye.

The night he'd learned of Dinah.

His teeth clenched. He couldn't think of her without primal anger.

And then the mess of Ian Wallace. He'd been revolted in so many ways, but the funny thing was he'd been almost *proud* of Denise! Instead of hovering behind sharp words and orchestrated scenes, she'd actually broken free and bashed the bastard. Good for her! If anyone needed to set their inner self free it was Denise, and there was certainly no better target than Wallace.

John couldn't work up regret over the man's death. He'd done it to himself. Set it up. Hurt people. Used and abused needy souls, then taken the cheap way out when the going got tough.

His mouth tightened grimly. Unfortunately, Denise hadn't survived the experience without a few more wounds to her psyche. She was better. He could see that, though he tried to spend as little time as possible with her. It bothered him to see her; he could admit that. It bothered him that she looked so much like Dinah, and that his feelings were raw and untethered and therefore unpredictable.

But he'd asked Denise to take Melissa Birker's place in *Lady Paradise*. The part was nothing Denise had ever done. It was subtlely layered and softly written. Anyone playing Katie would have to walk on cat's feet or it wouldn't work. Melissa had charged through like the proverbial bull in a china shop, and Frankie, or no, John had walked up to her the last time she'd blown the scene and said, "Goodbye." Of course it had pissed her off. And Frankie had screamed and gesticulated and generally made a noisy, time-wasting scene, then walked himself.

So . . . back to the drawing board.

And then he'd thought of Denise. He'd refused to have her as his star. He'd been on that ride before and no amount of coercion by Walburn or that whiney agent of hers would make him change his mind. But for Katie . . . the idea jolted him. He felt that buzz of electricity, a sort of sixth sense when he knew he was on the right track.

In an excited frame of mind, he'd driven straight to the Malibu house and interrupted a session between Denise and her shrink. Fleetingly, he'd wondered if she was sleeping with Dr. Stone, but just as fleetingly, he'd dismissed the thought because it truly didn't matter to him.

"Wanna be in my movie?" he'd drawled. All acrimony and fury and hate had left him, transfused with a sense of calm and acceptance he found slightly startling. This was Denise, after all. The woman he hated. Yet, it was simply over now, and because she had extraordinary radar where he was concerned, she sensed it immediately—and also accepted.

"Are you serious?" Her aquamarine eyes held his.

He told her about firing Melissa. She chortled at the story, and though Dr. Stone frowned, Denise jumped to her feet like a schoolgirl and hugged John spontaneously.

Incredible. And so welcome. But he still couldn't be around her at length, so he stayed at his apartment and slowly came to the conclusion that she should have the Malibu house. It was only fair.

But what about Dinah?

With a slam of brakes, he pulled into his spot at his office, glancing around for Hayley's new Range Rover. The woman had strange tastes. For someone so determined and dedicated, she was a mystery. You woulda thought she'd bitten into this role like a tiger into raw meat, but no, she was tentative and distracted. If he hadn't seen her audition tape for himself, and met her personally and therefore witnessed her aggressiveness, he wouldn't believe it possible. Something had happened. Some epiphany.

Whatever the case, she was not the same, and this meeting was because it was time to have it out with her and figure out what the hell had gone wrong.

He strode into his production offices and the receptionist leaped to her feet, white-faced. "Rodney Walburn was just rushed to UCLA Hospital with a heart attack!"

John digested this bit of startling news. "Is he going to be all right?"

She shook her head and turned up her palms. "Titan wants to talk to you," she added.

He knew what that was about. He owned a percentage of the studio, courtesy of Sampson. Rodney's underlings were probably already scrambling for position, hoping to be the next studio head appointee.

"Hayley Scott's waiting in your office," the receptionist called as an afterthought as he strode down the hall.

Which reminded him of all the problems with *Lady Paradise.*

"You look like death warmed over," Hayley said to herself and the empty room at large.

She'd caught her reflection in the base of the chrome lamp on the credenza behind Callahan's desk. Whoa. It was enough to give her the heebie-jeebies. Worse, she looked better than she felt.

For nine months she told herself it was because of Ian Wallace. God, that had been awful. It had haunted her all through these heady days of unrelenting success. Stuck to her conscience like a leech throughout location filming in Colorado, for the scenes of Toni's youth, and yes, Hollywood Boulevard, for the misery of Toni's present. Hayley told herself the reason she was so upset was because she expected to run into some of her old pals like Gloria Carver, but in truth, she knew she could brazen her way through anything. Hell, if worse came to worst, she'd just tell the damn truth! She was no hooker; she'd just been "soaking up the local color."

It would make great copy after the film was released.

But that wasn't what troubled her. Nor was it the memory of Ian Wallace's blood-soaked, unconscious form, or Denise's palsied response to beating him senseless.

It was the truth that bothered her. The truth about the past. And the fact that Connor Jackley *knew* she'd remembered.

She remembered Denise screaming, spattered with

blood, the chunk of granite beside her smeared brick red and stuck with bits of hair. And she remembered the "O" of Thomas Daniels's mouth as his dead eyes stared up at Denise in disbelief—which hadn't slowed the battering one iota, by the look of things.

She remembered the murder.

Now, flinging herself in one of the black leather and chrome chairs surrounding Callahan's desk, Hayley covered her eyes with one hand and choked back a cry. She was derailed, her soul destroyed. There was no going back. No way to concentrate on a career she'd felt was the one—the only—goal in her life.

And Connor . . .

He was to her what Dr. Stone was to Denise. Savior, confidante, friend. Except Hayley could tell him nothing without incriminating her sister. But the truth was eating away at her like acid, and Connor Jackley was watching. Watching and waiting and pretending he wasn't following through with the investigation.

He was talking about moving to Wagon Wheel. He'd grown up in Bend and had family in Wagon Wheel. He wanted her to visit the area with him. Wanted to share with her his plans for the future.

But it was all a lie. A trap. A way to entice and lure her into his dreams. Never once had he said he cared about her. Never once had she intimated that he was rapidly becoming her whole life. Gone was the smart-ass, would-be superstar actress who used people to get what she wanted. Gone was the waitress whom Jason had dubbed, "The worst employee on earth."

Gone was everything. And in its place was everything she'd ever wanted—careerwise.

Why don't you want it anymore?

Turmoil inside, like a whirlpool swirling and swishing

and rushing and gurgling until she thought she'd lose her mind. Dragging in a half-breath, she fought for control. The film was almost finished. She'd done well, but it had taken every bit of wisdom and patience on John Callahan's part to achieve the result she should have been able to produce effortlessly.

And now they had to do the scenes over with Katie because Melissa had plowed through the part as if it were a caricature rather than a serious character.

And John had hired Denise.

Turmoil inside. War of the senses. A loss of reality and focus.

Maybe I'm nuts like Denise. Maybe I'm crazier.

Why couldn't she forget? Thomas Daniels had deserved his death as much as Ian Wallace had. But it was the way Denise had done it. The bashing, bashing, bashing, and the hysterical screaming that was one part fear and two parts glee.

The door banged open and Callahan appeared in a rush, shooting her a hard look from head-to-toe that only made Hayley more cognizant of her drawn face and pale color.

"You must have lost ten pounds when you couldn't afford an ounce," he stated shortly. "Are you sick?"

"No."

"Pregnant?"

"No." She half-laughed.

"Drugs?"

"Give me a break."

"Has someone been harassing you? Someone involved with the film?"

"No."

"Has some tragedy occurred that I know nothing about? Something that's sent you into a depression?"

Hunching her shoulders, she shook her head.

"Don't tell me it's Ian Wallace because I won't believe it."

"No," Hayley felt like screaming at the top of her lungs but couldn't muster the effort. "Are you unhappy with my performance? Do you want me to do something over?"

"I want you to gain weight. You don't even look like the same person I hired to play Toni. I want you to resolve whatever's bothering you, because, damn it, Hayley, I've got a lot riding on *Lady Paradise* and I don't want you to screw it up!"

Harsh words. She flinched, yet she couldn't blame him. He'd taken a chance on her, and she'd let him down in a way neither of them could have anticipated.

"We're going to take a break," he decided suddenly. "A week, maybe two. We'll film the scenes with Denise that don't require you, but there aren't that many of them. I need you, Hayley. Back the way you were. Whatever it takes, fix this problem, and come back to production *whole.*"

She left his office in a daze. If she told on Denise, the film would be over anyway, wouldn't it?

She drove directly to Connor's apartment. She'd spent a lot of hours here. He'd become a fixture in her life; the first man to breach her defenses and earn the label "friend." Not lover. She couldn't face that. Nor had he shown any inclination that way. But then to him she was a source, his best way to learn the truth, because Dinah didn't seem to know it, and Denise, well, she'd either buried it so deep she couldn't remember, or else her conscience—unlike Hayley's—allowed her to keep it secret.

Maybe that's why Denise was so screwed up.

When she got to the apartment, he wasn't home.

Vaguely she remembered talk of him taking another trip back to Oregon. Had he already left?

She was still sitting in her car, completely lost as to what to do next, when Connor's black sedan turned into the apartment parking lot, pulling into the spot next to hers. He smiled at her and Hayley's heart felt like breaking.

Sliding down his window, he waited for her to do the same. It was an effort. She had to reach across the seat and crank the thing down.

"Hey," he said softly, his gray eyes searching hers.

"I was afraid you'd already left."

"I'm leaving tonight."

"Oh."

He flicked a glance at his dashboard clock. "You want to come?"

"To Oregon? I'm—I'm working."

"I talked to Callahan, Hayley. He said he forced you to take some time off."

"You were asking about me?" she asked faintly.

"Come with me," he ordered with more urgency.

"You think I'll crack, don't you?" she said, with a resurgence of her old humor. "Don't bet on it."

He was deliberately blunt. "It's killing you. It's not a game anymore."

"I don't know anything."

"Then come with me and find out."

He knew she was lying. He'd known forever. Hayley felt herself being sucked down deep into some thick muck which pulled and pulled and pulled. Soon she'd suffocate. He was right. It was killing her.

"All right," she said wearily. "I'll go . . ."

Chapter Seventeen

"Start over," Stone said in his annoyingly shrink way. Denise glared at him and slouched in the chair. Did he purposely make his office chairs uncomfortable? Did he expect her to blurt out all the little nasties of her past just so she could get the hell out of here?

"We moved to Wagon Wheel when I was sixteen," she said in a sing-song voice. "I don't remember my real dad. He left before I was six."

"Where did you live first?"

"Portland . . . Medford . . . Bend. We moved a lot because my mother was always looking for work as a waitress, and we had trouble paying our bills." Denise gave him a look. "We ditched on the rent a lot."

"So, your mother was having trouble making ends meet, and then . . . ?"

"She met Dear Old Stepdaddy, Tom, and we moved from Bend to Wagon Wheel."

"What did you think of him?"

Stone didn't actually steeple his fingers under his chin, but he sure as heck emanated the impression. She'd revised her opinion of him. Not only was he fixated on sex, he was fixated on the past. "You're not one of those weirdos who believes in that delayed memory stuff, are you? I mean, if I start remembering that my stepfather forced me into a Satanic cult, and I watched him and his beer-drinking buddies sacrifice a one-month old baby, I'll have to give you up as my therapist *and* sue you for False Memory Syndrome."

"I don't think either of us has to worry about that," he said patiently. God, his patience would drive her crazy if she wasn't already there!

"Oh, yeah?" She lifted a brow in disbelief.

"Because you're fighting your memories back. But they're right there, in your throat, choking you."

The words hung in the air. *Choking you.* An ominous frisson of fear rippled down her spine. Sometimes he scraped unbearably close.

"Tell me," he urged softly, watching her.

Denise grasped the wooden arms of the chair, her hands slick with sweat. They'd danced and danced about this. Every shrink she'd ever seen had performed this same two-step.

"What did you think of your stepfather?" he asked again.

Denise considered. Guilt beat inside her head. Maybe it was time to confess.

She swallowed, hesitated, then finally said, "You're not going to like it."

"How did you feel about him?" he pressed.

"I was attracted to him," she shot back. "I *liked* him."

Silence. Not the answer he'd expected? No . . . not the answer she'd expected to give. He'd been loathsome and crude and dirty, and she'd hated him. Hated him with such passion it had seemed surreal.

Stone stared at her, gauging the truth of her words, she supposed. "You liked him?" he repeated.

"He was . . ." She couldn't say it. Just couldn't say it.

But Stone was waiting. His dark eyes seeing everything. For a moment she thought he'd whispered her thoughts. It seemed like he spoke.

"Sexy," she muttered, turning away, lips quivering.

There. She'd said it. Admitted her shame. Yes, she'd flirted with him. She'd done it knowingly. Until he responded and then it had been too late. Much too late.

"Did your mother have any previous boyfriends?"

"Lovers, you mean?" She heard the snarl in her voice but couldn't prevent it. "None that mattered. Thomas Daniels swept her off her feet, and I wanted him." She folded her arms around herself. "For God's sake, Stoner, it's freezing in here. Can't you afford to turn up the heat?"

"It's on an automatic timer. Maybe I could find you a sweater."

"Forget it." She got up from the chair and walked to the windows, staring at the well-tended bougainvillea and jade plants scattered outside.

"So, you found him attractive."

"At first," she answered quickly. "Only at first. And yeah, I led him on, but then I really didn't want to do anything, y'know? But he didn't get the message. He kept coming after me, and coming after me, and coming after me. If Dinah hadn't been there, he would have gotten me."

"She saved you?"

"She always saved us." Denise smiled wryly. "Without Dinah, Hayley and I would have been sunk. She nailed him with a bowling trophy and a high heel and some other things. He hit her a time or two, but she was quick. Dinah knows what to do."

"So, Thomas Daniels never forced you into sexual relations."

"I . . ." She struggled to speak and shook her head. "No."

"But there were some times when he came close?"

She was taken back, suddenly, to the smell of the basement—damp, dirty, musty. The extra room was there, the one with a cot and Denise was freezing cold, shivering, pressed up against the concrete wall while Thomas unwrapped his belt.

"You like this, don't you, little hot pants?"

She watched the belt uncoil, mesmerized, listening to the tattoo of her heartbeat. No Dinah. Dinah wasn't here. No Mama, 'cause she was sleeping on the bed, too tired to help. And Hayley couldn't know. Couldn't let her know 'cause she was too young.

The first slap took her breath away, then she felt nothing. His fists followed, thick and red and full of power and hate. She felt nothing. Then he stripped out of his clothes and she watched in silence as he stroked himself and initiated her into this, their soon-to-be nightly ritual. She felt nothing. Nothing but a sense of the inevitable. Because she deserved it. She always deserved it.

"Deserved what?" Stone leaned forward, tuned in. Apparently she'd spoken aloud.

Denise licked her lips. Stared down at her trembling palms. "I lusted after him. I wanted him. And I deserved to have him."

That stopped him for a moment. *Surprised, Doc?*

He recovered. "You were a kid with a crush on your mother's husband. It's normal."

"Oh, no, no." She wagged a finger at him. "No fancy mumbojumbo. I wanted him, and I got him. The cruel bastard! I dreamed about him. Us. In bed together. I wanted him. I let him know in a hundred little ways. A flirtatious smile. A slip of the hand in his. Shit, I just brightened up when he walked in a room."

"Until?"

"Until I saw what it was doing to my mother," Denise choked out.

"Until he acted on your flirtatious ways," Stone corrected gently.

"I think my mother knew." Her voice was softer and softer, barely audible. She couldn't hear the words. Couldn't face them.

"Was he sleeping with your other sisters?"

"NO!" The shriek that jumped from her throat startled her. Now her lips were quivering, too. She covered them with one shaking hand.

"How do you know?"

"Because they hated him."

"But you hated him, too."

"I was the one who wanted him," she shot out through clenched teeth. "Not Hayley."

"Why did you say Hayley and not Dinah?" he asked after a long moment.

"Because he couldn't have Dinah," she answered rapidly.

"But he could have Hayley?"

"She was *fourteen!*"

The cry reverberated through the room. From a great distance Denise viewed the scene with humor. He'd done it. He'd wrung a confession from her. From a memory she'd fought hard to repress.

"Thomas Daniels forced himself on Hayley when she was fourteen." Stone said the words, but she could tell he didn't want to say them either.

She nodded jerkily. "It was always when Dinah wasn't around. He was shrewd. He was so godawful shrewd. But he couldn't fight Dinah. Everytime he hit her, she hit back. But if she'd known about what he did to us, she would have killed him."

"So, you hid it from her."

"Oh, yes. Always. And I told Hayley that nothing happened. 'Remember, Hayley. Nothing happened,' I said. And she believed me."

Floodgates. Opening slowly with a rush of poison behind them. Denise the sick-o, was now Denise the Blabbermouth. Blah, blah, blah. Bad words. Bad memories. Bad, bad times.

"So, am I cured, Doc?" she asked bitterly. "Now that you know all that you suspected to be true. You should be proud. Give yourself a medal. You've done what no man has done before, and I feel brand new. Hallelujah!"

"I'm sorry you had to protect them," he answered, his voice sounding faraway and ripply.

"Protect them? I didn't do a goddamn thing."

"You kept his attention focused on you. You tried to save Hayley and you tried to save Dinah, too."

"You're nuts, Doc. You make no sense," she said wearily.

She heard him walk around his desk. He was right behind her. His breath on her neck. "I know what you thought. 'If I keep him occupied, maybe he'll forget about my little sister. But I've got to be careful, because if Dinah finds out, she'll kill him. She really will.' "

"Fuck you, Stoner!"

"You think Dinah killed him and you've been burying everything and keeping it inside and destroying yourself with it."

"I'm not that deep, shrink," she blasted. Now her whole body was shaking and shock of all shocks, he placed a comforting hand on her shoulder. Wetness in her eyes. Tears. She turned her palms skyward and watched them drop hotly onto her skin.

"You're just not very good at hiding things," Stone answered. "Especially from yourself."

Her skin felt seared from his touch. The urge to turn into his arms was overwhelming. She fought it, but he was too close and too important to her. Swallowing, she slowly rotated, wrapping her arms around his neck and silently seeking comfort. At first he resisted. He let her hold him, but he didn't respond. But then his hands crept tentatively across her back and he returned the embrace.

"I've wanted you to hold me," she admitted, her voice muffled against his shoulder.

She felt him shake his head. "You've been sending off sexual signals to keep me from finding out about you." A beat. "You're still doing it."

"This isn't sexual."

"Isn't it?"

She vehemently shook her head, dragging herself back from him in an effort to prove her point. But damn the man. He was right! She was already thinking about sex with him. Already feeling triumphant that she'd breached his first line of defense.

Shocked at herself, her feelings must have shown on her face because Stoner actually cracked a smile. "Hey, Denise, you're too attractive to resort to this. Give yourself a break. People will still like you, if you don't sleep with them."

"They don't like me either way," she admitted with painful honesty.

"Yes, they do." He sighed, his breath stirring the blonde hair at her crown. "So, what are we going to do about Dinah?"

"What do you mean?"

He held her at arm's length, staring at her through

those eyes that knew her far too well. "You think she killed Thomas Daniels."

"Who? What?" Denise laughed.

"Dinah."

Her veins were ice. "Wow, do you jump to conclusions! No way."

"You're acting again."

"Oh, sure. Like you know so much about it."

"Your whole body's shaking from fear, Denise. I *know* you think she did it. The question is: what are you and I going to do about it?"

Denise blinked, scared. For once in her life she had no answer.

Connor rented a midsize sedan at the Portland Airport and they began a three hour drive around Mt. Hood toward central Oregon. He glanced at Hayley, huddled in the seat beside him, and did the unthinkable. He reached over and brushed her hair away from her face in a tender motion.

To his amazement, she didn't overreact. She just closed her eyes and leaned toward his fingers.

"I've talked to Dempsey and the sheriff's department about a job. I'm definitely moving back," he said.

"I know."

"I want you to come with me."

"Oh, sure." She half-laughed. "There's really an abundance of good film roles in Nowheresville, Oregon."

"I'm serious, Hayley."

She looked at him, then. Understanding crossed her face. A brief flare of pure happiness, then the curtain of guilt and fear.

"You have to tell me everything," he warned gently. "That's why we're here. Before we go back, I want to know the complete, unvarnished truth."

She didn't respond and Connor settled in to drive, determined to have all the answers no matter what it took to get them.

". . . Three, two, one . . ." The production assistant circled his hand and indicated that she was on camera.

Dinah stared at the single eye of the lens. It was surprisingly easy and impersonal, this verbal reporting stuff, though she certainly got impassioned over some of her subject matter. With practiced ease, she slid into her editorial on the slimy, step-on-your-neighbor's-grave-for-a-good-story, tabloid tactics of the media. Pure irony, since she was the media, but right now, the message was the important thing.

A minute and a half to say everything she had to say. More time than they liked to allow, but enough to get the point across. She spoke casually, her voice rising as it always did at the end.

". . . what is the price of fame?" she finished. "And whose life is it, anyway?"

The production assistant signaled the cut-off. Dinah grabbed her papers and hurried from the desk, stepping over snaking cables and aiming for the gray double doors at the back of Studio One.

John Callahan stood there, as expressionless as a sphinx.

"What's wrong?" Dinah asked anxiously. "Denise?"

Something in his eyes flickered. "No, it's not Denise."

"What then?"

"I want to talk to you."

Dinah's aquamarine eyes widened. Today she wore make-up, for the camera, and she'd actually sold out and put some blonde highlights in her hair, once again for the camera. She hated it, but she wasn't completely stupid.

Except where Callahan was concerned.

"What about?" she asked, leading him from the studio to the inner carpeted hallway.

"Hayley."

"Hayley?" Dinah repeated, giving him a once over.

"I'll take you to dinner," he ordered by way of invitation, "and we'll talk."

He took her to his apartment which was just as masculinely designed as his bedroom at the Malibu house. Prints by unknown artists in shades of taupe and black and peach accented a cool room with off-white carpet, rust brown leather couches, and wrought-iron floor lamps. It wasn't fancy, nor was it homey, but since Dinah felt like a fretful interloper anyway, it was just fine.

"So, where's the food?" she asked.

He opened the refrigerator where someone had left an array of cold salads. "I asked my housekeeper to make us up something."

"You knew I'd say yes, huh?"

He set several bowls of pasta salad and salad greens on the counter, then eyed her in a way that made her fight not to wriggle in discomfort. "I planned to do my damnedest to persuade you," he said, motioning her to a black leather barstool.

They ate in silence, the minutes stretching out.

She sipped red wine and stared straight ahead, hating

herself for the simple fact that she wanted him to sweep her into his arms and make hot, passionate love to her all night long.

Ratwoman, she told herself in taut fury. *You're a ratwoman!* Ratwomen let men walk all over them and kept coming back for more.

Except that, she reminded herself sternly, he didn't want her.

"Something's wrong with Hayley," he said in his slow-talking drawl.

"Wrong?"

"She's completely changed."

"Like you know her so well?" she asked, hating her jealous, barbed tongue.

"I know that she was selfishly determined and brilliantly focused and now she's neither."

"What does that mean?" Dinah really heard him for the first time.

John's gaze swept reflectively down her face, focusing on her throat where her heart beat, strong and even. "Something happened to her, and I think it happened during that whole Ian Wallace mess. Either that did it, or something related to it. She just can't keep it together and this damn film is going to collapse around us all if she doesn't find a way out."

Dinah inwardly snorted. So, that was it. His precious film. "You want me to talk to her?"

He shook his head. "She's gone to Oregon. Jackley's still working on your stepfather's murder—"

"What?"

"—case," he finished, frowning.

"Why did Hayley go to Oregon?" Dinah demanded. "To *Wagon Wheel?*"

John nodded. "He thinks she can help. So, we're film-ing the scenes with Denise that don't—"

"Why did he take her?" Dinah broke in again. "Why *only* her?"

"Beats me," John replied, staring. She knew she was acting like a maniac but she couldn't help it. "Hey, if it brings her around, more power to him."

Dinah's face set in hard lines of concentration. "He should be talking to me."

"Jackley?" John gave her a long look. "Why? Do you know something?"

Dinah regarded him coolly. She hadn't kept secrets this long to suddenly spurt them out like a fountain. "When did they leave?"

"Couple days ago." She could feel his own brain click-ing away, tallying up.

"I'm going, too."

"Whoa!" he declared, grabbing her as she slid off the stool. "You know the truth, don't you?" he said in amaze-ment. "You do!"

"It isn't what you think."

"How do you know what I think?" When she didn't immediately answer, his eyes narrowed and he said, "This all has to do with Daniels, doesn't it? That's why Hayley's been like walking death. You *know* who killed him, and so does she." A beat. "Denise," he whispered.

"No." She shook her head vehemently.

"Yes," he answered.

"Oh, John." Dinah sighed and sucked air between her teeth. It was over. All over. And she was suddenly glad. "I'm the one who stuck his body in the culvert, not Denise."

Chapter Eighteen

Springtime was still frigid winter in central Oregon. Cold, arctic, blasting air rushed off the mountains, sometimes forming into snow, sometimes turning to needles of rain so cold they took your breath away.

Hayley stood at the edge of the field, her hands tucked inside the insulated navy blue parka. Connor's. He'd wrapped her in the oversized coat, his eyes twinkling as he looked at her tiny form inside.

She wanted to reach out and stroke his beard-shadowed face. She couldn't make herself do it, and the moment had ended.

Now, the whistling wind filled her ears, so cold it gave her an instant earache. Her eyes squinted and she gazed at the soggy stalks of field grass, feeling slightly sick.

The culvert where Thomas's body had been found was about fifty feet away. The field was in back of the house where they'd all once lived, but no one had ever looked in the culvert. The place had gone into receivership after Daniels's disappearance, and the subsequent owners had leased the property to a middle-aged, retired couple who never set a foot out of the tiny crabgrass-infested backyard. The fence that had once surrounded the periphery had long ago fallen into disrepair and ignoring its gray, weathered, broken slats, two boys had ridden on horseback into the open area and come across Daniels's body.

She'd told Connor a little bit about her past, how she'd shied away from her lecherous stepfather, how she'd squirmed when girls at school had whispered about his numerous affairs.

But she hadn't told him about Denise.

Now, however, the accusing silence of the place coupled with the angry whine of the wind preyed on her soul. She had little resistance. None, really.

He'd taken her to meet the players in this dark farce. His nephew, Matt, and his close friend, Mikey. His own sister, Mary, who spent half the time regarding Hayley with pity and understanding; half the time haranguing her brother into rejoining the force. His laconic brother-in-law and the sheriff, Gus Dempsey, who clearly thought Denise was guilty, and who was eager to close the book on the whole damn thing and forget it.

And then there'd been the curiosity seekers, the ones who came to see *her*. Ex-schoolmates, ex-friends, ex-everything. Hayley Scott, Denise Scott's little sister, an aspiring actress who may, or may not, have knocked off her mother's vile husband.

And wonder of wonders, a balding thirty-ish man with flashy taste and more money than sense had introduced himself to her as Jimmy Fargo, Denise's long ago love. He'd driven down from Seattle at Connor's request, she'd learned, and he was eager to be a part of the investigation.

"Yeah, she was pregnant," Jimmy had told them, settling back in a squeaking chair in Dempsey's office for a big, long yarn. "I gave her money for an abortion, and she did it. I regret it now, though. We shoulda had that baby and been a family." He smiled in a way he undoubtedly thought was full of regret but managed to look merely slimy. "I'm doing alright now in Seattle. Sold my parent's place here, got quite a pretty penny for it, then invested in real estate in Seattle. Made a fortune!"

"Then, why did you sell your story to a tabloid," Hayley asked, feeling dirty just being near him.

"Well, sure, there've been a few lean times. And, besides, I think the public has a right to know the truth. After all, she's down there making tons of money and acting like she's so good and all. I thought people should know, that's all."

Throughout this exchange, Connor said nothing, but Hayley could feel the waves of disgust emanating from him. Jimmy Fargo was a weasel. He'd been cute and kind of cool in high school, but he'd turned into an ogre of mega-magnitude.

"You're certain the child was yours," Connor had finally asked.

Fargo's face turned a dull, ugly red. "You bet it was!"

"I was just wondering if there was any other man in—"

"*I* was her man, okay? Me. Nobody else. She killed *my* baby!"

Hayley had turned away. She couldn't look at him. He was another part of the problem that had led to the killing, and she couldn't bear to look at him.

Jimmy then went on about Denise and how nobody believed him that she was Denise Scott, the movie star. It was clear he was upset that some of her fame and notoriety hadn't rubbed off on him and he meant to set things right. Finally, Connor held the door for him and Jimmy reluctantly got to his feet.

"I remember you had that concussion," he'd added at the door, wagging a finger at Hayley in recollection. "Couldn't make it to class and all. Denise said you fell, but

Mr. Saunderson called county services and went to see if you were all right. I remember 'cause it was right before she left. Before you all left," he added bitterly.

Fuzziness. Hayley almost recalled that same memory but it eluded her somehow. She was afraid to chase it. Afraid it might reveal even more memories she didn't want to see.

Connor managed to hustle Jimmy outside. He paid him for his time, hoping he'd head back to Seattle, but Jimmy was having none of it. He was determined to hang around like a bad smell and stink up everything.

Hayley shivered and pulled the parka closer. So, now she was at the scene of the crime and Connor, apparently, was waiting for miracles.

"How're you doing?" he asked as he tramped across the dead stubble toward her.

"Okay."

"Let's go back to the motel."

She nodded. They walked across the field side-by-side. Hayley's eyes had a will of their own. They glanced at the spot—*the* spot—where it had happened. She knew exactly where it was.

Instantly she felt the familiar increase of her heartbeat, the flood of warmth and then its quick disappearance, like the turn of the tide. Anxiety attack. She hadn't had them in years. Had buried them under layers of forced sanity. She was *not* like Denise.

His gloved hand suddenly encircled her arm. She stumbled anyway, gazing in horror at a circle of ground behind the house, just outside the yard, in a thicket of overgrown blackberry vines and jack pines.

"What is it?" Connor asked from faraway.

A woman shrieking and screaming. An arm swinging downward, bludgeoning an inert body. The body bouncing and twitching with each blow. Blood, blood . . . so much blood. Denise, rocking to and fro, her hands covering her face, her clothes splattered red. A piece of granite sticky with blood and hair.

"Hayley?" he asked, grabbing her shoulders, shaking her, his breath white gusts against the gray sky.

She stared at him through tortured eyes. "He deserved to die."

Connor gazed at her, feeling her anguish as his own. Her brittle shell had broken so completely and left the unformed woman. Knowing she would resist, he reacted to his feelings anyway, dragging her to his chest, cradling her close.

He didn't expect anything more. Not now. Not today. It was all unraveling anyway. She would tell him in time because he'd ripped the scab off this wound and she was writhing with pain. He hated himself for it, but, like Denise, Hayley had to come to grips with the past if she ever expected to be whole.

So, he was surprised when she spoke again, and her words turned his veins to ice.

"It was me," she said quietly. "Because he kept trying to . . . because he followed me and Denise, and came into our rooms . . . and he . . . and he . . ." A shudder ran through her whole body. "And he touched me. And hurt me." He felt her swallow. "I killed him. I had to."

Connor closed his eyes, resting his chin on the top of her crown, sick. Daniels did deserve to die. He did. With a wrench of his heart he heard the echo of his sister's admonitions. *You're going to put one of those girls in jail . . . You're going to ruin her life for the sake of avenging Thomas Daniels . . .*

He just hadn't expected it to be Hayley.

* * *

It was later. Much later. He'd taken Hayley back to the
Wheel Treat You Right Motel, Wagon Wheel's only decent lodgings, regardless of the silly name, and now Connor was driving in his sister's Ford Explorer, footloose and
bothered. His feelings were all tangled up. He was close
to the truth; like a bloodhound he could scent it. But it
hurt.

The Explorer bounced up the rain-slogged ruts to a
gray-shingled house with a trim lawn and a carport where
an older model Plymouth wagon looked as if it had just
wheezed to a stop.

Connor cut the engine, pocketed the keys, and made
his way around the mud puddles to the front door. The
sky was slate gray and close and when the door opened,
letting out the aroma of cinnamon and nutmeg, Connor
breathed deeply, an ache building inside him he couldn't
control.

"Yes?" a woman with tightly curled gray hair asked.

"Mrs. Saunderson? I have an appointment with your
husband."

"Oh, yes . . ." She held the door open wide and Connor stepped inside.

Saunderson sat by a tidy fire, glasses slipping down his
nose, working his way through the paper's daily cross-
word puzzle. He glanced up at Connor and waited while
the younger man took a seat. Then he said simply, "I
can't tell you anything more than what I said on the
phone. Hayley Scott was in my history class and she came
in with bruises now and again. Her sister always said it
was just accidents, but I didn't believe it. Called the
county, and went to her house, too. That last time she was

concussed, but Daniels wasn't around to question. He was already gone."

Already dead, Connor guessed, his gut tightening.

Saunderson sighed heavily. "There was talk of sending Hayley to a foster home, since no one but the twins were around, but nothing happened, and then they all left."

"When you went to the house, what were your impressions?"

Reflectively, he pulled his glasses off his nose. "That something terrible had happened and they were all desperately trying to cover it up."

Denise sprayed Chanel #5 liberally on her throat and wrists, inhaling deeply. The scent penetrated so deeply it amazed her. She was awake. No perpetual sleepwalking. No fuzziness and lost hours and delusions. She was *awake*.

Confession must be good for the soul, she decided wryly, gazing at the Santa Fe motif of her bedroom. Odd. It felt like a stranger's room. Everything, in fact, gave her a creepy feeling that she was living out someone else's life. She was entirely disconnected from her room, the house, the lifestyle, even John . . .

She had to remind herself almost hourly that yes, this was Denise Scott Callahan's life, and that yes, she was Denise Scott Callahan.

New thoughts. Eerie feelings. Stone was chip, chip, chipping away at her, and for reasons she didn't entirely understand, she was letting him. Maybe it was because her bipolar-crapola-manic-depressive problem was under control. Or, maybe she'd just reached that age when victims supposedly can face what happened to them in their youth and dredge up the buried memories. Or, maybe it was Stoner himself.

Whatever the case, she was better. She could feel it inside. Like great ice floes breaking apart and floating away.

Push the poisons out . . . out into the great void of space.

Denise closed her eyes and held out her fist, slowly opening her hand until her fingers splayed and stretched, mentally pushing, pushing, pushing—until all the baddies suddenly spurted from her fingers and shot away.

Opening one eye, she glanced at her straining hand. A giggle caught in her throat. The exercise that had saved the remnants of her sanity didn't work anymore. She *was* better.

She'd worked today and the production crew had been warm and relaxed and so easy to be with that she could hardly credit it. With her history, she would expect them to hate her, or at the very least, distrust her. But they didn't walk on eggshells around her, and they didn't treat her with extra deference—a quality she would have demanded in her diva-bitch days! No, they were all there to get the job done, and the job had got done remarkably quickly. John's assistant director was a great guy who knew how to make everyone feel comfortable, though she wished John would return from his sudden trip to parts unknown. She still worked best with him.

So, now she was waiting for Stoner. She'd begged a dinner out of him, the Freudian cheapskate, and though he'd been loathe to agree, he'd finally caved in.

He hadn't taken his belief that Dinah was Thomas's killer to the police. Though unspoken between them, he clearly knew Denise would lie, cheat, and steal to protect her twin. And if Dinah truly bashed the bastard over the head—Denise was still unclear on the details, there—it was in self-defense. No question.

Except there *would* be questions. She'd always known

there would be questions. No self-respecting lawman could keep from asking questions.

Which was why Hayley's involvement with Connor Jackley was such a problem. He had COP stamped all over him, regardless of how sexy he was, and that was bad news any way you read it.

She was in the kitchen, mixing pesto, sundried tomatoes, and ground mozzarella into a paste when the feeling stole over her, standing the hair on her arms on end. She stared at her forearms, watching the gooseflesh raise before her eyes, hearing a rushing in her ears.

Dinah.

The message came in a block. She understood it as she calmly walked toward the closet and reached for her coat. A message. It wasn't often she got one. She was usually too self-absorbed, too undone to tune-in to that special communication line between twins.

But this one was powerful and she was clear tonight. Clear and alert.

The doorbell chimed at the exact moment she pulled the front door open. Standing on the flagstone steps, Stone was surprised enough for her to scare a smile out of him.

"Well, hi. Perfect timing."

"Can you drive me to the airport?" she asked, shrugging into her coat.

"Where are you going?" he asked.

"Wagon Wheel. Dinah's there, and she's in trouble."

He'd insisted on coming even though she didn't want him. She truly didn't want him here. Things were much too complicated as it was.

"Go back to L.A.," Dinah ordered for the billionth

time, but Callahan dogged her heels from the rental car to the front door of the sheriff's department of Deschutes County.

Bursting through the front door, Dinah didn't expect the impact she made. Mouths dropped and someone punched an intercom button and stuttered out, "G-g-gus, you'd better g-get out here."

A rather homely looking man appeared. As soon as he caught a look at her, and then John who'd followed right on her heels, a friendly smile split his face. "Well, hullo," he greeted them both, pumping Dinah's hand, then John's. "So, you came up here with Jackley, too, huh?"

"Have you talked to my sister?" Dinah bit out.

"She's been talking to Connor."

"Has she?" Dinah didn't crack a smile.

"Could you help us locate them?" John suggested, belatedly introducing himself and Dinah which the sheriff waved away until he heard—really *heard*—Dinah's name.

"Ah'm sorry," he declared. "I thought you must be Denise, since you're here with Mr. Callahan. Well, Connor's probably at his sister, Mary's. I'll give you the address."

He scribbled down the information, so helpful and courteous that Dinah immediately distrusted him. She didn't like the small-town goodwill. She remembered how it was when they were the poor girls living with Thomas Daniels. The looks. The pity. The avid interest.

Nope, she didn't trust Sheriff Gus Dempsey at all.

"I don't want you coming with me," Dinah declared when they were outside and climbing into the rental car. John, however, just slid his lean form in the passenger seat, content to let her lead.

It was a lie anyway, Dinah thought, gritting her teeth. She did want him with her. Although she was scared shitless that he would learn more than he'd bargained for.

She couldn't let it happen.

Hayley sat in an antique rocker in the corner of the kitchen, chilled to the bone. Rocking gently, she distanced herself from the chatter going on around the dinner table. Connor's sister, Mary, was sweet, and her husband, Kurt, didn't say much but his silence was companionable. The kids were great, especially Matt, who wanted so badly to be part of this miserable affair. His older sister, Heather, just stared and smiled because, Hayley had realized wryly, she was in the room with a bonafide actress.

Wait'll she gets a look at Denise.

It was silly, a real cosmic joke, in fact, that Hayley, now that she was an actress, didn't feel like one at all. The goal she'd fought for like a bulldog had no substance. There was nothing there. And she'd ended up back here in Wagon Wheel anyway—the hellhole of her nightmares, had she cared to remember.

Connor came over to her, dropping a palm lightly on her shoulder. "You didn't eat anything."

"I'm not hungry."

For an answer he walked back to the kitchen, snagged a couple of dinner rolls, came back over, and offered her his free hand.

Reluctantly, she accepted and they strolled onto the backporch of the rustic cabin. Kurt was a builder and he'd put the house together bit by bit, weekend by weekend, until it was nearly complete, fashioned entirely out of wood. Wood floors, wood ceilings, wood walls, and wood beams. It was bare and beautiful, and nothing like the threadbare carpets and scarred linoleum of the house she'd shared with Thomas Daniels.

But Wagon Wheel was the same. She'd forgotten the way it smelled, its rural vastness, its complete dislocation from the noise and traffic and accelerated beat of the city.

It scared her.

He propped himself against the porch rail as Hayley sank onto the dusty cushions of a creaking swing. The air was so cold it took your breath away. Hayley huddled inside herself. "Have you called the sheriff?" she asked dully, knowing he would, praying he wouldn't.

"No."

"Why not?"

"I can't do it until you make me believe you killed your stepfather."

"I told you I did."

He shrugged, as if he could just shrug the whole thing away. "I've got to have more."

"More than a confession?" she demanded with a trace of her old fire.

"Tell me about the night it happened."

"I'll tell the sheriff. I don't want to go through it twice."

He tore one of the rolls in half and handed part to her. "Eat," he commanded.

"What's with you?"

Connor looked at her in that way that got under her skin and sent her stomach somersaulting. "I can't decide whether you really believe you did it, or if you're protecting one of your sisters."

"I'm not protecting my sisters."

"I talked to your history teacher this afternoon, Mr. Saunderson."

Hayley recoiled. "And?"

"He remembers you were concussed right around the time Daniels disappeared."

Her smile was humorless. "Well, there you have it. He hit me and I killed him."

"You don't even remember, do you? Something's come back to you, but you really don't remember." He leaned closer. "What is it that's come back?"

Hayley hesitated. The urge to tell him was growing stronger.

"Connor?" Mary called from inside the house. One hand fiddled with her neckline and she glanced nervously over her shoulder.

"What?" he asked a bit sharply, annoyed at being interrupted.

She lifted her palms and without waiting to be announced, a tall, incredibly fat woman worked her way through the backdoor and joined them on the porch. She wore a denim smock and a pair of moccasins, and she breathed heavily, as if the mere effort of breathing was near fatally taxing—which it was, Hayley supposed.

Hayley glanced at Connor who was clearly surprised by his visitor. "Hello, Candy," he said, "this is Hayley Scott. I'm not sure you ever met."

Candy gazed at Hayley, waiting. Hayley shook her head and Candy said, "No."

"Candy is Thomas Daniels's daughter," he explained for Hayley's benefit, though he'd already mentioned her during one of their long talks on the subject. Hayley nodded, feeling uncomfortable around her.

"The whole town's talkin' about Daniels's murder," Candy stated flatly. She glanced around for somewhere to sit, but apart from the railing like Connor, there was only the swing. Hayley got to her feet but Candy waved her back down. "I figured I had as much right as anybody to know what's goin' on." She threw a sideways glance at Hayley. "He was a bastard."

"Yes, he was," Hayley agreed.

"And I'm glad somebody killed him."

Hayley smiled, but a shiver started somewhere inside and her lips began to tremble.

Candy turned her glimmering eyes on Connor. "You tell Gus he should give up on this thing. It's old, and it don't matter anyways. Sheriff Urganis—the sheriff before Gus," she related to Hayley, "looked into the whole damn thing and there was nothin' there. Didn't Gus tell you that?" she demanded of Connor.

"Urganis didn't know Daniels had been murdered," he pointed out. "Gus has to follow through."

"Oh, sure," she muttered, disgusted.

"There's something I didn't ask you before," Connor said reflectively. "Your last name is Whorton."

"Oh, I was married once." Her lips flattened. "Cheated on me with a waitress from Redmond. I didn't like him much anyway."

Hayley couldn't help staring. There was something about Candy that reminded her of Daniels. The bright blue of her eyes, or maybe the shape of her chin. It was eerie.

"He spoke of you once or twice," Hayley told her. "I never really thought about it, though."

"I saw all of you," Candy revealed. "All the time. You were all so pretty, and I wondered why your mama let him in."

"She wasn't the best judge of character," Hayley admitted, recalling Daniels' rough, manly ways. The shiver escalated to a shudder.

"I got married real young," Candy mused. "I had a crush on Jimmy Fargo, too, but he was with Denise."

Hayley cocked her head, surprised by how much

Candy knew about her family. "That's when Jimmy Fargo was cool."

They both laughed softly.

Connor sat in half-shadow, listening quietly. It was a trick of his to melt into the scenery. Keep the customer talking. And Candy and Hayley were bonding in a way he would never have suspected.

It unnerved him.

"Did he . . ." Candy hesitated. "Did he try anything with you?"

Her voice was small, pathetic. Connor closed his eyes and knew without a shadow of a doubt that Thomas Daniels had made a pass at his biological daughter as well.

Hayley knew it, too. She swallowed. "I can't think about it, too much. My mind just . . . hurts."

Candy nodded. "Write this down in your book, cop," she sneered, patting her enormous belly. "All this blubber's for a reason. That's what the shrinks on "Oprah" and "Sally" say. Protection. My old man made it with me and so I just started eatin' and eatin' to make myself so ugly that he'd leave me alone. You believe that?"

Connor didn't respond.

"I think it's true." She turned to Hayley. "I was glad when he left. Real glad. But I kinda worried about you guys."

Hayley shook her head quickly. "We had Dinah. Dinah took care of things."

Candy hesitated. "You tell Denise that none of it matters anymore. There's no evidence, so she should just keep quiet."

Connor rubbed his face. Candy was still stuck on her theory that Denise was the culprit. A cowardly, selfish part of himself wished it were true.

Hayley's smile was sick. Candy looked around some

more for a chair, then decided it was time to go. "Stop by," she told Hayley on the way out. "He can show you the place." She jerked her head to indicate Connor, then she sidestepped through the door and into the house.

Silence, except for the rustle of wind through the trees, icy cold, cutting into her despite the weight of her jacket.

He sat down beside her and picked up one limp hand. "The sassy hooker I met on Hollywood Boulevard wouldn't react like this."

"She never existed."

"She kept you going for nearly ten years. She's there. Bring her back. You need her."

"I just want off the planet."

"You're afraid I'll find out something about Denise."

The words cut to the bone, too true to argue with. They took her breath away because she hadn't realized it: she was protecting Denise.

"Come on, Hayley," he said in a softer voice, one full of concern and, dare she believe it, affection? "Fight back."

Of their own volition, her fingers reached for him, tentatively touching his chin, questioning and unsure. He dragged her closer, comfortingly. Their heartbeats melded.

She whispered, "I used to be able to focus on a field of dry grass and huckleberry bushes, somewhere in the mountains. It kept me sane. But now I think that field is where . . . he was killed. It came over me out there, like a bad, bad memory. God, I can't think!"

His chin rested on her crown. She closed her eyes and gave herself up to his protection. She'd never wanted to be close to a man, and she found this inordinately scary.

"Y'know, I always said I was a virgin," she went on through dry lips. "But it was a lie. I didn't know it, but it was a lie."

"You're you." His voice was a growl in his chest. "That's all that matters."

She drew a shaking breath. "No, it's not."

His lips were against her hair. Now her whole body was trembling. "Tell me," he whispered.

There was a disturbance inside the house. Exclamations. Connor turned his head to listen, then watched in amazement as Mary ran out breathlessly, hands clutching at her throat again.

A long-legged woman strode outside behind her. In the dim light it took Connor a moment to recognize the newcomer.

"Dinah?" he said in surprise.

"Dinah!" Hayley came alive.

"Well, hello," she greeted them. "Is this a private party or can anyone join this pow-wow?"

Hayley rushed into her arms as John Callahan appeared beside her and Connor drawled, "Why do I get the feeling Dinah's here to fix things . . . again."

Chapter Nineteen

It was late, especially for a school night, but Matt Logan had no intention of going to sleep until he'd gotten all the facts written down. Juggling a flashlight and a pen and notepad, he huddled beneath the blankets of his bed, fully clothed. He had to take good notes for Uncle Jack. He didn't care what Mom said. He was important. He'd found the skull, hadn't he? It bugged him that everybody seemed to forget that!

Chewing on his lower lip, he wrote six big question marks in a row. He could tell Uncle Jack was worried about his actress friend. He must think she knocked off old man Daniels. Matt didn't believe it, though. She was too pretty and nice.

Matt had listened hard at the back door to their conversation until Mom shooed him away. Heather had snitched again. She'd smirked at him and he'd wanted to smack her, but if he did, he'd be the one who got sent to his room, not her. Besides she could scratch with those icky, long fingernails and it really *hurt!*

Scribbling down names, he made a face as he wrote Candy. Yuk. She was fat and weird. He'd bet five dollars that *she* did it.

And now this other sister had arrived and Matt itched to know what they were all talking about down there.

Maybe it was time to find out.

Carefully, he cracked open his window which screeched as if it had lungs. He clamped his hands over his ears, scared, but nobody came to nail him. When he peered outside he realized why. They were gone. The back porch was quiet and empty.

Knowing he was begging to be caught, he sneaked out of the room and crept down the stairs. They were all in the family room off the kitchen now, talking by the fireplace in low, serious voices. But it was that other one— that new sister—who was doing most of the talking.

Pencil at the ready, Matt settled on the second to last step and craned an ear to listen.

It wasn't easy to confess. She'd never planned to do it. For over eight years she'd kept the secret close to her breast until it had become a fable, a fantasy, something less than real.

Funny, she'd always believed it would remain that way. Or, if by some bizarre twist of fate, the truth were revealed, then it would be Denise who cracked. Not Hayley.

But one look at Hayley's huge eyes and wan cheeks and Dinah had realized her sister was breaking apart. That brilliant, diamond-hard facade Hayley had adopted soon after the accident, the one Dinah had begun to believe was the true Hayley, had completely collapsed.

So, it was time to face the music. They were waiting. Faces turned to her. Expectant. Worried. Dreading the truth, just as she dreaded telling it.

"I came home early from school," Dinah began. Hayley watched in horror; Connor frowned in concentration;

John stood with a cool, watchful aura of distrust and disappointment. Her throat closed in on itself, but she tore on, knowing if she stopped she'd never be able to finish. "I was playing Whitney Houston, one of her first albums, before she was very famous, and I was blasting it through the windows and outside. Hayley knocked on the door and yelled at me to turn it down but I paid no attention.

"Mama was dead, and I didn't care where Tom was. We had a cat . . . a cat named Bobo," she admitted, her voice faltering a bit as she shot John a nervous glance. "Tom had been home and he'd kicked Bobo so hard the cat had run away, limping. I hated him. I really hated him."

She paused for a moment, her jaw locked, but then she shook off those ragged, leftover feelings. "Denise was with Jimmy Fargo. At least I thought she was. They were as thick as thieves then, and he was bragging about sleeping with her. He disgusted me. So did dear old stepdaddy, but I could handle him, although it did cross my mind that I might have to kill him someday.

"It got later and later. Hayley went out, I guess. She was gone for a long time. When she came back, she called for help, and I finally went to see what was wrong."

Hayley murmured, "I tripped when I was running back to the house."

Dinah nodded. "That's right. She'd fallen down hard and apparently passed out. And she was screaming about something out in the woods. Somebody beating someone again and again. I made her lie down. She was confused—concussed, actually, though I didn't know that at the time. I grabbed the axe by the back door and went outside."

John stirred uncomfortably. Dinah's pulse beat hard,

her feelings threatening to overwhelm her. She loved him and she hated that he was witness to this.

Connor said, "You took the axe with you to the clearing."

Dinah nodded again. "But I didn't use it, if that's what you're thinking. I walked out there and Denise was rocking herself and crying. Thomas's body was there." Dinah swallowed, her mouth dry as sand. "He'd been beaten so badly you could hardly tell who he was.

"Denise was covered with blood," Dinah finished, forcing the words out. "I took her home. Hayley was on the couch, dazed. And Denise started babbling about all these things he'd done to her." She inhaled and exhaled quickly, several times. "I put her in the shower, but she just went on and on. Hysterical. Crying and crying. And then she started bleeding. She miscarried later that week."

Dinah stopped abruptly. The pop and crackle of the fire punctuated the silence. Gazing at John, she longed to be taken in his arms again and soothed and comforted.

"Did she admit to the killing?" Connor asked softly.

Dinah slowly shook her head. "She wasn't coherent. But if you believe half the things she said he did to her, then she killed him to stop him. I have no doubt that it's his fault she miscarried."

Connor slid a look Hayley's way, checking for corroboration.

She smiled wryly, a faint reminder of her former, more selfish self. "I just remember an arm smashing downward and her screaming." She swallowed. "But . . . but I think it was my arm . . ."

"Don't accuse yourself of something to protect someone else," he shot back sharply.

"I'm not," Hayley said wearily.

"Don't," Connor warned, then he turned back to Dinah. "How did his body get in the storm drain?"

"I put it there. I dragged him across the field and shoved him inside. I was glad he was dead. I still am."

Connor regarded her thoughtfully, both impressed and slightly uncomfortable with her steely eyed resolve. He had to agree. It probably was self-defense and Daniels did deserve to die. "What did you do with his clothes?"

Dinah regarded him blankly. "He was naked when I found him."

"Do you think Denise removed them?"

"I never saw them anywhere."

A strange loose end. An untidiness. It bothered him. But there were lots of untidy things about murder. "I'd like you both to talk to Gus Dempsey tomorrow, and Denise needs to be a part of this, too."

"No!" Dinah and Hayley shouted in unison, surprising both Connor and John.

Dinah went on quickly, "She's finally on track. This whole thing nearly killed her, and she's been killing herself ever since. Please don't mess this up."

Connor hesitated. "How about if I talk to Dr. Stone?"

"Fine," Dinah agreed, shooting John a glance. What was he thinking? What did he think about Denise now? About *her?*

He stood near the fire, his expression grim and reflective. She dared not move closer to him; his vibes clearly said her approach wouldn't be welcome.

"I'll call Hayden Stone tonight," Connor said grimly, heading for the phone.

"Denise is a royal pain in the rear end," Dinah couldn't help from saying, "but she's a victim. I don't want her hurt anymore than she already has been."

Connor paused. Glancing over his shoulder, he read

the faces of his three guests and came to the not-so-hard-to-reach conclusion that they all believed Denise had murdered her stepfather. Not Hayley. Not Dinah.

Denise.

A terrible, selfish part of himself hoped it was true.

The Wheel Treat You Right Motel's sign sputtered and hummed in green neon. John Callahan walked beneath it, so conscious of the woman beside him he felt tied to her presence by an invisible rope.

"Dinah," he muttered, as her foot reached the first step of the outdoor stairs that led to their connecting rooms.

She hesitated, turned around, her face serious and pale in the uncertain light. They stared at each other, so much to say and no way to say it.

His lips twisted into a bitter smile. "I don't care about any of it except that you couldn't tell me the truth."

"I'm the protector," she said by way of answer.

He wanted to tell her he loved her. Damn it all. Why was it so complicated?

Dinah closed her eyes. He could see the shudder that swept over her. Unconsciously she leaned toward him and he gathered her in his arms and kissed her face and neck and hairline. She sank against him and he half-led, half-carried her up to his room.

"I don't want to care about you," she murmured.

"But you do." He almost smiled.

"You're an arrogant, egotistical chauvinist who once married my sister."

Gently balancing her against his shoulder, John twisted the key in the lock and pushed open the door to his room—an unattractive hovel currently blasting heat from its baseboard units. As the scene for a romantic reunion, it couldn't have been worse.

"You're everything I wanted her to be," he admitted. "She just couldn't be it. It's no one's fault."

Her breath was warm on his neck. She hesitated, finally pulling away to arm's length so she could read his expression. "I don't know whether to be insulted or flattered."

He lifted one brow. "I brought some condoms. Flavored."

"Oh?"

"Cherry-lime rickey."

"Make me puke." She smiled. Her first genuine one since he'd learned who she was. Then a frown creased her smooth brow. "Everything's so scary. I can't . . ." She glanced toward the bed. "Do you understand?" she asked bleakly.

"You're turning me down."

"I've just got things to think about."

"When this is over . . . when we're back in L.A. . . ." He left the thought unfinished, but Dinah got the message. They were going to be together. It was meant to be. *He* meant it to be.

She would die for it to be.

"When we're back in L.A.," she agreed with a lighter heart, then slipped through the connecting door to her room.

Matt skittered upstairs, heart thumping, poised at the upper landing, ready to flee from sneak attacks. A frigid blast of air swept through his open bedroom window and surrounded him in the hallway.

What would a real policeman do? What would Uncle Jack do, if he was on the force again?

He'd go to the scene of the crime. They always did that. Searched for clues and stuff.

Looking over his shoulder to the source of the icy air, he thought about how dark and cold it was in the clearing tonight. His blood froze in his veins.

What'sa matter? You scared, shit-for-brains?

With new fortitude, he set his jaw and tiptoed back to his bedroom in search of his darkest, warmest coat.

Connor set the receiver back in its cradle, his fingers lingering, his thoughts moving rapidly. Dr. Hayden Stone was nowhere to be found though Connor had left messages both at the doctor's home and with his emergency number.

It was late; John and Dinah had left several hours earlier. Hayley had fallen asleep in the guest room and he was considering dropping onto the couch for the night.

A crunch of gravel.

Connor looked out to the drive and saw a dark figure hurrying away. Someone from the house?

Lightly he moved upstairs, hesitating outside Hayley's room. Part of him wanted to step inside and climb into the warmth of her bed. They were heading in that direction. Rapidly. Too rapidly, maybe. Or from his point of view, not rapidly enough.

Cracking open the door, he peeked inside.

The room was empty.

"Shit!" Denise muttered through her teeth. The word, though spoken softly, seemed to echo through the trees and meld with the wind. As if in answer, a lash of icy rain peppered the side of her face.

She stopped short, momentarily lost. It had been eight years since she'd followed the path from her house to the wildflower-strewn ledge where she'd met Jimmy Fargo for those moments of unrelenting lust. She wasn't exactly a nature hiker, anyway, and in the darkness she couldn't see her torn nail—compliments of a wild moment with a spiderweb and a pine tree—but she could feel its rough surface.

Swallowing, she counted her heartbeats, aware this little midnight foray was right up there with totally crazy. But she'd met Jimmy many a night, late, after she'd escaped from *him*.

Thomas Daniels. She shook her head. Why had it taken so long to remember? She must possess amazing powers of repression for she hadn't recalled anything but her sick feelings whenever she thought of Wagon Wheel. Bipolar-crapola? Partly. But plain old "I don't want to think about it" mostly.

Dissociation, too. *I hurt, but I won't feel, because if I feel, I die.* Better to pretend it had never happened. Even with celebrities coming out of the closet in droves to tell of their abuse—hey, it was the chi-chi thing to do—she still couldn't touch those memories.

Stone had pushed her. Stone had made her recall everything awful that had happened to her at the hands of that sick-o Ian Wallace, and made her realize she was perpetuating the cycle of victim.

She *was* a victim; she knew that. Her stepfather had sexually abused her innumerable times and she'd lied and told Jimmy he was the first and that they were having a baby together. Desperate, desperate measures. The hope that he would take her away from all this. The realization that Jimmy—hunk that he was—would never be man enough to help her.

And then that final evening . . .

Denise kept walking, fighting her way through damp bushes and sticking pine branches which threatened to poke out an eye. Breathing hard, she finally reached the upper ledge, then promptly sat down on the moist, pine needle-littered ground.

"I'm pregnant," she'd told Jimmy, tears welling unsuspectedly.

He'd been talking about his pick-up: black satin finish, oversized wheels, roll bar, and gun rack. The words rolled off his tongue like compliments to an adored lover. Her announcement stopped him cold, mouth open, eyes blinking comically.

"Pregnant?" he repeated dumbly. "Jesus fucking Christ!"

"I wanted to know what—you thought we should do," she stumbled on. "Make some decisions."

"Hell, we've only done it *twice!*"

"What do you think?" she asked desperately.

"Get rid of it. I don't care. Jesus! You think you could use some protection! I don't want a baby."

A bad, bad moment. The realization that she was going to have to tell Thomas the truth.

She'd sleepwalked through the whole next day at school. Jimmy wouldn't talk to her. Whispers. Pointing fingers. She and Dinah and Hayley weren't considered cool. They were pretty and poor and had only been around a couple of years. No one knew them; no one wanted to know them. But everybody knew Thomas Daniels.

And then . . . the rest was still a blur, pictures in fast-forward. She must have told him. She could remember serious yelling, and she had a mental picture of him in the fading sunlight, standing in the driveway waiting for her, his face livid with rage.

He'd yelled and hit her. Nothing new. She'd tried to scream for Dinah but there was music everywhere. A cacophony of sound. Beautiful and oddly terrifying because she couldn't hear the smack of his fist against her face—nor could she feel it.

Time passing. The clearing. And then, very clearly, she remembered the stink of his breath and the taste of his slobber and the *hunh-hunh-hunh* of air leaving his chest as he jumped atop her. His idea of how a man should have sex with a woman. His stepdaughter. Her.

She'd rarely tried to stop him. Dissociation. The feeling of floating away. She dreamed of being an actress. Someone else. Anyone other than the pathetic shell she was. She'd told Hayley her dreams and Hayley's expression had changed. She felt it, too.

And that's when Denise knew. He'd been after her, too. Hayley. Little sister. Still unformed and defenseless. Where the hell was Dinah? Dinah the good. Tough, determined, smart, and relentless.

"Don't worry," she'd told Hayley. "Dinah will kill him for us."

But that night, with Thomas rutting away like the sorry pig he was, Denise thought of Hayley under his stretched belly, Hayley getting slapped and hit, Hayley feeling the rough possession of his ugly cock.

For a moment she'd lost her mind entirely and reached up and clawed at his eyes. "I'm pregnant!" she'd screamed out the truth. "I'm pregnant! And it's yours!"

And the bastard started hitting her abdomen, great smashing punches she struggled to avoid. She screamed and felt the rock beneath her hand.

She remembered the first hit.

More time passing. And then Dinah, picking her up, soothing her, assuring her she'd take care of everything. It came pouring out then. All the abuse. All the pain. All the degradation.

"Not anymore," Dinah assured her. "Never, never again."

And blood everywhere. On her hands. Splattered all over her. Trickling from her mouth. And then, later, down between her legs as Thomas Daniels' cruel method of abortion proved effective.

Now Denise huddled into a ball, her arms around her knees, rocking softly, remembering. So, this was what Stoner wanted her to feel? All this horrible, numbing pain. Well, she felt it all right! And she wasn't totally convinced it was better for her than the years of self-deception.

Except there was no more sleepwalking. No more lost periods. Sure, her bipolar-manic-depressiveness cropped up in weird ways. Nerve-deadening depression and looney forays into the mountains at the stroke of midnight.

She half-smiled to herself. But this wasn't the result of any mental disease. This was escape.

Blackness yawned over the edge of the ledge. She recalled worrying the ground would give way when she and Jimmy attempted their rudimentary lovemaking here. She walked to the very brink, squinting in the darkness. The clearing was right down there. That's where it happened. That's where he killed her baby and she smashed in his brains.

She'd done it. Oh, yes. She'd done it.

"I'm glad," she said aloud.

The Sadim Touch. She'd always possessed it. It was over now, and all too late.

Closing her eyes, she felt the emptiness of space all around her. She shouldn't have run away from Stone. She shouldn't have lied and said she'd wait for him to take her to the airport. She should have let him come.

But then he'd be here to stop you.

"I love you, Stoner," she whispered into the wind. She really did. She loved him.

Suddenly, she remembered the music. Whitney Houston. The day was clear and cold with a whistling wind that snatched at Whitney's voice. But the volume was cranked up high and Whitney sang with glorious gusto.

And Thomas was there. Chasing her to the clearing, throwing her on the ground.

But there was someone else there, too.

Denise's lips parted in shock, tiny lights flickering inside her brain, bright and elusive. *There was someone else!*

Mud slipped beneath her shoe. Her foot slid, snagged on Oregon grape, slid some more. Denise waved her arms, seeking balance. A silent cry filled her throat. Dirt gave way, dropping in chunks.

Who? Who?

And suddenly she saw her. So clearly it was as if she stood in front of her. In wonder, Denise stared, agape.

It's you!

Her foot slid. She grabbed with her toes but all at once there was nothing. Nothing beneath. Clutching at air, she screamed, "Stoner!"

In slow motion, she toppled over the ledge headfirst and into the dark, dark void of space.

* * *

The scream lifted the hairs on the back of Matt's neck. Abruptly, he turned and ran, tripped over a wet, mossy log, fell into pine needles and scratchy, clawing field grass. His heart deafened him. He was in the clearing by the culvert.

"Shit!" he blubbered out.

He lay still, scared to move.

It's the wind, moron! Scaredy-cat-stupid-shit. Just the wind.

Cautiously, he lifted his head, lips quivering. Hating his own cowardice, he climbed to his feet. The sound had come from the west.

Bent low and moving like a guerrilla, Matt worked his way to the mud pit below the outcropping ledge. Damn, he needed a gun! Some kind of serious protection. Old man Daniels mighta been chock full of Satan's malice, but somebody'd bashed in his head pretty good.

Matt stopped short. His heart jumped and skittered.

A woman lay in the mud, her leg twisted behind her at an angle it shouldn't be.

"Jesus Christ," he muttered, more prayer than profanity.

Out of the corner of his eye—movement. He glanced back. Somebody there. In the bushes. Somebody watching.

She came out then, waddling. Her huge bulk grotesque in the black gloom. Dimly Matt realized she was hurrying. Hurrying to the woman in the mud.

Candy-Dandy, the sheriff had called her and here she was, right in front of him.

"You did-did it," he stuttered through numb lips.

She looked straight at him. "Had to. He woulda killed her. He killed her baby."

Her monotone voice scared a tickle up his spine. His

teeth chattered. But this was no time to be a pussy-whipped baby. Screaming out his Injun *whoop-whoop-whoop*, he rushed forward to help the lady in the mud, Candy Dandy on his heels.

Chapter Twenty

Primping in front of the mirror, Dinah smiled wryly at her new appreciation of cosmetics. Being in front of the cameras had forced her to change. A little. And tonight, being as special as it was, she'd even done something extra. She'd plugged in her hot rollers and—GASP!—curled her hair!

Of course, everyone else at the premiere would be decked out Rodeo Drive style, but she, Dinah Scott, had fixed her own hair and bought her silvery silk gown off the rack.

"I love L.A.," she murmured dryly.

Picking up the bottle of cologne, she noticed the brand and hesitated. Chanel #5. Her sister's.

She was, in fact, in her sister's bedroom at the Malibu house.

Except it was her house now.

Bobo stretched against the aquamarine and pink coverlet across Denise's bed. Extending his claws, he opened his mouth and yawned, curling his tongue and revealing vicious teeth. Unable to resist, Dinah set down the cologne and scooped up the luxuriating feline, hugging him close. Bobo purred like a motor, used to these sudden death-squeezes; Dinah's overwhelming need for reassurance.

Back at the dresser, Dinah grabbed up the bottle of Chanel #5 again. The bedroom door opened and John leaned against the jamb, looking fabulous in a black tux. "When are you going to move all that into our bedroom?" He indicated the perfume and various make-up paraphernalia littering Denise's dresser.

"It's not mine. I promise I'll buy my own." She grinned. "Never thought I'd need the stuff, but tonight's BIG."

He grimaced. "I hate this shit."

"So, do I. But it would be worse if you'd taken Rodney Walburn's job at Titan."

"Never." He gave a mock shudder.

"They're still after you," she said, referring to Titan's board of directors.

"Why don't we run off to Vegas and get married?" he diverted.

Dinah laughed, but her amusement faded when her eyes zeroed in on the slim gold band he held between his thumb and forefinger. "You're serious?"

He slid her a look, a smile playing at the corners of his mouth. "I'd do about anything to get out of going to a premiere."

"Hah." They were planning a wedding. Marriage was foremost on both their minds, but there were a few items left to clear up. "We have to go," she reminded. "For Hayley. And for Denise."

John nodded, sobering. "Then let's get a move on, my love. The sooner we're done, the sooner we can get to new business."

"Monkey business." She spritzed the cologne and grabbed a silk Indian shawl she'd fashioned from a sari.

"Marriage business. You and me and some greedy Vegas marriage-maker at the Love-And-Roses Drive-Through Chapel."

"You're such a romantic." Dinah grinned, sliding her arms around his lean waist.

John kissed her slowly. "I love you," he said.

"I love you."

They smiled at each other.

"So much for small talk." He took her arm and led her down the gallery. "To *Lady Paradise* and the vulture paparazzi."

"God. As long as they don't ask me about Denise's fall again."

"You should never have left the motel to go find her," John couldn't help saying for about the billionth time.

"I had a premonition," she rejoined, just like she always did, and then she shuddered, remembering the sound of Matt Logan's wild cry—just like she always did.

She'd been at the edge of the field. She'd taken the rental car, frightened deep in her soul. John had been right behind her, however, having jogged the three miles from the motel after discovering her missing. He'd suspected where she'd gone and followed. They'd both heard Matt Logan's loud whoop.

And then they'd found Denise, unconscious, her leg twisted at an ungodly angle. Matt stood by, wide-eyed. And Candy just stared.

"Get an ambulance," John barked at Matt who ran as if his feet had wings.

And then Hayley appeared, walking to the scene as if in a dream.

After that, pandemonium. Flashing lights and crowds of people and Denise carted away on a collapsible gurney. Candy had calmly confessed to Connor, but it was such a cut-and-dried case of self-defense, Dinah didn't see how she could ever be convicted.

Still, a rage burned inside her at all the years of torment—torment Candy Daniels Whorton could have saved them all from. But in truth, Candy didn't seem to get it. Her serene passivity was unnerving, to say the least. She kept saying, "He had to die," as if that explained everything, and maybe it did.

But in the end, it hadn't helped Denise.

Now, she cuddled close within John's protective arms. "I love you," he said again, this time a bit more desperately.

Dinah swallowed and closed her eyes, holding the moment. They'd walked through the fire. It was over.

Her dress was the palest peach and covered with fringe, Roaring Twenties' style. Hayley brushed her hair down straight, examined her brows, decided this was as good as it was going to get, strode into the living room of Connor's apartment, and struck a pose. "Da Da!"

He was seated on the sofa wearing a white shirt without a tie, black pants, and a glower.

He'd never looked more handsome.

"If you give me grief about going tonight, I will make your life a living hell."

"Too bad your buddy, Jabba, can't be there. I would have loved to introduce him to 'The Watcher.'"

"Threats." Hayley smiled but it hurt. There were no secrets between them anymore, though sometimes, the way he looked at her made her wonder if he truly trusted her. He hadn't forgiven her for sneaking out the night of Denise's fall.

But time would heal that. She'd learned that much about trust. She trusted him whole-heart, and he was coming around to feeling the same way.

They'd even actually managed to make love a few times—more and more frequently, in fact, as she'd let the walls of resistance come crumbling down. At first she'd been so scared. She'd cried out when he'd simply brushed her flesh with his fingers.

But now . . . now . . .

Well, hell, earlier this afternoon she'd had the courage to don her tan suede vest with the leather thongs, black vinyl skirt, and thigh-high boots.

"Wanna take a trip around the world?" she'd propositioned, and Connor had thrown her on the bed and tickled her until she was gasping for breath and shrieking for mercy.

Then he'd touched and caressed and kissed, and she'd slid into a warm pool of ecstacy which made her feel humble with gratitude that she'd ever found this man, ever deserved this happiness.

But he wanted her to move to Bend with him. Sure, she could still have her career, but he was going to be a hick, country lawman.

Well, why not? She'd played a dual role most of her life. She could do it for real. She *would* do it for real, for Connor.

"You know, I've often thought of visiting Jabba's grave and checking out the headstone," she reflected, tugging on Connor's hand, dragging him to his feet. "Think the F-word's chiseled prominently on there somewhere?"

"Don't get any ideas." Connor grinned, wrapping his

arms around her. "I can think of a better way to spend the evening," he murmured into her hair.

"Nope!" She tugged on his hand. "We're going right now!"

He resisted, his gaze thoughtful, and she knew he was thinking about Candy again. He'd interviewed and interrogated and spent hundreds of all-nighters trying to wring more out of Candy than merely, "He had to die." He wanted answers. Something more. Something that didn't exist.

So, while Candy was at home, released on bail and awaiting trial, Connor Jackley stewed about her story and wished for some kind of closure that didn't exist.

"I'm just glad she finally came out with the truth," Hayley said now, managing to drag him to his feet. "And Denise corroborated that she was there. What more could you want?"

"I feel sorry for Candy, that's all."

"You would have preferred it was Jimmy Fargo," Hayley sniffed. "Typical chauvinistic male. I'm just glad it wasn't one of us!"

"Me, too," Connor agreed heartily. Then, a sly grin stealing over his face, he attempted to lead her to the bedroom.

"Later," she promised with a smile of her own. "Come on, or we'll be late."

Limping slightly, Denise sucked in her gut and examined the white satin gown in the cheval mirror of her new Bel Air home. The rock on her left finger was too enormous to be real but it was. Denise Scott Callahan Stoner. Nice moniker. Jeeezus. Life was good.

Of course, she was a gimp. Her left leg a twisted ruin.

"So much for playing sexy young sirens," she muttered aloud, examining the indented lines of surgery that circled her knee and cut across her shin.

But she was lucky to be alive, to quote a cliche. Thanks to that screaming kid and Dinah's telepathy and Stoner's miraculous appearance at that podunk hospital.

She'd awakened to learn she'd gone face down in muck three-feet-thick. It had nearly suffocated her, but hey, it had also saved her life, and apart from her shattered leg and a minor head injury, she was relatively unscathed.

But the press had been everywhere! Wagon Wheel, Oregon was on the map and the Wheel Treat You Right Motel was now a national landmark of travel "must stays."

The story came out in a deluge. She was suddenly Wagon Wheel's tragic heroine while her stepsister, Candy, was cast as the villain/victim. A great story. Truth stranger than fiction. But most of the attention was focused on Denise and yes, she could admit it, she'd reveled in it.

In the middle of the craziness, Jimmy Fargo had managed to wheedle his way past the barrage of nurses and doctors to bring her a single rose. The slimy creep. Did he seriously expect her to forgive and forget and jump back eight years to high school?

She hadn't seen anything of Candy. The poor girl had been grilled mercilessly by Connor Jackley and had become, from all accounts, a broken record. Denise had been left to fill in the details, which were sketchy at best, thank you very much.

She'd told them it was Candy who'd bludgeoned Daniels, and she'd remembered that Candy had asked to walk home with her that fateful day. She could now recall the wild Whitney Houston music and the enveloping fear for her baby.

The rest was still kind of a twilight blur, but who really cared? She'd remembered the most important parts while she'd been recovering in the hospital. It had all been so overwhelming. When she thought of the medical staff, and press, and just everything coming down on her, it really ticked her off.

But she'd had a savior. A Shrink-In-Shining Armor. Dr. Hayden Stone had appeared in Wagon Wheel and rescued her from the worst of the trauma.

Denise grinned. Thank God for Stoner. Her husband. Her lover.

Of course, the gossip-mongers had clucked their tongues that Denise Scott Callahan's psychiatrist was now her husband, but that story was only a dead-end, side alley to the main street headline: STEPSISTER MUR-DERS FATHER TO SAVE DENISE SCOTT CALLA-HAN STONE!

Soon to be an NBC Movie Of The Week.

Luckily, she'd been able to finish *Lady Paradise*. They'd even fashioned her accident into the script, a beating from an overzealous pimp. It added another dimension to the story and made great promotion copy as well. One of those yarns to reveal on "Oprah;" the studio hungered for her to keep the publicity machine humming.

Throwing open her antique wardrobe—a companion to her walk-in closet—her series of canes beckoned her. Should she take the handcrafted mallard head, a gift from an adoring fan? Or go really tacky and bring along the solid, rhinestone-studded monstrosity Dinah and John had commissioned for her?

Dinah and John. . . . Denise shook her head in wonder,

but hey—things happen. It was strange that she felt so little about their union, she supposed. She *had* been jealous, but then she *had* been a sick-o. Past tense, if you please.

Well.

Snatching up the rhinestone cane, she studied her appearance. Her hair had been artfully designed by Ola, her newest hairdresser. Ola never cracked a smile, spoke in grunts, wore prison gray, and looked like Don Rickles, but she didn't bug Denise and she could do hair. Boy, could she do hair! Tiny rhinestones winked out of layers of pinned tresses, a windblown effect that had taken three hours to achieve.

"Nice package," Denise said to her reflection, wincing a little. She still couldn't look at herself without remembering those painful moments of self-examination she'd managed while her world was a whirling kaleidoscope that left her dizzy and sick.

A knock on the door and Stone looked around at her. His brows lifted, but he made no comment.

"Tell your crippled wife how beautiful she looks," Denise commanded.

"You look beautiful," he said dutifully.

"I'm damn lucky they could shoot around my deformity. You know, I've been thinking. This could help win me an Oscar."

"You care too much about it," he told her, standing behind her right shoulder, staring at the mirror. Through the glass, she watched him close his eyes and inhale deeply of her scent. It thrilled her to her toes.

"I don't care about my leg."

"It's all you think about."

"No, it's not! Stop being a shrink." She saw the ghost

of a smile on his lips. "Aha!" she crowed. "You *were* being a shrink."

"I can't decide whether your injury was a good thing, or a bad thing. You're too focused on it, but it keeps you from dwelling on the past."

"And falling into a spiral of depression followed by bouts of manic behavior," she finished in a monotone. "Bi-polar shit-o-la."

"To the premiere," he said, unwilling to argue with her.

Hooking the cane over her arm, she slipped her free arm through his and let him help her out. In truth, her injury needed no aid from the cane any longer, but she liked the effect. And it was kind of like a smoker with his cigarette or pipe—some of the enjoyment was just in the playing with it.

It was like a shield.

"Tell me again what I raved about in the hospital while I was lying near death," she said as they descended the stairs to the lavish oaken foyer with its sinfully thick Aubusson rugs. A twinge. She remembered Carolyn's rugs and that whole sordid episode.

"You pleaded with Candy to save you. And your baby."

Hayden Stone held the door for his wife. This was a familiar refrain. About once a week she needed to hear it, to be reminded, to know she wasn't to blame.

They were on the first steps to recovery, and unlike Connor Jackley, Hayden Stone accepted Candy Daniels Whorton's confession wholeheartedly. It would just take time for Denise to truly believe the pain was over.

* * *

FLASH! The bulb blasted serious illumination, turning the heads of those in the crush who were outside its brilliant range but caught in its power.

Three women stood smiling in front of the camera. Three sisters. The one in silver covered her eyes and searched behind the photographer for her companion. The one in peach fringe struck another pose and wiggled her tush, giggling, but backing off when the crowd swelled forward. The one in white lifted a flashing, rhinestone-studded cane and blew a kiss.

The premiere of *Lady Paradise* was a huge success and the picture of the three women became an instant classic.

Epilogue

Slice . . . slice . . . slice. The action appealed to Candy. Carefully she cut the picture from *People*, pasting it just as carefully next to the newspaper clipping. There they were. The three angels. Her blue eyes regarded them with a mixture of affection and envy. How she wished she could be part of their beautiful life!

She re-read the picture's caption for the *nth* time: *Denise and Hayley Scott at the premiere of* Lady Paradise *accompanied by their sister (Denise's twin) Dinah.*

Candy sighed. Setting down the scissors, she scooted back the chair, etching the cheap linoleum floor with more scuffs which would fill up with dirt and add to the general air of neglect. With an effort, she raised her bulk to its full height, then paused and lit a cigarette, squinting against the smoke burn.

Her eye caught the newspaper clipping. Words jumped out. ". . . runaway hit . . . Callahan scores again . . . two sisters, twice the joy . . . best film of the Christmas season . . ."

She was glad for their success. She just wished she had some of her own.

Waddling toward the back of the trailer, she pushed at

the door to one of the spare bedrooms. It budged an inch, then got hung up. Candy kicked at it, swore, then reached around and started throwing boxes and debris out of the way.

Opening the door wide enough to admit her bulk, she eyed the room with disinterest. It was stuffed to the gills with junk. Boxes and debris and her mother's cheap doll collection, mementos Jane Daniels couldn't part with. Candy'd thrown everything in here after her mother died.

But there was one item that was hers.

Tromping on sacks and boxes, oblivious to breaking glass and crushed plastic, she dug through stuff in the corner until she found the wooden trunk which was hers, and hers alone. She'd locked it, but the key was on the cobwebby windowsill. Smashing spiders and gunk, she retrieved the key and twisted the lock.

The trunk creaked open. A waft of noxious air widened Candy's nostrils. Gingerly, she picked up the shirt. Darkish brown patches of old blood decorated it. Twisting the garment on her finger, she examined it from all sides, then did the same with the pants.

She really didn't know why she'd stripped him, but she had. While Denise swayed and rocked and moaned and screamed, as if she were in some kind of trance, Candy had calmly finished bashing her father over the head and ripped off all his clothes.

God, but he'd deserved it!

She remembered the day so clearly. It had been one of the last before Christmas break. Candy, fourteen, had been a freshman, and like most of the kids in high school, she'd envied Denise Scott's good looks and ebullience even though Denise was really just poor white trash. As for Dinah, nobody much cared about her; she was too serious. And Hayley was just a shadow.

But Denise had Jimmy Fargo for a boyfriend, and he was everything all the girls at Wagon Wheel High desired: good-looking, rich, flashy, and popular. That day, Candy worked up the nerve to speak to Denise who seemed unusually subdued and distracted. Candy took her unspoken consent as affirmation and proceeded to walk home with her, proud to be in her presence.

But Denise was a glaze-eyed sleepwalker, silent and otherworldly. They reached the edge of her property and she stopped short, unwilling to let Candy approach any closer. But Candy was curious about dear old Dad's new family and so she dawdled even after Denise hinted for her to leave.

It was late afternoon. From the upper windows, Whitney Houston's clear voice rang loudly. Ignoring Denise, Candy strode right in the house and there he was. The shit. Waiting at the kitchen table with that knowing smirk, a spider in his web, waiting for Denise.

Oh, she'd seen it all so clearly. She'd been his victim once. She knew. And when he saw *her*, his face turned livid red, and he hit her open-handed. He always knew how to hit.

Then he pushed Candy aside and came at Denise who was standing in the doorway, looking confused. With a small cry, she backed away, but he chased after her, yelling obscenities at her, calling her a whore.

As Whitney sang on, Candy stumbled outside, following after them. Rage burned in her heart. She caught up with them in the clearing, but by that time Denise's skirt was over her head and she was struggling and slapping at him.

And then she was screaming. "Stop! Stop! I'm pregnant! And it's yours!"

Candy's heart liked to stop right there. The ugly, stink-

ing bastard! Then he made his fatal mistake: he started
punching Denise, hard, right in the stomach, over and
over again while she whimpered and curled up protectively, futilely trying to save her baby.

He had to die.

Calmly, she'd picked up an outsized rock—a small
boulder, really—and smashed him over the head and face
so many times that she fell away, exhausted.

Time passed. Denise lay still. The moon was high when
Candy awakened from her reverie. It had turned the
frigid ground ghostly white, making the shadows seem
darker. His clothes were in her hands and he lay like a
beached whale in the pale, unforgiving light, covered with
black stripes of blood.

She'd touched Denise. She was cold as death herself.

That's when Denise started screaming in earnest. A
keening wail so creepy that Candy skulked away, hurrying
back to the trailer over five miles away, sneaking in and
washing up and locking his clothes in the trunk.

But she was spotted. She hadn't really thought much
about hiding her crime; that had come later. But bad luck
followed her. Sheriff Urganis, who was carrying on with
Mama at the time, witnessed Candy sneaking in the back
and scrubbing for all her life. The horny jerk-off was
actually waiting outside the bathroom door when she
emerged. He *knew.*

Then the three angels left town, but did Sheriff Urganis
give up, or blame dear old dad's disappearance on them?
Oh, no. He came looking for Candy.

He stopped by the trailer every evening; said he was
waiting for Mama to get home. Uh uh. He was waiting to
catch her.

So, she'd done what she had to do. She'd sent an
anonymous letter to the sheriff's uppity wife, explaining

about his little trysts, and that prim old lady kicked his sorry ass out of there. Rumor ran like brushfire. No more reelection. Nosirree.

One more mean, crooked bastard taken care of.

Candy snorted in satisfaction, then settled back in the kitchen, lighting another cigarette and watching the watery, winter sun set outside her dirty window.

She supposed she could tell all to Connor Jackley. He certainly wanted her to. But he only wanted the truth to assure himself that all of the angels really were innocent. He didn't care about Candy.

So, let him wonder. It didn't make no goddamn bit of difference anyway. The three angels were safe and she was free.

Candy picked tobacco off her teeth and dreamed.

DISCOVER DEANA JAMES!

CAPTIVE ANGEL (2524, $4.50/$5.50)
Abandoned, penniless, and suddenly responsible for the biggest tobacco plantation in Colleton County, distraught Caroline Gillard had no time to dissolve into tears. By day the willowy redhead labored to exhaustion beside her slaves . . . but each night left her restless with longing for her wayward husband. She'd make the sea captain regret his betrayal until he begged her to take him back!

MASQUE OF SAPPHIRE (2885, $4.50/$5.50)
Judith Talbot-Harrow left England with a heavy heart. She was going to America to join a father she despised and a sister she distrusted. She was certainly in no mood to put up with the insulting actions of the arrogant Yankee privateer who boarded her ship, ransacked her things, then "apologized" with an indecent, brazen kiss! She vowed that someday he'd pay dearly for the liberties he had taken and the desires he had awakened.

SPEAK ONLY LOVE (3439, $4.95/$5.95)
Long ago, the shock of her mother's death had robbed Vivian Marleigh of the power of speech. Now she was being forced to marry a bitter man with brandy on his breath. But she could not say what was in her heart. It was up to the viscount to spark the fires that would melt her icy reserve.

WILD TEXAS HEART (3205, $4.95/$5.95)
Fan Breckenridge was terrified when the stranger found her near-naked and shivering beneath the Texas stars. Unable to remember who she was or what had happened, all she had in the world was the deed to a patch of land that might yield oil . . . and the fierce loving of this wildcatter who called himself Irons.

Available wherever paperbacks are sold, or order direct from the Publisher. Send cover price plus 50¢ per copy for mailing and handling to Penguin USA, P.O. Box 999, c/o Dept. 17109, Bergenfield, NJ 07621. Residents of New York and Tennessee must include sales tax. DO NOT SEND CASH.